BARREN

Passing-of-Life

◆━━━◆━◆━━━◆

JON ANTHONY PERROTTI

Version M (masculine pronouns)

Brief Overview of *BARREN* So Far

In Book 1: Taking of Name, *a uedin, Elenn, learned of his barren condition and had to make peace with the fact that he carried no embryo and would never have passing-of-life, the glorious end that all uedin look forward to all their lives. We learned that the condition was likely to turn him into a kind of pathetic monster, deranged of mind, dangerous to others, and destined to meet a miserable demise in the desert when the condition reached its full-blown manifestation. His struggle was not against persecution, since the uedin race was shown to be evolved and compassionate; it was simply a struggle to bear the burden of his unhappy fate. A medical breakthrough introduced a limited intervention, but Elenn was reluctant to accept it. It might create the pretense of normal life, arresting many of the symptoms of barren syndrome, but it would not address the central ordeal—it would not give fertility to a barren uedin or make him any more likely to ever know the passing-of-life. While Elenn wrestled with despair, various events shaped his life and led him to his ultimate choice to accept the treatment and live bravely with the knowledge of his condition and its implications.*

In Book 2, Elenn is swept up in the disastrous unintended consequences of the medical intervention. The intervention has had the indirect result of "feeding," a quasi-erotic practice in which one barren uedin consumes live skullsap directly from another through the catheter and indeed becomes addicted to it. The capital responds by asking the barren to resist their desire to feed and emblemize their commitment by wearing hoods to keep their skullwombs and catheters covered at all times. Elenn becomes part of a squadron of barren guards charged with the duty of monitoring the hooded community. Elenn and his squadron partner, Nula, strive to preserve the oath of the hood-takers even as they struggle with their own temptation. They are conflictingly drawn to one another but ultimately enter into a close emotional partnership marked by a pact of abstinence and mutual loyalty.

A detailed synopsis of Book 1 can be found at the beginning of Book 2. The following is a detailed synopsis of Book 2, provided to refresh the reader's memory about events and subplots which precede the commencement of Book 3.

Synopsis: *Of Guards and Caretakers*: *Book 2 of the Barren Trilogy*

In Part 1, *Feed or Be Fed On*, we learn that much time has passed, as evidenced by the fact that the blind child-uedin whom Elenn met in Book 1 has grown up, taken name (Jutef), and is now an apprentice caretaker to the barren. He, along with two other apprentices, is in the woods outside the western gate with Benar and Yenca harvesting mola beans from trees. Benar gives the newly-named apprentices advice about how to work with the barren. On the way home, Jutef tells them that he almost became a reed-crafter but chose instead to join the caretakers to the barren. Yenca recalls his own decision to become a caretaker to barren after his experiences with Domas before Domas's passing. Later, Yenca and Jutef have a conversation in which there is mention of the current rumor about many barren showing symptoms of the syndrome despite catheters being in place.

In the next sequence, Elenn is doing a mind-stilling exercise at the spot where he once came close to drowning. While he is in a trance, an unknown uedin comes up to him, undoes Elenn's neckstrap, and places his mouth directly on his neck to suck skullsap from him. Elenn experiences intoxicating pleasure from this, even though he knows that it is the notorious "feeding" that is taking place. We soon learn that the stranger who intruded upon Elenn is a server, and he is later caught in a courtyard area next to the temple kitchen while changing from a stolen master's robe back into his own server clothing. He confesses everything. As a server messenger spending much time outside the temple compound, he has been exposed to and has gotten caught up in this "master habit" of consuming skullsap. He imagines that it is a common practice of masters and inappropriate only because he is a server, but when he does it, he experiences something that he can only compare to passing-of-life. He addresses many levels of superiors in the temple until he reaches the Most High, who happens to be unexpectedly young. The messenger's confession is received with shock, for the idea of consuming skullsap is highly offensive. He is taken away, and it is finally explained to him that he is barren, and he will have the make a choice. He may either leave the temple to face his future alone with no direction from the servers, or he may drink poison and die. Meanwhile, we learn that the Most High is, in fact, Tilke, and he has learned to accept pain and difficulty without resistance as he has drawn closer to "the Soft One," Lern Beyana.

In the next scene, the Fieldburning is taking place. Elenn has gone up to a hillside to offer help, but his help is not needed, and he goes back down to watch the spectacle with the capital crowds. He encounters Yenca near the North Route Bridge. They talk about Domas's concerns about the syndrome before his passing. Yenca tells Elenn about a proposal to have the barren wear hoods to prevent them from feeding, and he asks Elenn to attend the masters council to support the proposal. Just as Elenn says that he will consider the request, he is summoned by the guards. A lost and confused server has shown up near the North Route Bridge. Elenn and the other guards take him back to Flatpools

Station where he says that his name is Pavis and explains that he has run away from the temple to avoid having to drink poison, the recommendation of servers to their members with barren syndrome. Elenn tries to explain to Pavis that feeding is something to be avoided, but Pavis clings to his belief that it is a different kind of passing-of-life. Elenn feels great pity for Pavis because he has been rejected by the community of servers, but when he tries to console him, Pavis wants only to feed and begs Elenn for his neck. Elenn rebuffs him, and Pavis escapes into the night. He wanders to Jutef's hut where he and Jutef have a conversation and learn about one another. Pavis agrees to cooperate with the masters with Jutef as his counselor.

Some days later, Yenca receives a letter from Elenn, and it is understood that after the confrontation with Pavis, Elenn has made up his mind to support the hood proposal. Yenca then visits Benar, and we see that much is stirring in the capital with yet another barren—in addition to Pavis—demanding the attention of the caretakers to the barren. Yenca talks with Benar about the two barren uedin of recent events, and Benar tells Yenca that Pavis is taking an assignment with the distribution masters and is going to live as a master outside the temple. Yenca tells Benar about the hood proposal, and Benar dismisses it as implausible.

In Part 2, *The Barren Take Hood*, we see the advancement of the hood proposal. At a meeting of the masters council, medic master Ferin reports that the catheter intervention is being rampantly negated by feeding. This news throws the masters into a panic until Yenca shares the hood proposal. Jutef, when asked to speak about his original idea for the proposal, completely reverses his position and decries his own idea, but Elenn speaks in favor of it, and his status as a guard who happens to have the syndrome gives him much influence. The council decides to embrace the proposal and inaugurate a statute that will require hoods for all barren.

One night when Elenn is drinking yeastdrink with his fellow guards, the party is interrupted by Wanba who reports that the Quarterhouse hatching pool, full of wetuedin, has been defiled by the dead body of a master, clearly a barren who has committed suicide. It is a scene that offends uedin values on a deep level, and very early the next morning Elenn secretly escorts Pavis to the site and makes him look at the corpse in order to drive home the point that barren syndrome must be taken very seriously. In great anguish, Pavis concedes that he will go along with the plan wherein all the barren are asked to wear hoods and renounce feeding.

When the day comes for the hood-taking ceremony, Elenn sees the crowd of newly-named uedin who have just learned of their barren status, been given catheter implants, and are now assembled to be given hoods. They are clearly distraught, and Elenn is at a loss about what he can possibly say to give them hope. The ceremony itself is glum and depressing until Benar, who has privately inhaled sourember smoke, lightens the mood with his antics. A new era has come to the capital with a large number of hooded masters now intermingled in its population, barren uedin who are pledged to an oath of abstinence from feeding.

The introduction of hoods gets off to a good start, and Elenn initially feels very positive about the new statute. During a side adventure, he goes with fellow guard Nemis to spend a night at the grainhouses of Murro. Elenn and Nemis share stories and joke together under the stars at Murro, and Elenn is very pleased to know that his fellow guard accepts him as a comrade and doesn't hold his barren status against him. In the morning they inspect the grainhouses, and while checking on the damage to one of the towers, a large flying bug suddenly flies out and causes Nemis to lose his balance and start to fall. Elenn catches his arm, and with strength made possible only because of his enlarged barren body, he raises him back to the high ramp and saves him from a fall that might have killed him. On the way home, they discover Pavis in a compromising situation with a young hooded master under the Clay Bridge. It is the first time since the hood ceremony that Elenn has reason to believe that some hooded masters may be unable to keep their oath. This danger is reiterated in the next chapter where we see Yenca petitioning Wanba to enlist the help of the guards in monitoring the barren to make sure they don't break their hood oath. Wanba is very resistant, but when Yenca suggests putting the responsibility on hooded guards like Elenn, Wanba agrees to consider the request.

In Part 3, *A Great Struggle*, a squadron of hooded guards is formed to monitor the barren. They understand that they are being asked to take on a special and difficult task. Elenn meets Nula and they have their first conversation about the fact that Elenn uses the word "barren." Soon after the formation of the hood squadron, we find Elenn seriously contemplating his role as a hooded guard when he is described taking a bath and meeting his elder guard, Ribol. The humble Ribol gives an account of a teacher from his early childhood, a Master Leci, who disappeared, presumably to face his death in the desert. Elenn hears this and other memories from Ribol, and later, alone in the bath, he comes to some acceptance about his new assignment as a hooded guard.

Soon we see the hooded guards in their first days of the squadron. Elenn and Nula are very compatible, and they find that when they interact with the hooded masters, they encounter support and even admiration. They are practically idolized by Serka, a young hooded outfield worker they happen to meet. They talk about going to the outfields to visit Serka and his companions someday. Elenn later meets with Benar and, after hearing some of Benar's opinions, decides not to say anything about his private temptations or attraction to Nula.

The time comes when the wet-ones are ready to take leg, and Benar and Yenca go to the caretaker-only event. They witness the birth-like uedin event with joy, but Yenca cannot help thinking about how the syndrome will impact the new generation.

The first time Elenn and Nula encounter barren masters breaking their oath, Nula is very uncomfortable reprimanding them for something that he, in fact, craves. When two offenders are caught in the act, one escapes, but the other has to be delivered back to his counselor. Nula feels terribly conflicted having to force him to face his counselor in great humiliation.

We can assume it is some time later that Serka, the young hooded outfield worker, is called from his work to greet the squadron guards who have come to visit him. Serka, along with his fellow hooded outfield workers Jeber and Leol, are very excited by the visit and do their best to honor their guests. They consort around a bonfire into the night, and the outfield workers listen to Elenn's wisdom and advice about their barren condition. Nula recognizes a great naivete in the outfield workers and sadly realizes that he has no such innocence. The next time we see Elenn and Nula encounter barren feeding, they have become more assertive in their roles as squadron guards, though Nula secretly feels increasingly conflicted. Again, one offender escapes and the other is captured and taken to his counselor, but this time the one who ran away is later found dead, having killed himself by jumping over a cliff. Elenn later has a conversation with Yenca, and they talk candidly about what appears to be the rising failure of the hood statute. Elenn tells Yenca that Benar is a suitable counselor for him because he doesn't ask the questions that have no answers.

It is later in the novade that one morning, Nula fails to show up for duty, and Elenn learns that he has taken ill. Elenn goes immediately to the infirmary, and he learns that Nula is believed to have something wrong with his heart and lungs, which could be very serious, though Nula has not been told of the danger he is in. After visiting the clueless and cheerful Nula, Elenn goes on to notify Nula's counselor, Yinob. Yinob displays a curious regard for Elenn which suggests that Elenn has been a frequent subject of discussion between Nula and his counselor. Elenn goes from there to Flatpools station, where he asks Ippal to substitute for Nula for the day. Their afternoon shift goes well, and Ippal agrees to fill in as Elenn's partner guard until Nula is ready to report back for duty. Ippal shares a secret with Elenn. He shows him a little mouse that he discovered in the station house, has been keeping in a paintbrush box, and hopes to set free outside the capital. They plan to go to the drystream the next day to release it. Ippal admits that he is very nervous about the possibility of encountering barren uedin feeding, the thought of which makes him very uncomfortable. However, when they get to the drystream the next morning, they encounter no feeding, but rather a solitary barren in derangement. The barren stomps on the mouse and makes his condition obvious by his speech and behavior. Treated with kindness, he becomes docile as they take him into the capital and to the infirmary. After the barren is received there, Elenn asks to see Nula again. By this time, Nula has been told about his diagnosis, and he is deeply depressed and afraid. Elenn tries to give him encouragement, and Nula, in appreciation, does his best to appear calm and assured. Elenn returns later in the evening to check in on Nula again, and Nula wants to talk about feeding. He wants to experience the thing that some barren uedin are referring to as "passing-of-life." At first Elenn balks, but he reflects quickly on Nula's condition, and he decides to give Nula his wish. The two partner guards, in the shadows of the infirmary room, do the thing that they have been committed to preventing.

Part 4, *In the Midst of Fiasco*, opens with a meeting of high servers inside the central temple. We are introduced to Nekur, a no-nonsense high server who is skeptical and even disdainful of the current infatuation with the new young server who has risen rapidly through the ranks to become "Most High." The Most High is indeed in his own world, focused on communion with the Soft One. Nekur tries to maneuver the discussion so that more practical-minded high servers like himself can take over the operations of the temple. He attempts to manipulate the situation with a sly recommendation that the Most High come out of withdrawal. He expects the Most High to refuse and thinks that the refusal will serve as further evidence that change is needed in temple management, but he is flummoxed when the Most High takes his suggestion seriously. Afterward, the interior ponderings of the Most High are described, and we are reminded that he is, in fact, Tilke. A direct message from the Soft One prompts him to return to full server activity for the sake of his health and wellness.

Back at Quarterhouse, Benar invites Elenn for yeastdrink. Elenn confesses that he has shared necks with Nula. Benar admonishes him but is not greatly surprised and says that he never expected the hood squad to manage their duty anyhow. He has no faith in the hooded guards and foresees the regular guards taking over the monitoring of the barren. This response causes Elenn to feel ashamed about his decision to share necks with Nula. Later in the conversation, Elenn learns that a hut outside the capital walls is being proposed by the caretakers. After leaving Benar, he goes to Crafting to visit Nula. His conversation with Benar is fresh in his mind, and he tells Nula that neck-sharing between them will not happen again. The despair evident in Nula's reaction prompts Elenn to make a statement of his devotion to Nula, and they share a moment of deep understanding that they both know will bond them for life.

In the next chapter, Nula visits his counselor, Yinob, and is very open about all that has happened. The idea of transitioning from guard to caretaker is discussed, and Nula is given the opportunity to envision a different kind of future for himself. At the next meeting of the alliance between the squadron and the caretakers, Nula reports that he is pursuing the transfer. The prospects for a new caretaker hut are also discussed. Jutef, who brings the proposal, does not reveal his private motivation—he sees himself residing outside the capital walls so that he can prepare for an eventual attempt at pilgrimage for his own passing-of-life. The sacrifices involved in taking up residence outside the capital walls present a problem. It is not something that caretakers or guards can simply be assigned to do. Finally, Elenn volunteers to join Jutef and occupy the new hut, on the condition that the hut be built to accommodate three. He requests that Nula, his former squadron partner, be the third resident.

The story then jumps to a future point when the new hut is in mid-construction. Nemis, the regular guard who went with Elenn to the grainhouses of Murro, has come to lend a hand. He arrives early before anyone else is there, and he sees a young hooded master walking along the drystream. It turns out to be Leol, and they have an awkward conversation in which Nemis tries not to be accusatory even though it is clear that Leol is out looking to feed. Nemis tells him that the construction is for a hut that will eventually be occupied by Elenn and Nula, and that he is expecting Elenn to arrive later on. Leol finally admits that he shouldn't be there, and he doesn't want to meet Elenn. He runs off and makes his way back to the western outfields. He resolves to tell his companions where he has been and what he has learned about the new caretaker hut, but when he gets home, he accidentally walks in on Serka and Jeber feeding and is greatly traumatized.

In the final chapter of the book, the new caretaker hut is described as complete and occupied. Elenn has carried water from a well inside the capital and returns to find that a visitor is there with Jutef and Nula. It is Pavis, and he appears to have turned into a decent and likable master. Pavis is there to accompany Jutef for a walk. After they leave, Elenn and Nula talk about how "sharing-of-life" may be a better concept for barren uedin than "pass-ing-of-life." They go out to get the water Elenn has carried back, and they pause to appreciate the beauty of their new surround-ings. Talking and laughing together in the final lines, they leave the reader with a sense of their pleasant and harmonious new life.

BOOK 3

PASSING-OF-LIFE

Part 1

GRIEF AND RUIN

Jutef Mourns the Loss
of His Hut Companions

JUTEF SHUFFLED FORWARD WITH IRREGULAR steps toward Nula's rock pile while the morning twilight opened around him into a sunrise whose brightness he could not see, but whose warmth he could feel. The path was indicated here and there with rock markers that the squadron guards had put in place for him so that he could take walks to various spots in the area around the hut. Jutef had walked this particular path to the bottom of the drystream bed back and forth many times. He knew where the rock markers were and took conscious steps from one to the next, tapping his cane on the ground as he went, his head up and to the right as he concentrated. Proximity and distance could only be judged by the time it took him to get from one spot to another. He found that he could get about pretty well as long as there were familiar rocks in familiar places to reassure him.

The greatest thing he had to learn was how to be lost. How to be lost and keep moving, using whatever vague hints that might lead him *toward* instead of *away* from the right direction—that was what he needed to manage without being overtaken by fear and hopelessness. This would be critical for his passing-of-life. To address his fears, he really needed to ask someone to go with him walking out in the grassland between the drystream and the hill country. Someone should go with him and let him try to go further and further out without helping him get back until he could endure the disorientation no longer. It was a hard thing to do, but there was no one to help him do it, even if he should feel courageous enough to try. Nula was gone, and Elenn was . . . out there somewhere.

He came to the spot where a mound of rocks was piled to mark the place where the squadron guards had buried Nula's body in the ground. Nula had requested that his body be buried shallowly at the bottom of the drystream so that the Great Rains river would carry him away at the end of the novade. It was a request inspired by his favorite poem. After Nula's death Jutef had memorized the poem to honor his dear friend, and arriving at the grave, he couldn't help bringing hands to face and saying the lines out loud.

"*A silver streamfish followed one, clear from the Lake Ceulan, but when one stopped here to take leg, the streamfish just swam on,*" Jutef spoke to the reedgrass around him and the ground under his feet. A tear trailed his cheek as he said the lines. "*If one had chosen not to stop, but go where the streamfish go, one wonders where one might would be, what nowheres one doesn't know . . .* "

Jutef got down and sat on the ground in the same spot where he always sat when he came to Nula's grave. "Oh, Master Nula," he said to the pile of rocks, "you are most unfortunate for coming to this end, but sometimes I think you are fortunate. You wouldn't want to see how Master Elenn has completely fallen apart since your heart failed you. He is hardly a uedin now. He is just as overtaken with feeding as any of those poor wretches we tried to help."

He sighed, leaned back slightly, and raised his face to receive the warmth of the morning sun. What would become of him now? He was extending his time living in the hut by concealing the fact that Elenn was gone for days at a time, and when Elenn did return, he was often incoherent with derangement. But at this point, nobody in the capital had high expectation when it came to the hooded masters. They were always allowed to return to their regular jobs and regular domiciles, but there was little to do about their level of functioning.

All of the squadron partnerships had turned into teams of three, with two regular guards to work with each hooded guard. But Yenca had told Jutef that in Elenn's case, his two squadron partners, Ippal and Nemis, put more time and effort into keeping an eye on *him* rather than working with him to deal with other hooded masters. Trouble was evident when Elenn started asking them to leave him alone when they were on duty together. From there it deteriorated into his not even showing up in the morning, or worse yet, deliberately losing them during their rounds and then going off by himself and avoiding them. He was in a very self-destructive mode. Jutef didn't know what to do about it.

Pushing himself up with one hand, Jutef moved forward into a crouched position on his feet and reached with the other hand toward the rock pile. He found the large familiar rock and planted his one hand there, as usual, and ran his other hand slowly over the rock pile, feeling its rugged outline. He was becoming quite familiar with the shape of the rock pile. The rocks collected from the bottom of the drystream were nowhere near smooth, but their sharp edges were worn away by Great Rains rivers over time. It would be just another couple years before the next Great Rains. Unfortunately, the coming of Great Rains was looked at with different feelings now. The child uedin would be tested before their Namesgiving, and if recent novades were any indication, it could be a dreadful time of dealing with harsh truth. Even Master Benar, who lost his temper often but rarely got discouraged, seemed to get very quiet and spoke with trouble in his voice whenever there was ever any mention of the next generation of wet-uedin coming.

Jutef heard what sounded like a woodflute coming from the direction of the hut. Wasn't that a woodflute? It would be Master Pavis. He stood and faced eastward, feeling the rising sun again, and edged his way around the stone pile and back onto the path that led up and out of the drystream bottom. He could not hurry this walk or he would trip. Pavis had always been very patient with him, but these days Pavis was feeding a lot, and there was no telling what state he would be in. Jutef did his best to work his way carefully along the path, with each step tapping his cane to find the markers. As he got about halfway up the bank, he heard the sound of Pavis's flute clearly. It wasn't playing anything recognizable. It sounded like a child-uedin playing with a woodflute like a toy. Was that Pavis?

He made his way up and out of the bank, and he moved faster on a well-worn path that led back to the hut.

"Master Pavis!" he called out, but the woodflute kept on. He strutted forward as quickly as he could, and called again. "Master Pavis!"

The woodflute stopped.

"Master Pavis," he called ahead, "I'm coming now!"

He heard the sound of running feet coming toward him, and Pavis was there quickly, breathing hard from running.

"Master Pavis—"

"Hello, hello, a beautiful sunny morning!" said Pavis.

"Did you have deliveries near the north gate?" asked Jutef.

"Master Jutef, you have been so kind to me . . . " said Pavis, and Jutef could immediately tell by his voice that he was in some slight derangement.

"Are you wearing your hood, Master Pavis?"

"Yes, I'm wearing my hood," said Pavis.

"Let's go back to the hut. Give me your shoulder."

Pavis came and took Jutef's hand and guided it to his shoulder, then walked the remaining distance back to the hut. Jutef was reassured to feel that the thick woven flap of the hood piece was in place under Pavis's robe, but he knew from the weird voice that Pavis had been feeding recently. He wouldn't have the clarity of mind to listen to Jutef's advice. He decided to send Pavis for water. That would clear his mind. They could talk after he got back.

"Are you busy now, Master Pavis? Can you help me with something?" asked Jutef as they reached the familiar ground around the hut.

"What do you want, Master Jutef? I will do it for you," said Pavis.

"We need water, and I haven't seen Master Elenn for a few days. Have you seen him?"

"Yes, I saw Master Elenn! I *did* see him!"

"Where?"

"At the project."

The project . . . Jutef wanted someday to visit the project where so many of the hooded masters had been put to work. It was one hopeful thing amidst all the trouble in the capital these days. The masters council had approved a plan to build an observation deck at one of the grainhouses at Murro. One of the reasons for the project was to provide healthy work for hooded masters who couldn't keep up with their vocations in the capital. It would not be an easy excursion for Jutef, but he hoped that Yenca would take him there one day.

"Master Elenn is at the project? How long has he been there?"

"He's not there anymore."

"But you saw him there."

"Yes, but he left."

"When was he there?"

"I saw him a few days ago."

"Did you speak to him? Is he all right?"

"I didn't speak to him," said Pavis. He seemed intent on answering Jutef's questions in the simplest terms and had no inclination to provide any details. Jutef decided it would be better to attempt conversation after sending Pavis to get water. Hopefully he would come back with a clearer head.

"Will you take our water buckets to Bells and fill them for us?"

"Oh yes, Master Jutef, I will do that for you, gladly."

Pavis followed Jutef as he made his way to the hut and went inside. Jutef gave Pavis the empty buckets. "The carrying pole is leaning on the side—do you know where it is?"

"Yes, I know," said Pavis.

"Tell the masters at Bells that you're getting water for the caretaker hut. They're used to us coming."

"All right. It won't take me long," said Pavis.

"Good. When you come back, we can talk." Jutef sat down and listened as Pavis went back outside, around the side of the hut to get the carrying pole, and off toward the north gate. Jutef reached down to find the piece of basketry that he was working on and a sheaf of reeds. He pulled a reed from the sheaf to start weaving. He found the spot where he had left off and counted the twists in the row. Over, under, twist, over, under, twist. He leaned back and worked his fingers, quickly snapping the crisp reeds as he bent them around one another and moved along the curve of the basket. His mind wandered as he worked. He wished he could contact Ippal and Nemis about Elenn's absence without drawing the attention of the other Flatpools guards. Maybe Pavis would copy down a message for him and deliver it to one of them discreetly.

Jutef tried to concentrate on his weaving, but his mind wandered all the more. He was now considering whom he could ask to take him to the project site in Murro. He had two reasons to go. He wanted to go because many of the hooded masters were congregating there to help with the construction, and caretakers to the barren had established a presence there to address their needs. As a result, there were fewer uedin showing up at the caretaker hut that had been built just for that purpose. Jutef wasn't upset about this—he didn't care if the hooded masters were being helped elsewhere, he just wanted to know about how they were being helped. And now, a second reason was that Elenn had apparently shown up there at some point, and maybe Jutef could find out more.

As soon as Jutef relaxed enough to stop worrying, he grew drowsy. His hands rested on his lap, finally letting slip the bent blade of reed between his fingers, and he fell quite asleep.

He was having the same dream again. He was a child-uedin at Bells, and no one was there. He walked from room to room asking, "One is here, is anyone there?" But there was no answer and no sound of movement. He started to cry, but it did no good. No tutor or caretaker came to him. He finally stopped crying and simply wandered lost in the domicile with no idea what room he was in or how to get back to a familiar location.

He was startled awake by the sound of tapping on the door-tarp. Master Pavis was back. He usually came right in without tapping the door tarp. Jutef quickly found the basket on the floor beside him, put it on the table, and got up to meet Pavis.

"Master Pavis, you were gone a long time." He would let Pavis decide if he wanted to admit to feeding again.

"Can I drink some of your water?" asked a voice. It wasn't Pavis. It was one of the hooded masters who came now and then to the caretaker hut, especially when he was despondent and deranged after a feeding encounter. Jutef had convinced Elenn and Nula, before he died, not to ask this uedin's name. He was very ashamed, and they didn't need to insist on having his name. They told Jutef that he wore a miller's robe. This familiar anonymous hooded master was thirsty, and providing a drink of water was one of the most fundamental ways that Jutef offered aid to those who came to the caretaker hut. Unfortunately, there was very little water left. Where was Pavis? It had been a mistake to send him, Jutef now realized.

"Come in, come in," said Jutef. The master entered. Back in the days before Nula's death, Jutef would wait for Elenn to say one of two lines that would communicate an important detail to Jutef. He would either say, "Good to see you in your hood," or "I see you're not in hood, but don't worry." Then Jutef would have a better idea about who had come. But now, the only way to find out was to ask directly, which Jutef felt uncomfortable about, but he had to do it.

"Are you in hood, master? I am alone here today."

"It has already been off, but I put it back on," said the visitor.

"That water jar has a little in the bottom. You may take what you want, but I'm sorry we don't have any more." Jutef listened as the visitor went to the water jar and poured a small amount into a cup that sat beside it.

"I'm very sorry about that kind barren who died. He was a very good uedin."

"That was Master Nula. Yes, he was very good."

"Where is the hooded guard?"

Jutef paused, wondering what to say to this guest, and then answered simply, "I don't know. I was hoping you had seen him."

"No, I haven't seen him for a long time."

"Neither have I," said Jutef.

"He's probably feeding," said the visitor with a hopeless note in his voice. The hooded masters were greatly affected by the fact that the hood squadron was being taken over by regular guards.

"If you would stay inside the capital for any length of time, you would find that not all the hooded masters are giving in like the ones you encounter out here."

"We take our turns, don't we?" said the visitor bitterly.

"Master, have you thought of going to the project at Murro?"

"I'm sure the barren are all feeding there, worse than anywhere," said the visitor.

"No, I've heard that they are doing well there. There are many unhooded masters working alongside them, and the caretakers are there too."

"Have you been there?"

"No, I haven't. I want to go."

"I don't."

"Why not, master?"

"It won't do me any good," said the visitor.

Jutef decided then to ask the visitor to take him to the project. "You may not want to go, but would you be willing to accompany me there, as a favor?"

The visitor didn't answer at first. "I need to stop at the mill, to let my seniors there know that I am all right."

"That's a very good idea. We'll have to walk through the whole capital all the way to Southgate, so we should stop to tell your seniors that you're all right. We should stop to tell your counselor as well."

"I don't want to see my counselor," said the visitor.

"That's fine. Whatever you wish. Can you stay here tonight, and we'll leave in the morning?"

"All right. But after I take you to the project, I'm not going to come back with you."

"That's fine. I'll find another caretaker there to help me."

"Do you have any food?"

"I have some dried fieldpears. That's all." Jutef got the fieldpears and sat with the visitor as he ate them quietly. Jutef was actually hungry, but the visitor was hungrier, and he let him have them all. Later he directed the visitor to use Nula's old mat and wheel-shaped pillow for his bedding, and they slept till dawn.

Jutef asked first thing in the morning if the visitor was still willing to escort him to Murro, and he was glad to hear that he was willing. Jutef tied empty water gourds to his belt. They would need water for their hike to Murro. They would fill the gourds somewhere in the capital on their way through. It made Jutef nervous to leave the caretaker hut completely unattended, so he had the visitor write a note for him, telling Elenn that he was looking for him and was leaving for Murro and that he would be back in a day or two.

When they got close to the north gate, the visitor said to Jutef, "Someone left two water buckets connected to a carry pole beside the path here. Are they from your hut?"

"Just leave them there," said Jutef.

Primary Advisor to the Most High

Nekur read the message and felt an immediate disappointment. It was another request from the Most High. He had been hoping for a report from one of the high servers who had once been his allies. Nekur had always understood the reason that servers hid things. The further you went up the ranking in server society, the closer you got to the Most High. Of course there were times in temple history when the position was more ministerial, and at such times it didn't matter so much. But when there was a perception of genuine communion, servers sensed that the Soft One was susceptible to distress conveyed to her when the Most High was unnecessarily exposed to strife. The belief, therefore, that the current Most High was in a communion completely unprecedented had a very squelching effect on communication throughout the temple compound.

When the Most High asked him to be his primary advisor, Nekur's role among the high servers changed completely. He was empowered to exercise a great influence on every aspect of temple life, and yet it immediately got very difficult to know what was happening. He was quite buried in the machinations of server discretion. He had requested reports from the high servers with whom he had once shared a great confidence. He knew that barren syndrome was a problem outside the temple, and he remembered the strange case of the young messenger who had requested counsel some years back, the one who was ultimately determined to have the syndrome. But were there others? And was there ever any confirmation of the strange scenario the messenger had described? This had been a matter of concern to him, and he had always intended on getting the facts about it, but now it seemed impossible. If his former allies knew anything, they were afraid to let their information get any closer to the Most High.

The message could be deciphered, *"Please come at your convenience with recommendations for the upcoming meeting of the high servers,"* but it was written in a very shaky hand. Before the Most High had come out of seclusion, he had often dictated his messages for one of his assistants to write down, but since he had rejoined daily routines, the Most High had taken to writing out all correspondence by himself. Unfortunately, Nekur could easily see the increasing shakiness of the Most High's handwriting with each successive note. The characters were only legible because Nekur knew what the Most High was trying to write.

"Does the high server have any response?" asked the messenger.

"No, there's no need to return a message. I will go to him now."

When he reached the central chamber, the Most High was playing a game of shell-toss with one of his assistants.

"The Most High should play the eye block. That will undo my circle," said the assistant. He was telling the Most High exactly what to do.

"Pardon my interruption," said Nekur. The assistant immediately turned to look at Nekur holding the door tarp back while the Most High continued gazing absently at the game table.

"Most High, the primary advisor is here," said the assistant.

The Most High finally looked up. "Come, high server, I'm glad you are here," he said.

The assistant picked up the game table and carefully moved it aside with the pieces in place so that the game could be continued later. Nekur entered and waited for the Most High to invite him to sit, but the Most High looked at him blankly.

"Would the Most High like his primary advisor to be seated?" asked the assistant.

"Yes, yes! Please come and sit," said the Most High.

Nekur raised hands to face and took the seat cushion beside the Most High.

"Did you bring me a list of recommendations to give the high servers?" asked the Most High.

"I don't have a list, Most High, but there are a few things we could discuss," said Nekur.

"Please tell me," said the Most High.

"Well, for one thing," said Nekur, "We have a number of tenth and eleventh generation servers who are getting close to their time of departure. We should give them turns at morning greeting."

"Very good," said the Most High. I will bring this up first thing. Do you think we should start with a mind-stilling?"

"Would it be easier or harder for you to take part in the meeting if we started with a mind-stilling?"

"I think it would be harder for me, but easier for the Soft One," said the Most High.

"Let's do without the mind-stilling. The high servers must see the Most High as alert as possible."

The Most High nodded. "Yes, and the Soft One will want me to engage actively."

"That brings me to another recommendation. We should exclude the flat pose from general shiftings and limit it to the younger servers' training."

"I have had a difficult time with the flat pose," said the Most High.

"Exactly. And we don't want the Most High to have to withdraw from general exercises if we can help it."

"Will the servers worry that they're denying the Soft One . . . ?"

"They won't worry if you make the suggestion," said Nekur.

"Very well. But I'm not sure if limiting it to 'younger servers' is the best way to say it. Remember, I am only third generation myself."

Nekur looked at the Most High and tried to mask his sorrow. Indeed the Most High looked like he was at least sixth generation. "You may tell them that the flat pose is to be limited to training and practice for the younger servers, and you don't need to explain anything or account for the fact that you are also young. They will not question your decision."

"Is there anything else?"

"Is there anything you have thought about yourself?"

The Most High paused. "There is nothing at this time. The high servers may want to address concerns with me."

"The only thing being talked about now is the Feast of Moons' Crossing. There is some discussion that we should keep it small to minimalize disruption."

"What do you think?"

Nekur wasn't sure what he thought. It was a sad signal to him that his advice was sought on a matter such as this. The Most High had no sense of his own authority. Nekur had once been eager to have this kind of influence, but now that he had it, what seemed most important, strangely, was that the Most High should thrive. Would a traditional feast be too taxing on him?

"Would you enjoy a feast, or would you find it too exhausting?" asked Nekur.

Tilke's head dropped. He gave the impression of indecision and exhaustion.

Nekur read the signal easily. "When the high servers propose a smaller feast to minimalize disruption, tell them that you agree for the sake of the Soft One's tranquility."

"Very well. In truth, a smaller feast will be less disruptive to her."

Nekur realized that every one of the Most High's comments revolved around his preoccupation with his communion, the same communion everyone in the temple, including himself, naturally thought of as something to protect. But it was a communion that looked like misery for the poor uedin who occupied the position of the Most High. His thin frame hardly filled his server wrappings, and the dark circles under his eyes further saddened what was already a face of disturbing premature age. The fact that he dragged himself through server exercises and took meals with the other high servers provided evidence that he was *trying* to be active, healthy, and fit—it was not, unfortunately, providing the desired results. Nekur, cool-minded as he was, didn't like what he was seeing. This third-generation uedin might die in the temple and never go to his own passing-of-life. How could the Soft One ever allow that?

Jutef Finds Elenn at the Murro Project

The hooded master never gave his name to Jutef. Jutef had hoped to get him to talk a little more freely, but he was too withdrawn. He spoke up only to say that he didn't want to stop at Bells to fill the water gourds and that he would fill them when they got to the mill where he planned to speak with his seniors. That suited Jutef well enough, since he knew that he would be interrogated at Bells, and he still wasn't sure what he was going to say about Elenn's absence. Still, he wished that when Nula was living, and Elenn was keeping oath, they had together gained a better acquaintance with this unfortunate hooded master.

When they got to the mill, the hooded master asked Jutef to wait at a distance while he went in and talked to his seniors. Ordinarily such a request would have seemed rude, but Jutef understand that one who declined even to share his own name would hardly be interested in making introductions, especially involving a blind uedin who so stood out and drew attention. The hooded master came back with the filled water gourds, and Jutef quickly drank and nearly drained one of them, but he didn't ask his silent companion to refill it.

Once outside the South Gate and over the Clay Bridge, Jutef noted how the sounds of the capital streets died away and were replaced by the steady crunch of their feet on the road. Because of the project at Murro, they crossed paths with occasional others coming back to the capital, some of whom made an informal greeting of commentary on the cool weather. Jutef, knowing that the uedin walking beside him was probably avoiding contact, deliberately smiled and responded to anyone who spoke to them. One of them, rather than talking about the cool, addressed Jutef directly.

"Master Jutef, hello!"

"Hello, hello . . . " said Jutef nervously. He didn't recognize the voice, but he was afraid it might be someone whose voice he *should* recognize. "Is it, . . . you're from Quarterhouse, aren't you?" It was either faint memory or guessing, he couldn't be sure which.

"Well, yes, kind of. I'm with the Flatpools guards."

"A Flatpools guard?" Jutef was very glad to hear that.

"Yes, name of Ribol," said the guard.

"Master Ribol, perhaps we have met, I'm sorry I don't recall."

"I don't suppose we've actually met, but I know you was living with Master Elenn, right? Outside the north gate?"

"That's right," said Jutef.

"Well, let me tell you, Master Elenn is at the project right now. But he's not doing very well."

"Not doing well . . . ?" Jutef said. He was surprised that this guard seemed to know Master Elenn well, though he didn't remember Elenn ever mentioning a guard named Ribol.

"It's sad to see it," said Ribol. "He's a fine uedin, down deep, I'm sure of it."

"Thank you, Master Ribol. I was afraid Master Elenn might be doing poorly, but I'm glad to hear that he's at Murro."

"Yes, it's a very good project. When that young Master Nemis kept bringing it up, I thought it was a little crazy, but now that the hooded masters are involved, I think it's a very good thing. Are you going to help at the project young master?" Ribol addressed the hooded miller.

The miller, to Jutef's surprise, spoke right up. "I'm just accompanying Master Jutef. I'm not planning to work at the project."

"Well, the way they have it set up over there, you don't have to work if you don't want to. But most of the hooded masters there really want to. The ones that aren't working are just the ones that can't handle it on a given day."

"I'm glad to hear they have such an arrangement," said Jutef.

"Some of them just can't handle it, that's all. I'm sad to say, Master Elenn can't handle it right now."

"Did you speak to him?" asked Jutef.

"No, I didn't. I thought it would be better not to, so when I see him when he's doing better, he won't need to feel ashamed."

"He's that bad?" asked Jutef.

"Well, it's probably just that I'm not used to seeing such things," said Ribol. "You know him better than me. You should talk to him, definitely. He seems to be camping by one of the other grainhouses, the one at the very end of the row."

"I'll try to find him," said Jutef.

"There are other caretakers there. They'll help you."

"Did you know any of the caretakers there? Was Master Yenca there, by any chance?"

"No, none of the older caretakers are there. It's all the young ones coming out to Murro."

"You have been helping at the project with some regularity, I take it?"

"Flatpools is letting me come here half time and do my other duties half time. I've lost count of how many times I've been back and forth on this road."

"I've been wanting to visit the project for a while now," said Jutef.

"Well, I hope you have a very good visit. I'm sure you're going to help Master Elenn."

"I hope there's something I can do."

"Master Elenn will talk to you. I'm sure he will."

"Thank you, Master Ribol. I'm sorry that we're traveling in opposite directions. Maybe I will visit the project another time in the future, and I will talk with you again."

"That would be very nice, Master Jutef. I wish you the best! Best wishes to you too, young master!"

Jutef raised hands to face and held them there for a moment to give Ribol a chance to raise hands before he lowered his. Then he focused on the grip of his hand on the cane so that he could reorient himself with regards to direction, and they continued on the road to Murro.

When they reached the grainhouses, Jutef heard the sound of voices, as well as the sounds of sawing and chiseling, and the familiar sound of a log transporter. He had heard one in operation once before when he had visited the construction site for the caretaker hut. This one was creaking loudly in the distance. They must be moving or positioning some very large logs.

He spoke to the miller. "Master, I know you don't want to stay, and I appreciate your coming all this way with me," he said, "but I just need one more thing from you. Do you see anyone with a caretaker's robe? If you can help me find another caretaker, I won't bother you for anything else."

"One of the grainhouses has a scaffolding on the side. There are a lot of uedin in groups there. Maybe there's a caretaker, " said the miller.

Jutef could smell campfires and hear talking as they got closer.

"There's someone with caretaker's robe," said the miller.

Jutef held his hand up, "Will you guide me? Let me put my hand on your shoulder?" The miller silently took Jutef's wrist and led his hand to his shoulder. They walked toward the sound.

"Master Jutef! Hello! I'm Kelo, from Bells!" said a voice. Jutef was often in the awkward situation of being on the wrong end of a unilateral familiarity. He had grown up at Bells, and everyone there knew him from childhood. While other unnamed had been indistinguishable, everyone knew the little blind child-uedin and easily remembered him as Jutef once he took name. But for his part, Jutef had left Bells to join the caretakers to the barren at Quarterhouse before he could learn the names of his peers from Bells.

He imagined they could all tell when he was pretending to know them, but it seemed like his only polite option. "Master Kelo, I'm glad you are here," he said.

"There are no senior caretakers here, only our generation. I'm surprised, actually, to see you here."

"Haven't they been coming at all?"

"Master Yenca was here once. He hasn't been back."

"Do you know why the senior caretakers aren't coming?"

"Yes. They don't like to see the hooded masters feeding."

"They feed *here*?" said Jutef, appalled.

"They do," said Kelo.

"It doesn't surprise me," commented the miller.

"Well, I didn't expect to hear that," said Jutef.

"The ones working right at the project sight don't do it, but there are many here who are in derangement. They eat and drink from the supplies we bring, but they don't work."

"What do they do here?" asked Jutef.

"They feed all the time."

Jutef was stunned to hear this about the project. He was speechless.

"You see why I don't want to be here?" said the miller.

"The builder masters are able to ignore it?" asked Jutef, finally.

"The ones who find it too troubling don't come back."

"I wonder if the masters council knows about this."

"That's what Master Yenca was here to do. He was asked to report to the masters council on behalf of the caretakers. We tried to convince him that the outreach here is critical."

"I see . . . " said Jutef, but in fact, he was upset and perplexed to think that he was left out of the discussion. "Well, perhaps this explains why we hardly get any visitors to the caretaker hut, specifically put there to help the hooded masters."

"They're all coming here," said Kelo.

What bothered Jutef the most was the idea that many syndrome-afflicted uedin were not even working on the project. They were only congregating here to feed. This was a sickening thought. How could caretakers allow this to happen? They would lose their uedin identity if they were not held in check. At the same time, Jutef had to take responsibility for not keeping up with the news of the capital. He had avoided Quarterhouse because he was trying to cover up Elenn's absence. That reminded him, and he spoke. "We saw a Flatpools guard on the way here. He told us that Master Elenn of the hood squadron was here. He resides with me at the caretaker hut. Have you seen him?"

"Master Elenn—the one who spoke at the hood-taking ceremony—yes, he's around here. It's very sad that he went from spokesperson and hood squad guard to derangement. You do know he's deranged, don't you, Master Jutef?"

"There have been signs of it, but I'm afraid it's going to be worse than I thought," said Jutef.

"I think before you meet him, you should spend a day with us. Give yourself a day to learn about what happens in the project. That might help when you talk with him."

"I am curious about the project. Are you involved at all in the work of the project, or are you just here to look after the hooded masters?"

"I learn a lot from working with the hooded masters who stay at the project site. We try to give them as much support as we can, to keep them from following the others."

"It's just a rooftop deck they're building, right? I didn't think it would take so long as it has."

"Do you know Guard Master Nemis? He's a regular guard with the hood squadron now."

"Yes, I know Master Nemis. I understand that he was instrumental in getting this project underway."

"He has kept the project going. He and the current members of the hood squadron focus a lot of their work here now."

It was then that Jutef felt a pang of indignation. Not only did everyone neglect to tell him that all the hooded masters were congregating at the project, but the squadron guards were even focusing their work there while leaving Jutef completely out of the loop. He suspected it was because they saw him as disabled.

"Please help me find Master Elenn right now," said Jutef, suddenly irritable. "I don't need to learn more about the project before I speak with him."

"Master Jutef, I hope you don't mind, I'm going back to the capital," said the miller. "Will you be able to find someone to help you get back home?"

"Yes, I'll find someone."

"Uedin are back and forth every day," said Kelo.

"Then please excuse me. I hope you have success here," said the miller. Jutef sensed in the pause following that the miller was raising hands to face.

He raised hands in response. "Thank you, master. I understand your reasons for leaving. You will be welcome at the caretaker hut as long as I am there. I hope you will visit me." But the miller didn't say any more, and Jutef listened to his footsteps going away.

"Will you help me find Master Elenn?"

"It shouldn't be too hard. Let me ask some of the hooded masters around here if they've seen him recently. You must be tired from walking all day. Why don't you sit by the fire here and I'll bring you some salted porridge. You can rest while I go find out what I can."

"If you find Master Elenn, will you bring him back here?"

"I don't think he'll come here. We'll have to go to him, after we find out where he is."

"All right. Porridge sounds good, actually." Jutef let Kelo direct him to a resting log in which seats had been roughly hewn. The dip of the seat was surprisingly comfortable, and the campfire was just close enough to send a little wave of warmth his way. Kelo was gone for a minute, and then returned with a bowl of salted porridge, which tasted just right to Jutef after his trek through the capital and all the way to Murro.

"I'll be back before dusk. There are other caretakers close by— just call out. I think someone will come right away if you need anything."

"Thank you, Master Kelo, I very much appreciate your help."

"That is what we do, isn't it, Master Jutef."

"Yes, you're right," said Jutef thoughtfully, "that *is* what we do." This reminder of his caretaker vocation made Jutef think about his anger regarding being left out of communication, perhaps because of others considering him to be disabled. It was true, they might be bypassing him, and that was unpleasant to think about. But more than that, it was Jutef's concern for the hooded masters that made him feel aggravation when he was denied his opportunity to help, however he might. "It's very good to be around another caretaker, Master Kelo. I'm so glad you were here to meet me."

Jutef felt Kelo's hand light on his shoulder and give it a friendly squeeze. "I'll see you soon," he said, and left Jutef alone.

Jutef returned to his porridge. It was made from fresh-milled barley, and it made him think of the miller. There was reason for hope, in that miller's case. The miller was determined to go back to his domicile and work. Deep down, the hooded masters all wanted to fulfill their duties. This project was supposed to be a temporary occupation for those who couldn't stay with their vocations. Even if it wasn't working out exactly as planned, the intention was a good one, and surely the effort would pay off in some manner. Meanwhile, someone had gone to the trouble of bringing fresh-milled barley and fresh herbs to make a fine salted porridge all the way out there in the fields of Murro. Jutef couldn't help but be impressed.

Jutef was just starting to do the little stretches and wiggles that one does when coming out of a mind-stilling. As a rule, he didn't have a very good temperament for any of the exercises, except for droning, which he especially enjoyed in the company of others. But the mind-stilling had gone moderately well, and he felt a small peace of mind.

"Master Jutef, are you awake?" It was Kelo. The fire, he noticed, was burning warmer, but he felt cool night air on his back.

Jutef sat up straight. "Yes, Master Kelo. I'm awake. Did you find Master Elenn?"

"He's inside the first grainhouse. By the time I got there it was too dark inside, and I didn't bother going in. But we can go in the morning."

Too dark? What nonsense! "Could you take me to the grain-house now? The darkness doesn't matter to me."

"You don't want to wait?"

"I really don't. I am too eager to see Master Elenn."

"Let me get a lantern."

Jutef waited as Kelo went for a lantern. He adjusted his cloak on his shoulders, fastened it in the front, then reached down and grasped his cane.

"All right then, I'm ready," said Kelo, and Jutef rose from the log seat. Jutef didn't protest when he felt Kelo take his free hand and lead it to his shoulder so that he could guide him. They walked what seemed like a long distance. To Jutef it felt like he was on the road back to the capital. Then he realized that they had passed a number of empty quiet grainhouses on their way and he hadn't known it because the miller had said nothing. Finally Kelo led Jutef off the road and through a field of tall grass until he halted and said, "This is the first grainhouse. Are you ready to go in?"

"Yes. Let me call for Master Elenn. Are there going to be many others in there?"

"I don't know. Another barren master out of hood was helping me look for Master Elenn, and he went in to check for me. When he came out, he said that Master Elenn was in there." Kelo rolled the door partly open and stepped in ahead of Jutef.

Jutef followed him in and called out in a clear voice, "Master Elenn! Master Elenn are you here?"

There was no answer. The inside of the grainhouse was foul with stench. Whoever was staying in there didn't even go outside to toilet.

Jutef called again, "Is Master Elenn of Flatpools here?"

"Look on the second level. Some uedin are up there," said a voice.

Glad to hear a voice respond, Jutef called out, "Is Master Elenn among them, do you know?"

"Don't know anyone here, don't know any names," said the voice.

Kelo spoke to the stranger. "There's food and water at the project site if you need it," he said.

The stranger groaned slightly in response.

"How do we get to the second level? Stairs?" whispered Jutef.

"There are ramps that go along the walls and lead to an opening," said Kelo. "But there are no rails. You'll have to hold my shoulder and stay right behind me."

"All right. Can you see well enough with your lantern?"

"It would have been much better in daylight, but I can see well enough."

Jutef followed behind Kelo with his hand on his shoulder. Kelo moved slowly to allow easier movement for Jutef. They crossed a large space, then turned and started working their way up an incline. At a certain point they turned and continued up along another wall, then again, and again. They reached the top of the fourth ramp, and Jutef could hear the sounds of heavy breathing and movement, and he knew they were at the second level. He stepped onto the flat floor after Kelo and followed him to the interior space. He spoke out again, this time not so loudly, "Is Master Elenn here?" There was some groaning, and Jutef asked Kelo, "What do you see?"

Kelo whispered back, "There are some very unhealthy uedin here. They're naked and filthy. I've seen many deranged masters coming around the project site, and some have been in very bad condition, but I haven't seen any like this."

"Is Master Elenn here? Would you recognize him?"

"I'm sorry, I don't think I would have recognized Master Elenn even when he was well."

"Master Elenn, are you here?" Jutef called out again. One of the hulking figures limped toward them.

"One of them is coming," said Kelo.

"Leave us," said a phlegmy voice, all rasp. Though a voice might change in derangement, Jutef felt sure he would be able to recognize Elenn's. This was not he.

"We won't bother you," said Jutef. "We're looking for Master Elenn, a hooded guard."

"Put out the light!" yelled a voice from the far side of the space.

"I can't put out the light, I won't be able to see to get down the ramp," said Kelo, to Jutef more than anyone.

"I'm sure I can find my way out," said Jutef. "I have my cane, and all we need to do is stay very close to the wall."

"But the walls in the grainhouses aren't regular walls. They're at an angle. I don't want to put out the lantern. I'll hold my sleeve in front of it so it won't be too bright."

"How many uedin are here?"

"It looks like at least six or seven . . . I can't see in the far corners."

"Let us go past, Master," Jutef said to the barren standing in their way. He was sure that he had been around many this bad and worse since moving to the caretaker hut. He wasn't afraid of them. Strange, he thought, how masters who can see get afraid of the dark, and it makes them afraid of everything. He raised his hand to the barren's shoulder and repeated himself calmly, "Let us go past." He heard the sound of heavy footsteps, thudding. The uedin was barefooted, but large enough to make the floor planks creak below him as he walked away.

Jutef whispered to Kelo, "Well if you're not going to recognize Master Elenn, the only way to find him is to speak to each one of them and try to get them to answer back. I'll know his voice."

Jutef let Kelo lead him around the second level. "Let's come back to these two," whispered Kelo, "they are . . . "

"I understand," said Jutef. They were feeding.

One of the barren they found sleeping. "Perhaps it would have been better to wait for morning," said Jutef, "but now that I'm here, I don't want to leave if there's a chance Master Elenn is here."

"Are you going to wake him up?"

"I'm going to put my hand up to his face for just a moment. I think I'll be able to tell if it's Master Elenn."

"Yes, well, please be ready to move back quickly if he wakes up angry,"

Jutef knelt and ever-so-lightly brushed his hand across the sleeping uedin's face. The uedin sluggishly flopped his hand over his cheek and nose as if to shoo away a fly. "It's not him," whispered Jutef quickly.

They went back to the two whom they had almost interrupted. They were both lying flat at odd positions with one another, obviously finished.

"They'll be very muddled in their minds right now," advised Kelo.

"Of course. But I'm going to try to get a sound out of them."

He used his cane to gently determine where the first one was lying, then got down on his knees again, leaned toward where he thought the uedin's head was, and said in a quiet but clear and steady voice, *"Master, if you can hear me, just say 'yes'."*

"Yes."

"Thank you, you're all right. Sleep now."

Kelo reached for Jutef's hand and helped him up and led to the other uedin lying there.

Again Jutef leaned right over him and spoke clearly, *"Master, if you can hear me, just say 'yes'."* The figure in repose did not say anything at first, but then mumbled something indecipherable but revealing of voice. Jutef sighed and whispered disappointedly, "It's not him either."

"That was the last one on this level. There is one more level."

"There's a third level?" asked Jutef, surprised.

"Yes, all these grainhouses have three levels. We'll have to check there next."

"I'm really grateful for your help," said Jutef.

"It's all right, Master Jutef. This is what we do."

Kelo led Jutef again around a series of ramps. This time he had a sense of the lengths getting shorter and the space getting smaller. He reached up with his free hand and felt the wall. Indeed the wall angled in as it rose.

When they got through to the third level, Jutef gave Kelo a chance to hold up his lantern and look. He finally asked, "What do you see?"

"Looks like there's no one here, but . . . wait . . . Someone is sitting at the top of the highest ramp."

Jutef was confused. "Didn't you say there were three levels? We're on the third level now."

"There are three levels, but the third level has ramps going up the walls just like the lower two. I don't know why. They just stop at the ceiling. Obviously a deranged master is up there, just sitting up there."

"Master, if you can hear my voice, please say 'yes.'"

There was no response.

"I must go up," said Jutef.

"If I lead you up, you won't be able to get around me. The ramp is very narrow up there, and it runs right into the ceiling."

"I'll go very slowly. I'll manage."

Kelo took Jutef to the lowest ramp, then watched and waited while he made his way up and around, feeling the wall with one hand and using his cane to find the edge of the ramp as he climbed.

"Master, can you hear me? Are you Master Elenn?" called out Jutef. Still, no response.

"Just please be careful, Master Jutef! Watch your head—the roof is just above you!" called Kelo.

"Are you there, Master?" said Jutef to whoever it was.

"You're right in front of him."

Jutef finally felt the tip of his cane slide against someone. He hunched down on his feet, feeling the slope of the ramp.

"Master Elenn?" he said. He could hear breathing. Was it his wishful thinking, or did it sound like Master Elenn's breathing?

"Excuse me, I must, I'm . . . I'm going to touch your face."

Jutef didn't know how deranged this uedin might be, or how it might upset him to be touched, but he put out his hand and brushed it over a face. It was him! It was Master Elenn!

"It's him!" cried Jutef.

"Is he conscious?"

"I think so," said Jutef, and then leaned over him, less warily. "Master Elenn, it's me, Jutef. I've come all the way from the caretaker hut. Are you awake?"

Elenn slightly groaned, and then said, "It doesn't go up any more . . . "

"Master Elenn, please wake up! I'm taking you back to the capital."

" . . . can't get any futher . . . "

"Master Elenn, don't you know me? I'm Jutef."

"Oh . . . Master," said Elenn.

"Yes, that's right! I'm taking you back!"

"Master . . . Master Jutef . . . I'm never going back . . . "

"Oh yes. Oh yes, you must. You have to come back to the capital. You're very ill."

"No, Master Ju . . . never going back . . . "

"Master Elenn, you are a guard of the capital. You must go back."

"I'll come down later. I don't want to share neck right now."

"Come with me down the ramp. Will you come? It's not to share necks. We're going to go outside. How long have you been inside this grainhouse?"

"I'm not a guard, not anymore . . . " said Elenn.

"You are a guard. Be a guard! Master Nula would have wanted that!"

"Nula, I will share with you, now I will," said Elenn, confused.

"Master Elenn, you know that Master Nula is gone," said Jutef.

"Now I will share. Will you give me your neck, or do you want mine first?"

"Master Elenn, let's go now. Let's go down." Jutef reached across, felt for Elenn's hands, and took them into his own hands. He found the hands to be larger and more powerful than he could have imagined. Just then, Elenn pulled his hands away, grabbed both of Jutef's wrists, and made two hard jerking twists, breaking both of Jutef's arms at the same time. Jutef heard the bones crack and splinter at the same time that he heard his own scream erupt. Currents of pain shot through his arms to his neck and down the length of his body. The pain was so intense that he wanted to pass out, but he could not.

"Aaaahhhhhhhhhhhh!" screamed Jutef, "MMMasssterrrrrrrrrrrr!"

Elenn's Request

Henik had no idea what to expect when he went to the infirmary to check on Elenn. Would he even know Henik, or was he too gone? Ribol had already been there twice since Elenn's arrest. He said that Elenn spoke but made no sense. But a letter from Medic Master Gorik said that Elenn had regained his senses enough for questioning by the Capital Guards, and Henik was chosen to go.

Henik knew from Jutef's report that Elenn had somehow knocked him off a high ramp at one of the grainhouses at Murro. Jutef had fractured both arms in breaking his fall. The senior guards had been unaware that Elenn had drifted from the project and had completely given in to feeding. He was a serious liability to the guards now. And yet, even at this point, Flatpools still considered him one of theirs. According to code, Elenn could not be held responsible for things he did when he was out of his mind. The senior guards all understood that this was a time that exercised the spirit of this code.

He followed the junior medic to the syndrome ward. It was full. Henik was a seasoned guard, but he had never been around so many deranged barren at the same time, and he struggled to maintain his guard's composure when he arrived at the ward. It felt nightmarish to him. It was very clean, orderly, and well-lit, but the sound of barren uedin yelling and crying was dreadful to hear. Henik was relieved when he found Elenn, though wearing no hood, sitting quiet and attentive in his room.

"Master Elenn, your comrade guard is here to see you," said the junior medic.

Elenn stood and brought hands to face, but he said nothing.

Henik was glad that at least Elenn was behaving somewhat normally. The six days of monitoring must have been enough to see a decrease of derangement. "Master Elenn," he said, "the guards all send their greetings, but I am mainly here to question you about what happened at Murro before you were arrested."

Elenn didn't speak.

Henik continued, "You know that Master Jutef was hurt, don't you?"

"Yes, I know," said Elenn darkly, "I hurt him."

"Well, it was bad, but the medic masters are glad he didn't break his neck. It could have killed him."

"I hurt him," said Elenn again. He was doing well, thought Henik, but he was not yet himself completely.

"Master Elenn, what do you remember? Do you remember anything?"

"I—broke—his arms," said Elenn, his voice strained.

"Master Jutef broke his arms in a fall," Henik explained to Elenn. "You didn't really break them."

"No—I *did* . . . " said Elenn, looking Henik in the eye with great torment.

"You—what do you mean?" Henik looked at the deep anguish in Elenn's eyes. What was he saying?

Elenn slowly lifted his freakish hands and looked at them with horror. "I broke his arms . . . with my hands."

Henik felt his own face change into disbelief as he perceived what Elenn was saying. Could Elenn have actually broken Jutef's arms with his bare hands? It was unimaginable, and Jutef had not reported anything like that, but . . .

"Jutef said he fell from a high ramp."

"No." Elenn gazed downwardly, thinking about what Henik was telling him.

"You broke his arms, with your own hands?"

"Yes . . . I did," Elenn whispered.

"Can you show me without hurting me?" asked Henik, and he cautiously held out his arms for Elenn to take.

Elenn's head leaned slightly to the side and he regarded Henik with sadness.

"You don't want to show me," said Henik with understanding, "It's all right. But we don't know if that's what really happened. You were not in your right mind. You might have dreamt that." Somehow, though, Henik's resistance to the idea could not hold up. He had a feeling that Elenn was telling the truth.

"Master," said Elenn finally, "You remember when I had to get this?" Elenn turned his head to the side and pointed to the neck strap in the back.

"I remember. You wanted to refuse it." Henik remembered how moved he had been when Elenn, then just an apprentice guard, didn't want the catheter implant because he didn't want to live a long time with no passing-of-life ahead of him.

"You told Master Wanba . . . to let me decide."

"Yes, I remember. But you decided to get the implant. We were all glad you did."

"But you see, . . . it didn't help."

"It *could* help," said Henik, sternly, "If you didn't *abuse* it."

"Master Henik, . . . you told me you would take me . . . out of the capital."

Hearing this, Henik remembered his promise. He had told Elenn that if he chose not to get the implant because of his objection to living long with no passing, Henik would look after him, and even take him out of the capital to seek a death by the elements. "But Master Elenn, that was only going to be if you didn't get the implant. You did get it."

"I shouldn't have," said Elenn.

"Well, you did, and you have helped many other syndrome barren to cope. You have to get better, and return to guard duty . . . "

"Don't you see?" Elenn pleaded, "I can never return to guard duty?" He held up his large hands.

Henik looked at the miserable and syndrome-ruined uedin before him, and he imagined how he would feel if he were in such a state. If it were he who had deteriorated to such a degree, he would not want to be forced to recover what could not be recovered. Henik couldn't lie to Elenn. The truth was too obvious. Elenn would never return to guard duty. He was simply past that point. Henik, as he had once before, a novade ago, saw the terrible necessity that Elenn was facing. Elenn *needed* to die.

"Master Henik, . . . you will help me."

Henik looked at the floor in discomfort. He didn't want to try to convince Elenn to extend his deterioration.

"Master Henik, *please* . . . "

"Yes, Master Elenn," said Henik gravely, "I will help you."

Feast of Moons' Crossing

Henik took a sip of yeastdrink and tried to answer Wamba's question as diplomatically as possible. What would be necessary to assist Master Elenn in a quick recovery so that he might return to the hood squadron? At this point he could not hope to spare himself the unpleasantness of lying—the best he could do was make his dishonest answer as ambiguous as possible.

"I believe it will take some time before Master Elenn is ready to return to the squadron, Master Wanba."

"You said that he raised hands and greeted you like a guard when you saw him," said Wanba, "and that he could listen and talk to you."

"It's true. We'll just have to see how much he improves," answered Henik, though he knew himself that Elenn was no longer on the road to improvement. Henik himself had intervened at the infirmary to secretly testify that Elenn had a plan to put himself away at the southeastern desert, and that it was a plan that Elenn had contemplated even before he had ever received the catheter. This influenced the medic masters' decision to reverse the procedure and remove Elenn's catheter so that he could take the course of action he chose of his own free will. They had decided to perform the operation without notifying anyone, and Henik knew that it was his own testimony in support of Elenn's request that had influenced them to do so. It all made him very nervous, but there was no backing out. He was going to usher Elenn out of the capital and all the way to the edge of the southeastern desert. It would take all night to do this without drawing attention and ruining the plan. Moon's Crossing was a perfect night to do it, since everyone would be distracted by the spectacle in the sky, and besides it would light up the entire way to the edge of the desert.

He had told no one except Deben, who agreed to go along. Elenn had indicated no desire to say goodbye to anyone. He seemed to settle, with full mental clarity, into a resolve about what he was choosing to do, and Henik couldn't help but respect Elenn's choice to do what barren uedin had apparently done in generations past.

"Well, I do appreciate your visiting him, and your description confirms what I thought," said Wanba. "Elenn is a guard deep down. He will do right."

Henik was glad when Wanba stepped back, took a good sip of his own drink, and didn't eye him for some kind of response. Maybe eventually the guards would be able to see that Elenn was doing the right thing, but he also knew they would disapprove of it's happening without full consent of the senior guards and masters council. Wanba was already turned around and talking to someone else. Hopefully he would never know about their plan. The infirmary would report that Elenn had disappeared on the night of Moon's Crossing. Only he and Deben would know that Master Elenn was assisted.

Deben came over and spoke to Henik. "Too bad Master Elenn couldn't have come to this feast," said Deben, "Too bad he couldn't have come and said goodbye to all his comrade guards,"

"He didn't want to say goodbye to anyone," said Henik. "Master Benar of Quarterhouse is his counselor, and I know he will be deeply offended knowing that Master Elenn neglected to say goodbye to him. But he refuses."

"What about Master Jutef?" suggested Deben, "He's lived with Master Elenn at the hut since it was built. He's healing from the fall, of course, but I'm sure he would have wanted to say goodbye."

"There's only one thing on his mind now, and that's to leave," said Henik. "This is not a departure for passing-of-life, and good-byes are not an option for Master Elenn. We needed to make it as easy as possible for him."

Simol stood near the door of the meal hall facing the tables where the guards were still talking and mingling over their cups. He held up a hand to get the guards' attention. The talking ceased, and they all gave their attention to Simol. Simol raised hands to face and said, "Master Wanba asked me to remind you all that he will be remaining at Central Station for the duration of the Moons' Crossing, and if any of you need assistance with anything, you may find him there. I have been given the honor of reading the Poem of the Two Moons," he said, and commenced to read.

> "The greater moon bounds across the sky
> In a hurry to reach his destination.
> He's filled up from the well of foolishness,
> And now he is thirsty for the water of wisdom.
> The further he gets from the well of foolishness,
> The more wise does he become.

> "The lesser moon walks at a very slow pace
> As if dragging himself through the heavens.
> He is filled up from the well of wisdom,
> And now he is thirsty for the water of foolishness.
> The further he gets from the well of wisdom,
> The more foolish does he become.

> "See how they meet at the center of heaven,
> Both half foolish and half wise.
> Because they are wise, they understand
> That they are thirsty for different things,
> But because they are foolish they can't imagine

Why one should thirst for what the other left behind.
Because they are wise, they decide to help each other,
But because they are foolish, they end up giving
One another the wrong directions.

"Greater moon and lesser moon
Each go off in wrong directions
They miss the wells for which they seek
Go clear around to whence they came.
Once again foolish, once again wise,
Each must begin all over again.

"The moons linger a moment at crossing
And light up the capital from the night sky.
Uedin look up at the bright encounter,
How we resemble the criss-crossing moons!
We are half foolish and half wise
Giving directions and taking our chances."

To the Southeastern Desert

Elenn looked at the folded blanket and rolled up bedding neatly put away in the corner of the infirmary room. Even though he knew he wouldn't have been able to sleep, maybe he should have lain on real bedding one last time—might it not have been a comfort to him? But it was too late now. Henik would be here for him soon.

He brushed his heavy hand over the green fabric of his robe. He had apparently been given some light robe to put on when he had been arrested, and he had worn that for many days while he was recovering from derangement. But Henik had insisted that he should wear proper guard's garb for the departure. He was glad that no one said anything about a hood.

Master Gorik had removed his catheter that afternoon. Gorik had made small incisions at either side of the implant, removed it—a very painful moment—and then closed the cavity and stitched it. A balm was put over the wound to reduce pain, and it seemed to work. Elenn knew that by the next morning he would start to experience derangement again, and this was going to be his last time to feel that strange collapsing sensation.

Many of the medic masters were either feasting at their domiciles, or perhaps, already on their way to the main plaza for Moons' Crossing. The ones who remained at the infirmary were politely staying out of the way. The senior medics must have given instructions to the staff so that no one would interfere with Elenn's departure. Elenn was deeply thankful to Henik for speaking to the medics on his behalf. There was no way to ever repay him.

He did notice the bright glow of the two moons in the alley-way outside the window of his room. Earlier in the evening, an apprentice had brought in a tray with food, and there had been a little honeycake with it, a treat to remind him that the capital would be celebrating. He had no interest in eating anything. Henik had suggested leaving tonight so that he could get Elenn to the southeastern desert as quickly and easily as possible on well-lit paths and at a time when they could steal away unnoticed while everyone was gathered in the central plaza.

Elenn heard the sound of footsteps in the alley. It sounded like more than one uedin.

"Master Elenn!" Henik's voice said in a loud whisper as the footsteps approached.

"Who's with you?" asked Elenn.

"Master Deben is coming with us," said Henik.

"I hope you don't mind," said Deben, now appearing in the window, though his face was in shadow.

"I have spoken to Master Deben about your decision. He knows everything."

"Thank you for coming, Master Deben. I'm sorry you will miss the celebration at the plaza."

"We'll see Moons' Crossing wherever we are," answered Deben.

"By that time, I'm hoping we'll be in the canyon," said Henik.

"It will be best if you come in to get me," said Elenn. "If we encounter any infirmary staff who are worried about me leaving, it will help to have other guards escorting me out."

Henik and Deben went around to enter the infirmary from the front, and shortly afterwards, a young medic appeared at the door of Elenn's room.

"Your comrade guards are here for you, Master Elenn. Master Gorik told us that you would be going out for Moons' Crossing. Just please be careful—your surgical wound is still fresh."

"Thank you, Master," said Elenn. He felt odd leaving without taking anything with him, but he followed Henik and Deben through the infirmary and out the front entrance. Elenn could hear the sound of the crowd all the way over at the central plaza.

As they walked out of the central district and toward eastgate, the streets in that part of the capital were quiet and empty.

"You've timed it well, Master Henik," said Deben.

"I knew by now everyone would be gathering at the central plaza," said Henik.

Elenn hardly looked around as he walked, Henik in front of him and Deben behind. It had been a very long time since he had walked the capital streets. He was leaving forever, but he felt no nostalgia. A dismal feeling clutched his chest when they reached the capital gate, but it was offset by a glaze of disorientation that he now felt coming over him, a result of his catheter having been removed. They paused briefly at the gate, and he felt felt as though he were engulfed in a cloud of grief, and yet the grief seemed faraway and irrelevant. It was the first hint of derangement, that familiar sensation of disconnect.

They passed through and stood in the light of the two moons just outside the gate. Henik waited a moment there, and Elenn was unsure what he was doing. For a moment he was convinced that they had only planned to escort him to the gate, and that he would have to get through the canyon by himself. Immediately he worried that derangement would confuse him and make him circle back. But when he saw the tears on Deben's face, he realized that they weren't saying goodbye yet, they were pausing to let Elenn reconsider his choice before leaving the capital.

"Master Elenn," said Deben with emotion, "Are you very sure . . . ?"

"Thank you, . . . I'm sure. Please, let's go."

They walked into the eastern slopes in the bright moonlight. Elenn's attention was inconsistent. One moment he had a sharp awareness of what he was doing, and the next moment his mind wandered. Henik was in front of him, the skullwomb on the back of his head facing Elenn like a taunting reminder of his feeding habit. His mind flicked to recollections of trailing and be trailed by barren uedin with titillating tell-tale hoods to signify the promise of ecstasy they held beneath the white knit. Then he thought of the dark putrid corners of the grainhouse where he had spent days in darkness. For some reason his mind wandered to the thought of the hole they had dug in the moist soil at the bottom of the drystream for Nula's body.

"Look, it's almost Moons' Crossing. Let's stop," said Henik. They stood on the rocky ground of the slopes and looked up at the moons. The greater moon had caught up with the lesser, and now they were drawing close to each other.

They watched in silence as the larger moon eclipsed the smaller and waited for a minute to pass as the smaller edged out, a small bright ball first bulging and then emerging from the larger. Elenn thought of a lecture he had heard as a child-uedin about the Moons' Crossing. At the time he could only imagine it. It was described with a patronizing show of excitement by one of his early tutors. He had now seen it for himself many times—enough times. As brilliant as it appeared from the vantage point of the quiet and empty eastern slopes, it did not move him. He stopped looking up and waited for Henik to meet his gaze, then nodded once to acknowledge that it was over and that he was ready to walk again.

Before long they reached the beginning of the Haka Cliffs. The pathway down to the base was smooth and gradual. *Master Jutef could make it out here with his cane. I wonder if he's ever been here.* But then Elenn remembered that he had hurt Jutef, and that he would never see him again. The cliff edges rose and fell on both sides as they walked deeper in. The light of the moons, now edging away from one another, started casting double shadows everywhere.

Be strong and remember your oath! The phrase started to repeat in Elenn's head, antagonizing him. They were words that now cruelly mocked him. *Be strong and remember your oath! Be strong and remember your oath!*

44

After a while, Elenn noticed first just a sandy grit on the rock path under his feet, then eventually, pockets of sand on the canyon floor. They were getting closer. Finally, when it was nearly dawn, the valley opened up into a landscape of rock formations half buried in dunes. Henik first slowed his pace and then came to a halt, guiding Elenn and Deben to do the same.

"Master Elenn, the medic masters said derangement would hit you within hours. Are you feeling anything yet? Are you able to carry on alone?"

"Yes," said Elenn, "I think this is far enough. You two can go back."

He then looked at Henik and saw his mouth move, but in the dizzy onset of derangement he was completely unable to decipher what he was being told. Henik kept looking at him for an answer to a question that Elenn hadn't heard.

"I'm sorry, Master, what did you say?" Elenn took in the expression on Henik's face. *He's realizing that I'm starting into derangement. He's looking at me so sadly.*

"I asked you if you would like to recite the Names," said Henik. Then he added, "I can't imagine how hard this is for you."

Into Elenn's mind popped an image of a very large weed growing in garden soil. In his mind, he had hold of it with both hands, trying to pull. "It is very hard." *It is hard to pull the weed. It should be easier.*

" . . . could you say the Names? If we tried, could you say them?" *He's concerned that I can't say the Names because I'm slipping into derangement. Could I say them? I don't know. I don't care. I have nothing to give to Lern Beyana but my going away.*

Henik saw that Elenn was unprepared to recite the Names. "Master Elenn, it's all right, we don't have to recite the Names. But if it gets very painful for you, it may help you to say them."

"Thank you . . . both . . . for coming this far with me," said Elenn. "Please, now go back to the capital."

Elenn looked at the faces of these two guards, the last uedin he would ever see. Henik looked pained with worry. Deben had tears in his eyes.

Deben said to him, "Master Elenn, I remember the day I found you in the library, when you were newly named. I told you it was just a bad dream. I'm sorry . . . I'm sorry I couldn't help you." His voice cracked, and his eyes filled with tears.

Henik put an arm around Deben. He now also had tears. "We will miss you greatly, Master Elenn," he said. "You were a fine guard."

Elenn felt a trickle of sadness cut through the numbness. But there was no wish to *attach* it to, no notion of what *ought* to be. He slowly lifted his arms to raise hands to face. Deben and Henik quickly stood up straight and held their hands to face in guard-like respect, holding until Elenn brought his hands down. He nodded once, then turned his back to them and started walking away from the canyon into desert. He walked a long time before turning around to make sure they were gone. He walked on.

Eventually the greater moon disappeared below the northeast horizon, while the lesser lingered in the pre-dawn sky. When the sun itself broke above the horizon, Elenn was far enough into the southeastern desert that he could only see dunes when he looked back from where his tracks led. He continued walking, aware enough to change directions slightly to go a little south of the point of the sunrise so that he could go directly into the heart of the desert.

A blazing sun climbed the sky in front of and then over him as he trudged on for hours. The heat grew intense. By the time he saw his shadow moving slightly ahead of him, derangement was hitting him full force. Only after he felt his headache worsen by afternoon did he consider that he might be suffering from the heat. Thirst and dry mouth were also now coming on. Yet he felt no desperation. Instead his mind was compulsively repeating the hood oath. . . . *wear this hood for the rest of my life, and by doing so, bring no trouble . . .*

When the early evening sun fell on his back, the heat subsided, but the headache worsened and his throat became parched. By sunset, he was feeling the first flashes of panic in the midst of confusion. *Should I try to turn back? I'm going to die! My body will dry up and disintegrate into this sand!* What had been a slow but continuing march turned into a broken progression. He would stop, overwhelmed by the realization of his doom, not knowing what to do or where to go, and then, finding it unbearable to stand still, push himself on in any direction.

He completely lost track of time. At some point later, he opened his stinging eyes, feeling the scrape of his dry eyelids. It was night. The moons were out again. Now it was very cold, his head was throbbing, and his whole body ached. He didn't remember lying down. Had he collapsed? Without trying to get up, he just lifted his head a little to discern his tracks in the sand, coming to the place where he lay and stopping there. The slight movement it took to thrust himself up and look about felt like heavy work, and when he dropped again, his head swam with dizziness, and he slept more.

When the light of the morning woke him, he was able to stand and walk again, but his disorientation was more severe. He talked to Henik and Deben, imagining them to be still with him. They interrogated him.

If you cannot wear your hood, then how can you wear guard's garb?

I don't have my hood.

You swore that you would wear it for the rest of your life.

I wore it as long as I could.

He couldn't stop his comrades from torturing him.

You abandoned the squadron, abandoned your oath, and threw away your hood. But you still wear a guard's robe?

Leave me alone! Just let me die!

You will die in guard's garb, even though you left us?

Enough! Enough!

Elenn finally stopped and, with slow and shaky movement, took off his guard's robe, undergarment, belt, and footwear. He looked at them lying together on the sand.

He stood over the pile of clothing. Naked, he turned around, to shout in all directions, "I AM NOT A GUAAARD!! I AM ONLY BARRREEEEENNNNN!!!!!!" Then he walked aimlessly away, leaving the heap to the wind and sand.

Still walking at mid-morning, he was reminded of his nakedness by the hot sun. His dry skin baked. He noticed that his bandage had fallen off somewhere and the surgery scab was dry. But again, he was stopping, walking short stretches, and stopping. *There is nowhere to go. There is no reason to walk anymore.* But he walked a few more short series of strides before he finally fell to his knees and scooped handfuls of sand into his hands and threw them in the air hopelessly. Then he lay on his side in the sand, trying to create a pool of shadow in which to escape, like the dark space in a face pillow. *Lehera Beyana yana ya, Lerna Beyana ulrana uedina, Lern Beyan kiman kiman uedin olorrr, Hunna Bah muh Lor, Mei nar Lalem Lalem Paremm . . .*

Rescue in the Desert

Elenn slipped into a feeble semi-consciousness. His throat was sore, his nose burning inside, his eyes hot and dry. The scab on his neck below his skullwomb was stinging, as was the entire back of his body and feet, blistered with sunburn.

The movement of shadows darting over his face made him open his eyes. He couldn't see well, but a figure, darkly silhouetted by a sunset, was walking around him, then leaning over him. Elenn thought it was Henik, come back to rescue him. He tried to speak but could manage no more than the hint of a groan. He felt himself being picked up and carried like a small child-uedin. He didn't have the strength to protest being taken back to the capital. He surrendered his will along with the full weight of his body, letting his head hang back and his arms fall limp. The jerking and jiggling that went with being carried was fully absorbed, as he had no muscle strength to hold himself tense to resist them.

Something was wrong. Something didn't make sense. He was barely conscious, and pain occupied his mind, but the inkling of some oddity pestered him. What was it?

His eyes were stuck closed, the lids glued together by dried secretion. He tried to open his eyes, feeling the sticky seams of his eyelids give way, drawing his eyelids apart. Henik was carrying him away from the sunset toward the darker dusk of the eastern sky. The capital was in the other direction.

But was it even Henik? It occurred to Elenn that considerable strength would be needed to carry his large frame . . . was Henik strong enough to carry him so effortlessly? And then, in an instant,

Elenn realized that whoever carried him was not wearing guard's garb at all. It was not even a normal robe. It was some kind of vest of dried leaves. The jostling continued, but Elenn faded back into sleep before he could wonder further about who was carrying him.

The next time he regained consciousness, he was lying on a cool stone floor. One side of his field of vision was in the dark, the other bright with blue sky. Figures of uedin sat around him. One of them was using a curved piece of wood to spoon some kind of soupy mixture into his mouth. It was warm and wet but nearly tasteless, with mashed fleshy bits in it. He swallowed. It hurt to swallow, so chapped and raw was his throat. The uedin feeding him looked down at him. It wasn't a face he recognized.

"He's awake," the uedin said to the others. He used the same words as capital uedin, though it sounded a little odd. He neither smiled nor showed any emotion. "Rest, new one. Don't worry. You have arrived safely." Others now came and looked down at him, all with expressionless faces. They were large but lean, with bronzed faces and strange clothing of woven leaves and tendrils. They looked old, but strangely preserved. Their faces were languid and quiescent. None of them spoke; they only watched him, calmly.

Elenn decided to attempt speech. He opened his mouth, but at first he could only murmur. The uedin put down the small wooden spoon to let him speak. Elenn tried again. " . . . where am I?" he whispered hoarsely.

"Welcome," said the one looking down at him. "I am Yulig."

The soup was just slightly warm, and it was the perfect temperature for his sore mouth and throat. It gave him a very pleasant, peaceful feeling.

"What is this?" Elenn asked when the uedin brought the spoon to his mouth again.

"It is whitesponge. We mash it with water and warm it in the sun." The uedin's voice sounded so calm—Elenn found it calming to hear him talk. He shortly fell back to sleep.

The Village of the Childless

On his second day, Elenn was feeling rapid recovery. The porridge of whitesponge had not only nourished his spent and sunburnt body, it had also soothed his thrashed and grieved mind. Gradually he got a sense of where he was and what was happening. It was clearly a dwelling carved into a bluff, and it appeared to be part of a network of connected dwellings, given that other uedin were constantly coming and going. They spoke the same as any master, and Elenn could only ask himself, since they obviously had come from the capital at some point, how were they able to *be* there, unbeknownst to the uedin in the capital? Could an outvillage actually be forgotten? The dwelling was clean and dry, carved out to smoothness and furnished with various woven grass matting and sit-stools. A number of uedin seemed to lounge there around him, serving no purpose but to wait for his recovery.

A large uedin, clearly appearing to have the frame of a barren, entered on brisk feet. Elenn and he looked at each other, recognizing their shared condition.

"Well, we are getting larger," said the uedin.

"Yes, he is a big, young new one," said the one who had been feeding him.

"New one, what is your name?"

"I am Elenn."

"Elenn, welcome," said the large barren, neglecting to address him as "master". No one had ever called him just "Elenn" except for Nula. These uedin apparently didn't consider themselves as masters or any such thing. "I was called Pelto in the capital," said the barren. He had the same disarming calm as the uedin who had fed Elenn the warm porridge.

"How did you find me?" asked Elenn. He wasn't sure whether he was glad to be saved.

"It was a bright night. We do night walks in the desert. You are our reward."

Elenn had to ask, "Are you and I the only barren here?"

Pelto looked at him squarely. "We are all barren here. There are no child-uedin here."

Elenn looked around at the other uedin sitting around them. These more normal-looking uedin were also barren?

"Everyone here—barren?"

"We came here just as you did."

Elenn tried to comprehend how a village could form around barren who had come from the capital over time. "What—you don't suffer derangement?"

"What is 'derangement'?"

"The madness . . . of barren syndrome," said Elenn, still weak.

"You mean the raving for the desert? That is the great trial of all childless uedin, but you are lucky, and you have reached us. You will not have to suffer it any longer."

"How is that possible? As long as we live, we produce skullsap."

"Skullsap?" Pelto seemed perplexed by the mention of it. "We are barren. We have no need of skullsap."

Didn't these barren uedin even have a basic understanding of their condition? It did seem strange though, that except for the one he was talking to, they did not exhibit the large frames associated with the syndrome.

"Why don't they look like us?" he asked about the others.

"Barren did not grow so large in the past. These barren are many generations older than either of us."

"They don't look much older than fourth generation or so,"

"Fourth?" Pelto smiled. "I am sixth, myself."

Elenn looked incredulously into Pelto's face. "You are sixth generation?" It was impossible. Pelto looked like a third generation peer to Elenn.

"Yes, I am sixth. Yulig, who found you, is tenth."

That uedin was tenth generation? He had neither the speech, nor the face, nor the slow movement of a ro-uedin. How could the uedin who had fed him that soup be *tenth generation*?

Pelto noticed Elenn's surprise. "I was also surprised by this when I first arrived here," he said. "We barren do not age the same as uedin who go to passing-of-life."

"How can that be? Of course we age . . . " said Elenn.

"It has always been that way," said Pelto.

"Are you saying you *don't age*? What happens to you?"

"We don't grow frail like capital uedin, but we do eventually die. We all die. We have had two deaths since the last Great Rains. Both were twelfth generation uedin."

Uedin in the capital usually went to their pilgrimages during their tenth or eleventh novade. Twelve novades was an exceedingly long time to live. "How many are here in the village now?"

"We were down to forty, but now, with you, we are forty-one."

Elenn thought about how he was being included in their number. "How long have you been here?" he asked.

"I have been here for three novades," said Pelto, "and no one has followed me for all this time, until you. Clearly there are fewer and fewer barren uedin taking leg."

Elenn didn't know where to start. "The capital is on the verge of collapse because there is a great epidemic of barren syndrome now. Barren uedin number in the hundreds." He looked at Pelto to see how he would react.

Pelto looked puzzled. "But none is trading lives in the desert . . . Why?"

Trading lives? The uedin in this lost community had a very different way of looking at barren life. "You see this?" said Elenn, turning around to show Pelto the scab on his neck. "The medic masters have developed a catheter implant that drains skullsap out of us and spares us from derangement. All the barren uedin in the capital have it."

"So you believe it is our skullsap that makes us rave for the desert?"

"Yes, and it also makes us grow large."

"I don't think your theory is correct. The childless know that new ones have been getting larger and larger—I have been told that I myself am proof of that. But the older uedin here had the same skullsap, and they never grew as large as us. And why are you large, then, if you had this catheter thing?"

Elenn did not answer. How could he explain what had transpired in the capital—the advent of feeding, the hood statute, the current chaos?

Finally, Pelto said, "Eat the whitesponge when they bring it to you. Next time I see you, you will explain. It will be easier for you."

Indeed, an ease came over him within days. The turmoil that had driven him from the capital and plagued him right up to his collapse in the desert seemed to be evaporating. He felt no self-consciousness as he was introduced to one after another of the small tribe. He couldn't help but notice the deference shown to him, strange as it seemed that a newcomer should be given such status. The younger among them, he learned, could be distinguished as slightly larger and taller than the older ones, but otherwise their tranquil faces did not provide much indication of age.

Elenn was shown around the network of dwellings and its surroundings on his third day with them. They told him that they had inherited the cliff dwellings from a line of barren uedin who had apparently gravitated to the area for unknown generations. Elenn found it very strange that they did not seem to maintain a record of their history, but their sedate manner suggested that it mattered nothing to them. Some of the dwellings were natural caves while others were hewn into the eroded bluff that faced the desert. There were shadowy pockets of vegetation where moisture seemed to settle from water trickling out of some of the caves.

They never seemed busy, but they focused on various chores. A few varieties of succulents and herbs were cultivated in a small plot just outside one of the caves. The dwellings themselves were maintained scrupulously. Staired pathways led in various directions around the complex of dwellings and caves. Other paths led away from the bluff. Elenn was told that they went on excursions for resources like grass and scrubwood, and they also walked the desert on given nights—a ritual responsible for Elenn's own rescue. The one activity that Elenn did not find at all enticing was the harvesting of whitesponge. It grew in one of the caves, and seeing the tunnel of darkness at the mouth of the cave reminded him of the tin mines at Redrock outvillage. He had always thought it would be awful to have to work in the dark like that. The memory of Redrock was a connection to his career as a capital guard, and it came with a sensation of shame and misery, making him question whether his rescue was fortune or misfortune.

Elenn was confounded by the fact that no barren had reached the village for three full novades. It meant that Pelto had arrived before Elenn had even taken leg, and no one had reached the village in all that time. Elenn knew that the common pre-catheter understanding of the barrens' destiny was that they eventually made their way into the desert in order to die there. Apparently that turned out to be the case for most.

"Have you ever found dead uedin in the desert?" he asked Pelto. They were walking back to the Yulig's dwelling where he was still receiving hospitality. Elenn imagined with odd detachment how Yulig might have found him dead if it had been one day later.

"Yes," said Pelto, "We leave them there. It is always a terrible disappointment to find them. But our night walks can only cover a small area at a time."

"You just leave dead barren out there?" asked Elenn, mildly surprised.

"You have to understand, we don't mean to deny them any honor. There is no better place for their bodies to deteriorate. In fact, we bury our own dead in the desert sand."

"I suppose it is the destiny of a barren to have his bones be scattered across the sand after all," commented Elenn.

"It is not a troubling thought when one has found peace here. We have a simple life, and the whitesponge sustains us."

It was true, there was a calm about the village that seemed to put his mind at ease.

"Pelto, let me tell you now why I am large, even though I had the catheter."

"Very well," said Pelto, patiently.

"I don't know why the older uedin here are not as large as we are, but they are still larger than capital masters. It is our skullsap that makes us large."

"I see how that could be true," said Pelto.

"It also causes us to go into derangement—what you call the raving for the desert."

"And you had the catheter, but you still grew large, and you still came into your raving for the desert."

"Yes, I will explain," said Elenn. "Something strange happened to the capital barren after we received catheters. We got caught up in a very unnatural situation."

"Yes?" Pelto was quietly attentive.

"We learned that we could . . . we could consume skullsap from one another. It affected us in a very powerful way, much more powerful than any sourember or yeastdrink."

"Consume from one another? Why would you do that?"

Elenn sighed with the difficulty of explaining. "Its effect is irresistible."

"I see," said Pelto. Do you collect your skullsap for this?"

"No, it has no potency once it touches air."

"So how do you consume it?"

"We put our mouths directly on the opening."

"On each other's skullwombs?"

"Yes."

"Hard to imagine," said Pelto, with no sign of disgust.

"It is that practice that has now come to obsess the barren population in the capital—and they are many. It's referred to as *feeding*."

"And they linger there, and grow large and have the raving, but they don't come across the desert," said Pelto. He was trying to understand.

"It has been a very great trial for us, and for all the capital. We have tried to control it. We wore hoods on our heads and took an oath to keep the hoods on and never feed."

"They don't know it, but they are trying to rave so that they might make their way here," Pelto surmised. "They are stranded in the capital." His voice stayed relaxed no matter what he was talking about.

"But Pelto, their numbers are great. The entire second generation is one quarter barren, and many believe that the soon-to-be-named will have an even higher incidence. They could never be absorbed into this village. And I'm sure the whitesponge would run out over time if we tried to give it to them."

"You have the wisdom of your newness," said Pelto. "It is best to let the matter unfold as it will."

"Do you ever worry that the whitesponge will run out?"

"We will never harvest it all. It is vast."

"You don't use any lanterns here. How do you see it to know that it's vast?"

"It's smooth and soft on the cave wall—it can be felt. It extends very deep into the cave. It takes a period of many hours to explore it."

Elenn imagined climbing through a cave in total darkness. It sounded quite awful to him. He was somewhat curious about the whitesponge, but not enough to motivate him to venture deep into a cave for hours with no lantern.

It wasn't long, however, before he was invited to go in, and he felt it would be ungrateful to show disinterest. He pushed himself, first to accept the invitation graciously, and then to suppress his anxiety as the time came to enter the cave where the whitesponge grew. It was near the lowest corner of the cliffside village. He was with Pelto, Yulig, and one other.

"I know you have too many names to learn," said the other smiling uedin who was coming along. "We have met, but let me tell you my name again. I am Leci."

All the barren uedin in this village had a similar ease. They were nothing like the tormented wretches in the capital. "Thank you, Leci," Elenn said, starting to get used to saying names without putting "master" before them. "It's true that there are many names to learn at once."

"I will not mind however many times you should forget my name," said Leci with a smile, which made Elenn feel that he certainly would remember the name.

"Elenn, do you remember this cave?" asked Pelto. "I brought you here when I showed you around the village the first time."

"Yes, I remember. It reminds of the copper mines at Redrock Village. I was there once as one of the Flatpools guards," said Elenn, peering into the cave. One could see only about ten paces in.

"I heard that you were a guard, but I didn't know that you were at Flatpools," commented Leci, following Pelto in. Pelto went first, then Leci, then Elenn, and Yulig followed behind Elenn. Darkness surrounded them immediately as they started in. Elenn found it difficult to gaze forward into the darkness instead of turning around to see the diminishing light at the mouth of the cave.

"How long have you been here, Leci?" asked Elenn.

"I have seen seven Great Rains since coming," answered Leci.

"What generation *are* you?" asked Elenn. He never ceased to marvel at the unguessable ages of the uedin living here.

"I am ninth."

"Put your hand up against the wall here," said Pelto, halting to speak to Elenn. "Do you feel that?"

Elenn reached up, expecting to feel the sponge. "This is smooth, but hard," said Elenn. "I thought you said it was soft." He realized they were in pitch black darkness at this point.

"This is not whitesponge. This is a spot where it used to be. The cave wall is very smooth wherever we have harvested." The sound of Pelto's voice was loud and clear in the silent stillness, with only a slight echo.

"Oh, I see," said Elenn. The cave wall here was, indeed, remarkably smooth compared to the rough texture of the rock at the cave's entrance—so smooth in fact, that it had more the feel of glazed pottery than rock.

"We'll keep feeling our way from here," said Pelto. "You can keep your hand up and slide it along. Don't worry, there are no rough edges. It is smooth all the way till we get to the sponge."

Elenn continued following, adjusting his pace to the sound of the others' footsteps. It was reassuring to slide his hand along the smooth wall.

After a long stretch of time, Leci interrupted the monotony with a question for Elenn. "So if you were a Flatpools guard, did you spend much time at Quarterhouse?"

"I grew up at Quarterhouse," answered Elenn.

"So did I." said Leci. "I stayed there through my apprenticeship. I was going to be a tutor."

"Is that right?" Elenn was fascinated. "You said you were ninth generation . . . Let's see, did you know Master Domas? Or Master Hera?"

"I don't remember Master Domas. I had Master Hera when I was unnamed myself."

"Who was there when you were apprenticing?"

"It was a very difficult time," said Leci, "I don't recall names."

"I see," said Elenn. He realized that Leci's memories of the capital were painful. That seemed to be true of all the uedin here.

After a short pause, Leci disclosed, "I only got through the first half of my novade as a newly-named when I was struck with the raving for the desert. But I did get to work with the unnamed during their early years. It is a nice memory—working with the little unnamed."

"They are adorable when they're very small, aren't they?"

"Yes, and I had them when they were very small, indeed. Only a few of them could say my name. I was going to be their 'Master Leci,'" he said wistfully.

When he said "Master Leci," Elenn immediately made the association. *Master Leci? Yes, he had heard the name before! Could it be? Was this the tutor whom Ribol had told Elenn about in the bathhouse?*

"You are . . . Master Leci?"

"Just Leci now," he said with a bit of a chuckle.

"I heard someone speak of you once," said Elenn.

There was a long pause before Leci responded. "I doubt that. I barely knew anyone at Quarterhouse, and no one knew me. I didn't even complete my apprenticeship."

"A child-uedin," said Elenn. "It was a child-uedin who knew your name—and remembered you."

"The unnamed I worked with were very small," said Leci. "They were too little when I left. They certainly wouldn't have remembered me."

"One did. The one whom you taught to put on his clothes." Elenn waited for Leci to respond, and when he said nothing, Elenn reiterated, "I tell you, I spoke with a master who remembered having a Master Leci when he was unnamed. Master Leci was very kind to him, and taught him to dress himself. But he disappeared before the child-uedin took name. That had to have been you!"

"He would have to be seventh generation by now . . . " said Leci.

"He is! He was my fellow guard at Flatpools! His name is Ribol."

"Well, that's remarkable," said Leci. "I sometimes wondered if any of my fellow apprentices ever remembered me, but I never imagined one of the unnamed would."

"He definitely remembers you. He was upset as a child-uedin when you disappeared."

"It serves us no purpose to remember our early lives in the capital," said Yulig, who was following behind Elenn and listening to the conversation.

"I think I agree with you, Yulig," said Pelto, from the front. "I used to remember my trouble there, but the less I remember it, the better I am."

Elenn was beginning to understand that the uedin in this lost colony had little attachment to the capital. Their memory of it was void of nostalgia. Unlike Elenn and the hooded masters who received a great deal of support, these predecessors had experienced their derangement, their "raving for the desert" as they called it, with practically no understanding of what they were going through or why. Their early lives in the capital must have been like a nightmare to them.

"But it's remarkable, isn't it?" said Leci, to acknowledge Elenn's recollection of his name. "I never think of anyone in the capital, but someone there thinks of me."

Elenn said no more about Ribol. He understood that Leci had few happy associations with his time at Quarterhouse. He suddenly thought of Jutef. Jutef would have experienced this cave very differently with no notion of the dark. He would feel the same cool, damp air, and run his hand over the smoothness of the wall just as Elenn was doing, but he would have none of the anxiety Elenn felt from the darkness. *Dear Jutef . . . I didn't even say goodbye to you. But how could I? After the horrible thing I did to you?* Elenn did not always remember the things that happened when he was in derangement, but he remembered breaking Jutef's arms. The memory sickened him, and he felt he could understand why the uedin here said they had nothing to gain from recalling their old lives. No matter what or whom he recalled—Master Benar, or Nula, even going all the way back to Hela—everything about his life was poisoned by the trouble visited upon him by his barren condition. There was nothing in his memory that escaped its sour influence.

"Here we are," said Pelto, suddenly stopping. The wall had remnants of dried sponge where it had been recently harvested, and when Pelto and Leci moved forward a few more steps, Elenn felt and found the moist and soft texture of the sponge under his hand.

"It starts here," said Yulig, "and goes on for a very long way."

"We'll just go forward a little bit. We aren't going to explore it today."

"I can feel where others have run their hand over it. There's a trail," said Elenn.

"Yes, but we try to touch it softly when we explore," said Yulig.

They moved forward a short distance, and Elenn got the general idea of how the sponge grew in a thick, unbroken coat over the cave wall.

"Someday we will come back, and I will take you to the end of the cave, and you will see how far it goes," said Pelto.

"It grows all the way to the end of the cave?"

"Yes. We think maybe the cave was formed by the sponge itself."

"How interesting," said Elenn. Now he was aware of the smell of the whitesponge. It was like the peculiar aroma of the porridge he had been eating since his arrival, only stronger.

"We will cut a little bit to take back. We have a lot of dried sponge, but it's best when it is fresh." They turned and went back the short distance to the edge of the sponge where Elenn listened and waited as Pelto cut pieces from the wall. He heard the clean swipe of the rock tool making a muffled scrape as it cut through the soft flesh and glided along the smooth wall beneath.

"Here," said Pelto, "try a piece of fresh sponge." He reached to Elenn, touched him on the shoulder, and placed a small piece in his hand. Elenn put it in his mouth an began to chew it up. It was soft and moist, like the doughy inside of a freshly baked melonseed bun, only cool instead of warm, and with a flavor that matched its unique aroma.

"It's wonderful," said Elenn. "I can see how barren uedin could survive here, eating this."

On the way out, Elenn briefly pondered why the barren uedin living there had never ventured back to the capital, in order to establish a clear route for barren to come there. Wouldn't they have been able to save all those uedin who died wandering? But the sedative effect of the fresh whitesponge made him consider that it was perfectly acceptable that only a minority of barren uedin found their way to the village to survive. It wasn't worth worrying about. How marvelous it felt to worry about nothing at all.

Part 2

TERRIBLE OPTIONS
AND DESPERATE MEASURES

Servers Respond to a Necessity

Ferin was so relieved to be away from the infirmary and the crushing stress there, that to him, the meeting felt like a welcome recess. He was at Central Station to meet with a temple emissary along with the senior guard there at Central, Master Amit. The emissary was yet to arrive. Amit was serving him a tea made from fresh, not dried, milkgrass. He hadn't had any like that for what seemed like novades.

"They will probably send Server Rafo," said Amit. "The last few times I hosted meetings between servers and masters, it was Server Rafo who came to represent them."

"Yes, come to think of it, there was no server's name mentioned in the letter. I don't think I've ever had correspondence from the temple before this. I'm aware of the value they put on unnameliness, but it's so strange to get a letter that's completely unsigned."

"Well, it wasn't even addressed to you by name, was it?" Amit took pride in his familiarity with the temple.

"You're right. It was just addressed to 'head medic master' at the infirmary."

"I have fairly regular meetings with them, and they still don't ever contact me by name. It's always 'senior guard.'"

Ferin took a good sip of the tea. These days he was too caught up in the commotion of the infirmary to even enjoy a meal or a cup of tea. He tried to relax. He wasn't particularly looking forward to the meeting with the server, but sitting and waiting with Amit was better than dealing with the chaos at the infirmary.

"We usually host meetings between temple emissaries and members of the masters council. I think this is the first time they've asked for a meeting with a medic."

"Well, I'm pretty sure I know what they want," said Ferin tiredly. "They want to start catheter implants for servers."

"Why do you think that?" questioned Amit. "Their method of dealing with the syndrome is a grim one, but it allows them to keep to themselves and keep all things confined to their compound. Why would they want to start introducing catheter implants?"

"Well, since the masters council confirmed that no uedin was being coerced to drink poison, I know we've had a no-intervention policy, but with the syndrome numbers as high as they are, it's bound to come up again. I think the servers are probably anticipating the inevitable."

Amit's expression suggested disagreement, and Ferin knew what he was thinking—that the catheters were more harm than good. He was constantly having that conversation with other medic masters, and he didn't want to debate it with a guard. Derangement was largely circumvented by the implant, and even if only a minority of the syndrome masters allowed it to work, its net benefit for the capital should not be negated just because there were so many who *didn't* allow it to work.

"You must be overwhelmed at the infirmary these days," said Amit, diplomatically changing the subject.

It was true. Even besides the cases of severe derangement, they were getting too many injuries on a daily basis. "I'm afraid it's very hard on the apprentices," said Ferin. "They are doing procedures that ordinarily they would only have to observe." Fern wanted to say that he didn't see how the infirmary would be able to function if it got any worse, but he declined to voice the thought.

"Well, we just have to keep prioritizing. Most of the capital guard response is focused on the four gates."

"Are you restricting movement?" asked Ferin, though he was not surprised.

"We don't stop anyone from coming and going, but we deal with severe derangement when we see it."

A rapping on the door tarp indicated that an emissary had arrived. The server entered. He looked to be of six generations or so, close to Ferin's age.

"I am Rafo," he said, raising hands to face. Apparently it was acceptable for a server to speak his own name when interacting with masters.

"I am Ferin, senior medic at the infirmary," said Ferin, returning the gesture.

Amit greeted him with familiarity but used no name. "Server, please come and sit. I have fresh milkgrass."

"That sounds very good, Guardmaster. It is good to see you again. You know you're not just hosting today . . . We want your participation." The server spoke friendly words, but his face looked steeled for something.

"Yes, I saw that. I hope I can be of service however possible."

"Thank you for being available. How are things here at Central Station? Are you still dispatching guards to Murro?" Ferin noted that his manner was not so different from a master—perhaps it was because he was an emissary and used to conversation outside the temple.

"Not so much these days. The Southgate guards seem to have it under control."

"What's it been now, a year or two since they finished the project? And hooded masters are still congregating there?"

"Just one year it's been, but I must say, I thought the hooded masters would have cleared out by now."

"Have you been up on the rooftop deck?"

"No. I will go at some point, but right now Murro is more or less a caretaker station."

"I would love to see the view of the capital," said Rafo. They all understood he would never go. It was unusual for a server to be outside the temple compound let alone outside the capital.

Ferin sat down with Rafo while Amit poured tea. Rafo nodded and smiled at Ferin, inviting him to join the conversation. Ferin tried to think of small talk about weather or festivals, but he decided to just get right to the point. "The letter I received said that my assistance was needed for a matter of great importance to the temple," he said, dispensing with niceties, hoping his doing so would not offend.

Rafo seemed quite fine with Ferin's directness. "There are actually two concerns—one pertains more to the guardmasters, but they are both related," said Rafo.

"What is it that pertains to the guards?" asked Amit, pouring a frothy green liquid through its own steam into Rafo's cup.

"You are aware that we have very limited grounds and gardens within the temple compound," said Rafo.

"Yes, well, servers have always come out to the central courtyard from time to time for shifting practice," said Amit.

"We have a problem related to our limited grounds, but it involves a very unpleasant matter."

Amit nodded, "I'm sure if there's any way the guards can assist you . . . "

"We were slow to realize the extent of the barren syndrome epidemic. It has been our tradition in the temple to offer barren servers a choice." Rafo looked at Ferin to see if he knew what Rafo was talking about. Ferin could see by the worried look on his face that Rafo hoped he wouldn't have to explain.

Amit dutifully filled in, "The masters council is aware of your practice, and I'm sure Master Ferin here also knows about it. As you know, we have a policy of non-intervention."

"Are you reconsidering your practice?" asked Ferin.

Rafo looked at him somewhat sadly. "We are reconsidering some things, but not the choice we require of our servers with barren syndrome," he said, with a note of apology in his voice.

"What does it have to do with limited grounds in the compound?" asked Amit.

Rafo paused before answering, anticipating how the issue might be upsetting to masters. "We need to dispose of our dead. When there was one or two in a generation, we buried them in the compound. There are too many now."

Ferin imagined young uedin drinking lethal doses of sleep medicine, their bodies being buried in corners of temple gardens and promptly forgotten. As a medic, his initial reaction when he first heard about the server practice was disapproval. But he had seen so much suffering and indignity with deranged barren at the infirmary, he was feeling less inclined to condemn the servers' tradition.

"I see," said Amit. "You don't have enough space."

"We are thinking it might be best to bury them outside the capital walls. Of course it will require the masters council's approval."

"What do you seek from the guards?" asked Amit.

"We only want the guards to adhere to the non-intervention policy as long as it remains in place," said Rafo. "We want your assurances that all stations will be in cooperation."

"As long as the masters council maintains the policy, the guards will comply," said Amit. To Ferin, the thought of dead uedin being buried here and there outside the capital walls was certainly an unpleasant one.

"We think it would be best if all guards were informed of our intentions," said Rafo.

"I agree. The guards must know what's happening," said Amit.

"Are your servers with syndrome informed that there is a treatment for their condition?" asked Ferin.

"You mean the catheter implants? The idea of using catheter implants has not gained favor in the temple, but any barren server who opts to leave the temple can learn about that on his own."

"They deserve to know that it's available," insisted Ferin. Then he asked, "If it's not about treatment of syndrome uedin with catheter implants, for what reason did the temple ask me to meet with you?"

"As I told you, we have two related concerns," said Rafo. "One is what to do with bodies of our servers who choose to end their lives. The other concern has to do with the method of self-extermination. All we have is sleeping medicine. I'm sure you're aware it's a very disruptive event when one dies by drinking sleeping medicine."

Ferin knew that an overdose led to convulsions, but he was not familiar with the sequence of reactions up to death. He imagined it must be horrible. "I have no doubt that it's a dreadful event," he said.

"We are in need of a more quick and efficient means," said Rafo. "This is why we are seeking your expert recommendation."

Ferin thought about what he was being asked. They had no interest in implanting catheters in their servers with syndrome. They wanted to find a quick and easy mode of self-extermination for them. He was not happy about being asked such a thing. "I'm not prepared to give you any kind of recommendation like that," he said.

"Medic Master, we do not ask you to prescribe or administer anything. We ourselves do not pressure our servers with syndrome to take this course of action. They act on their own accord. But as their frequency has grown, we are forced to see that sleeping medicine is insufficient for this purpose. Surely the medic masters must be able to provide us with a better method—a better method for achieving a quicker and less miserable death."

Ferin's training, experience, and years of working and living with medic master customs all suggested that it wouldn't be proper for a dedicated medic to tell anyone how to kill himself. But this server was sincere, and he made a very good point. Dying by an overdose of sleeping medicine was bound to be a drawn-out, excruciating demise. There had to be some easier way to do it.

"The problem is, your practice requires that the server who chooses to die must act independently, right?"

"Yes, your understanding is correct."

"Then I'm afraid we're limited to poisons. The alternatives to sleeping medicine would not be any easier or quicker—in fact they might be worse."

"I see," said Rafo. "And if the server could receive assistance, would that open up other options?"

"Well of course, the obvious route to a very quick death would be the cutting of the head from the body. That would involve more than 'assistance'—it would require some poor uedin to carry it out and then somehow try to forget doing it."

"Shield the Lern!" said Rafo. "Well, I certainly won't report that as a recommendation!"

"No, I never meant it as a recommendation at all, but you asked what would work if a barren server had 'assistance' . . . "

"No, I'll tell them there are no medical solutions, and that alternative poisons might be worse than sleeping medicine."

"Server, will you also tell them that I believe *all*—whether they're in the temple community or any part of the capital—*all* uedin with syndrome should be initially given catheter implants. It's the best treatment we have at this time."

"I will tell them," said Rafo.

"Server, I feel I should mention something also," said Amit. "Once you start burying the bodies of dead servers outside the walls, there is bound to be reaction. The guards will act as directed by the masters council. But I'm sure the caretakers will be aghast."

"Is there something we can do to minimize disruption?" asked Rafo.

"I'm only saying you should be prepared for a negative reaction."

"Do you think it would placate the masters of the capital if we were to clearly inform our barren servers about the option to receive a catheter implant should they leave the temple?"

"Yes, I do," said Amit.

"I agree," said Ferin.

"Well then I will strongly advocate for that . . . though I'm not sure it will do any good."

"Why not?"

"We are not completely shut off from the realities of the capital that surrounds us," said Rafo. "We know enough about the trouble in the capital to make it obvious that the catheter implants, in the end, do not work."

Ferin looked down at the floor in frustration. Perhaps a meeting like this wasn't such a nice break after all. He might as well get back to the infirmary. There he could keep his opinions to himself and stay busy with the tremendous amount of work there was to do.

Ippal and Nemis at the Western Gate

One could tire of respect. Nemis recognized it as something he wouldn't say out loud, but it was true. Nemis was tired of respecting the authority that dictated his life these days. He stood with Ippal in the bright morning sun, taking advantage of the strip of sunlit area between the chilly shadow of the capital wall and the woods. They were there to guard the western gate, and their task there seemed entirely unnecessary, as there was nobody passing either way at that gate. All the traffic in and out of the capital was headed south to Murro, and the regular guards of the Southgate District, somewhat jealous of their territory, had a very close watch on the gate there.

Murro. The thought of it troubled and saddened him. The construction of a rooftop observation deck at the grainhouse there had been his own idea, but in the end Murro turned into a miserable place where the hooded masters went. Better to let the Southgate guards watch their gate. He didn't want to see the stream of hooded masters going back and forth to Murro. He took a deep breath and stretched his neck and shoulders.

"We haven't seen a single uedin," said Ippal. "Do you think it's going to be like this all day?"

"Who knows? I think it's going to be a long day," answered Nemis, resigning himself to the tedium of standing watch. He much preferred patrolling. At least when they patrolled, they could keep moving. It was so vexing to have to stand around in one place for an entire day. There was nothing to do but think, and Nemis was already thinking too much. He couldn't talk to Ippal anymore. They had exhausted all suitable subjects. Ippal wasn't likely to want to discuss how one could tire of respect, for example. Ippal didn't seem to tire of it.

Nemis knew that part of his frustration rose from the fact that he had ended up in the hood squad, something that was not originally intended for a regular guard. He had agreed to do it because Master Elenn needed help. At the time, he hadn't even minded when the situation had gotten very demanding, when Master Elenn started having periods of poor judgment. But then Master Elenn just seemed to give up, and before long he disappeared. Nemis and Ippal had searched for days, until Deben finally told them that he and Henik had secretly escorted Elenn to the southeastern desert—to die. So their long and difficult struggle with Master Elenn had ended in sorrow and loss. What started as a favor to his Flatpools comrade turned into a "temporary" assignment on the hood squadron that he knew was never going to end. How long had it been . . . was it a year yet?

There was an open space separating the forest from the capital wall where a trail ran along the outside. To keep the woods from encroaching, a dense vine had been planted as a groundcover. After a while, out of boredom, Nemis started studying the meandering vines. Nemis always did like plants. Plants, and rocks, and stars—those were things that interested him. He didn't know the name of this particular vine. He thought of cutting a piece and taking it back with him so he could go to the library to look it up.

"I'll be back in a minute," said Ippal. He was going to relieve himself. Nemis continued looking down at the vine-ribboned ground next to the trail. Ippal walked the short stretch of West Road that led to the edge of the woods and ducked in. Ippal was a decent enough partner guard. He cared deeply about the hooded masters. He probably never minded that he had ended up a regular guard on the hood squadron. Nemis knew he *shouldn't* mind it, especially since the rest of the regular guards were all dealing with the same syndrome-related problems anyhow. But, as a regular guard on the hood squad, there were times when he simply felt out of place. For example, the emphasis on the oath created an awkward situation for him. The hooded guards often recited it to remind the hooded master of their responsibilities. There was nothing to stop Nemis from telling a hooded master, "Remember your oath!" but somehow it didn't seem right for a uedin without barren syndrome to tell one with the syndrome how he should be acting. When it came to regular guards serving on the hood squadron, they always said that the hooded guards were being provided with "back up." What nonsense! How could you call it "back up" when the regular guards were running the whole operation? The hooded guards were incapable of their jobs at this point. It seemed to Nemis that every single one of them was faltering. Master Elenn's deterioration and disappearance was the most notorious example of hooded guards getting caught up in the feeding, but *all* of the hooded guards were doing it.

Nemis looked up from the vines, and he saw that Ippal was on the edge of the woods talking to a large, obviously barren, uedin. The uedin wore no hood, but his appearance left no doubt. It was becoming common to see them without hoods, though everyone still politely referred to them as "hooded masters." He immediately went over. As he approached, he noticed an unpleasant smell. The barren clearly had not bathed for a very long time, his hands and face were filthy, and his robe was splotched and stained.

"You're completely in the wrong place," Ippal was saying. "You need to start at Southgate and cross the Clay Bridge and then follow the road till you see the trail leading off on the left-hand side. That goes to Murro."

"Doesn't he even know where he is?" asked Nemis.

"He's a little bit *confused*," said Ippal. That was the word they used when they didn't want to say "deranged."

"Master, can you tell me your name?" asked Nemis. A series of questions usually helped to determine level of derangement.

The greasy-faced uedin looked back at him, hesitated a moment, and then pleaded with a whispering voice, "Will you please just let me pass?"

The desperation was clear, but the speech and expression did not suggest derangement to Nemis.

"Are you trying to get to Murro?" asked Nemis.

"Yes."

"Master, you look like you've been outside the walls for a long time. It might be better for you to follow the outside trail around to Southgate instead of going through the capital." Nemis didn't want to tell him that he was filthy and he smelled bad.

"You must tell us your name, Master," demanded Ippal.

"I will not," said the uedin miserably, a blank stare in his eyes.

"It's all right," said Nemis, and he signaled to Ippal with a firm look that they would not insist on having the uedin's name. Letting him in at the gate was another matter. Unless they were being ushered to the infirmary, hooded masters in any degree of derangement were supposed to be discouraged from entering the capital unattended. At one time they were directed to the caretaker hut outside the north wall, but these days it was generally understood that there were more resources for them at Murro. There was a permanent camp there, provided with supplies and staffed with guards and caretakers.

Ippal turned to Nemis and, dispensing with discretion, asked plainly, "Do you think he's in derangement?"

"I don't think so . . . " Nemis answered, and then addressed the stranger directly, "Master, have you been feeding? Are you in derangement?"

"I was," said the uedin with a tired-sounding voice, "I was feeding, and then I wasn't, . . . and then I was again. I don't know how long I've been outside."

"He doesn't sound deranged right now," commented Ippal to Nemis.

"No, I don't think he is," agreed Nemis, "but he needs to get to the caretaker camp. And he shouldn't cut through the capital by himself."

The uedin rubbed his eyes and face. He was exhausted and despondent. "I'll do as you say. I'll follow the trail around to Southgate, and head to Murro from there. Do you have any water?"

Nemis untied a gourd from his belt and handed it to the uedin. He guzzled the water, and the guards exchanged a glance of common concern. The uedin had been roaming for some time. He was in a pitiful condition.

"Maybe I could walk with him through the capital," suggested Ippal, "You can stay here."

Nemis thought about it. "Then you'll have to explain it to the Southgate Station guards . . . What will you tell them?"

Before Ippal could respond, they were interrupted by a sound coming through the western gate. Nemis turned around and looked. Before anything appeared, he identified the sound of a rickety wheel cart approaching. Then he saw server wrappings. It was a group of four servers moving a flatwagon through the gate. It took a few seconds before he understood what they were transporting.

Ippal and the barren uedin remained silent, and they all watched as the servers pulled the wagon toward them. Sure enough, there were a number of wrapped bodies on the wagon. The servers were hauling the bodies of dead barren to bury in the ground outside the capital. Nemis was surprised that there had been no warning that they would be coming. Apparently none of the stationhouses had been alerted. Otherwise, he and Ippal would have been notified.

It was a terrible thing that was happening inside the temple compound. About a moon-cycle before, Master Wanba had called the Flatpools guards together to let them know that the masters council had agreed to let servers bury dead barren outside the capital wall, and the guards were not to interfere. Then Nemis had heard from Deben that group suicides had occurred twice in the temple, with full permission from the temple administration. Barren servers had cooperatively killed each other with double-handed blades. They apparently acted in small groups, one taking the worm position so that the second one could cut his head off. Then that one would hand the double-handed blade to the next and take the same position to have his own head cut off.

As the wagon drew near, Nemis looked in and saw that there were indeed three bodies wrapped in undyed cloth. They appeared to be wrapped up tight with their heads put back in place, though one could tell by looking that the heads were weirdly askew under the wrapping. There was no blood leaking anywhere; the bodies must have been drained and washed.

They all stared for a moment, comprehending the scene. Nemis looked at the barren uedin to see how he would react. He was staring at the servers and their wagon, transfixed. "I heard about this," he said, "Barren servers choose to die . . . "

Nemis said nothing because he didn't know what to say. Piled on the flatwagon along with the bodies were some spades, shovels, and a pickaxe. Ippal looked distraught. Nemis decided that he would do the talking. He stepped forward and raised hands to face. The servers all stopped, and everyone raised hands to face.

"You are here to bury some dead uedin in the ground," said Nemis.

"Yes," answered one of the servers. "Your masters council has agreed to it." The server who spoke had nervousness in his voice. He had probably been assigned to serve as spokesperson as needed. Nemis took a good look at his face. He could see that this task was not easy for him or the other servers. Nemis was glad that the masters council policy was to not interfere and that he would not need to confront them.

"Something is strange," said the anonymous barren uedin, staring at the bodies. "Their heads are not right."

The spokesperson cast his eyes downward, hoping to avoid questions. Nemis and Ippal knew why the heads were askew, but they said nothing.

"I thought that barren servers died by drinking poison. Why are their heads like that?"

The server spokesperson answered him with respect. "Yes, Master, you are correct that our barren servers choose to die. They die in groups now."

"But why are their heads like that?" insisted the barren stranger, horrified.

The spokesperson was clearly uncomfortable having to explain, but he answered directly, "They use double-handed blades, one cutting the head of another. Their heads have been cut from their bodies. It is quicker and less painful than other methods."

There was a moment of silence as this explanation was comprehended, and then Ippal, unable to hold back his disgust, commented sharply, "It's just not right!"

Nemis mildly admonished him. "Master Ippal, it is not our place to object," he said, "We are not to interfere. You know that."

Ippal cast his eyes down, reproving himself for the outburst. "I beg pardon from the servers," he said.

"Of course it is very troubling," said the spokesperson server. "But you should know, the servers among us who have the syndrome are not pressured to do this. They choose this end for themselves."

The anonymous barren master did not appear troubled so much as perplexed. "If one cuts the head of another, who cuts the last one's head?" he asked.

It was a question that Nemis himself had wondered about. Did some server actually volunteer to cut off the last barren's head with the double-handed blade? What a horrible job that would be!

The server seemed to hesitate, uncomfortable describing the grisly operation. "We now have many with syndrome in the compound," he said. "When a group agrees to carry out the self-extermination together, they use shelltoss pieces to determine who will have to assist last. Whoever that is, he must use the double-handed blade to cut the head of the last server to die for that time. He must then wait for others to approach him, and when a new group is ready, he will receive assistance first."

Assitance? What a strange way to refer to getting one's head cut off. Nemis was shaken, imagining it all, but he kept his reaction in check. He looked at Ippal who was staring again at the bodies on the cart, looking very upset.

"These servers cut each others' heads off," said the anonymous master desolately, " . . . assisting one another in dying."

"When did these servers die?" asked Nemis.

"In the early morning. They sat in mindstilling all night and completed the task at daybreak."

Nemis thought to himself that regardless of the unpleasantness of the situation, this spokesperson and these servers who were there to bury the bodies were not at fault for any of it. He sympathized with them. They probably had also had to wash and wrap up the bodies. They didn't like any part of what they were doing, but they had to do it.

"Let us help you," he said.

The spokesperson exchanged glances with the other servers, sharing some relief. They weren't going to refuse this offer. "That would be greatly appreciated. Master. We don't want to bury the bodies close to the gate. We would rather bury them in the forest. Can you suggest a good spot?"

"There are paths leading into the woods all along the road, but most of them are too narrow for that wagon. We can come along with you to help you find a good place to dig that you can reach."

"Thank you," said the server, then asked, "Are there many masters traveling this road?"

"Very few," said Nemis, "but there are some. Does it concern you?"

"I would be most thankful if one of you could remain at the gate to warn any master who might see us. Otherwise I might have to explain everything, and it's very difficult . . . "

"I understand," said Nemis. He looked at Ippal. "Master Ippal, will you stay at the gate?"

"Yes," said Ippal. He then turned and addressed the barren stranger. "Master, you will need to follow the outside trail along the wall to the south gate and go on straight to Murro from there."

"I will go later," said the barren, indicating his intention to follow Nemis and the servers and watch them bury the bodies.

"Master, perhaps you should just go ahead to Murro," said Ippal, sounding a bit more insistent.

"I want to see where these bodies are put in the ground," said the uedin.

"We must respect the servers. They just want to do their job quietly and return to the temple . . . " argued Nemis.

"I'm going to see where the bodies of the barren servers are put in the ground!" insisted the barren one.

"He wants to see. It is all right," said the server.

Ippal, as it was agreed that he would remain at the gate, gestured respect to the servers by raising hands to face.

The four servers took hold of the wagon and pulled it forward as Nemis and the barren followed from behind. Nemis decided it would be better to bury the bodies a good distance out from the capital wall where there would be fewer uedin passing who might notice the broken ground. He let the servers pull the cart a fair span down the road, past most of the trail entrances that led off on one side or the other, until they were at a very quiet and shady place.

"I think this place would be good," he announced. "There is room on the side here to dig a large pit."

The servers pulled the wagon to the side, and Nemis and the barren then stood by and watched as they distributed the pickaxe and spades, settled on a specific spot, and started to dig. They worked slowly and methodically. The barren uedin stared at the wrapped bodies on the flatwagon. Nemis knew that this must be a very troubling thing to see for a master with the syndrome, but he could think of nothing to say or do to make it less disturbing. The barren uedin seemed almost hypnotized, gazing at the wrapped bodies and listening to the alternating rhythms of the pickaxe and spades slashing into the ground.

Suddenly, there was the distinct sound of metal hitting rock. A protruding edge of rock revealed itself at the end of one server's pickaxe. The server bent and dug around it as the others made room for him, but it appeared that the rock was of substantial size, not easy to dig out. When it seemed that he had exhausted himself trying to dig out the rock, another server stepped in to dig at it for a while, but their digging only exposed more rock. It was turning out to be a rock of considerable mass.

Just as another server stepped down to assess the unwelcome rock, Nemis turned his head just enough to catch the strange look on the barren uedin's face. It was a look of sadness and anger at once. Nemis worried for a moment that it might have been a mistake to let Ippal go back to the gate and leave him alone with the barren. What might the barren do if he was in fact deranged to some degree and should happen to get very upset? Nemis barely had time to glance back and see how the server was again digging around the rock, when the barren stepped forward and cried in an anguished voice, "Give the pickaxe to me! Let me do it!" The server stopped digging and looked at his fellow servers.

"I—don't think that would be wise . . . " said Nemis, but the server, without even seeming to hesitate, stepped out of the pit and handed the pickaxe to the barren uedin. The way the barren uedin took the pickaxe and practically lurched toward the pit where all the other servers were standing gave Nemis a terrible scare. But the barren heaved the pickaxe hard and drove it nowhere else but into the ground beside the rock. It cut deep through the soil and struck against rock with a piercing clink. Dirt and stones flew as he ripped the pickaxe back up and swung again, this time nearly burying the whole head of the tool deep in the ground. As he tore into the ground with ferocity, Nemis joined the servers in stepping back out of the way.

The barren finished digging once more around the rock and then tossed the axe aside, bent down, took hold of the rock and yanked hard. The rock shifted from its deep position, and a small cloud of dust was emitted from around the edges. Nemis and the servers then watched in amazement as he lifted the massive rock up, moved in under it, and screamed an awful scream as he powerfully hurled it through the air. Nemis was astounded by the sight of such a weighty object sailing through the air. It landed some ten paces away with a deep thunk. Nemis sprang to attention, trained as a guard to respond to any urgency. This barren could have killed one of them throwing that huge rock. The way he screamed suggested that he was emotionally upset, and if he had some derangement, he could be very dangerous.

The uedin approached the flatwagon, and the servers drew back. He reached toward one of the wrapped bodies.

"No!" cried one of the servers.

"Please Master, we must leave this affair to the servers!" called Nemis.

But the servers stood by as the barren reached down and took the first wrapped large barren corpse into his arms.

"We must be careful with the bodies!" objected the server.

But the barren hugged the corpse to his chest and stepped back, dragging its legs off the side the of flatwagon.

"Master, stop!" yelled Nemis, but the barren ignored him and turned toward the pit with the wrapped body in his arms.

"His head! Hold his head up!" cried one of the other servers.

The barren adjusted his hold so that one arm held the back of the corpse, and the other arm crossed behind its neck so that his hand could support the head. His large hand cupped around the skullwomb.

One of the servers stepped forward to try to help, but the barren said, "No . . . I will . . . " and proceeded to carry the weight by himself, dragging its legs down into the pit and finally letting it down easy in a face-down position. He looked down at the body he had just laid there and let out a single great sob.

He trudged back to the flatwagon to get the next body, but one of the servers shouted out, "Master, please at least let us help you. These servers were our friends. They belonged to us. We asked for this duty."

The barren stopped and looked at them all.

"Master, please honor their wishes!" urged Nemis.

"Come then," said the barren. He turned and reached for the second corpse as they all came close. He held the torso while the servers supported the head and limbs of the body, and they all shuffled together carrying it to the pit, and lowering it down with great care and respect. Then they slowly turned it around, leaving it again with its skullwomb up.

They did the same with the third corpse, after which the servers began to recite the Names, and Nemis joined in. The barren did not recite, but stood quietly with them, gazing at the three face-down bodies.

Back at the gate, Ippal arched his back and stretched his neck from side to side. Standing in one place made him stiff, and pacing was tiresome. He looked through the gate at the empty street and windowless Crafting District warehouses on the other side. There had hardly been anyone passing by inside the gate let alone coming through to the West Road. That was fine; he didn't mind being bored here instead of burying dead bodies in the ground, the thought of which nearly gave him a feeling of panic. It was disturbing enough getting to know hooded masters and thinking about never going to passing-of-life. Seeing them dead like bugs absolutely horrified him. He was glad the servers requested that one of them stay behind to warn travelers, even if there weren't any travelers to warn.

He had watched as Nemis and the barren had followed the servers and their flatwagon down the road into the forest. Then he could not see them, but he could still hear them. During the hour that followed, he had listened to the sounds that came from the distance where they were burying the bodies. He heard when metal struck rock the first time, and then when it happened again some time later. After a while he had heard some shouting and listened carefully in case Nemis might call him, but he didn't hear his name. He could only wonder what has happening. Later he heard what sounded like a cry coming from the barren, and then, after a long time, he heard the reciting of the Names.

When a droning began, he knew it might last for hours, and he worried that he might be stuck there waiting all day, but then he saw Nemis and the barren come out of the shadows of the tree-lined road walking toward him. As they got closer, Ippal could see that Nemis had a look of acceptance on his face.

"Everything go all right?" Ippal called to his partner.

"Everything's fine. The servers will probably be there a few hours. Hear them?"

"Yes—droning. What was that shouting earlier?"

"The master wanted to help with the digging and burial of the bodies . . . We had to sort things out."

"He helped?"

"Yes. If he had any confusion before, he appears to be fine now," said Nemis.

"And are you still unwilling to give us your name?" asked Ippal.

The uedin regarded him with a look of exhaustion, and finally said, "I am Chibo. I'm a groundskeeper at Whiteroof."

Hearing the names of the hooded masters—in this case, one who had misplaced his hood somewhere—always made Nemis feel a little more appreciation for their plight. "Do you still want to go to Murro, Master Chibo?" he asked.

"Yes. I'll go along the outside trail."

"It's probably a good idea. You will encounter less questioning if you go that way," said Nemis.

"Here, take this," said Ippal, and handed him another gourd of water.

"Thank you, masters," said Chibo, though he did not make eye contact. He held hands to face momentarily and then turned and walked down the trail through the vine-covered ground.

The guards watched him walk away.

"Did he really help?" asked Ippal.

"He practically dug the pit and buried them by himself," said Nemis. "but the servers were very patient with him."

"I can't believe they're allowing their barren to kill themselves."

"Maybe it's better than stretching out their derangement with catheters and feeding just so they can live in squalor like our barren masters," said Nemis. Ippal was shocked to hear Nemis say this, but he knew that many of the guards probably felt the same way.

A Terrible Plan

Jeber stepped around the smoldering remains of burned garbage in the lot behind a domicile where he was told he would be able to find the cooking master called Tono. It had been a cloudy day, and now it was unusually dark for the hour. Other than a fat scavenger chick picking at some rotten scraps, it seemed that nobody was there. Maybe Tono wasn't there . . . and maybe it would be a relief if he weren't. Jeber wasn't completely sure that he wanted to find him.

When Jeber first heard that hooded masters had carried out a group self-extermination, he was shocked along with everyone else in the capital. It was known that barren servers had been dying this way, but no one expected such a thing to catch on with masters. One of the dead masters, a groundskeeper from Whiteroof by the name of Chibo, was blamed for introducing the bloody ritual outside the temple. That was the first time. It had now been repeated twice, and while no information was public, enough rumors had leaked from the capital guards that all the hooded masters knew how the self-exterminations played out. Even though the ritual always resulted in three deaths, it took four uedin to carry it out. After cutting off the head of the third, the fourth uedin had to wait for a new group to form. He was referred to as the "waiter." Unlike servers who carried out their death ritual with approval from their administrators, the hooded masters were choosing self-extermination secretly and without permission. The guards were currently questioning hooded masters all over the capital, trying to find out who the "waiter" was.

One of the guards had asked Jeber, too. Fortunately that was before he had heard that Tono was the waiter.

In private discussion between barren masters, sympathy for those who followed Chibo to death sometimes bordered on admiration. For Jeber, admiration and glorification had nothing to do with it. Jeber's despair was deep. There was no passing-of-life to come, and nothing but more suffering and degradation to look forward to. Other hooded masters might still think they had something to live for in the capital, but he did not. He just wanted his life to be over.

The scavenger chick stirred and flapped its wings, and when Jeber turned to look behind him, he saw a hooded master wearing a soiled apron and carrying a pot of peelings and husks. His largeness indicated an advanced stage of syndrome, but he was clearly still working and not in derangement. He saw Jeber right away and must have noticed the interested look on his face.

"I'm not looking to feed," he said, and dumped the vegetable peels on top of a small pile of rotting compost.

"Neither am I," said Jeber.

"Then what are you doing here?" Tono turned the pot upside down and hit the bottom to get rid of any clinging bits.

"Are you Master Tono?"

Tono stopped and looked at Jeber squarely. There was something in his expression that made Jeber feel unwelcome. "Yes, I'm Tono."

"Master Tono, what I'm about to ask you . . . Please forgive me if I'm wrong."

Tono picked a piece of peel from the bottom of the pan and flicked it on the ground. "I know what you're going to ask me," he said.

"You are the . . . " Jeber was reluctant to say the word.

Tono drew a little bit closer and said in a hushed voice, "Yes. I'm the waiter."

"I want to join your group," said Jeber. He looked straight into Tono's eyes and held his gaze for a long time. For Jeber, there was a world of struggle and a lifetime of inner turmoil, so convoluted and complicated that he would never be able to explain his reasons for saying the thing that he was saying, but that simple statement was all the explanation he cared to give.

Tono looked back at him with a grave expression. "You want to join my group? Do you know what you're saying? Have you thought about it enough? Because there will be more waiters in the future . . . I'm sure of it. There will be more chances to do what we are doing."

"I don't want to think about it any more. I'm sure of it."

"Master . . . what is your name?"

"I am Jeber."

"Master Jeber, it is a dreadful act that we are intent upon. You cannot imagine it."

Jeber was impressed by Tono's concern and air of warning. But the thought that Tono was a serious uedin who was choosing this path despite its dreadfulness only deepened his resolve.

"I know it will be a terrible moment. But it will happen quickly. And then it will be over."

"You need to consider the kind of courage it takes. I'm not talking about the courage to die. I'm talking about the courage it takes to cut the head from another uedin. You must do that before your own turn. Have you thought about that?"

Jeber tried to maintain his confident stare, but in truth he hadn't really contemplated that factor. Tono immediately saw the unsteady look in his eyes. He shook his head and started to walk away. Jeber reached up and caught his shoulder.

"Please!" he pleaded. The last time he had pleaded in that way, he recalled, had been when he was begging another barren master to share necks with him. That was the life he wanted no more of. "I can do it. I can do it if I tell myself that the other master's head is *my* head, and that I am cutting off my own head."

Tono stopped and looked him in the eye. He seemed surprised and satisfied with the argument. "That's exactly right. That is exactly what you must do."

"Will you let me join you then?"

Tono thought carefully before answering. "If you are sure," he finally said.

"How many masters have agreed? Do you have two others . . . besides me?"

"Two?" said Tono, "I had three the day after it happened—the day after I drew the empty shell and became the waiter."

"Then you already . . . I don't understand."

"There will be nine of us if you join. Eight will die. One will have to be the waiter. I will not have to draw a shell. Being the waiter once is hard enough."

"Nine? But I thought it was always done with a group of four."

"It was. But we are not servers. We don't have to follow their ritual. And also, because we are not servers, we must act in total secrecy. A few masters know that I am the waiter, but nobody knows when or where I will arrange this thing to happen. No one must know."

"I understand that. The capital guards are trying to find you and stop you—stop us."

"And that means we cannot even say goodbye, not to anyone. Don't even write a note to anyone. It could be found early, and you would be apprehended."

"I understand," said Jeber. "Have you decided when and where we will meet to do it?"

"I decided the day after I became the waiter. It will be before sunrise on the morning of the lesser moon's half phase. We're going to meet behind the first grainhouse at Murro, the one everyone just passes."

Jeber thought about it for a second. "That's the day after tomorrow," he said.

"Yes. I gave myself too much time. It was a mistake. That's why we have nine instead of four. I hope no one else comes to find me. Let them find the new waiter after we are done."

"The day after tomorrow . . . " Jeber repeated. How strange it was to think that he was going to die in two days.

"If you change your mind, don't come to tell me. Just don't show up. Whoever is there will be part of the self-extermination. After it is done, if you have changed your mind, I don't care what you do or who you tell. You won't know who the new waiter is, and it won't matter what you say to anyone."

"I don't see how I would change my mind," said Jeber.

Tono placed his free hand on Jeber's shoulder and smiled a sad smile that reflected their shared understanding. "It's not only for ourselves that we do this, you know. Barren will be the ruin of the capital. We must sacrifice ourselves in order to save it."

"Yes, I believe it's true," said Jeber. "The servers understood it first, didn't they."

"Eventually everyone will understand it," said Tono. " . . . It's getting dark. I must get back to the kitchen. Good master, I will see you the morning after tomorrow before dawn at Murro. Remember, there can be no good-bye to anyone. I'm sorry."

Jeber raised hands to face and turned to leave the lot. A ro master was just walking around the corner with a tea pot. It was still light enough to see his discomfort when he discovered that two barren masters were there in the scrap lot together. Jeber could see the suspicious look on his face. He clearly thought that they had been feeding. At an earlier time, Jeber would have greeted the ro and tried to repair his distrust. But this time Jeber just walked past him. He was sacrificing enough. He didn't owe anything to anyone anymore.

Secret Death Chain at Murro

The day before the lesser moon's half phase was one of the most difficult days that Jeber had ever experienced. His anxiety made him tense up so much that by evening his neck and shoulder muscles felt as though they were twisting inside of him. He didn't want to see anyone he knew from the workhouse, so he stayed far away from the western outfields and roamed the capital. His presence at the workhouse had been inconsistent for a long time; they would assume he was feeding or wandering. He wanted to go early to Murro and just spend the night there. He knew that Serka and Leol showed up there some days, but they usually didn't stay into the night. To avoid encountering them, he waited until late afternoon before leaving the capital. He would go to the caretakers' camp and keep company with hooded strangers until he felt it was a few hours past midnight, and then he would make his way back to the first grainhouse.

As evening fell, he sat at a campfire with an apprentice caretaker and a few hooded masters recovering from derangement. He said nothing and let everyone think that he was recovering as well. He got up only twice, once to get food, and then later to get water. While he was getting water, a hooded master tried to get his attention to see if he wanted to share necks. Jeber ignored him and returned to sit on the log bench and stare into the fire. When the hour got late, the caretaker and the hooded strangers got up to leave.

"Master," whispered the caretaker, "There's bedding in the grainhouse when you're ready to sleep. The fire is nearly burned out. There is more firewood over there if you need another log."

"Thank you, master," said Jeber. "I'll be joining you very soon," he lied.

Once alone, Jeber stayed only a short while longer. He figured he might as well go ahead on over to the first grainhouse. There might be others among those planning to do the thing who would be there early. He didn't want to talk to any of them—he just wanted to wait with them. But it was nowhere near the appointed hour and there was no hurry. He walked very slowly, ambling as though he had nowhere to go, but directed himself back along the path and gradually to the dark edifice that was the first grainhouse. When he went around to the back, it was as he had hoped—there were several uedin already there, waiting quietly. It was too dark to see any of their faces. Jeber was glad he couldn't see them and they couldn't see him. He did not greet them in any way, but went right to the wall of the grainhouse and sat facing out with his back against the wall. He stayed that way for some hours, briefly dozing and awakening a few times, until others came. He didn't know if one of them was Tono or not because it was too dark to see well, and nobody was speaking. Finally, when all nine were there, he heard Tono's voice and picked him out from among the shadow figures. He was holding a long wrapped object. Jeber knew that it was the double-handed blade.

"We're all here. Apparently no one has changed his mind," said Tono. "The first thing we must do is draw shells." He put down the wrapped blade and untied a bag from his belt. "You can't see very well, but you can feel the etching on the shell pieces. Seven of the eight shell pieces have characters etched on them. One is blank. I will not have to draw. I became the waiter when I drew the blank piece, the last time a group met for this purpose. After we draw, we will act quickly. We will form a line here. Whoever has the blank shell must go to the end of the line. When we are all in place, I will hand the blade to one of you and then I will take the worm position. You all know what to do. Our time of thinking about doing this is over. It is our time to act.

"There is one very important matter that you must all understand. This double-handed blade was made to cut through thick stalks and brush. It is heavy and sharp—enough to do what we are doing. But the neck of a uedin is stronger than you think. You must swing hard and bring it down with full force. You must not hold back. When I was part of the group the last time of doing this, someone didn't swing hard enough. One of the masters had to be struck multiple times. He screamed, and it was a very terrible thing, both for him and for the master who faltered with the blade. Use your full strength and swing the blade as hard as you can, because you don't want that to happen."

Jeber was terrified. Tono, when they met before, had warned him that the courage needed to cut the head from another uedin was greater than the courage needed to die. He had understood that. But he had spent the day thinking mostly about his imminent death and not about having to cut the head from the body of another uedin. His mind flooded with fear.

"Does anyone have any words that need saying at this time?" asked Tono. The way he said it made Jeber think that Tono didn't really want anyone to speak. This was a self-extermination, and there was no decorum or ritual that would be anything but burdensome to them at this point. Their full concentration had to be on completing this tremendous, simple act. Even so, Tono paused long in case anyone wanted to speak. But all remained silent, until he finally said, "I'm going to hold this bag open for all of you to draw a piece. Come and draw one quickly." Tono held open the bag, and the masters surrounded him.

Jeber was among the first to reach in the bag for a shell piece. He drew it out and felt on both sides. All the masters withdrew with their shell pieces while he was trying to feel whatever etching was on it. He heard one of the masters say "ah," and he thought for a quick instant that the one who said it had gotten the blank shell, but he realized at the same time that it had been an "ah" of relief, and at that moment he realized that it was *he* who had a piece with no character etched on it.

No! Oh, no! I am the waiter! I will have to cut the head off the last uedin this morning, and I will have to go back to the capital do as Tono has done! I can't do it!

His thoughts began to spin. Could he refuse now? Was it too late? What could he say? But the masters were moving quickly, just as Tono had instructed them. Tono handed the first master the blade and quickly got down into the worm position. "Now!" he cried. Jeber couldn't believe it was happening so quickly. The master standing over Tono raised the two-handed blade high over his head and brought it down with all his might. Jeber did not see the blade strike Tono's neck, but he heard it chop, and then he heard the sound of something squirting on the ground. It was Tono's blood squirting out, Jeber knew. *Oh no! Oh no, this cannot be happening!*

But Jeber's shock could do nothing to slow things down. Already he heard, "Now!" as the second master to die ordered the next master to swing the blade to his neck. Again, the horrible sounds, the chop and the squirting . . . and then movement, another getting down to the worm position, and another "Now!"

" . . . don't want to be left! I don't want to be left!" Jeber muttered, but the master in front of him did not turn around or acknowledge him. All eyes were looking ahead at the dark forms moving into place as the progression of masters getting down and swinging the blade continued.

"Now!"

. . . . . .

"Now!"

Jeber felt a kind of frozen numbness come over him. His mind suddenly emptied. He listened and waited, until the master in front of him took the blade. Jeber could see that the one in front of him was trembling, and he watched him lift the blade hastily and swing hard. Jeber didn't see where the blade landed, but it must have missed the needed angle for a clean cut, because the kneeling master let out a terrible scream, rolled to his side, started shaking, and began to wail.

The master holding the blade froze for a moment, comprehending the dire situation. He briefly turned and looked at Jeber with a shocked and helpless face. Jeber said to him, "You must finish it—you must!" The injured master continued to scream as he lay on his side, a hand over his shoulder, and moonlight revealed blood spurts pulsing through his fingers.

The master raised the blade once more with a small cry of desperation, held it high, swung it hard, and this time cut all the way through the master's neck. Jeber heard the head roll into the weeds. The master stopped for a second to look at the body twitching at his feet, and Jeber heard him gasp. He thrust the blade into Jeber's hands. The grip was sticky with blood. The master got down on the ground and drew his legs under him, pulled his arms in, held his head down, and called out, "Now!"

Jeber hesitated just a moment until the master there at his feet screamed with desperate insistence, "NOW!! NOW!!"

Jeber felt weak, but he knew his strength. He knew that his barren size gave him plenty of strength to cut through the master's neck with one hard blow. He raised the blade high over his head and looked down at the trembling master in front of him, bent forward in position. He would make it quick and final. He used all the muscles in his body to swing the blade as hard as he could. The blade, clenched in his hands, flew downward through air and struck. It cut cleanly through the master's neck, and Jeber saw one closed eye spin around with the head as it separated from the body and rolled away. Blood spurted into the grass from the chopped neck.

Jeber inhaled and exhaled after the exertion of swinging the blade. There was dim light from the morning sky beginning to dawn. He looked at the row of bodies and heads in front of him, some still seeming to be bracing themselves in place, knees tightly drawn in and arms firmly held at either side, as if still anticipating the strike even after their heads were cut off.

"Aa, aa, aa . . .!" He wanted to scream but fear let him only produce this strange whimper. He looked at the two-handed blade in his hand. He wanted to throw it, but he knew he could not. He needed it. It was the blade that would be needed to cut off his own head and end this nightmare. On shaky legs, he hurried to find the cloth that Tono had used to wrap it. It was on the ground, inches from Tono's severed head. He picked up the cloth, wrapped it around the blade, tucked it under his arm, and started running down the path and toward the capital. By the time he reached Clay Bridge, the sun was rising in the east, coming up over Murro to expose the horrible scene that he had left behind.

Eight Stars

Pavis tapped lightly on the door-tarp. He was going to accompany Jutef to Quarterhouse. Jutef had accepted an invitation to eat mola stew with Master Benar, a senior caretaker to hooded masters. Jutef had admitted to him that he didn't care for mola, but he wanted to accept Benar's invitation. Pavis did not know Benar personally, but he had heard a lot about him, as Jutef and Benar had become very well acquainted since Master Elenn's demise. Pavis felt connected to them through Jutef, the only friend he had ever had. "Master Jutef, are you ready?"

"Yes, I'm just about ready," said Jutef. He leaned his cane against the table to free his hands so that he could pull a cloak over his shoulders. "It's windy today."

Pavis liked the tone of Jutef's voice, as it suggested a casual mood. "It's not as windy inside the walls," he said.

"I think I'll wear my cloak anyhow," said Jutef, "but I may leave my cane here and hold your shoulder while we walk if you don't mind."

"Of course," said Pavis. He actually liked it when Jutef held onto his shoulder. Jutef's hand made him feel valued.

"Have you heard anything else about those hooded masters at Murro?" Jutef asked as they ducked and stepped by the door tarp.

"Now some barren are referring to them as the 'eight stars'. I have no idea what that means."

They went out of the hut and started on the path to the capital gate. After half a minute's walking, Jutef offered an educated guess. "It's probably something from a poem," he said, his hand already on Pavis's shoulder. "I have never been good at remembering poetry."

"Before I left the temple, I thought that all masters knew all about poetry," said Pavis, "but not all do. I don't know any poetry at all."

"Master Benar will probably know. He's a Quarterhouse master of seven generations. You know what Quarterhouse is like . . . They eat and drink poetry for breakfast every day."

"Well, anyway, a lot of the barren are calling them the 'eight stars', and from the way they talk, it seems that chopping off each others' heads is the most wonderful thing you can do." Pavis noticed how Jutef neither laughed at his quip nor made comment. Jutef knew he had complex feelings about the death chains. He had known Chibo very well in the early days, just after they had all taken hood.

"Master Pavis, *you* are a hooded master now, . . . do *you* know who the waiter is?"

"No, I have no idea. I haven't really talked to anyone about what happened at Murro. I've only overheard others talking."

"Would you even tell me if you *did* know?" Pavis understood from this question that Jutef, like everyone in the capital, was preoccupied with finding out who the waiter was.

Pavis thought about this. He probably *would* tell Jutef. But then he would also have to tell him that he didn't think the self-extermination should be stopped by the masters council or the capital guards. Even though Pavis himself had once, given the opportunity to drink sleeping medicine and die in the temple, chosen not to do so, he now increasingly felt that barren uedin indeed deserved to have that option.

Jutef noticed his delay in answering and said, "I'm sorry, I shouldn't even ask you to tell me. I don't ever mean to question you about things you don't want to talk about."

"No, you mustn't worry about that, Master Jutef," said Pavis, "If I knew, I'm not sure if I would tell you or not. The fact is, I don't know," said Pavis. They arrived at the gate and passed through.

"I'll bet the hood squadron has every guard in the capital employed trying to find out who the waiter is," said Jutef. "I wonder how Master Nula and Master Elenn would be dealing with this if they were still here," he added, somewhat ruefully.

Pavis saw a chance to change the subject. "I can't believe you've been living alone in the caretaker hut all this time," he said. "and no other guard or caretaker has offered to join you there."

"Master Yenca offered. And so did one of the Flatpools guards—Master Ribol—do you know him?"

"No. He's not with the hood squadron, is he?"

"No, but he often patrols the road to Murro, and he's become well acquainted with the hooded masters."

"If two masters offered to join you at the hut, why are you still alone there?"

"Masters Yenca and Ribol have important work to do. They aren't needed at the caretaker hut. Only a few hooded masters come by occasionally to talk with me or ask for food. The real need is at Murro. Both of them spend a lot of time there. Besides, I've adjusted to living alone. When the alliance agreed to let me move outside the wall, there were many—Master Yenca included—who didn't think I would manage. But I'm showing them that I can manage just fine. You know those paths that the guards prepared for me with marker stones? I go right past them now. I'm going up the outside bank of the drystream now."

"Just don't get lost, Master Jutef."

"I wonder if I could ask you to come with me sometime. I want to explore on my own and just have you follow me, just in case I need help getting back."

"Of course," said Pavis, "I'd be glad to do that any time. And also, if you want to practice getting around more by yourself, I don't have to walk with you every time you come into the capital. I will understand if you don't ask me."

Jutef gave Pavis's shoulder a squeeze. "But then who would I have to talk to?" he asked, and laughed.

They reached Quarterhouse and made their way to Benar's hut, where they found him setting his table with great concentration. Three bowls were laid, two matching and one unmatching, each with a large spoon. A small lidded kettle occupied the table's center, steam rising in rivulets from around the lid. Benar looked up and smiled when he heard them arriving.

Benar turned and faced Jutef directly and said, in a very loud voice, "Master Jutef and Master Pavis, welcome! Please come in!" Pavis realized that Benar was trying to speak very clearly so that Jutef, who could not have the benefit of seeing him, might at least get the full benefit of his clarity of speech—but why was he talking so loudly? Pavis's first impression was that Benar was a rather foolish uedin.

"I'm so glad you could come. Master Pavis, I'm finally getting the opportunity to meet you. I've heard very good things about you."

Pavis felt a little ridiculous when Benar continued to speak too loudly even when talking to *him*, but he understood it was probably for Jutef's sake that he did so. It didn't hurt that Benar was complimenting him. "Thank you, Master Benar," he answered in a normal, perhaps even quieter-than-normal, voice. "I know that you meant to invite Master Jutef. I really only came to assist him walking here."

"Well I'm glad you came. I've always wanted to ask you about server life. You know, you have life experience that no other master has."

"I find that I remember less and less. It's been nearly a novade since I left the temple."

"I certainly can smell the mola stew," said Jutef, sensing that Pavis didn't want to talk about his server past. "There's no smell quite like it."

"I've never had it before," said Pavis.

"Well, get ready for something very delicious," said Benar. Jutef softly elbowed Pavis to give him the hint that maybe the mola stew wasn't as delicious as Benar said it was.

"I believe it's a Quarterhouse tradition," said Jutef, discreetly avoiding further commentary on the taste.

"Yes it is. There is something about a mola stew that comes from the Quarterhouse kitchen."

Pavis noticed the half-heartedness of Jutef's nod of affirmation, and then was surprised when Jutef suddenly broached, "Master Benar, what are your thoughts about what happened at Murro?"

"Well, I think it's absolutely dreadful what happened!"

"This is the third time, right?"

"Yes. The guards need to find the so-called 'waiter' and put a stop to this once and for all."

"I just hope the soon-to-be-named don't find out what's happening. They're bound to have a high incidence of syndrome among them . . . "

"Well we just have to deal with one problem at a time, don't we? Now let's sit and have some of this stew while it's fresh and hot."

Pavis sensed that Benar was the type of uedin who didn't like to talk about troublesome things. He pulled a chair out from the table and put a hand on Jutef's arm to guide him to his seat. Benar used a dipper to fill the three bowls with the steaming brown stew. He politely took the bowl that didn't match to be his own. Pavis took his own seat and looked down into the steaming bowl, pausing to admire the texture and color of the stew. He picked up the spoon set there beside his bowl, took a nice spoonful of the steaming stew, and brought it to his mouth. The smell of it was very strange, subtly reminding him of something rotten. He opened his mouth and put in the spoonful of stew. Indeed, it was like nothing he had ever tasted before. He wasn't sure if he liked it or not, but he at least found it edible.

"Ah . . . seems like it's been so long since I've had a good bowl of mola stew. Well, I guess it was just last year. What do you think, Master Jutef? Is it as good as last year's mola?"

"Oh, every bit as good, I think," said Jutef.

"And you, Master Pavis? Do you like it?"

Pavis didn't exactly *dis*like it, but he felt that he needed to get used to the flavor. "It's not bad," he said.

"Not bad?" Benar seemed a little disappointed that Pavis's appreciation of the stew went no further than "not bad," but was too busy enjoying his own stew to argue about it. He scraped the last drops of stew from his own bowl and reached for the dipper to refill it. "Master Jutef, I hear that you're doing very well at the caretaker hut," he said, advancing polite conversation.

"I'm managing all right," said Jutef.

Pavis knew it was a great point of pride for Jutef, so he said, "Master Jutef is indeed doing very well with very little help. He even goes for long walks all over the territory north of the capital."

"That's amazing! I think you have dumbfounded all of us in the alliance! Master Elenn would be very proud of you!"

Pavis knew that Elenn was the link between these two very different caretakers. How different they were! Jutef was so thoughtful. And Benar was so . . . well, . . . *loud.*

"I still get a great deal of help from the guards, and from Master Pavis here," said Jutef.

"Do you remember when you were apprenticing here at Quarterhouse, Master Jutef?"

"Oh yes," said Jutef. "I was just thinking of that. In fact, I went with you and Master Yenca to harvest mola beans. Do you remember?"

"Yes, well, we tried to give you every experience of a Quarterhouse caretaker, even though you came from . . . oh . . . where was it? Bramble?"

"Bells," said Jutef.

"Oh yes, Bells. Well, we made every effort to welcome you to Quarterhouse. And we miss you, now that you've gone to live outside the wall. But you were with us long enough to feel like one of us, weren't you? We share many things in common, wouldn't you say?"

"We certainly do," said Jutef. Pavis knew that the love of mola stew was not one of the things Jutef shared with the Quarterhouse masters. For his part, Pavis found it palatable enough to eat, but he had to keep reminding himself to have another bite.

Benar noticed that neither of his guests was enjoying the stew as much as he was. "I'm sorry I don't have anything else to offer you today . . . " he said, but he didn't seem to be too full of regret as he filled his bowl again, this time with enough stew to reach the brim and dribble down the side. "Master Pavis, what sort of thing did they feed you when you lived in the temple?"

"We ate a lot of boiled grain porridge."

"Plain?"

"Sometimes they put vineberries in it."

"Vineberries? Servers put vineberries in grain porridge?"

"Yes."

"We don't use vineberries much at Quarterhouse," said Benar between gulps of stew. "Once in a while someone will make vineberry tea." He had the bowl up to his face and was using his spoon to scoop the stew into his mouth. "More, anyone?"

"No thank you, it was very good but I've had enough," said Jutef.

Pavis had more or less decided that mola stew was not much to his liking, but he wanted Benar to think he liked it. "Just a bit more," he said. Then, as he held his bowl for more, he asked, "Master Benar, have you ever heard a poem or reference to the 'eight stars'?"

Benar looked at him with a puzzled expression. "Eight stars? Hmm . . . why? What is it about eight stars?"

"A lot of hooded masters are referring to the eight who died at Murro as the "eight stars." Do you have any idea where that might have come from?"

Benar looked at him with distaste. "Well, yes, . . . there's a poem. Post-fasting period. I think it's Malta. . . . Hooded masters are referring to those uedin who chopped each others' heads off as the eight stars?"

"I've heard it more than once."

Benar made a disgusted face as if he were about to spit out his stew. "It sounds like they're actually *praising* them!"

"I think many hooded masters *are* praising them," said Pavis.

"That is absolutely shameful! I won't have any of that from any of my counselees!"

"Do you know the whole poem, Master Benar?" asked Jutef.

"Let's see, how does it go . . . *'Eight stars decorate my eyes. Should I throw back my hood for more? But no, my precious will be lost'* . . . Something like that." Benar shrugged and burped a small burp. The poem obviously had no special meaning for him. "But the idea that they are quoting a poem to remember those dead masters . . . I don't like the sound of that. I'm just glad none of those eight wretches were my counselees. I can't help thinking that whoever their counselors were, they didn't do a very good job."

"Master Benar, I think you are too severe," said Jutef. "We who are unafflicted don't know what it's like—"

"Oh, rubbish! Our hooded masters manage very well when they just stop feeling sorry for themselves. Look at Master Pavis! Master Pavis, if I'm not mistaken, you could have chosen to perish in the temple—right? But you decided to join us masters and live, did you not?"

"To be honest, I didn't leave the temple so much because I wanted to live as because I wanted to feed."

Benar blinked and looked a bit unprepared for this answer, but it didn't dissuade him. "Well, that was nearly a novade ago. You were very young. But now you're well adjusted, and it's very good to see that you keep your hood on."

Pavis was mildly annoyed by the satisfied smile on Benar's face. He decided to share a secret that he had never really said out loud before. "I have often thought," he said, "that I should have drunk the sleeping medicine."

Jutef reached across the table and took hold of Pavis's wrist. "Oh, Master Pavis, I hope you don't think that," he said with earnest.

"I'm only saying that it is not an unusual thought for a barren to have."

"You never seriously thought—You wouldn't think of joining one of those chains, would you?" insisted Benar with disapproval.

"Not now," said Pavis. It struck him that Benar had an elevated notion of his own opinion, and that a bit of honesty might suit the conversation very well. "But there have been times when I might have. For me, the chance to die came when I didn't want to, and when I wanted to, I didn't have the chance."

"Do you wish your chance had aligned with your later desires?" asked Jutef.

"Well, no . . . " said Pavis.

"Why not, Master Pavis?" asked Benar.

"If I had died, I wouldn't have been able to eat this delicious mola stew," said Pavis, and he scooped up the last cold spoonful from the bottom of his bowl and ate it.

Yinob Bends the Truth

A year in the life of an unnamed is a very long time. The last year before taking of name they grow up incredibly fast. Yinob had a new level of love and concern for the soon-to-be-named at Bramble as they spoke more about very serious matters. They were sunning the bedding. There were ropes strung back and forth between opposite veranda railings at one end of the courtyard for hanging the blankets, and the pads were being laid out on the pavestones. Bramble didn't have a very large courtyard, and the pads had to be spaced very tightly in order to get them all aired. A group of unnamed was completing the chore, and Yinob was helping and supervising. They all knew what to do. He hardly had to direct them at all. They chatted while they worked.

"I think when one has one's ecstasy, it's like something is pulling one, just like a clingstone pulls on needles," said one of the child-uedin. "It either pulls one to the Lake of Ceulan if one is an unhooded master, or it pulls one to the Home of the Wind if one is a hooded master."

"But does one know where it's going to pull one when one leaves for one's pilgrimage? Or does one have to just go and find out?"

"Master Yinob, when a uedin leaves for one's pilgrimage, does one know where one's going?"

"None of us knows exactly where the Lake of Ceulan is," answered Yinob carefully, "and none of us knows where the Home of the Wind is either."

"But does a ro-uedin always find the way? Can a ro-uedin get mixed up?"

Yinob was never very comfortable talking to the unnamed about what happens at the end of a uedin's life, particularly now that nearly half of them had tested positive for barren syndrome. Caretakers and tutors had taken to telling them that unhooded masters went to the Lake of Ceulan, and hooded masters went to the "Home of the Wind." The unnamed clearly liked the idea of passing-of-life. Their faces showed discomfort with the idea of the wind telling them how to get to its home where "all things would be beautifully understood." It was too ambiguous.

"Oh no, a ro-uedin always finds his way, one way or another."

Many of these unnamed knew themselves to be future hooded masters. Yinob was thankful that they seemed to cope with their differentness, but it pained him to know that no matter how tame a version of barren syndrome the tutors and caretakers might present to them, they knew they were recipients of misfortune. He didn't know how to make that any easier for them, other than trying to make light of it—and that sometimes felt a little disrespectful.

"How was the trip to the library yesterday?" asked Yinob to change the subject.

"It was good. The library master gave us honeycrumble. It was a little stale, but we ate it," said one of the unnamed.

"I don't suppose you did any *reading* while you were at the library, did you?" teased Yinob.

"One read something interesting," said a child-uedin unfolding a blanket. "We know that ancient uedin used to eat the muscles of animals, but one never heard that ancient uedin kept them in large numbers in the western outfields."

"But *servers* never ate animals' muscles, did they?" asked another unnamed, "Masters did, but servers didn't—right, Master Yinob?"

"I'm pretty sure they did too," said Yinob. "Before the codes were written down, the servers were just starting to read the thoughts of Lern Beyana. They didn't know how much she disliked it when uedin ate the muscles of animals."

"One heard that the unnamed of Quarterhouse ate a master when they were wetuedin. He fell in their hatching pool, and they ate him."

"One heard that too," said another.

"What! Where did that terrible story come from?!" Yinob raised his voice. The unnamed were silent. Of course they didn't know where it came from.

"What? What did the Quarterhouse unnamed do?" asked one of the unnamed who had not heard the story.

"Some unnamed are apparently hearing a false rumor about the unnamed at Quarterhouse. If you hear anything about the unnamed of another domicile, don't believe it, and tell the child-uedin who told you that it should not be repeated again. Do you understand?"

"Yes," said the child-uedin.

"Do you *all* understand?"

"Yes, . . . Yes, . . . " they all said.

"Now that one, and that one," Yinob pointed to two of the unnamed, "Go get the big baskets of wheel-shaped pillows on the veranda."

"Yes, Master," they said and ran off to get the pillows.

"Master Yinob, please don't be cross. One doesn't believe the stupid story about wetuedin eating a master who fell in their hatching pool. Someone just made it up as a scary story."

"I'm glad you have the good sense to recognize that," said Yinob.

"Master Yinob, what are the Eight Stars of the Capital?" asked an unnamed whose voice, a little low and raspy for a child-uedin, Yinob had not heard that day.

"Eight Stars?" Yinob never imagined that these unnamed would be exposed to such things. He had no idea how to respond. He decided he would pretend to know nothing. "I don't know anything about that."

"Someone said Master Holra was talking to a groundskeeper about the Eight Stars of the Capital for a long time. But nobody knows what that means."

"I don't know either. They were probably talking about . . . some kind of flower or something." *How irresponsible of Master Holra and whoever it was—talking about something like that when the unnamed were close enough to hear!* "Here they come with the wheel-shaped pillows. Put them on top of the pads, straw side up."

The unnamed quickly made a game of tossing the wheel pillows to one another and placing them in the sunshine. Yinob let them play. He was terribly concerned that they seemed to have heard something about the Eight Stars. It was no wonder. The self-extermination at Murro had occurred the night before last. By the time news of the group suicide made its way around the capital, they were already being called the "eight stars." It appalled Yinob to think that someone had been irresponsible enough to mention it in front of the unnamed. Even before this, the masters council was starting to face pressure to *allow* self-extermination chains. Hooded masters were advocating for its approval, arguing that masters should have the same option as servers. Some of the tutors at Bramble supported the proposal. Yinob had very mixed feelings about it. He understood that many of the afflicted thought it was their best option, and he sympathized. But as a caretaker working now with the soon-to-be-named, he thought it would be terrible to endorse such a thing. Unfortunately, most of the masters in the capital didn't work directly with the unnamed and didn't see it his way. Worse yet, it was obvious that clandestine planning among hooded masters was leading to these self-extermination chains, and the masters council had no idea how to stop them. If there were any more, the council would very likely be forced to act in the only way they could—probably by sanctioning some controlled form of the practice. Watching the unnamed playing in the sun, he felt sick with the thought that they were facing entry into such a dreadful reality.

Nekur's Realization

Nekur watched with gratitude as the attendants gingerly guided and lowered the Most High into a seated position on cushions and placed a thick quilt behind his back. They let him rest against the wall of the small room that had been converted into a vapors chamber. Nekur was touched to see the tenderness with which they treated the Most High. Nekur was, at this point, in awe of him. While one attendant wrapped a light blanket around the Most High's shoulders and covered his knees, the other gave a last stir to the pot of steaming hot water loaded with medicinal herbs and placed in the corner.

In a soft and kind voice, "There. Are you comfortable, Most High?" asked the one tucking the edge of the blanket around his feet. The Most High had his eyes closed and didn't answer. The attendant turned to Nekur and said, "Make yourself comfortable, high server. As soon as we shut the door, the vapors will fill the space. We'll be waiting right here—just let us know when you are finished."

Medicinal vapors had worked to give the Most High an increased vigor and lucidity for temporary periods, and this was the second time vapors had been used specifically for a meeting with the primary advisor. In the last four moon cycles, the Most High had declined rapidly. Nekur hated the memory that cropped up again and again when he met with him. He was ashamed to think that with ulterior motives he had once recommended that the Most High take meals and exercises with the high servers. It was with the full expectation that his suggestion would be reject-ed—a scheme to demonstrate to the assembly that the Most High was too frail to be wielding authority. Now that the Most High was plainly unable to take meals and exercises with them, and was tragically losing his ability to act in authority, Nekur made every effort to assuage his guilt by insisting that the Most High be consulted to the very last shred of his capacity. But it was not only to assuage guilt. Nekur was quite convinced that any direction coming from the Most High was of absolute benefit to the temple and the capital. He had had a complete conversion.

He sat opposite the Most High and looked at his hanging tired head as it disappeared into darkness as the door was shut for them. The aroma of pungent herbal steam was thick and pene-trating.

"Most High, the assembly of high servers asked me to convey their deep wishes for your recovery."

As they were now in complete darkness, Nekur could only wait for the Most High to respond. But there was no answer.

"They miss you," Nekur said, eyes practically tearing up as he said it. "They look forward to your return . . . " Nekur's great fear was that the Most High would never join high server activities again. It was a very real and horrible possibility.

"The kindness of dear ones . . . " murmured the Most High, *" . . . the kindness of all dear ones . . . "*

This was the sort of response from the Most High that always gave Nekur a strange feeling. It was ambiguous and distant. Per-haps the Most High was not alert. He decided to wait for a few minutes to see if the stimulant vapors would wake him up a bit.

"Breathe in the vapors, Most High. Just rest and breathe deep." Nekur sucked in air and exhaled loudly to show the Most High what he wanted him to do.

Finally, when Nekur noticed that his own mind was gaining stimulation and wakefulness from the vapors, he tried speaking to the Most High again. "Do you recall our discussion about high rule, Most High?"

"Whatever they want is fine . . . " answered the Most High, a little more alert. Nekur felt an instant of sentimentality hearing a tone that sounded more like the Most High in his good old days.

"Well, you know how they are," Nekur said with a reassured humor, "the servers want to believe that they're making a difference," and he chuckled lightly. But in truth, he had changed his opinion about high servers who needed to think they were doing something important. They had good intentions. Since growing to understand the wisdom of the Most High, Nekur was reassessing many of his former opinions.

"*Let us be at peace,*" said the Most High. Nekur relaxed as if gladly receiving a command.

After taking a moment to relax his mind, Nekur continued. "Many feel that high rule would be a comfort at this time. The assembly is requesting a set period, continuing until Namestaking. That would be a good time to end it, don't you think, Most High?" Namestaking was not as important in the temple as it was outside, but servers did participate in the ceremony, and it marked the beginning of a period when newly-named from outside would come to inquire about entering. "High rule should not be in place when newly-named come to inquire. Do you agree?" asked Nekur.

"Primary advisor—when is the next meeting of the assembly?" asked the Most High in voice that again sounded sweetly familiar.

Nekur didn't want the Most High to be overly distraught about his inability to attend. "The next meeting will be sometime soon, Most High. I will let you know. Don't worry about anything."

"No, we won't worry," said the Most High. "*. . . What happened to Pilka will not happen to Tilke.*"

Nekur was stunned to hear this combination of words. A few moon cycles ago, certain high servers were admonished for making heretical remarks, associating the Most High with a corrupt server from temple history. The association could be taken to suggest that the Most High was himself corrupt.

The high servers who were admonished were acquaintances of Nekur. He had once considered them allies when he was part of a faction vying for influence in the assembly. Fortunately, he had already been serving as primary advisor when the references to the corrupt server were made, so he was spared from directly having to hear them blab the unmentionable original name of the Most High, associating it with the name of the other. The thought of the historical name made him cringe—and he certainly didn't expect to hear it uttered by the Most High.

"Most High, how is it that you know about this controversy? Is the Soft One apprehending it?"

"... *I will not let harm come to him,*" said Most High.

Nekur was confused. He would not let harm come . . . to whom? To the one who made the heretical remark? But it was not just one server who had been admonished. "It is not one server who repeated the offending idea, Most High. There were a few. But they have repented."

Nekur thought it would be best not to get into too much discussion about the corrupt server of the distant past. Nekur had learned more about him when the assembly had admonished the controversial high servers who mentioned him. The corrupt server who had been indiscreetly referenced had lived during the Claybridge era. He had been obsessed with getting attention, and he had tried to demonstrate to everyone that he loved the Soft One more than his own passing-of-life, so he had sat in a mind-stilling and had never come out of it. He had died of dehydration and starvation, forfeiting his passing-of-life. The Most High at the time of the corrupt server's generation had quickly discerned that such a mistake brought great distress to the Soft One, and the server was pronounced corrupt. The mere mention of his name was thought to bring sorrow to the Soft One.

"Harm will not come to him," said the Most High.

Something in the strange way he said it made Nekur wonder. Did the Most High not understand that it was not one server, but a number of them, who had associated him with the corrupt server? Or was he talking about someone else? "Harm will not come to *whom*, Most High?" Nekur asked cautiously.

" *. . . Harm will not come to Tilke . . . Your most high."*

Nekur could not see the face of the Most High in the dark of the small vapors chamber, and suddenly he wanted very much to see it. What was the Most High talking about?

"Most High, I don't . . . I don't underst—"

"Primary advisor, may I tell you what pains me?"

Nekur caught his breath. "Yes, of course, Most High. Please tell me."

"The thing which they hide from us."

"What do they hide, Most High?"

"The uedin with nothing in their skullwombs . . . "

"Yes, Most High," said Nekur, "you mean the barren servers?"

" . . . and masters," said the Most High.

"Is it their presence that offends the Soft One, Most High?"

"Their suffering offends me," said the Most High, *"and now they die in groups."*

Offends *me*? It sounded like the Most High was speaking on behalf of the Soft One, saying the words that the Soft One might say. And what about barren uedin dying in groups? Nekur knew that some number of servers, more than expected, were turning out to be barren, and he knew that they were consistently choosing, unlike the messenger server from a novade ago, to drink the sleep medicine. But the barren masters were doing something else—something that involved surgery and the wearing of hoods. Nekur had heard some mention of it from one of the emissaries before he had become primary advisor. "Is the Soft One apprehending events outside the temple, Most High?"

"I follow many."

There, he had done it again. The Most High was speaking directly as the Soft One. Nekur felt a chill come over him, and his heart began to race. Lern Beyana was speaking. She was speaking, through the Most High, directly to *him*.

"What . . . Am I . . . ? Am I speaking directly with the . . . ?"

"You may continue . . . to call me Most High . . . " said the voice, *"I am used to hearing it . . . "*

Jeber's Quandary

Jeber carried the basket of fieldpears he had picked to the door of the food cellar, but when he heard Master Ghera speaking with someone down there, he decided to leave the basket at the door. He didn't want to talk to anyone. He stood for a moment, deciding what to do next. He rubbed his face and then ran his hands over the knitted hood that covered his head. He quietly walked back to the workhouse, climbed the stairs to the loft, pulled his bedding from the shelf, and dragged it to a shadowy corner. If anyone asked why he was sleeping in the afternoon, he would say that he felt ill. Without bothering to remove his socks or work clothes, he lay down on the bedding, pulled a blanket over himself, and settled his face into the wheel-shaped pillow.

He was trembling. His whole body ached with tension. On the night of the bloody event at Murro, he had fled back and passed straight through the capital and to the outfields to spend a sleepless night hiding in the tool shed. The two-handed blade was still hidden there behind a jumble of garden tools. He knew it could not stay there long, but he didn't know what to do next. He had spent the last two days avoiding all contact. Leol and Serka were gone somewhere—he was glad that he didn't have to talk to them. He was sure that the news of the self-extermination took no more than a day to reach every ear in the capital, and there were probably barren masters looking for the new waiter. He didn't know how to connect with them. He wanted it all to be over, but he was paralyzed with fear.

He tried to relax, face cupped in the pocket of darkness from the wheel-shaped pillow. He kept recalling the scene of decapitated bodies in the early morning light beside the grainhouse at Murro. He kept recalling the sound of the last one to die there screaming at him, *"Now! Now!"* What cruel luck it had been that left him with the blank shell. How he wished he could cry out, "Now!" and put an end to this miserable situation. His mind shifted from one disturbing image to another. He thought of the meeting with Tono in the empty lot, the scavenger chick flapping about as Tono emptied a pot of kitchen scraps. He thought of Tono saying, "It is a dreadful act. You cannot imagine it." How true! He thought about the miserable hours he spent peering into the campfire at Murro. He recalled the face of the barren master who tried to get his attention to share necks . . . share necks! As if such a thing could have actually enticed him as he tried to ready himself for the act he was about to join behind the grainhouse! He thought of the blood spurting from the necks of beheaded uedin like sourfruit juice from a juice press. These were images he would never be able to rid from his mind. He remained with his face buried in the pillow for the next few hours, unable to sleep.

Finally, he heard voices below. Some of the workermasters were starting to prepare the evening meal. Soon the kitchen would be full, and he wouldn't be able to get out of the house without being seen. On an ordinary day, he would have gone to help them, but he knew that they would want to talk about what happened at Murro. The last time it happened outside the eastern gate, they had all wanted to talk about it—this time was no different. He knew how quickly news spread and how the regular masters reacted to the self-exterminations.

He waited until the workermasters were doing something on the far side of the room, and then he quickly darted down the stairs and ducked low under the door tarp so as not to make a sound. There was nobody else around the workhouse that he could see. He couldn't exactly keep up the hiding much longer—he would go back in and face everyone when the sun went down—but for now he just wanted to be somewhere out of the way where the other masters might leave him alone if they saw him. He decided to go over and sit on the bench by the fire pit. He didn't think he could achieve any kind of mindstilling considering the agitated state he was in, but if anyone came near he could at least act like that was what he was doing.

He sat on the bench with his back to the house and looked at the cold ashes and burnt chunks leftover from some long ago fire. He thought about how he would avoid conversation when he went back in the house at sunset. He would eat with a blank stare, and they would think that he had come back from a session of behavior that they didn't want to think about, and they would leave him alone.

By a chance glancing over his shoulder, Jeber noticed two figures walking toward the workhouse from the trees that grew along the capital wall. They were hooded. He stood and took a few steps to get to a higher hump of ground so that he could get a better look. Yes, it looked like Serka and Leol coming. They were walking slowly. They seemed to be talking to each other. As they got a little closer, they noticed him watching them, and their eyes were fixed on him as they approached.

No one made any gesture or greeting, and no one asked where another had been. They simply came together silently, all wearing heavy, serious expressions.

Finally Leol said, "We just came from Northgate."

"I was wondering where you had gone . . . " said Jeber.

"You know what happened at Murro—three days ago," said Serka, sure that Jeber had heard the news, but only confirming.

Jeber felt himself being scrutinized by Serka. He weighed his response in his mind before speaking. "I heard about it, yes . . . " he said, "Eight of them."

"Hooded masters are calling them the 'eight stars,'" said Serka, still watching Jeber.

"Eight stars? That's strange . . . " In fact, Jeber did find it very strange. He had no idea where that came from.

"Yes, strange . . . but that's what they're calling them," said Leol. After a moment, when nobody spoke, he added, "And there's going to be another one. Even bigger."

"How do you know?" asked Jeber.

"They're talking about it all over the capital," said Leol. He too seemed to be assessing Jeber's reactions.

Jeber started to feel very uncomfortable. Did they suspect him? Was there any way they could know that he was, in fact, the waiter?

"I heard that twenty masters are joining the chain," said Serka.

"They're calling it 'Chibo's chain,' because a groundskeeper master named Chibo started it," said Leol.

"Yes, I did hear about that," said Jeber. Actually, that much had circulated before the event at Murro.

"Master Jeber, we have been together since taking name," said Serka. "We have faced having barren syndrome together . . . "

"I know," said Jeber, now very nervous that his comrades were going to confront him about being the waiter, "It has been a very hard time for all of us. I don't know what I would have done without the two of y—"

"We don't have to pretend anymore," said Serka, his eyes tearing up. "We don't have to be strong anymore."

"What are you saying?" asked Jeber.

Serka just looked at him with tears in his eyes. Leol finally spoke. "Master Serka and I have decided that we want to join the chain. If there are twenty, we will make it twenty-two."

"How can you . . . ? . . . have you met the waiter?" asked Jeber.

"We haven't been able to find out who it is," said Serka in a choked voice, "but we are determined to find him."

"He's keeping his identity very secret," said Leol. "But there's a hooded master named Hemi who has the same counselor I do, Master Mebok at Whiteroof, and we think Hemi knows who the waiter is."

Jeber felt dizzy with the strangeness of his situation. He knew that Leol and Serka were about to ask him if he wanted to join the chain and die with them. This was his chance. If he told them that he was the waiter, they would be flabbergasted, but if he showed them the double-handed blade, covered in dried blood and wrapped in a cloth, they would believe him.

"All the capital guards are trying to find the waiter as well," said Serka. "They say that the masters council has extended a conditional approval, contingent upon cooperation of some sort."

"We don't believe it. We think the guards want to stop us," said Leol.

Serka put his hand on Jeber's shoulder and looked into his eyes. "Master Jeber, don't think that you must join us . . . We only ask that you won't tell any of the others at the workhouse, until it is over. We just had to let you know what was happening."

In the years of growing up with Leol and Serka, Jeber had known them from many different angles. Many a time, one of the three of them had been upset with the other two. Many a time they had made and broken promises together. He had shared necks with both of them in the early days of their struggle. But he had never seen either of them look at him with such morbid resolve. They were truly determined to die. But Jeber couldn't stand the thought of them ending their lives in the horrible manner that he had witnessed and participated in. He made a decision. It was going to require deception.

"I will join the chain with you," he said.

Serka immediately stepped forward, embraced Jeber, and began to shake with sobs. Leol put his arms around the two of them, and the threesome cried together. Jeber knew that his friends were crying with him to share a common pain and deep sorrow. While he did share their sorrow completely, he had an additional private grief that he cried for. Jeber didn't know what was going to happen with the chain of twenty or thirty or however many were planning to die together. He just knew that he wasn't going to be with them. The double-handed blade was going to stay right where it was, hidden behind shovels and rakes in the tool shed, until someday, some workermaster would find it—perhaps after all three of them were gone. Jeber was not going to be the one to provide any blade for them, nor any plan. He owed nothing to anyone. He would let Serka and Leol think that he was going to join them in death, but he would steal away in the middle of the night and leave them forever. He was going to do as earlier barren had done. He was going to go far and deep into the southeastern desert—so far that it was beyond any chance of making it back—and there he would die alone.

Awakening at the Bluff

Elenn and Pelto were on their way back from a night walk in the desert. Elenn had lived in the childless settlement for over a year—he knew because the warm season had come around full circle. A hot wind like the one they were feeling only happened at the peak of the warm season, and usually only in the last year of a novade, though that was still a year away. Did it matter anymore that a new generation was soon to be named in the capital? Did it matter that when the next Great Rains came, he would be fourth generation? The diet of sponge and its effect put Elenn in a very yielding frame of mind regarding all things, and while it felt strange to embrace a monotony that promised to continue until his last breath, he felt neither trapped nor anxious. His only thought about his past life was the lingering relief that it was essentially over.

The night walks were a pleasure. To Elenn, they felt like a new kind of exercise, easy and relaxed. There was no rule about night walks—no imperative for silence or brisk pace, no fixed intention or time frame. They went out on bright nights, consciously varying their course from one night walk to another so as to maintain familiarity with the desert region that surrounded them. There was always the quiet understanding that their community was made up of barren uedin who were found alive in the empty desert expanse.

He had learned during his time in the settlement that the uedin there were quite unattached to their old memories of the capital. There was no reason to ask Pelto if he ever thought about a new generation coming with the Great Rains. He could tell that Pelto wasn't interested in the capital anymore. Elenn himself had started to regard his own memories as quaint and unimportant.

They reached the foot of the bluff and went straight to the spot where strategically placed rocks provided a kind of stairway up to the complex of dwellings which they referred to as their village. When they reached it, they saw that there was someone there waiting for them. It was still dark, so they couldn't see who it was until they got closer. It was Yulig. He beckoned them urgently.

"A new one has been found alive," said Yulig. "Daga found him. He is near death. He has a glass piece in his neck, like you described you once had, but it is broken into pieces and the wound around it is very corrupted and diseased. He could die from fever."

"Broken into pieces? How could that have happened?"

"Daga was able to remove some of the broken pieces, but some of it is too embedded in his flesh. He wears the robe of the western outfield—it hasn't changed since I was a young master in the capital."

"Can he speak? Did he give you his name?" asked Elenn.

"Oh no . . . he is completely unconscious. He is much weaker than you were when we found you."

With no further discussion, they followed Yulig back to a room carved in the rock much like all the other dwellings. A small twig fire burned at the open side, but it did not provide enough light to see what the rescued uedin looked like. Elenn knew that it had to be one of the three hooded outfield workers—either Jeber, Serka, or Leol—all of whom he knew not very well, but a little. The outfield workers were young masters who had once mattered very much to Elenn and Nula when they were partner guards. He hadn't thought about them for a long time.

"I got the rest of the glass out of his neck," said Daga, "but we have no way to treat the wound."

"Flush it with water," suggested Pelto.

"I already have. And I'm trying to get him to drink, but he cannot swallow."

Elenn bent over the figure to see who it was. "There were only three barren masters at the western outfields," he said. "This must be one of them, but I can't see well enough to know who it is. Daga, is it alright if I stay till morning?"

"Of course," said Daga.

"I will get out of your way," said Pelto. "I'll come back in the morning to see how you are doing."

"I hope he survives the night," said Daga.

Elenn sat near the ailing new one and tried again to see his face through the dark, but he could not. He could only listen to the occasional gasping. He stayed there the rest of the night. He talked with Daga, sharing a little of his memory of the western outfield workers. There was nothing they could do but sit and wait for the morning light. After a while, Elenn nodded off, and images of the night desert flashed in his mind—of the stars, and of the darkly shadowed dunes. Finally, when the darkness of the night started to recede, he awoke, recalled why he was there, and drew close to the rescued uedin to see if he could make out his face. He gradually surmised that it was Jeber.

"Master Jeber! Master Jeber!" he coaxed, trying to get a conscious response. But Jeber did not open his eyes.

Daga took some minced sponge, added water to it, then cradled Jeber's head in one arm and tried to feed him the soupy mixture. Jeber was still unable to open his mouth or swallow.

"May I try?" asked Elenn. Daga moved out of the way so that Elenn could hold Jeber up, and he handed him the bowl. Elenn tried to drip some of the mixture into Jeber's mouth. Jeber coughed, and the mixture dribbled from his mouth.

Gradually the sun came up. They were still trying to get Jeber to swallow. In the sunlight, Elenn was able to look closely at Jeber's sunburned and wind-chapped face. Recent years of feeding had not only given him a large frame, it had changed his features from the delicate look that he had had as a youth to the rugged and hardened appearance shared by so many barren uedin. It was the look of the barren who lived at the capital. The sponge-fed residents of the settlement did not have such a look.

This time, when Daga tried to spoon fluid into Jeber's mouth, he drew back and turned his head to refuse it. Daga looked up and smiled to Elenn. It was good that Jeber was showing some response. He was regaining consciousness.

"Master Jeber!" said Elenn forcefully, and he jiggled Jeber's shoulder, but Jeber was nowhere near ready to open his eyes.

"Hold him firmly. We can't let him refuse nourishment," said Daga, and Elenn held Jeber tight around the head and neck so that a bit of the liquid could be spooned into his mouth. He choked a bit but then swallowed. When they saw him swallow, they knew he was going to live.

The first time Jeber opened his eyes, Elenn saw his eyes and felt a powerful emotion come over him. In Jeber's eyes, Elenn saw every beloved master he had ever known in the capital. Jeber's face may have looked like the face of a barren at full-stage syndrome, but his eyes were pure uedin. They relayed confusion, fear, and hopelessness.

"Master Jeber, it is me—Elenn . . . of the hood squadron." It felt so strange to say it.

"Master . . . How can you . . . ?" murmured Jeber.

"Don't worry. We were both rescued. Now you must just eat. Don't worry about talking."

"But where . . . ?"

"There is much for us to tell each other, after you regain your strength."

Jeber looked at him for a long time, lost in wonder. Daga was trying to feed him the white soup. Finally he opened his mouth to accept some of it.

The fever broke during the second night, and the following morning Elenn suspected that Jeber was strong enough to talk but was choosing not to.

"Master Jeber, do you remember me?" he asked.

Jeber did not answer, but he looked at him and his eyes showed recognition.

"You have been rescued, and you are going to live. This is a settlement of barren uedin who have been rescuing one another from the desert for many generations—how many we don't even know."

Jeber looked at Elenn, but still he declined to speak.

"Why don't you speak? What happened to your catheter?"

Jeber turned his head away and closed his eyes. Elenn knew that with time and whitesponge, Jeber would not only gain strength but also arrive at the peace of mind that they all had in common, and the two of them would be able to talk calmly. Elenn wondered, though, what kind of trauma Jeber had faced. Why was he refusing to speak? Certainly things had been bad when Elenn had left the capital a year ago, and the situation then had only been worsening. How bad had it gotten? Elenn considered that there might be no benefit to hearing about how awful things had become in the capital. There was a wisdom, he knew now, to letting go of memories of the capital. Maybe the best thing possible was for Jeber to quickly recover and let the memory of his suffering melt away.

By the Jeber was finally able to stand up, it was obvious that he was quite capable of communicating. Elenn stared at him insistently. It was time to speak.

Jeber eventually looked back, but with a dissatisfied look on his face. "I have been brought here against my will," he said. "This is not a rescue. It is a capture."

Elenn was stunned by Jeber's words. He could not deny that Jeber was speaking earnestly. Jeber was angry that he had not died.

"Master Jeber, you will see how with time, you—"

"Why do you call me 'master'? You've been talking to all the uedin who have been coming in here. You call none of the others 'master.'"

Elenn was taken aback. "I know you as Master Jeber . . . from the western outfields. I did not know any of these other uedin before coming here. They don't call themselves 'master.'"

"This is terrible!" said Jeber, shaking his head in despair. "I should not be here! I should not be alive now!"

"Jeber!" When Elenn shouted it—the name without "Master" attached to it, Jeber looked up at him pathetically. "Stop thinking that!" continued Elenn. "You must wait until you recover before you can say anything about your situation. You have to wait."

"*Wait . . .* " cried Jeber, collapsing back to his bed of straw, moaning, "*I am the waiter! I am not allowed to die!*"

Elenn looked at him in bewilderment. "What do you mean?"

"I . . . killed. I killed a uedin. I killed him with the understanding that I would be killed in return. But then I ran away."

Elenn looked at Jeber with complete befuddlement. What had happened? Something very awful, it was clear, but what was this about killing and being killed? He looked at Daga.

Daga, however, was more concerned that this new one whom he had rescued was of the mind that he was being held there against his will, not allowing him his choice to die. "Jeber," said Daga, using the name for the first time, "Why do you say you were captured?"

" . . . because I don't want to be here! Oh, leave me alone! You won't understand!"

"He's going to need to be left alone for a while in order to adjust," said Elenn to Daga. "I'm going to my own dwelling. Is there anything I can do to help before I go?"

"You are both free to come and go as you like," said Daga.

"Is there enough whitesponge for him?"

"Yes, there is plenty."

"Well, please let me know if I am needed," said Elenn.

"There is something I must tell the new one. Hear me say it before you go." Daga hunched down beside Jeber who was now lying face down. "New one, there is one thing you must know. You are not a captive, and I am not a captor. I found you and brought you here in case you should want to live, but if you wish to die now, you can run and throw yourself off the bluff. It has happened before with certain new ones. It will only sadden us for a short while. You are free to do as you wish. There is sponge porridge if you wish to eat it. If there is anything else I can do to aid your comfort, please let me know."

Elenn was unaware until that moment that there had been new ones who had failed to trade lives, who had instead thrown themselves from the bluff. It must be true, or Daga would not have said it. But how strangely sad it was to hear that it would only sadden them for a short time. Was that also true? Would Elenn also be sad for only a short while if Jeber threw himself from the bluff? But he accepted the wisdom of the elder uedin's words to Jeber. He raised hands to face and departed.

Discovery of Things being Upside Down

For four days, Elenn avoided Daga's dwelling. He told himself it was to give Jeber time to deal with his aggravation and adjust to the event of his being rescued. Elenn knew, however, that avoiding the disruption also helped him stay with the calm flow of life as he had come to know it since his own arrival at the bluff. The other childless were practically immune to mental stress, but Elenn still felt susceptible.

When Jeber appeared in the sunshine at Elenn's own dwelling, Elenn felt great awkwardness. He was not genuinely happy to see Jeber, but he knew that Jeber needed and deserved his full attention.

"Pardon my intrusion," said Jeber, standing with hunched shoulders at the front corner of the open-faced dwelling.

"Jeber," said Elenn, consciously dispensing with 'Master' at this point, "I am glad to see you here. I hope you know I've left you alone so that you could have some peace."

"I remember your kindness when you were a guard. You are still kind."

Elenn smiled. "You're doing so well! You've been through so much, but you're doing so well!"

Jeber turned his head away, refusing this assessment. "I am here. I have not thrown myself off the bluff. But I'm not doing well."

"I do want to ask you . . . What happened to your catheter? Did you fall backwards and break it?"

"No," said Jeber, casting his eyes downward dolefully, "When I left the capital, I had to go through the canyon, and there were other barren there looking to feed. I removed my neck strap and took rocks in both of my hands, and I smashed the catheter behind my head."

Elenn pictured this and thought about Jeber's last days in the capital—how clearly miserable they must have been. He recalled the crude confession that Jeber had made—of killing someone with the understanding that he would be killed in return. What was this?! There was no end to the misery in the capital. The memory of it was a wound that would never heal.

"Jeber, it is a great adjustment to live here, but the adjustment comes more quickly than you think. I marvel when I think about how quickly being here has changed everything for me."

"I don't know how I can live at all—here or anywhere. The only way I can live is if I forget that I ever lived. There is no capital. There are no western outfields."

Elenn looked at him thoughtfully. He didn't need to learn about whatever awful things happened to Jeber before he came. He only needed to help him forget those things. "You're right," said Elenn, "There is no capital, and there are no western outfields. They don't exist. But we do exist in this place, even though it's new for you. You must give it a chance. There are many wonders here, though you do not see them until you *learn* to see them."

This prompted Jeber to look out at the vista of the desert. "It is not beautiful and green like the outfields, but it does have its own beauty," he said. Elenn was greatly heartened by hearing Jeber make a positive comment about the bluff.

"Have you done a desert-watching with Daga yet?"

"A desert-watching? What is that?"

"We just sit and look at the desert. It's very simple, but it's also challenging."

"Is that what he's always doing? What is the purpose of it?"

"Oh, just to see the desert, and see how beautiful it is," said Elenn.

Jeber laughed a casual laugh. Elenn had the feeling that it had been a very long time since Jeber had laughed at all. The white-sponge was remarkable.

"Would you like to try?" asked Elenn.

"Looking at the desert? I *am* looking at it."

"No, you're not. Come." Elenn gathered woven grass mats and two small sit-stools and placed them just at the ledge that faced out to the desert. He positioned them with care and then invited Jeber to sit. "This is a desert-watching. We will just sit for a while without talking. Right at the edge here, it takes a little while to relax."

"Yes, I can see why," said Jeber, glancing down.

They sat on the sit-stools and faced the vast sun-baked landscape. "If you need to get up to stretch, go ahead. And if there's something very important that you need to say, go ahead and speak."

"I understand," said Jeber. He looked to see how Elenn was sitting and straightened his posture to imitate him.

Elenn inwardly acknowledged his intention that Jeber would find value in desert-watching, even though it was only his first time, and then drew his attention to the desert.

They sat and watched. The colors were rather bleached by the mid-morning sun, and the heat made a blur of the distance. Elenn remembered when sitting so close to the ledge at such a height had made him nervous, and that was probably the case with Jeber, too. He redirected his attention back to the desert. He noticed in the view that there was still part of the dark shadow cast on the desert by the bluff to the north of them, the one they called "the boot." Did Jeber think about Daga's remark that he was free to throw himself from the bluff whenever he wanted? Had Jeber gotten close to doing it? But again, he decided it was better not to think about that, and he concentrated on the horizon.

They remained seated and silent for a very long time, until finally Jeber stood to stretch out his legs, and Elenn decided that it had been long enough for a first desert-watching.

"That's enough," Elenn said, standing up. "You see? There's not much to it."

"I understand now what you meant when you said I was not looking at the desert. It's very hard to look at something with your whole mind."

"Exactly."

"I was not able to do it at all. I am too unhappy," said Jeber.

"So you sat down to watch the desert, and you just watched your unhappiness. That's all right. You will watch your unhappiness melt with time," said Elenn.

"Daga said something like that to me too."

Bending to pick up a woven mat, Elenn noticed a trail of ants crawling along the ledge. "Look," he said to Jeber, "Look at these ants!" They were moving in a single stream and then disappearing over the side of the rock edge. Jeber stepped forward and observed the ants for a while.

"Why don't they throw themselves off?" Elenn asked Jeber. It was a joke and also a serious query.

"Maybe they are too busy," said Jeber, smiling at Elenn. Like his laugh, Jeber's smile seemed like something that hadn't happened for a long time.

"Maybe they are *just busy enough*," Elenn joked back. He picked up the sit-stools to put them back in the shady interior. "I'm going to eat now," he said, "Will you join me?"

"Do you eat anything here besides whitesponge?" asked Jeber.

"It's amazing that we survive on *it alone*," answered Elenn. He went to an inner corner where a raised area of the floor served as a little kitchen for cutting and mashing whitesponge.

"Don't you crave yams? Or tea?"

"I used to. I don't anymore. The whitesponge actually satisfies all cravings. You won't think about sharing necks, either."

"I was wondering about that. The uedin here are all barren but they don't share necks."

"Well, you know of course that there was no sharing necks before the catheter implants were introduced."

"Yes, I know." He paused for a moment and then asked, "What was it like when they were introduced? I heard that you used to go around with neckstraps visible."

"It's true. Before our generation got the implants, there was no neck sharing at all. The childless here know only what I've told them about it."

"The *childless*?"

"Haven't you heard Daga use the word? We do not refer to ourselves here as 'barren.' We refer to this place as the childless village. We are the childless." By now, Elenn was cutting some fresh sponge into bits with a stone tool. He finished and transferred the minced whitesponge into two bowls.

"What are those bowls made from?" asked Jeber.

"They are made of sliced whitesponge. There's a way of treating it with mud and turning it into a tough material.

"Even the bowls are made of it . . . "

"We have very few resources here," said Elenn as he handed Jeber a bowl.

While they ate, Elenn noticed how Jeber was eating slowly, pondering the substance he was eating. Elenn was glad to see that Jeber was starting to understand the beneficence of the whitesponge.

When they finished, Jeber put down his bowl, thoughtfully turned to face Elenn, and addressed him by name without the honorific "Master" prefix.

"*Elenn*," he said emphatically. Elenn met his gaze and nodded for him to speak. "I am ready to speak with you now about what is happening in the capital," said Jeber. "I will tell you everything."

"As much as you wish," said Elenn. He was not sure how eager he was to hear it all.

Jeber reached for Elenn's hand and held it for a moment. Then he said, "A form of self-extermination has caught on in the capital. It started in the temple and was introduced to the hooded masters by a groundskeeper from Whiteroof. His name was Chibo. I never met him."

Elenn was silent for a while, comprehending the report. Then he said, "I think Master Nula and I had an encounter with Master Chibo once, many years ago."

Without hesitation, Jeber said, "Master Chibo is dead now."

Elenn took a moment to accept this. But he wanted to know more. "This 'self-extermination' . . . what is it? Do they kill each other in a fit of derangement?"

"No. It takes great concentration and self-control, actually."

"Please tell me," said Elenn.

"Master Chibo was the first to have his head cut off. He died with three others. They took turns—with a double-handed blade."

Elenn stared at Jeber, dumbstruck. He tried to imagine it. It was beyond horrible. "I . . . I don't understand. How does such a thing happen?"

"Master Chibo took the worm position so that the second master could cut his head with the double-handed blade . . . like *this*." Jeber stood and raised his arms up, hands together as if holding a double-handed blade, then swinging them down to demonstrate the action.

For a moment they were both silent. Elenn looked into Jeber's eyes and he finally saw the shame and sorrow there. Jeber was telling him these things cavalierly, but he was suffering with the memories of them. He had, after all, said that he had killed. What he was now describing was something that he had actually participated in.

"They took turns?" asked Elenn, feeling great compassion for poor young Jeber.

"Yes. After killing Master Chibo, the second master—I think his name was Akut—followed, taking the worm position and getting his head cut off."

"If they took turns, who killed the third?" he asked.

"There was a fourth. The one called the 'waiter.' The waiter had to be the initiator of the next group self-extermination."

"I see," said Elenn. He was aware that Jeber's tone was changing as he told the story. It was painful for him to talk about. "You say you never met Master Chibo, and yet you told me when you spoke the first time that you were a 'waiter.' Did this thing happen many times?"

"It happened three times. I was part of the last one."

"Were there always three to die and one waiter?"

"No. There were nine of us in the last one. I drew an empty shell, and I became the waiter. The eight other masters died."

Eight?! Elenn compulsively brought his hands to his face, as if in apology. He didn't want to imagine it.

"I watched them cut each other's heads off, one by one, until it was my turn. I killed the last one."

"Oh, Jeber," said Elenn, his voice distant as he fathomed Jeber's pain. "How hard it must have been to do such a thing . . . So you had to become a *waiter* . . . but you obviously didn't go through with it. What happened?"

"I decided to die alone instead. I came to the desert. I wanted to do what I heard you had done, and what many barren had done before in the past. I came to die."

"We all came to the desert with that idea, more or less," said Elenn.

"I have been thinking about that every hour," said Jeber. "I have been asking myself—what is the difference? What is the difference between dying in the capital and dying in the desert?"

"I suppose . . . the difference is that we have no way of saving the uedin who are dying in the capital."

"Why? If you know that whitesponge stops derangement, why has there never been an attempt to take it back to the capital?"

"Taking whitesponge to the capital is not possible. That has been the consensus of many generations of childless uedin here. We could never carry enough to do more than entice the population there to want more. And even if the uedin of the capital could somehow come through the desert to get sponge, it would all be consumed rapidly. There is enough to last for many generations with our sparse numbers, but there is not enough for the capital."

"Daga told me there is enough that we will never consume it all."

"If you're only talking about the uedin who live here, then that's true. I have explored the cave it grows in. It's incredibly deep. But there are nearly five thousand uedin in the capital, even with diminishing generations. And they have every kind of food there. All we have is whitesponge."

"But the food in the capital is nothing like this," said Jeber, holding up his bowl to see the little drop of soup drying up at the bottom of the bowl.

"The food in the capital will have to be enough for the capital," said Elenn. "If you're suggesting that we should take whitesponge there, I must tell you that such a thing would destroy us."

"But you know what will happen. Barren uedin who want to die are dying in self-extermination chains. None will venture into the desert. They will all die by the two-handed blade."

Though the tone of this remark was almost flippant, Elenn was stunned by the undeniable truth of it. The notion held from ancient times in the capital that barren uedin met their fates in the southeastern desert had resulted in the unseen existence and continuing replenishment of the population of the childless village. Barren uedin found their way there not knowing that a different life lay ahead of them even as they sought death. Now, that pattern had been interrupted. It was as if the frequency of barren syndrome had reached a breaking point. The capital itself was the new home of the barren . . . and they were determined to die *right there.*

"The whitesponge would never last . . . " said Elenn in protest, but as his gaze met Jeber's, he understood that his argument was meaningless. What was the point of preserving whitesponge for future childless uedin who would never come to trade lives? He had to think about that.

"I only wish . . . " said Jeber, " . . . I wish I could save my two hooded friends."

"Masters Leol and Serka," said Elenn. "I know that the three of you had a great bond of friendship."

"I don't know if they're alive or dead," said Jeber. "They were planning to join a death chain as soon as they had the chance. It's one reason I could not initiate. I couldn't bear the thought of it."

"You think Masters Leol and Serka might be dead?" Elenn hoped it wasn't true.

"There were more than twenty hooded masters trying to find me to join a self-extermination. I know from when I joined one myself that once the decision to die has settled in one's mind, all that's left is to get it over with."

"So you think they reorganized and started without you?"

Jeber sighed. "I'm afraid that may be . . . but I don't know."

Elenn was silent, pondering the situation in his mind. The childless had the aid of whitesponge to rid them of their cravings and provide sustenance, but an important aspect of their life was to watch for new ones. Those barren uedin who had a chance of becoming new ones were instead dying in some sort of give-and-take killings where they cut each other's heads off. There would be no more new ones.

"I think we need to go find Pelto and speak with him," said Elenn.

"Why? What is it we need to tell him?"

"He needs to hear what you have just told me."

"But I thought I was just supposed to forget everything that happened in the capital. And you said the whitesponge would never last even if it could be taken back."

"Yes, but the childless need to know if there might be no more new ones coming to the bluff ever again."

Part 3

THE GREAT CONVERSION

Mission to the Capital

Careful consideration was given to the option of waiting till after the Great Rains to make a trip to the capital with whitesponge. The desert would have plantlife then, and the canyon would have a running stream. But Jeber's account of the self-exterminations taking place was enough to convince the childless not to wait. A foursome including Elenn, Jeber, Pelto, and Daga were thus given the task of carrying a quantity of whitesponge to the capital.

In addition to the great loads of dried sponge bundled tightly with bands made from nothing other than strips of sponge itself, the bearers draped themselves with covers of woven grass that latched against their foreheads to stay in place and protect them from the sun. The shapes they made with the shag-edged straw covers extending forward to shade their faces and backward over their packs hid their uedin forms completely. It was initially shocking for them to see one another appearing as unnatural shapes moving beastlike across the desert, but as the sun grew harsh, they all clung anxiously to their covers and the crucial shade they provided.

The childless had come to an agreement to send the contingent to the capital with whitesponge despite great trepidation. Elenn shared their doubts completely, but it was because of the warning coming from him and Jeber that the mission was conceived. There was nothing to gain by dwelling on the fact that no good solution existed. Even though the introduction of whitesponge to the capital could result in all of it being consumed, it was unacceptable to carry on as they had been, quietly conserving the precious whitesponge while the barren uedin exterminated themselves in the capital. Their departure from the bluff felt, in any case, like a journey of last resort.

While water had always been available, however meagerly, from trickles that ran from certain caves in the bluff, the childless uedin living there had never devised any method for storing or carrying it. According to Yulig, attempts had once been made to form pouches from thin slices of whitesponge or tightly woven grass, but nothing had ever successfully held water. Each of the four carried, in addition to packs of dried sponge, a bundle of fleshy stems from a succulent that grew in pockets on the bluff. The moisture in them, they were told, was not enough to quench thirst, but enough to keep them from dying of dehydration.

Once the bluffs were out of sight behind them, the landscape was unyieldingly flat and unvarying. Elenn spent his mental energy worrying about how they would explain themselves when they reached the capital, but gradually his mind emptied until there was nothing but the hypnotic rhythm of the bouncing woven cover flapping with his movements as he walked. They spoke little, keeping a steady pace the whole of the day across the parched desert plain in a northwesterly direction. The brushweed that dotted the ground back in the regions familiar from night walks was nowhere to be found in the desert interior. Nothing but rock and sand surrounded them, and nothing but a fuzzy horizon lay ahead and behind. There were moments when Elenn suddenly feared that they were going in the wrong direction and would end up lost. How strange it would be, he thought, if the desert which they had all individually once entered to end their own lives were to now claim their lives as they attempted a return crossing. But they all knew now what they had not known then; the scorched emptiness of the desert was indeed vast, but it could be crossed in four or five days. They had only to keep a consistent pace and steady direction.

During the hottest hours of the mid-day and afternoon sun, they stopped their march and curled up under their shade covers to rest. It was then that Elenn first took one of the stalks and chewed the moisture from it. It did not provide liquid enough to swallow, but it coated his mouth and throat with a slightly sour-tasting juice that at least relieved the dryness.

They resumed their walking in the late afternoon and continued well into the night. There was a comfort to the cool and dark, not only because it was a relief but also because it was much like what they were used to during their night walks at the base of the bluff. As the night wore on, however, they grew tired and sleepy and eventually they withdrew once more under their covers to sleep.

During the second and third days, the travelers chewed the succulent stems till there was nothing left of them but stringy pulp. The sameness of the flat dry land, the burning sun, and the relentless walking hour after hour put Elenn into such a blank state of mind that stretches of time went by during which he had no thought of where they were going or why. He was nearly startled when Pelto came and spoke to him.

"We'll be going through the canyon before we get to the capital. We could encounter some *ro* masters there, right?" Pelto's voice was weak and hoarse.

Elenn had to take a second to remind himself about their situation before answering. "It's more likely that we will see hooded masters there, looking to feed." He knew that Pelto and Daga were unfamiliar with the population of barren uedin who had a feeding custom quite incomprehensible to them.

"Will we go right past them, straight through the east gate?"

"I think we should send Jeber in ahead of us to find a guard," said Elenn. He looked back to where Jeber and Daga were trailing slightly behind them.

"Can't we just enter with you in the lead? You were a guard yourself," said Pelto.

"No. Jeber is still wearing his master's robe, and he's only been gone a moon cycle. He won't cause as much upset as the rest of us."

"We can't wait long. We must have water."

"It won't be long. We'll be seeing some rock formations before long, and we'll reach the outer canyon."

When they did reach the rock formations and canyon, it was early afternoon of the next day. By then their eyes and throats were burning, their tongues dry and sore in their mouths. The first sign of a rock protrusion at the horizon gave them hope, and they picked up their walking pace despite their exhaustion and dehydration. When they reached the rock protrusion, it was nothing but a slight ledge, but Elenn recognized it from his years with the hood squadron. They considered themselves lucky to arrive at a place he recognized, given that it had only been with a vague sense of the capital's direction that they had traversed the desert.

"We're at the northernmost edge of the canyon. We can follow this all the way down. It turns into the canyon wall."

"How long will it take us to reach the east gate?" asked Jeber.

"It will take the rest of the day. We'll probably get there by nightfall," said Elenn. He noticed the exchange of glances between Daga and Pelto. Having lived for novades at the desert's edge, they had a keener awareness of the danger of sun and dehydration. But Elenn said nothing. They had no choice but to push on and make their way through the canyon.

The now solid ground they walked on was by no means any less ovenlike than the desert, and they held fast to their woven shade covers as they hiked in. Their anticipation at this point made the hours drag. As they walked, the rock ridge grew first to a high ledge at their side, and then, by evening, to a tall canyon wall more reminiscent of the familiar echoing place they all remembered from childhood excursions. Because of the angle of the setting sun, the face of the canyon wall was lit, but the evening air grew cooler as they continued along it.

Finally they reached the gully of the main drystream that ran along the bottom of the canyon. It was a band of dried brown weeds. They soon found the path that ran along it, and they knew that that path made its way up to the slopes and then directly to the east gate of the capital.

"Let's leave the shade covers here," said Pelto, tossing his on the ground.

They were back.

Northgate Guards Receive the Childless

Jeber was a little nervous about being asked to run ahead and find a guard in the capital, but he was glad to be doing so because he was eager—much more eager than the others, it seemed to him—to learn what had happened there since his departure. At the time he had fled the capital, he had heard from Serka and Leol that there had been at least twenty hooded masters trying to contact the waiter. Jeber was desperate to know what had transpired in his absence. He hoped that those twenty or so hooded masters, including Serka and Leol, had indeed held off their self-extermination and had waited for the real *waiter*. Yet he feared terribly that perhaps they had not waited. The discomfort of headache, dizziness, thirstiness and dry, sticky mouth retreated to the back of his mind as he quickened his step.

He was now at the Haka Cliffs, the section of the canyon closest to the capital. The walls of rock were now dark with shadow but still held warmth from baking in the sun through the day. It occurred to Jeber that he was close enough that someone might hear him if he called out. He didn't care if it was a deranged feeder or not.

"*HELLO!*" he yelled, continuing his jogging. "*. . . ANYONE OUT HERE? . . . HELLO!*"

But there was no answer. He thought it odd that there was no one at all—even there in the commonly visited Haka Cliffs. Finally he reached the bank where the path ascended into the slopes. From there he could see the east face of the capital. He ran to get closer so he could see if anyone was at the east gate. Gradually he saw that there was no one there. All the gates had been under squadron monitoring since the completion of the project at Murro, but there was no guard there. Perhaps it was because of the late hour that the gate had neither loiterer nor attendant.

He ran across the slopes straight to the gate and entered. There were a few masters still in the street. The first one Jeber saw was a ro-uedin carrying a basket of charcoal, and he ran to get his attention. The ro put down his basket when he saw Jeber coming.

"Hello young master," said the ro, pulling a handkerchief from his pocket to blow his nose.

Jeber was out of breath. "I'm Jeber, fieldworker . . . western outfields. I've been gone from the capital . . . more than a moon cycle . . . " He struggled to speak, partly because he was out of breath, but also because his mouth and tongue were so dry and sticky that it was nearly impossible to form words. "I need to find a guard," he managed, and then with desperation, "I need water!"

The ro walked up to Jeber and looked into his face, assessing whether he was deranged. "Come," said the ro, "I'll walk with you to Northgate Station. You can stop for water at the Bells domicile—we'll pass it on the way."

"Why no guard . . . at the gate?" asked Jeber.

"The guards are very busy these days. You've been gone a moon-cycle? How did you survive?" asked the ro, astonished that anyone could last so long.

"I can't explain now," gasped Jeber. "I have to find some guards. There are others on the way . . . following me."

Jeber knew his way to Northgate Station, but he was just beginning to realize the severity of his dizziness and disorientation. It was a good thing he had the ro to assist him. They passed a number of uedin in the streets. Jeber noticed no hooded masters. They stopped at Bells where two soon-to-be-named child-uedin were filling some jugs at the well.

"Unnamed," said the ro urgently, "please let this master have water. He was lost in the canyon, and he needs water very badly."

Jeber didn't bother saying anything about this misunderstanding. One of the unnamed filled a cup and handed it to him. Jeber took a gulp of water and choked.

"Slowly, slowly . . . " said the ro. "Take some small sips. You're having trouble to swallow."

Jeber took sips and felt the wonderful relief of water come to him. He drank cup after cup until the ro told him that he must stop and give the water a chance to quench his thirst. Indeed, Jeber had a moment of nausea as he suddenly felt his belly full with water.

"Sit for a moment," said the ro, "the guards will be at Northgate whenever we get there."

"No—I must hurry to them," said Jeber, "the others are on their way."

The ro and the unnamed raised hands to face at one another, and then Jeber and the ro continued on to Northgate. The ro tapped on the door tarp at the station office. Two guards came to the door, one the elder by a generation or two.

"Master guards, I have an outfield worker here who says it's urgent that he speak with you," said the ro. "He's been lost in the canyon. He says there are others." He moved aside so the guards could get a look at Jeber.

"What is your name?" the elder guard asked.

Jeber looked up to speak, but he felt his stomach heave, and in an instant he was vomiting a stomachful of water.

"Oh, I was afraid of that," said the ro-uedin with dismay.

"Is he sick?"

"He was overly thirsty and he drank too much water at once," said the ro.

"Are you all right, Master?" said the guard.

Jeber was now feeling very dizzy.

152

"Come in and sit down." The guards helped Jeber enter and sit on a chair.

"He said he has been in the desert and he needed water."

"Did he give you his name?" asked the elder guard.

"Yes . . . what was it? Jeda? Jeba? Something like that."

The guards looked at each other for an instant. "Are you Master Jeber of the western outfields?" the elder asked him.

"Yes," Jeber said between gasps.

"You were reported missing. Have you been lost this whole time?" asked the elder.

Jeber waited to catch his breath before answering. "I was not lost. I found a group of uedin living in a place . . . on the far side of the southeastern desert. Three of them came back with me. Master Elenn of the hood squadron is among them."

The guards exchanged glances again. "Master Elenn?" said the younger guard, "You have seen Master Elenn of the hood squadron?"

"He was among those living on the other side of the desert. He is coming now!" Jeber could tell by the looks on the guards' faces that they were confounded, but they realized he was not just deranged and talking nonsense. They believed him. Jeber spoke clearly to inform them: "Master Elenn and two other uedin are coming through the canyon now! They need your help immediately!"

"I don't think he's deranged. I think he's telling us the truth," whispered the younger guard to the elder.

"Masters, I'm quite convinced this fieldworker crossed the desert, just as he says he did," said the ro. "He just drank water as if he had had none for days."

The elder guard held a lamp up to get a better look at Jeber. "His robe is filthy."

"I've been gone for more than a moon-cycle," said Jeber.

"All right," said the guard. "Let's go find the others who came with you. You think they're still in the canyon?"

"Yes, and they must have water," said Jeber.

"I'll get gourds and an extra lantern," said the junior guard.

"Why were there no guards at the gate?" asked Jeber.

"Were you here when the eight hooded masters died together at Murro?" asked the elder guard.

"Yes, I was still here when that happened," answered Jeber. He most certainly had been. But now he just wanted to know what had happened since that time. He braced himself for whatever news he might hear.

"Since then, the hooded masters have been staying at Murro—almost all of them. Guards from every district are there with them. We know that one of them is the waiter, and we believe they are planning a mass self-extermination—it may be as many as a hundred hooded masters planning to die. The council wants to consult with the one they refer to as their 'waiter.' They're willing to sanction the self-extermination if the hooded masters will accept some stipulations. The hood squadron was asked to find out and report who this *waiter* is, but they haven't been able to determine who it is."

Jeber felt a flood of relief. Leol and Serka were still alive. Tears came to his dry eyes. "Bless the Lern! Bless the Lern!" he said. The ro and the guards looked at him with confusion. "There will be no more self-extermination!" he said with great relief and emotion.

"What do you mean? How can you know that?" asked the guard.

"I will tell the masters council later. Just come! We must meet the others quickly! They're probably close to the slopes by now!"

Elenn was ascending the ramp from Haka Cliffs up to the slope when he saw two lanterns coming toward them. Soon he could see that it was Jeber with two guards. As the guards approached, Elenn saw their amazed faces lit by the lanterns they carried. He knew that the coverings he, Daga, and Pelto were wearing on their bodies were like nothing ever seen in the capital before. Of course they also had the huge bundles of sponge strapped to their backs—even bigger now since Jeber's portion had been divided and tied on top of each pack. Elenn noticed the Northgate insignia on their robes. He recognized them but did not recall their names. Both of them were now staring directly at him.

"It's true!" exclaimed one of the guards. "Master Elenn of the hood squadron! You're alive!"

"Here," said the other guard, untying a water gourd from his belt, "You must drink slowly, just a small amount at first."

Elenn, Pelto, and Daga passed the gourd amongst themselves and shared its contents. "Thank you, guardmasters. We have been without water for three days," said Pelto.

"What are you carrying?" asked one of the guards.

"It's whitesponge," said Elenn. "It's a kind of healing food. We brought it for the hooded masters."

As soon as Pelto, Daga, and he had drunk water enough to feel ready to move again, they transferred their packs to Jeber and the two guards and followed them across the slopes to the east gate.

Inside the gate they stopped to rest and discuss their plans. "I think we should go directly to Master Embal's hut so he can report our return to the masters council," said Elenn.

"Master Embal lives in Crafting," said the elder guard. "The Crafting guards must have the honor of escorting you. Can you wait till morning?"

"Will you accommodate us at Northgate?"

"Yes, there's plenty of room in the bunkhouse."

"Are Masters Cebik and Umat still there?"

"They wear the Northgate guard's garb, but we don't see much of them. They are at Murro."

"Apparently all the hooded masters have moved to Murro in the last moon-cycle," said Jeber.

"I see," said Elenn. He was now following the Northgate guards through the capital streets. It felt strange to him to walk the capital streets after being away for a year. He knew it must feel even stranger to Daga and Pelto who had been away for generations. He felt extremely conspicuous wearing the leafy suit of the bluff, but it was dark, and the masters they passed on the street were busy and inattentive. He thought about the times he had walked the same streets toward Northgate, when he and Nula spent day after day walking every corner and alley of the capital and all around its exterior watching for hooded masters. So all the hooded masters were now at Murro? Hearing this news caused his mind to wander. If anyone had known that Murro would become the home of the hooded masters, the alliance could have had the caretaker hut built there instead of outside the north wall. And yet Elenn was glad that the caretaker hut had been built where it was, for he had happy memories of his days there with Nula and Jutef. He wondered if Jutef was still living there.

When they got to Northgate Station, Elenn saw how dark and empty it was. The guards of every district were apparently focused on Murro. They were given cold boiled grains with milkgrass tea, a simple meal that Pelto and Daga especially enjoyed after so many years of subsisting on a diet of whitesponge and little else. Later, as he lay on proper bedding in the bunkhouse, Elenn listened to the sound of insects chirping outside the north wall. It sounded like a great mass of uedin doing a droning exercise. It was so nice to put his face into a wheel-shaped pillow to sleep—he had forgotten how good it felt.

The Return Masters Cause Great Surprise

The new arrivals were awoken by the sound of morning greeting being called out from central temple. Elenn opened his eyes, sat up, and immediately looked to see the reactions of the others.

"Is *this* the dream, or was the bluff a dream?" asked Pelto, summing up their sentiment perfectly.

Except for Jeber, who had never lost his fieldworker's robe, they had no clothing but the coverings of the bluff. Elenn looked at his own primitive bluff covering, lying at the foot of his bedding, folded over. A clever patchwork of leaves and grasses, it served well as a protective garb for the desert's edge. But in the morning light, he could see all the desert dust caked into its weave making it a most unappealing thing to put on. Back at the bluff it would have sufficed to hit it against the rockface and shake it out. But they were in the capital now, and Elenn couldn't wait to get a bath and a fresh robe.

The Northgate guards had summoned Master Kobi, their senior guard, and presently he appeared at the bunkhouse, looking very terribly concerned. Shock registered on his face as he got a good look at them and realized they were indeed masters returned from extended absences. "Masters! . . . I . . . I can hardly believe it's true! Master Elenn, you've been gone since last hot season a year ago!" Kobi gave Elenn a look of urgent bewilderment. "Where have you been?"

"There is a community across the southeastern desert that the capital doesn't even know about. They call themselves 'the childless.' They are barren uedin of many generations."

"How did they get there?" asked Kobi, finding this report very hard to believe.

Elenn answered slowly, understanding that this was a lot to take in. "They all suffered derangement, sought death in the desert, and were rescued by forecomers who had done the same thing."

Kobi stared blankly at Elenn, trying to fathom this outrageous possibility. "What? How many are there?"

"Master Jeber reached us one moon-cycle ago. Including him, we number forty-two."

"Forty-two syndrome-afflicted uedin . . . ? Are they both masters and servers?"

"No, it doesn't appear that any former servers are among us," answered Elenn with a hint of lament.

"What sort of place is it? How have you survived there?"

"It's a village built into the face of a bluff on the far side of the desert. It's very harsh, and life there is stark, but we live on something called whitesponge. It grows in a cave there," Elenn paused before adding, " . . . and it has curative capacities."

"*Curative?* . . . what do you mean?"

"Whitesponge is curative on many levels," said Elenn with great seriousness. "That is why we have come. Master Jeber told us about the self-exterminations."

Kobi's eyes widened. "But . . . surely your *whitesponge* couldn't cure barren syndrome—could it?" he asked cautiously.

"No, Master Kobi. There is no cure for barren syndrome. But whitesponge does reverse derangement and eliminates the urge to feed. It aids in keeping peace of mind. The capital has never seen anything like it."

"There's no denying, the capital is in crisis. If your whitesponge could help us . . . "

"I'm sure it can help!" interrupted Jeber. "Once the hooded masters have eaten it, they won't want to do self-exterminations any more!"

"Well, I must contact the council and all the guard stations immediately," said Kobi.

"Master Kobi, we have been wearing those coverings since we left the village many days ago," said Elenn. Could we please have master's robes to put on now?"

Kobi assumed a look of embarrassed frustration. "We only have Northgate guard's garb . . . " he said.

"We know, of course, that guard's garb is not for just anyone to wear, but given our circumstance . . . " suggested Elenn.

"I can't do that," said Kobi uncomfortably. "The Quarterhouse guards are so proud of you, Master Elenn," said Kobi with distress, "I can't put you in Northgate guard's garb at a time like this. Master Wanba would never forgive me. Do you realize how famous you're going to be? All of you?"

"I just so wanted to get a good bath and put on a clean robe. Master Wanba will understand."

"I know him very well, Master Elenn—probably better than you do. He's very proud of Flatpools. But I'm going to send word right away to Quarterhouse that you're here. We can ask for garb to be sent immediately. My guards tell me that you want to go straight away to meet with a member of the masters council. It's Master Embal that you're going to see, right?"

"Yes, Master Embal has been very involved with the hooded masters since the hood-taking ceremony."

"If you don't mind, I'll tell Master Wanba to go there directly. He will want to join your meeting, and he will want you in Flatpools guard's garb, I'm sure."

A little while later, robes were brought to the returned masters from various locations in the capital. They were brought from Flatpools for Elenn and from the western outfields for Jeber. Kobi also contacted the weaving mill where Pelto had apprenticed and requested a robe for him, and Daga got one from Whiteroof where he once had spent a brief career. The freshly bathed masters donned robes of communities they had never imagined they would encounter again. They agreed that after their meeting with Embal, they would each go to their respective former residences to greet masters they once lived with. Daga carried a small box, provided by the Northgate guards, which he had filled with a few handfuls of finely cut whitesponge so they could show Embal what it looked like.

Kobi and the other Northgate guards walked with them through the capital until they reached Crafting. There, the four of them were transferred into the custody of the Crafting Station guards. Elenn recognized Huma, Crafting's senior guard, from the days when Nula was still a guard but restricted to light duty at Crafting's station office. Huma and Kobi both raised hands to face in a show of guards' honor and cooperation, but there were no introductions. Elenn was somewhat relieved that he didn't have to address Huma; the Crafting guards were working in their official capacity, and their focus was only on escorting the four of them to Embal's hut.

Elenn was marveling at the feeling that time had played a trick on him and the capital was the same now as it had always been. Then, he saw Yenca come out of a thread shop, look at him, and stop dead in his tracks. Elenn then stopped also, and the group came to a momentary halt.

"Master Elenn—you're alive! How can it be?" uttered Yenca in disbelief.

Elenn took a good look at Yenca and said, "Just please, don't tell Master Benar. I'm not ready to deal with him right now!"

Yenca's expression showed multiple levels of surprise and delight as he realized that this was indeed Master Elenn, joking with him.

"I'm sorry I can't talk now," said Elenn, bowing slightly into his half-raised hands and moving on. Yenca raised hands back, bidding them to go ahead and pass by, but the look of surprise didn't leave his face.

Arriving at Embal's hut, Elenn found Wanba and Henik waiting for them on the street. Wanba had his normal look of authority; Henik, on the other hand, appeared absolutely beside himself with perplexity. They greeted each other formally. Embal came out.

"I apologize, my hut is small, but let us all go in," said Embal. Embal was probably just as amazed as anyone else about seeing Elenn again, but Elenn thought that he had a very tired look about him. They all followed him into his hut. It was larger than Benar's and larger even than the caretaker hut, but it quickly felt crowded. In attendance for the meeting were the four returned masters accompanied by Wanba, Henik, Huma, and the other Crafting guard who came with him. A small table with chairs was only enough to accommodate four. Embal naturally invited the head guards, Wanba of Flatpools and Huma of Crafting, to take a seat, and he told Elenn to please take the remaining seat. The other guards stood by with Jeber, Pelto, and Daga. They spent a minute coaxing one another forward. Pelto and Jeber managed to convince Daga to take the spot directly behind Elenn. Daga, finally acquiescing, wanted to raise hands and face to them to thank them for the honor, and he reached to place the box of whitesponge on the tabletop. At the same instant, Wanba was adjusting his chair. His chair bumped the table and Daga's hand jerked just enough to let go of the box a second too early, and the box tumbled from the table's edge onto the floor. It landed on its side just under the table, spilling half the bits and shavings of whitesponge in a small heap.

"Oh, don't worry," said Embal, having no idea what had spilled, imagining it to merely be some sort of gift from wherever they had come from. Daga, on the other hand, gasped in horror at having dropped the precious whitesponge and spilled it on the floor. Jeber immediately got down on his knees and began to scoop it back into the box with the side of his hand. Wanba laughed dip-lomatically to relieve the embarrassment of the moment.

"Thank you, Jeber!" said Daga, causing Embal and the guards present to notice his disuse of the honorific "Master" when ad-dressing Jeber. They waited for Jeber to get all the bits off the floor and back into the box and then place it carefully in the center of the table. Daga raised hands to face with extra humility for having been responsible for the spill, and he stood behind Elenn.

A lengthy conversation commenced in which Elenn first ex-plained the situation fundamentally as he had done with Kobi the night before. This was followed by questioning which led him to a more detailed account of what he had seen and experienced since leaving the capital a year before. He told Embal about how he had joined the village after being rescued, what he had learned about the Childless uedin living there, how the sponge diet had transformed him, and finally how he was prompted to return to the capital by what Jeber had told him.

"Master Jeber was found near death by Master Daga about one moon-cycle ago," explained Elenn. "After he recovered, he told us what's been happening in the capital with the hooded masters doing self-extermination. And, . . . well, . . . Master Jeber has something important to tell you." Elenn turned in his chair and looked back at Jeber who was standing behind Daga, eyes low-ered as he took a breath to prepare himself to speak. He looked calmer than Elenn expected him to be.

"I do have something important, but first I want to say that what Master Elenn told you about whitesponge is true. I didn't know how much it would help me think with a calmer mind. That is the only reason I am able to be here now. It's the only rea-son I am able to tell you what I have to tell you."

Embal nodded and gazed down at the box. He seemed to com-prehend that the whitesponge was important to these returned masters, but he had an exhausted look nonetheless. Elenn thought he looked altogether different from the self-assured speaker for the masters council who had directed the hood-taking ceremony. "We understand that you all put a high value on your whitesponge," said Embal, "but what is the other thing that you want to tell us?"

"Well it pertains specifically to me," said Jeber. "You see, before I left the capital I was distressed because . . . " Jeber paused, thinking about how to say it as gently as possible.

"Because your fellow hooded outfield workers tried to talk you into joining them in a self-extermination?" asked Huma. Crafting guards had jurisdiction over the western outfields. Huma was obviously familiar with the case of Jeber's disappearance.

"Is that what everyone thought?" asked Jeber.

"That was the consensus about your disappearance. And many, including your friends—what are their names?" Huma paused and recalled, "Masters Serka and Leol. They, too, were upset about it. They seem to have blamed themselves for your disappearance."

Jeber was clearly vexed by this account. "That's why I want to tell you," he said, "I didn't just leave because I was afraid of self-extermination—though it's true I was afraid of it. But the real reason I was in distress was that . . . I was the waiter. . . . I mean, . . . I *am* the waiter."

No one spoke for a long moment.

"*You* are the waiter?" Wanba was stunned.

Huma was nodding. "I thought it might be so. I shared that idea with Master Nemis of the hood squad, but he said anyone capable of cutting off another uedin's head wouldn't run away when it was time for him to get his own head cut off."

Elenn noticed that Jeber's composure had gone from calm to troubled. He was confident that the benefit of the sponge would help Jeber stay on an even keel.

"I can't speak anymore for whatever I was feeling when I left the capital," said Jeber. "I can only speak as one who has recovered in many ways, just over the course of a moon-cycle."

163

"And that, of course, is because of that whitesponge again," said Embal, smiling condescendingly.

Elenn was startled when Daga spoke loudly behind him. "Yes, Master Embal, Jeber's recovery, and all our recoveries, are owed to the benefits of whitesponge." His tone caused Embal to stop smiling immediately.

Huma became a little defensive on Embal's behalf. "Master Embal is speaker for the masters council," he said to Daga. "Please show him proper regard."

Embal placated him. "Master Huma, thank you, but it's quite all right. Master Daga is reminding us that we don't know anything about the white sponge. Master Jeber, accept my apologies. You have gained much health in a month's time by eating your white sponge. Please go on."

Jeber continued with earnest, "Well, I became convinced, with Master Elenn, that whitesponge should be shared with the capital—with hopes that it would bring calm to all the uedin with syndrome who are suffering here."

Embal redirected his gaze to the box of whitesponge on the table. "The benefit that you speak of, whatever it is, . . . do you actually feel it coming on? Is it like sourembers?"

"No, . . . I think it's more like milk-grass tea, except that it's much more calming."

"So it is more or less a sedative?" asked Huma.

Jeber looked at Daga, the one who had rescued him and nursed him back to health with whitesponge. "Daga, do you think whitesponge is more or less a sedative?"

"Sometimes it is," said Daga, "but in a very beneficial way. It does not dull our minds."

"So you, Master Jeber, are the waiter?" said Embal.

"But I trust you have no intention of leading a self-extermination," said Wanba.

"No. I intend to introduce them to whitesponge," responded Jeber. "I hope you will help us do so."

"Well I'm not sure if all the hooded masters will immediately line up to receive a sedative," said Embal. "But I want to see for myself how strong it is. May I?"

"It's not at all like sourember smoke," commented Daga, "Don't expect anything like that."

"Do I just eat it like this?" Embal brought a few of the white shreds half way to his mouth.

"You can," answered Daga. "We have the custom of letting it soften in warm water, but you can chew it up, just like that."

Embal put the morsels in his mouth, chewed silently, and stared away for a moment, trying to categorize the mere hint of flavor it had. They all watched him chew and swallow a few more bits. He managed a smile with tired eyes and brought a half hands to face in a good-natured, chummy gesture, as if to say, "Doesn't taste *too* bad."

The masters, seated and standing, shared a momentary chuckle at Embal's little demonstration of eating. Then Pelto suddenly yelled out, "Oh! A mouse! Under the table!"

"Where?" Wanba moved his legs aside and peered down.

"There is it!" said Henik.

"I hate to say it, but I think it had a crumb of whitesponge—from when we spilled the box!" said Pelto.

The mouse darted across the floor, first to the shadow beside the door, then out under the door tarp and away.

"That tells us one thing," said Huma. "We'd better keep your whitesponge in sealed jars. There are a lot of mice around the capital during the hot season—they find their way to water because we have wells."

"Master Jeber, you were saying you hope that I can help you introduce whitesponge to the hooded masters. How do you see this happening?"

Jeber deferred to Elenn. "Master Elenn?" he said, hoping Elenn would have a ready answer.

"We would invite the masters council to oversee it," said Elenn.

"The hooded masters are not in any frame of mind to heed the direction of the masters council," said Embal. Clearly this was part of the trouble in the capital that weighed on him. "They're all residing at Murro now, outside the walls. It's like they're in their own capital there."

"The guards are fully taxed just trying to maintain order at Murro," said Huma. "You will need to reach out to the hooded masters directly—not through the masters council."

"Master Jeber, you must tell them that you are the waiter," said Wanba. "Then they will listen to whatever you say."

Reunion of the Hooded Outfield Workers

When the masters concluded their meeting and exited Embal's hut, they found Serka and Leol waiting outside. They still wore their hoods with the outfield worker's robes. Jeber was struck by the looks on their bold-featured faces. The uedin of the childless village on the bluff did not have the kind of bold features that the barren masters of the capital all seemed to have. Seeing his fellow workermasters reminded Jeber that he too had the face of a capital barren. Serka and Leol's faces conveyed morbid expressions. They did not convey joy at seeing him.

"It's true. You're here," said Serka grimly. Jeber quickly took stock of his friends' gloomy mood. When he had learned that there had been no self-extermination in his absence, he had been filled with relief and gladness. But now he immediately understood that Serka and Leol were still preparing to join a death chain. He raised hands to face, a formality owed to the fact that he had not seen them for a moon-cycle.

"I know . . . You thought I was dead."

Suddenly Serka noticed Elenn standing there, and the grave expression on his face changed to one of bewilderment. "Master Elenn of the Hood Squadron—You're not dead either!" He looked back and forth between Elenn and Jeber. "How do you explain this? Where did you both come from?"

Jeber waited a moment to see if Elenn would say anything, but he only nodded to Serka and gave his attention to Henik and Wanba, who were waiting to walk with him back to Flatpools.

"I'm sorry masters," said Elenn, "Master Jeber will have to explain." He raised hands to face and left with the other guards.

"I'll tell you everything," Jeber said, and thought about how to begin. " . . . but we need to go back to the outfields."

"Yes, I suppose you should report to Master Tamo," said Leol.

"Yes, and Master Ghera," said Jeber, "I'm sure I've caused him great worry."

"You caused us all great worry," said Serka. "Master Leol thought it was our fault that you ran away."

"It was not your fault that I left. But it was your fault that I came back," said Jeber.

"What do you mean by that?"

"Come. Let's walk. I'll tell you everything."

The three of them walked the short distance from Embal's hut toward the western gate. As they walked, Jeber told them about the childless village.

"Master Elenn and I have both been at a village that no one in the capital has ever seen before. It's on the far side of the south-eastern desert."

"An outvillage?"

"Sort of. It's inhabited by barren uedin who have been rescuing each other from the desert for many, many generations." He gave them a moment to let it sink in.

"So you were rescued?" said Leol.

"Yes. And Master Elenn was rescued the same way, a year ago."

"But both you and Master Elenn went to the southeastern desert to die, didn't you? After you were rescued, didn't you want to die anymore?"

"At first, I still wanted to die. But after being there a short time, everything changed."

"Why?"

"There's something called 'whitesponge' that the uedin eat there. It heals body and mind. It stops derangement."

They were nearing the gate. No one said anything. Jeber could tell that Serka and Leol were skeptical about whitesponge because they didn't ask any questions about it.

"I don't think you ever really wanted to die," said Serka finally. "And that's all right. Just because Master Leol and I made up our minds to find the waiter and join him in death, you didn't have to feel pressured. It's your own choice to live as a hooded master."

"I want you to eat some of the whitesponge. Then you'll understand."

"The whitesponge can't stop us from being barren, can it? It can't put embryos in our skullwombs, can it?" asked Serka.

Jeber could not tell if Serka was argumentatively countering him or asking because he truly thought that it might stop them from being barren. "No," he answered gently, "The whitesponge can't do that, but it does calm the mind and stop derangement."

They were now past the gate and were making their way up the road that follows outside the western wall.

"I don't need to have my mind calmed," said Serka. "I know what I am going to do."

"What about you, Master Leol? Are you also determined to die with the waiter?" Jeber knew it was unkind to pose such a terrible question to Leol, but he wanted to confront him.

Leol looked tormented. He did not like having to defend his decision. "Master Jeber, please . . . It's fine if you're contented to live on for many generations—it's good. I don't agree with what they've been saying at Murro about all hooded masters dying together."

"What? That's what they're saying at Murro?"

"Yes," said Serka. "A lot of hooded masters believe that the waiter is delaying because he wants the whole community of hooded masters to join him. There are many who are trying to convince everyone that we must all self-exterminate in one final act."

Jeber was shocked by this idea. "All hooded masters? All in one death chain?"

"I don't agree with it," said Leol defiantly. "Ever since you left the capital, I've felt that no hooded master should ever feel pressured to join."

"What about the soon-to-be-named who have the syndrome? They too should die? They don't even have their names yet!"

"*We're* not saying anyone should die," Serka snapped back. "We're just telling you what many are saying at Murro."

They reached the trail that cut through the tree stand and looked across the field to the western outfields workhouse and buildings.

"I never thought I'd see this sight again," said Jeber. He looked across at Leol, and Leol was smiling back at him, but when he looked at Serka, Serka only walked on with a downward gaze.

Before long they reached the edge of grounds around the buildings. Here, Jeber first slowed his pace and then halted and said, "Master Serka and Master Leol, before we go into the workhouse, I want to show you something . . . it's in the tool shed. It's very important."

"What is it?" demanded Serka.

"I have to show you," said Jeber. But we need to go through the field up there and come around the back. I don't want anyone but the two of you to see it."

"All right. Show us whatever it is you want to show us," said Serka. They followed Jeber around and over to the back of the workhouse grounds and then directly to the tool shed. Jeber silently opened the door and stepped in. Serka followed behind him, and, because the shed was so small, Leol remained at the door looking in.

The interior of the woodshed was lit up by the rays of sunlight that shone around them from the doorway. Jeber moved to a corner in the back where a collection of old and disused shovels and broken rakes were leaned against the corner in a bunch. He moved a couple implements aside, then reached in and downward with his hand. When he pulled out the two-handed blade, at first, Serka and Leol didn't know what they were looking at. Then he held it downward and into the light. Dried blood covered much of the blade all the way to the handle.

Jeber watched Leol and Serka shift their gaze from the blade to look at him with total shock. They didn't even speak.

"You see . . . It was me all along," said Jeber somberly. "I am the waiter."

High Rule in the Central Temple

A young server had joined the two ro-servers who had night duty in the temple kitchen. They were very glad to have the help, but they had to watch everything he did. He sometimes substituted the most impossible things when he didn't see the ingredient needed. He did it because he chose to risk ruining something rather than speak out loud and break the rule of silence. They told him many times it was perfectly fine to speak briefly if he had a question about anything, but he never spoke a word unless absolutely forced to do so. He was very obsessed with obedience, and he took to high rule much too seriously.

During the eighth year of the novade, a change in the mood had come to the temple that was unlike anything either of the ro-servers had ever experienced before. Neither of them found it to their liking. It was too strict. High rule being in place, there were no more games, no talking except for emergencies, and the atmosphere of the temple, which had already been dreary enough, was starting to feel uncomfortably oppressive.

The two ro-servers had worked together on night duty for many generations, and they did not try to hide their instincts from one another. They defied the silence rule with giddy rebelliousness. They would even ridicule the notion that talking should occur only during emergencies. "This is an emergency," one would say to the other, "Should I add more vinegar to the greens?" The other would respond, "Yes, and this is an emergency too: Just a little bit!" Then they would laugh until they saw their junior server looking at them with utter disapproval.

This night was different. They were preparing a soup of yam gruel thinned with milkgrass tea, and it was going to be taken up to the Most High himself. It was very important that they get it right. The head steward had left instructions that everything prepared for the Most High must now be thin enough to drink through a straw. In order to convey how important this was, he mentioned that the Most High was in danger of starvation. With this serious task in mind, even these ro-servers were inclined to refrain from unnecessary chatter, but one of them felt it important enough to ask, "Shall we test the yam gruel to make sure it's thin enough to sip through a straw?" He looked at his fellow ro server with seriousness. Indeed, this might be important enough to call an emergency without being facetious.

"Young server, please see if you can find us a straw in that bin of small utensils—over there by the grain sacks," said the other ro directly. The young server went to look for a straw and presently returned.

"There were two. I brought them both. One is regular size, and the other is a little thinner than regular," said the young kitchen helper. They were somewhat surprised to hear him speak openly now.

It would have been rude to sip directly from the Most High Server's yam gruel, so they poured a small amount of it into a little cup first and then stuck the smaller straw into it and motioned for the young server to do the test. He took the cup of gruel, put his lips around the straw, and tried to sip.

"The gruel is too thick," declared the young server. "And even after we thin it down, anything we send to the Most High Server should go with a larger straw. It will be easier for him to use."

They added a good pour of milkgrass tea and stirred the yam gruel again.

"Try now," said one of the ros, replenishing the small cup.

The young server sipped it through the straw and wrinkled his brow. "A little thinner," he insisted. More tea was stirred in and the gruel tested again. "That will do," said the young server.

"It's probably getting cold. Should we heat it?" one ro said to the other, not expecting yet more opinions from the young one.

"Don't heat it," said the young server impertinently. "Better to send it up lukewarm."

The two ro looked at each other and smiled. "Anything else you would like to say, young server?" asked one of the ro. "Perhaps you'd like to take charge when we make seed buns after this?"

The young server blushed and raised hands to face in humility.

The other ro went to the corner and gave a little tug to a rope that ran through the walls to the steward's office and rang a bell there so that someone could be sent to come and take the soup. A few minutes later, the steward appeared, and they gave him the gruel on a tray. It was in a small deep bowl with a straw on the side. He nodded and took the tray away. The kitchen servers went back to their work station to start preparing for the next day's meals.

The steward carried the tray through a number of corridors and corners, finally reaching the inner chamber. He lightly tapped the door tarp, and another server who stood watch at the door lifted it aside for him to enter with the tray. Two attendants were kneeling over the Most High, moving his limbs and working his joints. The steward silently placed the tray on a low table, raised hands to face, and backed out of the room without turning his back as the server by the door raised the tarp once again for him to exit. The attendants were massaging and manipulating the hands of the Most High, opening and closing them, working each finger to stretch it out.

Without speaking, one of the attendants rose, got the bowl of yam gruel, and carried it with the straw to the Most High Server while the other propped cushions under his back so that he could partially sit up. The first one held the bowl close to the Most High's face and put the straw in his mouth. He bent slightly forward to whisper in his ear, telling him to drink.

Both attendants looked very worried and dismayed. They had seen the Most High deteriorate from a young prodigy to this shriveled uedin. The silence rule did not permit them to speak about it, and in this case they had no desire to do so. The sadness of the situation was so clear that it didn't need mentioning. They both knew they were witnessing a tragic event. The Soft One had somehow overwhelmed the young Most High. Even though he was eating and breathing, there was little left of his former self. Various attendants rotated their duty, but all of them felt the same way. They were terribly discouraged. Yet they held on to their sense of duty to attend to the comfort of the Most High, even in his wasted state.

They were at the end of their shift. Hearing the sound of the door tarp being lifted aside, they expected to see the next pair of attendants arrive to relieve them of their duty. Instead, it was the primary advisor.

"How is the Most High doing today?" Nekur asked.

The attendants looked at each other with discomfort.

"High rule won't be over till Namesgiving," whispered one of them very quietly. "It requires silence."

"Oh, yes . . . " said Nekur. He fished in his sleeve for a note and gave it to them. They immediately saw that it had the assembly stamp on it. It was a permission to make an exception to the silence rule. "It's all right to speak. How has the Most High been doing?"

The two attendants looked knowingly at each other. "He's worsened, High Server. He has not spoken since the last time you were here. Sometimes he opens his eyes and tries to give us a smile, but it's been a few days since he's done even that."

"Do you think he's in pain?"

"It doesn't look like it."

Nekur looked down at the Most High. It was a pathetic sight. He looked disturbingly gaunt and weakened. He was wrapped about the abdomen with cloth but wore no other clothing other than the blankets of his bedding. "Well, I would say that he is as comfortable as he can be, thanks to the dedicated efforts of all you attendant servers," said Nekur.

The attendants raised hands to face to thank him for the acknowledgment.

"I see he is eating?" said Nekur.

"Yes, High Server, a little bit. He finished some of his yam gruel just now. The kitchen servers have been very eager to cooperate."

"And are you having any luck getting him to work his muscles?"

"No. At this point, we only try to stretch him out to keep him from curling up too much, and we move his joints to keep him from stiffening."

"The Most High loves when we do that," commented the other attendant, but then immediately cast his eyes downward, as if there were something inappropriate about the comment. Nekur, on the contrary, was very interested in this comment.

"You think the Most High feels relief when you work with him?" This would help him with his report to the assembly. He could emphasize that the Most High was enjoying his therapy. They would be pleased to hear it.

"Oh yes, the Most High appreciates everything we do. He also enjoys his food."

"Well, I will certainly share that with the high servers," said Nekur. It would be better to report any scrap of positive news than to simply state that the Most High was unconscious and dying.

During the year that had passed since his becoming primary advisor, Nekur had allowed the assembly to venerate the Most High, but he stopped short of telling them that the server who had risen to the position was now quite possessed by the Soft One, and that the Soft One had spoken directly through him. He feared that such knowledge could cause too much disruption. There was very little pertinent communication at any rate, and it seemed more sensible to just report on the condition of the Most High.

"We've even given him a bit of yeastdrink from time to time," said one of the partner attendants.

"Yeastdrink!" Nekur smiled and opened his eyes wide in disbelief. He laughed, "Well, that detail will entertain the assembly!"

"We think it's quite all right, on occasion," said the attendant.

Nekur looked again at the Most High on his bedding. "Servers, I would like to try to engage with the Most High, if I may," he said.

"That would be fine," said an attendant, "He may not speak to you, but he can probably hear you."

"We used to get him to respond by squeezing our fingers, but he hasn't done that for a while. You could try."

Nekur put his hand on top of the Most High's hand. He was surprised to find it very warm. He had imagined that it would be cold because surely the Most High in this state had poor circulation. He moved a finger to the palm of the Most High's hand so that he could squeeze it.

"He responds best if you whisper directly in his ear," said an attendant.

Nekur bent and whispered into his ear. "Can you hear me?" he asked. "Please let me know if you can hear me by grasping my finger."

"Ask him if he liked the soup," suggested one of the attendants. He will often respond if he is being asked if something is acceptable to him."

"Did you like the soup, High Server?" asked Nekur.

But the weakened uedin only lay in his bedding and neither squeezed Nekur's finger nor showed any sign of hearing him.

"I'm glad he has the strength to swallow," said Nekur.

"Of course he does. He drinks through a straw, and whenever we move him, he holds his breath while we're repositioning him," said one them defensively.

"He's quite alive yet," asserted the other.

"Indeed he is," said Nekur. "Let me try again." He took the Most High's hand and bent the fingers around the finger of his other hand. "Most High," he whispered tenderly, "Are you with us?"

The Most High did not grasp his finger, but he moved his head and arched his back somewhat. His eyes remained closed, but his lips moved.

"I think he's trying to speak," said the attendant.

Nekur put his ear close to the Most High's mouth to hear. "What did you say? Please say it again," said Nekur. He felt the breath of the Most High in his ear as he spoke the few words.

"The masters have what we need."

A Summons from the Temple

The returned masters knew that they only had the limited white-sponge of whatever bundles they had carried across the desert. It was a very precious amount, and it was intended as a sample for the capital, not as a supply for themselves. Yet they also understood that they could not deprive themselves of whitesponge either. If they were, for example, to return completely to the food of the capital and put the whitesponge aside, how long would it be before Pelto and Daga, neither of whom had ever received the umbilical catheter, would start to suffer bouts of derangement? So they took small rations of whitesponge from the stock.

Elenn thought frequently about how it steadied him. It gave him a calm mind when crowds formed around them wherever they went and when they were forced to repeat their accounts of the unknown village across the desert. It had given him courage to go out to the caretaker hut to visit Jutef. That had been at Nemis's suggestion. The year at the bluff had been a time to forget the things that Elenn loathed to remember, but now that he was back at the capital, the events of the past had to be reckoned with. The reunion with Jutef was marked by pain and shame, but Elenn managed to get through it without being overwhelmed by emotion. He was also able to walk down to the drystream bottom where stones still marked the location of Nula's buried body. Elenn did a mindstilling there.

During their third day in the capital, Elenn was talking to some of the second-generation Flatpools guards—young masters with whom he was not well acquainted. They were talking about the conditions at Murro. Jeber and his comrades from the western outfields wanted to go to Murro to introduce sponge to the hooded masters, and Elenn was very interested in hearing about how it had evolved into a kind of outvillage unto itself.

Master Embal suddenly appeared at the station house accompanied—surprisingly—by a *server*. The young guards immediately ended their conversation and stood to honor the sudden arrival of such an exceptional visitor to Flatpools Station.

"Master Elenn, I'm glad I could find you here," said Embal. His manner was friendly. "Are you in contact with the other returned masters?"

"Yes. Master Jeber is currently at the western outfields, Master Daga is at the weaving house at Crafting where he apprenticed, and Master Pelto is at Whiteroof. I will see them all tomorrow. We were planning to contact you again about the possibility of offering whitesponge to the hooded masters at Murro."

"We can most certainly discuss that," said Embal, "but right now I'd like to introduce you to the emissary from the High Server's Assembly."

The server raised hands to face. "I am Rafo," he said.

"I'm sure you know the senior guard of Central Station . . . ?" Embal asked Elenn.

"Yes, I know Master Amit," said Elenn.

"The senior guard and I have known each other since taking name. We are both eighth generation. I met with him this morning to tell him about the whitesponge. My reaction to eating your whitesponge was not what I expected."

"No?"

"You told us that it would have a sedative effect. I feel that in my case, it has given me vigor."

"Yes, I believe it may do that also sometimes," said Elenn.

"Well, the reason I've brought the emissary here is that I happened to tell the senior guard that I'd eaten some of the whitesponge brought back from the desert by the returning masters, and that it was like a remedy for me. The senior guard called immediately for the emissary. They've been in recent correspondence over a request from the servers for assistance from the medic masters. One of their high servers is ailing."

Embal looked at the server, inviting him to speak. Rafo said, "I asked Master Embal to bring me to you. Our Most High is in a very weakened state. The assembly of high servers is seeking help from the outside."

Embal interrupted. "Surely something so nourishing and potent as the whitesponge would have a good effect on the high server, don't you think?"

"The whitesponge is stored at Northgate," said Elenn. "All I have right now is my own small ration, which I would be glad to offer you. If you need more, we will have to go to Northgate."

Rafo looked at him with humility, which embarrassed Elenn. "Master guard, we are worried about the survival of our Most High. If you are willing to share your portion with us, the server community would be most grateful to you."

Elenn did not hesitate to withdraw the small cloth-wrapped piece of whitesponge from his pocket and offer it to Rafo, his other hand raised to face in courtesy.

The next morning, the return masters were reunited at Northgate where they sat together for a morning meal. Elenn was particularly eager to hear from Jeber what had happened at the western outfields. They were barely able to greet one another when their conversation was cut short by the arrival of a message.

"Who is it for?" asked Daga.

"It just says 'Hood Squadron Guard.'"

"That's you, Elenn," said Pelto.

"Look at the calligraphy—beautiful," said Daga.

Elenn opened it up. "It's from the temple," he said.

"What does it say?" asked Daga.

"Here, I'll read it to you. *To the Hood Squadron Guard accommodated at Northgate: The assembly wishes to convey its gratitude to you. The white sponge was prepared as you instructed and given to our Most High. Our Most High consumed a small amount and gained consciousness within an hour. His first instruction was to beckon the master who donated the special food. We hope you can come immediately. An emissary is waiting for you at the temple's main door. Lerna Beyana ulrana uedina.* That's all it says. It isn't signed."

"The Most High Server wants to see you!" said Pelto. "I've never heard of such a thing!"

"You must go immediately. Take a full length of sponge," said Daga.

Elenn was stunned. No master was *ever* invited into the temple. Servers came out, but masters never went in. He had adjusted to the attention he was receiving for having returned after a long absence from the capital, but he never imagined having an audience with the Most High Server.

"Is there some silk or something I can wrap the whitesponge in?" Elenn asked.

"There's no time for that!" said Pelto. "It says an emissary is already waiting for you!"

Daga got a sizeable piece of whitesponge from one of the packs. "This piece is still soft in the middle . . . It still has some moisture in it."

One of the young Northgate guards found a piece of plain white cloth to wrap it up. "It's not silk, but it's all we have here," he said.

Elenn wrapped the whitesponge tightly and tied the corners of the cloth together. He bid his companions good bye and left.

Elenn's First Audience
with the Most High Server

Following Rafo through the temple compound, Elenn felt very strange. He knew that the images of a delicate world dictated by the exercises and perpetual attention to Lern Beyana were fancies of innocent youth, but he still expected a pleasantly peaceful environment. He was unprepared for the awful gloom of the temple interior. A few servers that they passed looked startled by the sight of a master in guard's garb inside the temple, but communication was suppressed, and even he, as an outsider, keenly felt the imperative to silence. He followed Rafo through a series of corridors and finally to a small room where another server was quietly writing notes in a large bound tablet. Elenn thought for a moment that this was the Most High, but Rafo leaned forward and said in a whisper, "This is primary advisor to the Most High. He will accompany you to the inner chamber."

"Welcome, Master," said the primary advisor. "Is that a piece of the white sponge?"

"Yes," said Elenn.

"We're very grateful. Do you mind if we send it directly to the kitchen?"

"By all means," said Elenn.

"I'll take it there myself," said Rafo, and he received the cloth-wrapped block of sponge from Elenn, nodded farewell, and took it away.

"Our Most High Server has had a remarkable recovery since eating some of the white sponge that you gave us. He has even spoken a few words."

"I'm very glad to hear that it has been helpful."

"He asked that you be brought here. You realize it is very unusual for a master to enter the temple."

"Yes, I am very honored."

"It would not happen if it were not directly requested by our Most High."

Elenn raised hands to face.

"Now come. Let's see if he is awake." The primary advisor led Elenn through a few more corridors to a large door. Two servers were on either side in seated mind-stilling. They wore blank, lifeless expressions. The primary advisor tapped very lightly on the door tarp, and a server lifted the tarp from the inside. They entered. The room was completely void of any decoration, calligraphy, or even furniture. There was a platform taking up half the room which rose just a short bit from the floor. On that platform a server who looked like he could be fifth generation like Elenn was kneeling over a bundle of blankets.

The server looked up and acknowledged them but did not speak.

"Is the Most High awake?" asked the primary advisor.

"He was a moment ago," whispered the server. As Elenn watched the kneeling server look back down into the bundle, he realized that there was a uedin lying amid the shuffle of blankets. He followed the primary advisor to the edge of the platform. The server who had been kneeling there silently rose and left them alone. Elenn looked down.

What he saw there shocked and horrified him. What looked like a small ro-uedin was lying on his side with his eyes closed in a gaunt and starved state. He looked too old and wasted to still be alive. Such a sight was tinged with tragedy. By any standard, this was a uedin too frail for pilgrimage. And though the uedin's face had a look of age, a closer look made Elenn think that it was not the kind of age that comes from weather and time. It was the face of one who has become tired and old through worry. It was exactly the opposite of what Elenn would expect from one who lived a life of exercises. Yet it was a face strangely familiar.

When the uedin turned his head and opened his eyes, his gaze was already exactly focused on Elenn, and Elenn practically jumped backwards. He *knew* the person looking at him! How could it be? It was Tilke! He didn't understand how it was possible, but he was sure it was Tilke looking up at him. And while Elenn had grown to conspicuous size due to barren syndrome, Tilke looked to be just as small as he had been when he entered the temple less than a year after taking name.

To Elenn, Tilke's face conveyed a life of misery. How had it come to this? It was so unfair! Tilke had tried to follow Elenn into server life, and this is how he had ended up! Elenn felt responsible for what he was seeing. His eyes clouded with tears. He felt awkward because the primary advisor was there with them, but he couldn't suppress his emotion. He leaned forward and looked into Tilke's eyes. "I'm so sorry!" he said. Tilke just looked at him. In a moment, Elenn realized that his apologizing so emotionally might convey that he thought Tilke looked ruined. It might be a great insult. Indeed Tilke did look ruined, but hearing that said about oneself is bound to feel like an insult. Elenn swallowed hard and resolved to be strong. "Tilke? Do you remember me?"

The primary advisor drew in his breath and touched Elenn's arm to demand his attention. He made a disapproving face. "Where did you hear that name?" he whispered.

Elenn looked at him. "I know this uedin from a time when he and I were friends after taking name—before he came to the temple."

The primary advisor looked intrigued, but he warned, "Guard-master, the Most High is in great communion with Lern Beyana, and she always prefers not to hear any names at all."

Elenn nodded, suddenly feeling reverence. He looked at Tilke again. He didn't know what to make of the face looking back at him. He and Tilke had lived their lives in two completely different worlds over the course of two novades. One thing was sure— Tilke, now the Most High Server, *did* remember Elenn. The look of recognition was clear.

"I can see that you do remember me," said Elenn. "And I can only imagine what you must be thinking. I never imagined you . . . in this condition . . . " He looked into Tilke's eyes once again, and he couldn't bear to conceal his feelings. " . . . I *am* sorry. I *made* you come here, didn't I?"

"*It's all right,*" said the ancient Tilke face, "*You can be sorry.*"

Elenn felt the kindness behind the words, curious as they were. "Thank you," he said.

"*Yes, you can be sorry if you like, and you can be thankful if you like. It is fine with me.*"

These, thought Elenn, were the words of someone who had achieved a great depth of unnameliness. "You have become a great, unnamely server," said Elenn, smiling sadly. He nodded to show appreciation for Tilke's achievement.

"*Tilke is sleeping, my dear one,*" said the face. "*He has been sleeping for a very long time. His sleep is a great gift to me.*"

"What?" said Elenn, confused. "Tilke, are you sleeping or are you awake?"

The primary advisor placed a gentle hand on Elenn's shoulder. "Not even the other high servers here know . . . " he said.

"Know what?" He looked questioningly at the primary advisor, but the latter looked as though he was going to have a hard time explaining. Elenn didn't want to insult Tilke any more, but he nervously leaned over to whisper discreetly in the primary advisor's ear, "Is there something wrong with him?"

"No, nothing is wrong," said the primary advisor.

"*Your friend sleeps in a peaceful state,*" said the face.

"You mean Tilke sleeps? If I am not talking to Tilke, who am I talking to?" He looked up at the primary advisor again and found him to be wearing a very grave expression.

"Some time ago I realized it," said the primary advisor. "Lern Beyana is speaking through the Most High. No one even knows about it here, except me and the assistants to the Most High."

Elenn looked back at Tilke's face. An immensely strange feeling came over him and made his skin tingle. Could that be so? Could Lern Beyana be speaking through Tilke? He shook his head in wonderment. "But . . . I've always heard that Lern Beyana does not speak," he said, finding it too incredible.

"I don't know if the Soft One has ever spoken before," said the primary advisor, "but I'm convinced that she is speaking now."

Elenn couldn't help asking himself if perhaps Tilke had gone mad, believed that he was Lern Beyana, and now had the primary advisor convinced of it.

"*I must tell you what to do,*" said the face.

"What is it?" asked Elenn.

"*The substance that you brought. It must be given to all uedin.*"

"The whitesponge? But it will not last forever. We must try to conserve it for future generations, especially if barren syndrome continues."

"*You may give it first to those who have no life in their wombs. But then you must give it to all. There will be enough to last as long as it is needed.*"

"But how can you know that?" asked Elenn.

"*It is the only acceptable possibility,*" said the face.

"The Most High has called you here to tell you this," said the primary advisor. "There is no need to doubt the wisdom of it."

"*All uedin must know that this is my wish,*" said the face, and it closed its eyes.

Elenn was stunned and perplexed as he allowed the primary advisor to lead him out of the room and back through the temple.

Emissary Rafo was waiting to bid him good bye at the temple main door.

Nekur left the guardmaster at the door and turned around to make his way to his own cell. How remarkable a visit it had been! The Soft One had transmitted a message to the whole capital! "All uedin must know that it is my wish," she had said. That included all servers. Nekur decided that he would start with the assembly of high servers. He would have to explain to them that this request was not just coming from the Most High. It was coming from the Soft One.

Serka in the Peach Orchard

Serka stood against a low limb with a pruning tool and trimmed small shoots that were growing into the center of a tree. He was pruning the peach trees with a few of his fellow outfield workers. He didn't want to talk to anyone. Everything that Serka had set his heart on was now confused and thwarted. The news of where Jeber had been, the fact that he had returned with Elenn, and the claim they made about having a remedy for the barren—all these things had changed Leol's mind completely. But Serka was unable to let go of frustration and disappointment.

It had taken a great directing of will to prepare himself to join Chibo's chain and follow the Eight Stars to a final act of pure self-sacrifice. When he had finally made his resolve, the idea had given him a firm conviction that this was going to be the right destiny for him, and he had embraced it with determination. Then he had spent the month of Jeber's absence in guilt and regret, thinking that if only he had managed the situation a little more carefully, the three of them could have died together with hearts and minds united.

Serka blamed himself. If only he had been a little more courageous at the beginning, it would have been *he* who went first to find out how to join Chibo's chain. Yes, this was his own fault. As the thought occurred to him, he angrily cut a thick peach shoot and felt oddly satisfied with his own self-chastisement. He reached to clip a few extraneous twigs from a branch, and a thought occurred to him which he knew to be perverse. What if he had known that the double-handed blade was hidden in the tool shed? Could he not have pretended to be the waiter and come forward to lead the next self-extermination? How tempting that would have been! But when he imagined what it would have felt like to pretend to be the waiter, he knew that such a great lie would be unbearable.

"Master Serka!"

It was Leol.

"Master Serka!" Leol came running. "I've come from Flatpools Station!"

"Did you see Master Elenn?"

"Yes, we had a very long talk," said Leol, "I must tell you about it."

Master Elenn was a puzzle to Serka now. Serka had always respected and admired him, and he still did. But Master Elenn was back with this sedative medicine, and Serka was not interested in having any of it.

"Did he talk to you about the white sponge?" asked Serka.

"Yes, and it's very important that we give it a try." Leol was breathing hard from running. He looked up at Serka, waiting for him to respond.

Serka had to think about what to say. He wanted Leol to make his own decision. Perhaps Leol needed the stuff.

"Well, I suppose it could be good," said Serka.

"I want to try it, but I want you to try it with me. Master Elenn gave me some." He took a small cloth sack from his pocket. "We can eat some right now."

"Master Leol, I think if you want to try it, you should. It will calm you. But I don't think I need it."

"But maybe it will help."

"Help what?"

"Master Serka," said Leol, "I know what you're thinking about the double-handed blade."

"What? What do you think I have in mind?"

190

"Jeber is the waiter, he's not going to continue Chibos's chain. But the chain will probably continue without him. I know you still want to follow the Eight Stars."

"How is that stuff going to help?" asked Serka, pointing at the cloth sack with his cutting tool.

"It will help you be calm to swing the blade, . . . and then receive it."

This was something that Serka had not thought of. The reason Master Elenn and Master Jeber had come back to the capital with the medicine was to stop the chain. Serka didn't like the idea of living a numbed existence. But maybe the calm would enable them to carry out their final act with greater ease and efficiency.

"What about you, Master Leol? I know that the hooded masters at Murro are trying to persuade all of us to join. But if you don't want to, you should not join."

"I'm undecided. But I definitely want to try the white sponge. Master Elenn says that Lern Beyana wants all uedin to receive it."

"Lern Beyana? Why does Master Elenn say that?"

"He visited the temple. The Most High Server read the thoughts of Lern Beyana, and she said we should all receive the white sponge."

"Well, that's very strange." Serka knew that the servers sometimes read the thoughts of Lern Beyana, but why did she want all uedin to take a calming medicine?

"Outfield workers have always loved Lern Beyana," said Leol. "At least try it at the request of Lern Beyana."

It was true. They could hardly refuse to consume white sponge if Lern Beyana desired that they do so. Serka looked seriously at Leol. "Leol, if I eat some with you, you must promise me one thing."

"What is it?"

"If Chibo's chain continues, even if you are calm about it, you must not join just to follow me. You must make up your own mind."

"I promise," said Leol. He gave the small cloth sack to Serka. He would let Serka go first. Serka hesitated only a moment, looking down at the cloth sack. Then he opened it, reached in for a shred of the peculiar white substance, and put it in his mouth.

Leol Attends the Namestaking
Ceremony with Master Yinat

Leol had eaten some of Jeber's white sponge twice now, and he hadn't admitted it to anyone, but he clearly noticed that he was worrying less. Ordinarily he would have felt mildly resentful of the fact that he was the only one of the three who agreed to attend Namestaking with Master Yinat. The other two were lucky enough to have prior engagements.

Master Yinat tried the patience of all three of them. When they had first taken name and become apprentices, Yinat had agreed to take them along every time he went into the capital. He told them that Master Ghera, of his same generation, had put him up to it. He had told them to their faces that he regretted ever making such a commitment, but he was "stuck dragging them along every time he went to the capital." None of them had liked Master Yinat much, but they had all absolutely loved going to the capital, and they were all glad to put up with his unpleasant mood in order to have such chances. After a while, they had gotten a little used to him. Then apprenticeship ended. Strangely enough, Master Yinat kept expecting them to want to go with him to the capital, but they weren't apprentices any longer, and they could go to the capital whenever they wanted. Occasionally one of the three of them would go with Yinat, just to be polite. When Yinat invited them to go with him to the Namestaking ceremony, Serka and Jeber both said immediately that they could not. Leol resigned himself to the task of acting like an apprentice for the satisfaction of Master Yinat.

"Young Masters Jeber and Serka are very *important*," said Yinat as they passed through the western gate on the way to the central courtyard.

Leol wasn't sure if he was being sarcastic or not. "They're both very involved right now," Leol said.

"Yes, they are!" Yinat said. "They're very involved with the go-ings-on in the capital. They negotiate capital goings-on very well, probably because I taught them a thing or two."

Leol was mildly surprised to hear Yinat take this point of view. Apparently he wasn't being sarcastic.

Yinat continued, "You're not quite keeping up with them, are you? You're not nearly as important as they are."

Leol was quite used to hearing this kind of insensitive remark from Master Yinat. He noticed that it bothered him less than it ordinarily would have. Was it because of the white sponge, he wondered.

"It's true. I'm not as important as they are," said Leol. Maybe Serka was getting the calmness too. He hoped Serka would relax enough to talk to Jeber.

"Maybe if you paid better attention when I brought you into the capital, you'd have a better idea of the goings-on here," said Yinat.

"I have a fair idea of the goings-on here," said Leol, but Yinat wasn't listening.

"I have been wearing the same ceremonial robe for four genera-tions," said Yinat proudly, holding up his sleeve to inspect it while they walked. "Master Ghera has gotten fatter every novade. I think he's on his second or third one, but it still looks too small for him."

Leol knew that Ghera was Yinat's only friend in the outfields. "Did Master Ghera have other plans for attending Namestaking?" he asked.

"He's attending with Master Tamo and some of Master Tamo's acquaintances from Crafting," said Yinat. "But I saw him rushing about in the workhouse kitchen trying to get things ready for the dinner tonight. Master Tamo will not be happy if Master Ghera makes them late!" Yinat laughed a little gleefully. Leol considered that maybe Yinat's unfortunate quirk of personality was a way of coping with being left alone so much. Poor master.

"Your ceremonial robe looks too small for you, too," said Yinat. "But of course it's because of your syndrome . . . "

Leol knew it was true. The bottom hem of his ceremonial robe was just below his knees. He looked around at other masters who were now seen in the streets going in the same direction. Their turquoise ceremonial robes all went down to their ankles. He watched them carrying on conversations as they converged on the center of the capital, but they quickly hushed themselves when they entered the server-controlled plaza. The silent masses that waited around the circle of unnamed also included hundreds of servers in white and a sprinkling of guards in their green. Leol was immediately transfixed by the hugeness of the crowd. The whole population of the capital was in attendance. The silence of so many present at once was amazing to experience. At his own Namestaking a novade ago, it had not occurred to him to comprehend it.

Three young servers who appeared to be the same generation as Leol came forward and gingerly stepped between the soon-to-be-named who balanced on their feet. It was the formal hunched position often required of child-uedin. The three servers walked to the center of the circle and stood facing inward with their backs to the crowd. They were there to prepare the space for ceremony. Without any regard to the observers, they deftly removed their server wrappings and undergarments, stood naked for an instant, and then immediately sprang into a shifting. They did a series of classic shiftings. Between shiftings they took short breaks during which they rubbed their shoulders and moved their heads back and forth to recover from the strain of one shifting before going into the next.

Leol noticed the blank, anonymous faces of the soon-to-be-named watching the servers. He knew they were hiding a great nervousness. It was widely known that the new generation had been tested for the syndrome in early childhood. Those who tested positive for the syndrome were quite aware of their status. In a way, they were lucky in the sense that they had grown up knowing it. Leol would never forget the awful experience of learning that he had barren syndrome and then immediately receiving his hood. Serka had told him that this new generation was going to have a completely different experience. It will be up to the newly-named who have grown up knowing they have the syndrome to come forth on their own. They will arrange for their own catheter implants and join in the hoodstaking without being individually contacted. That seemed much preferable to the awful time that Leol had experienced. On the other hand, what could prepare the newly-named with syndrome for the troubled life of hooded masters these days, and how would they react when they learned about Chibo's chain? Serka had once said that nothing should be hidden from them. Leol wondered if his ideas would change now that they had started eating the white sponge.

The servers were doing their final shifting, the flat pose. Leol considered the fact that there were surely some of the soon-to-be-named who would choose to enter the temple. What about them? Shouldn't a newly-named with the syndrome know that if he entered the temple, he would most likely be coached to join a self-extermination? A server standing somewhere outside the circle in the area closest to the temple entrance hummed a series of three notes. The shifters gradually disengaged themselves from the flat pose, put their server undergarments and wrappings back on, and quietly exited the space. The soon-to-be-named sat back on their feet. Leol watched the servers preparing a large bowl of sourembers. Wind was very clearly blowing the smoke in one direction. An older server stepped in and whispered some instructions into the ear of one of the servers. That server in turn passed on the instruction to the other servers. After they got the bowl of sourembers smoking, they started their slow relay, passing the bowl back and forth as they made their way around the circle. One side of the circle received the smoke that the wind blew in their direction, but the other side got none. When they got back to the spot closest to the temple entrance, instead of stopping, they carried it a second time around through the throng of standing adult uedin to get to the very back of the crowd. Then they very slowly relayed the smoking sourembers back and forth around the crowd. They were trying to provide smoke to the uedin who didn't get any the first time around because of the wind. Since the wind blew the smoke away so fast, they slowed their pace to make sure everyone received it. Leol and Yinat were standing in the back, and when the sourembers went past, Leol got a very strong whiff of it. His attention turned to the wind.

The sourembers were taken away, and another server stepped into the circle and stood with hands folded to sing. Sound was not carrying well because of the wind, but the strange song that goes with the Leafsap ritual was immediately recognizable. It wasn't even really a song, thought Leol. The server squeaked and coughed and made the most peculiar vomiting sounds. None of it meant anything, from what Leol could tell. The song got louder and was now easily heard even with the wind blowing. Leol looked around to see where the clown would jump in. To his surprise, a server standing just ahead of him in the crowd suddenly stripped off his server wrappings and undergarments and dashed into the center of the circle. He started his silly dance around the singer, and a server chorus somewhere on the side started singing a more melodious version of singer's weird song. The server clown wiggled and flapped. Leol knew that the adult uedin were trying to suppress their laughter because they wanted to hear the sweet laughter of the yet unnamed. The clown pretended that he was fighting with the wind. He yelled and screamed and flailed at the wind. Finally, when he spat in the wind and the spit flew right back into his face, the unnamed broke into laughter, and the whole crowd erupted. Leol turned to see Yinat laughing heartily and he felt a sudden great affection for him. The clown put his hands on his hips and looked furious with exaggerated indignation at the crowd's laughter. He wiggled his behind and ran up to them, comically barking and braying at the unnamed as if scolding them for laughing, which made everyone laugh more.

When the fat-trunked shrub was brought forth on a wagon, the server clown resumed his dancing. The wagon was pulled around the circle, and certain soon-to-be-named took out needles and poked them into the soft-barked trunk. Leol immediately remembered how he had been one of the lucky ones to win a needle during the quizzing of Names Eve Observances and how proud he had been to jump up and stick it into the shrub's bark. The clown danced around the tree and picked off its leaves with expressions of "oops" and mischief. He dabbed at the sap that bled from the needle-jabbed trunk and broken-off leaves, smearing it in white stripes to decorate his body. Finally he picked the last leaf, smiled triumphantly at the crowd, and crammed it into his mouth. He chewed it up, swallowed, clapped his hands, and lay down on the plaza stones to take a nap. The server chorus now began a droning exercise which dramatically shifted the mood from levity to solemnity.

Leol couldn't well hear the quizzing that followed, for the wind continued to pick up. While the quizzing went on, his mind wandered. The first time he had seen the Leafsap, at his own Namestaking, he had thought that the server was lying down at the end to die. It had always bothered him.

"Poet, period, context." He heard one of the teaching masters say to whatever soon-to-be-named was being quizzed, and the youthful little voice began to ramble some recitation.

The idea that the server who danced the Leafsap was lying down to die had always been disturbing to Leol because uedin were never supposed to die like that. They were supposed to die with their heads down at the water's edge at Lake Ceulan. Uedin were supposed to take part in the passing-of-life. Leol sighed and tried to refocus on the quizzing of the soon-to-be-named.

The teaching masters were taking turns with the questions. One of them stepped into the circle and said in a loud voice to make sure it would carry through the wind, "*In the fourth novade after the wheatcrop failure and fasting years, fear that another failure would occur compelled the masters council to plow fields in a remote location. The poet Malta wrote a poem to reflect the discomfort that many uedin had about going into unfamiliar territory. Recite the poem.*"

Leol, as an outfield worker, found this question interesting because it involved the plowing of fields. The teaching master randomly chose one of the soon-to-be-named and tapped him lightly on the head.

The young one smiled and answered back with confidence, but his voice was not as strong as the teaching master's voice, and the wind nearly muffled it out.

"*Eight stars decorate . . . . . . Shall I . . . more? . . . But no, . . . will get lost.*"

Suddenly there was a small murmuring in the crowd. Leol thought it was because the teaching master had chosen to ask about the poem of the Eight Stars. Indeed, the unnamed likely had no idea of the association that their elders thought of immediately when they heard mention of the Eight Stars. Leol had a very deep respect and admiration for the Eight Stars of Murro, but somehow it didn't seem right to reference them at a Namestaking. Then he realized—the crowd wasn't rumbling about the poem; uedin were breaking the silence because an orange-brown cloud of dust could be seen forming in the eastern sky. A dust storm was coming!

The quizzing came to a halt, and a few masters and servers conferred on the side of the circle. The carts bearing the syllable blocks were hastily wheeled in, and the choosing of names commenced immediately. The pace was easily twice what Leol remembered from his own namestaking. A server darted around the circle with his willow branch touching one after another of those taking name. The anxious young ones practically ran forth, and they grabbed syllable blocks and announced their names without any contemplation. Within an hour, all of the new generation had name. Dust was already blowing in on the wind, and the air turned hazy. The servers who had prepared the space returned to do a few quick shiftings and led a hurried recitation of the Names of Lern Beyana to culminate the ceremony. As it ended, dust was starting to collect in Leol's nostrils, and he could taste it in his mouth.

"Come, come, come!" said Yinat. "We have to cross the field before the dust gets too bad!" Getting out of the courtyard, of course, was unbearably slow. Nearly the entire capital population was there for the ceremony, and everyone there urgently wanted to get straight home. Masters and servers alike stood nervously at one another's backs, waiting for the traffic to flow out.

"Oh, everyone needs to just move a little faster!" complained Yinat, but those within hearing could do nothing to accommodate his request. The dusty gusts began to sting Leol's eyes.

Finally, the crowd began to shuffle, and the shuffle soon turned into a scramble as uedin headed in all directions. Somewhat caught off guard by the fact that his request for faster movement was now being answered with such a chaotic rush, Yinat muttered in aggravation. Leol followed him wordlessly as they wove toward the western gate. By the time they reached it, visibility was decreasing dramatically. On the outside of the gate, the dusty gusts blew at them but the road was clear of other uedin. They went straight for the side path that led north for a shortcut to the workhouse. Yinat attempted to break into a run and immediately tripped over a vine, misstepping and twisting his knee. Through the thickening dust, Leol watched him take a few limping steps. He quickly surmised that Yinat had hurt himself and could hardly walk.

"You're hurt!" yelled Leol through the noisy wind.

"No I'm not!" protested Yinat, waving away Leol's attempt to help him walk.

Leol lingered to see if Yinat could indeed walk all right. He managed to limp along up to the spot where the trees parted and a path led through to the western outfields, but as soon as they stepped away from the capital wall, the wind carried sand that stung their faces and forced them to squint. Leol suddenly felt that he had to take matters into his own hands—they needed to get across the field to the workhouse as quickly as possible. "I'm carrying you!" he shouted to Yinat. He grabbed him by the torso and put him over his shoulder like a sack of grain. Then he started off across the field in great strides. Yinat made no protest. Leol felt Yinat's hand on his back, bracing himself to stop from bouncing as Leol ran. At one point he felt a little pat, and he thought he heard Yinat say, "Thank you, young master."

By the next morning, the dust cloud was gone. Leol felt strangely at ease. Was it just because the dust storm had passed without causing any major damage to the workhouse grounds or the crops? His mind kept going back to the picture of the server clown's acting out of what Leol had once erringly thought was supposed to be a uedin dying. It had bothered him since the first time he had seen it exactly one novade ago. The sight of it the first time, so long ago, had given him a sense of dread at the thought of dying that way. He still thought that he might prefer to die under the two-handed blade. But now, the awful feeling of dread that he felt about the subject seemed to be dissipating. He didn't know how he would die—only that it would be without passing-of-life. And yet, dying without passing-of-life now seemed less important than the pleasant clarity of the post-storm sky. He wondered whether Serka, who had also eaten the white sponge, was experiencing something similar.

A Meal of Whitesponge In the Temple

Serka's mind wandered as he waited with Jeber for Master Elenn of the hood squadron to arrive. He still thought of Master Elenn as a guard master of highest valor. Eating the stuff Master Elenn and the other returned masters brought back didn't change his mind about wanting to join Chibo's chain, but it did indeed provide him with a greater calmness of mind about it.

At first, after eating it, Serka had been just at the point of accepting that the puffy shreds were helping him to not worry, just as they had promised. But then Elenn had contacted him by letter. Elenn wanted him to accompany Jeber and him to a meal *inside the temple*. The idea made Serka very anxious—those puffy shreds notwithstanding! He understood why Elenn and Jeber, who had traversed the southeastern desert and resided at a settlement there, might be invited. But why was Serka asked to go along? It was probably because Master Elenn considered him a representative of hooded masters who wanted to join the chain. Indeed he did want to follow Chibo and the Eight Stars. Why should he be ashamed of that?

Master Elenn had requested that they wait for him to come to the outfields and meet up with them at the workhouse. Serka figured it was because Master Elenn wanted to talk with them before entering the temple. Ueden didn't speak too much inside there. He knew what Master Elenn wanted to talk about. Like Jeber, Master Elenn believed that if the hooded masters started eating those puffy shreds, they would be so at ease that they wouldn't want to make a self-extermination. From Serka's point of view, perhaps the stuff would put them at ease with *making* a self-extermination. But he would listen to whatever Master Elenn wanted to say. He only regretted that Leol was probably feeling terribly left out.

Master Elenn was apparently sensitive to that awkward situation too, because the first thing he said when he appeared at the workhouse was, "Is Master Leol anywhere around?"

"He's out weeding fieldpears," said Jeber. "I spoke to him. He understands that you can only bring two guests with you."

"I know why you chose me," said Serka. "I am outspoken about following the Eight Stars."

"I think it is important that you hear what the Most High has to say about us hooded masters," said Elenn.

"The Most High Server has something to say about us?"

"Either about us or *to* us. I believe that's why I was asked to return," said Elenn. "I was instructed to bring two hooded masters with me as guests."

"Well, if we are to be there by noon, we had better start," said Jeber.

Serka informed the other servers inside the workhouse that they were leaving, and they started out toward the capital wall. There was still dust on all the vegetation from the recent dust storm. They talked as they crossed the field.

"Master Elenn, you told us that you recognized the Most High Server. What do you mean? How could you recognize him?" asked Jeber.

"The Most High Server was raised at Quarterhouse," said Elenn. "We became friends after Namestaking. But then he entered the temple at the same time I joined the guards."

"The Most High Server is only in his third generation?" asked Serka.

"It's true," said Elenn.

"It must have been very interesting to talk about how you have led such different lives," said Jeber.

"We didn't talk about anything like that. I don't know if the Most High Server even recognized me."

"It's the syndrome," said Serka. "It doesn't just make us get large, it changes our faces too."

He thought it odd that Elenn didn't comment, but only when they reached the western gate did Elenn finally speak.

"The Most High didn't recognize me because he is not himself. I need to tell you both about that. I had doubts about it myself, but the more I think about it, the more I believe that the Most High Server is somehow possessed by Lern Beyana. It's very strange. You need to prepare yourselves for it."

"Is the Most High Server awake?" asked Serka, somewhat confused. He could imagine a server possessed by Lern Beyana—that seemed possible—but, since it was known that Lern Beyana sleeps, he naturally thought that a server possessed by her would also be asleep.

"Yes, the Most High Server is quite awake, and speaks clearly," said Elenn. "But when he speaks, it is as if we are hearing Lern Beyana speak. It's very hard to imagine, I know."

Serka thought about this. There was one matter that seemed to be a problem. Lern Beyana was troubled by uedin with barren syndrome. That was the whole reason that the servers developed a ritual for self-extermination. The masters adopted it to spare the capital, but it had all started with Lern Beyana. If uedin with the syndrome were so disturbing to Lern Beyana, would it be acceptable to eat and talk with a high server who was possessed by her and speaking in her place?

"Should we remove our hoods?" asked Serka.

"It won't be necessary," answered Elenn. "It is understood that we are barren uedin."

They reached the temple's main door to find an older server waiting for them. Serka joined Jeber and Elenn in raising hands to face.

"Greetings, Master guard. Master fieldworkers, welcome," said the server. "I am Rafo, chief emissary for the temple."

"Jeber of western outfields," said Jeber.

"Serka of western outfields," said Serka.

"I have a few instructions for you before we enter the temple," said Rafo. "The high servers have released word that we have a situation in the temple that we have never had before. The Soft One, Lern Beyana, has taken over the body of our Most High." The server's expression was deeply serious. "We are on high rule. You cannot speak once we enter unless you are invited to speak by the Most High. When you do speak, do not say your names or mention any other names. When I lead you to the hall where the Most High is meeting with you and the high servers, I will be walking very slowly, more slowly than you are used to. This is a new extension of our high rule, as we have noticed that the Most High seems to be more comfortable when we approach slowly."

"We understand, emissary," said Elenn.

"Please follow me now," said Rafo, and he led them into the temple. As he stepped across the threshold of the temple's main door, his walking became very conscious and very slow. They all followed in similar form. As Serka followed slowly through the various corridors, he noticed other servers, eyes downcast, also moving about with slow and careful movement. They finally reached the hall. For a second, Serka thought it was empty because it was silent and he didn't see any faces. Then he saw that there were about ten servers in the worm pose with their faces to the floor. The high server ushered them into the hall and nodded for them to take their places. Serka looked at Elenn to see what he was going to do, and when Elenn started to get down into the worm pose, he and Jeber did the same.

It seemed to Serka that they stayed in the worm pose, waiting, for a very long time. He wanted to look up when he heard shuffling and movement at the door of the hall, but he remained in the pose with his face against the floor. Something was being carried in. He waited. Whatever it was that had been carried in was placed at the head of the room, and there was another long extended silence.

"Dear ones, please sit up and face me," said someone in a calm and quiet voice. Serka raised his head. A small uedin—small enough to be newly named but looking too old for such a slight build—had been carried in on a chair and placed at the head of the hall. The high servers rose very slowly to a seated position but did not look around or make eye contact with the masters. They all fixed their eyes on the Most High Server. The master guests tried to match the slow pace as they likewise sat up.

"Dear one who is a master and a guard, and who came here once before . . ." said the Most High, *"Thank you for bringing these other dear ones to me. They are also uedin who carry no life in their wombs, are they not?"*

"They are," said Elenn. "They are both outfield workers. One of them, like I, went to the place beyond the southeast desert where the whitesponge came from. The other is one of the many barren masters who have made a plan to end their lives for the good of the capital."

"Yes, I know that a number of dear ones have done this, both inside and outside this temple," said the Most High.

"We are greatly honored to be here," said Elenn.

"Dear one who has plans to end his life . . . " Serka saw that the Most High Server was looking directly at him. The gaze was mystifying. *"Please speak to me. Tell me why you plan to end your life."*

Serka fought back his anxiety to answer. "We wish to exercise courage," said Serka. "We hope to rid the capital of the ill effect of our presence."

"It is very brave, dear one," said the Most High. *"All of you who have sought this solution are very brave."*

Hearing this, Serka felt a great and satisfying affirmation. Lern Beyana was indeed disturbed by the presence of uedin with barren syndrome, and their willingness to forfeit their own lives obviously pleased the Most High.

"I am unworthy of your compliment, Most High," said Serka in a humble voice.

"*But dear one, there is something you must understand at this time. It is your suffering more than anything else that has been troublesome to the capital, just as that has been the case with the dear ones here in the temple.*"

"We hope also to put an end to our own suffering," said Serka.

"*But there is more that is asked of you. All of you.*" said the Most High. "*It is not correct to end your lives.*"

"What is asked of us, Most High?" asked Serka.

"*It has been the purpose of dear ones with no lives in their wombs to be my keepers, and to deliver my substance to the capital. The two who came with you are fulfilling this. You must also do so.*"

Serka heard Elenn gasp slightly, but he didn't understand what the Most High was saying. "I don't understand, Most High . . . "

"*Dear one who is a guard of the capital, do you understand what I'm saying?*"

"I believe I do, Most High," said Elenn in a trembling voice.

"*Yes, you do. You and all the dear ones who found my substance and stayed near me did so because it was necessary for you to do so. Now you must travel a road back and forth from here to the place where my substance rests, and you must deliver my substance to all dear ones to consume until my substance is gone.*"

Serka looked around at the faces of the high servers. No longer sitting serenely with downcast eyes, they now wore shocked expressions. Serka began to understand.

"Oh, Most High . . . " said Elenn now, completely stupefied, "The whitesponge is . . . ?"

"*It is my substance,*" said the Most High.

"We must eat no more of it!" cried Elenn loudly, startling everyone including Serka.

But the Most High remained calm. *"No, my dear one, you must eat all of it."*

Elenn looked about the room to meet the gazes of high servers. They were just as stunned as he was. "It might last one generation—but not two," argued Elenn.

"It will be enough," said the Most High.

Serka's mind reeled to comprehend what was being revealed. The puffy shreds, what Master Elenn called "white sponge"—was that Lern Beyana's *body*?

"Primary advisor, please tell the dear ones at the door that they should bring it in now," said the Most High to the server seated beside him.

The server went to the door and motioned. A line of other servers came in, each carrying a tray-table bearing a very small bowl and spoon. The first one was placed in front of the Most High, then the masters were given theirs. Finally trays were placed before each of the other high servers. Serka looked at the whitish liquid in his bowl. He understood that it was a soup made out of the white sponge; it had the same smell.

The Most High reached out a thin arm and took the spoon on his tray. He took the lip of the bowl with his other hand. He then held them both out, like he was showing something to everyone. *"We eat this for our survival. My survival and yours. We are able to survive because we survive together."*

At first Serka didn't understand what was being said. He could tell by the expressions on other faces that it was a thing of tremendous importance. The servers around him, Master Elenn, *everyone* seemed to be overwhelmed with the greatness of what was happening. Serka didn't want to stare or appear conspicuous by gawking at the others in the room, but he looked around just enough to see the faces of high servers with tears in their eyes.

They lifted their bowls and spoons and ate as instructed. Suddenly, Serka had the realization that the servers, Jeber, and Master Elenn were caught in the emotion of a very strange and unimaginable thing, and he thought he understood what it was. There was a reason why they handled their spoons with shaky hands. They were eating the body of Lern Beyana.

Gathering of Hooded Masters at Murro

Once past the Clay Bridge and assuredly alone on the road to Murro, Pavis took his woodflute from his pocket and looked at it in his hand. He was away from the capital with no one in earshot, and it was a perfect time to practice tunes of his own devising. But in this case, his favorite distraction did not much entice him. He held it to his mouth and blew a few notes as he walked, but then gave up on it and put it back in his pocket. There was no urgency in his pace, even though he knew he would likely be the last to arrive. He had decided late to follow the rest of the hooded masters to Murro. The council had granted consent to a convention of hooded masters there, and there was heavy expectation that a mass self-extermination was about to take place. Somehow it had come to feel like an inevitability during the two moon cycles since the death of the Eight Stars. Hooded masters these days went outside the walls to find one another for feeding, and when they recovered from derangement they huddled in groups whispering about self-extermination. Pavis himself wandered off frequently enough that Jutef asked no questions when he left. From Pavis's point of view there was little real help or guidance from the caretakers or the hood squadron except to provide some liaison with the rest of the capital, but his friendship with Jutef was the one exception to that way of thinking. Jutef's hut had become home to Pavis. Pavis wondered if Jutef had any idea what was transpiring on this hot and dusty day. He tried to banish the question that pestered him—if the self-extermination was going to happen, as he imagined it was, would he feel drawn to it?

Approaching Murro, Pavis was confused at first when the area usually occupied by hooded masters appeared quite empty. As he got closer, he heard the sound of talking from above and realized that the viewing deck was completely full of uedin. It was a heavily built log deck much reminiscent of the observation deck at the Quarterhouse flatpool. He recalled his one and only visit there, when he was shown the half-eaten face of a barren master who had cut his own throat in the hatching pool. It was one of his most unpleasant memories. He hadn't anticipated that the hooded masters would be gathering on the grainhouse observation deck, but as he listened to the mumbling of voices, it occurred to him that it was indeed built with massive beams, strong enough to support a large party of uedin to look out at the view of the capital. He walked to the ground-level entrance of the grainhouse. There was no one there. The whole ground floor was filled with various materials and supplies reflecting its current use by the hooded masters who now occupied Murro permanently, but there were no uedin around. They were all up on the deck.

He walked up the ramp to the second floor, and then continued to the third. Some uedin were congregating around the door at the top of the third-floor ramp that opened to the deck, and Pavis could hear the voices from outside. One of the masters at the doorway wore guard's garb. As he got to the top of the ramp, he realized that it was Master Elenn of Flatpools—the very one who had taken him that awful night to see the dead master with the white, water-soaked gash in his neck. Pavis was hit with anxiety. He knew that Master Elenn, along with a group of other masters, had returned to the capital from a long absence. All sorts of contradicting rumors and stories were circulating about where they had been. Pavis had not seen Elenn for a very long time, but seeing him at this particular moment caught him off guard. He ascended the ramp. Elenn and the other uedin at the doorway had their backs to Pavis, looking out and listening to what sounded like an argument.

"Master Elenn," said Pavis quietly, getting Elenn's attention.

Elenn turned around and looked at him. As soon as Elenn recognized him, he smiled. Pavis was quite struck with the warmth of the smile.

"What is happening?" asked Pavis.

"Go on," said Elenn. "Go out and join the hooded masters on the deck." His kind eyes were an unexpected contrast to the dark feelings Pavis held about the imminent event. Elenn moved aside and tapped the shoulder of another master, unhooded, and small for a barren, who likewise moved aside so that Pavis could get through to join the others on the deck.

All the barren uedin of the capital were crowded around the perimeter of the deck, a few guards in green interspersed among them. They were listening to an exchange between two who seemed to be arguing. As Pavis made his way to the side of the deck, he looked to see who was talking. One of them was Hemi from Whiteroof, whom Pavis knew. The other was an outfield worker whom Pavis had seen before but whose name he did not know.

"What makes anyone think the waiter will show up?" insisted Hemi. "He has kept us all waiting for nearly two moon cycles!"

"He will be here!" answered the outfield worker.

"Who are you? How do you know the waiter is coming?" yelled Hemi.

"I'm Serka of the western outfields. The waiter is another outfield worker. We have worked together since taking name."

"If he doesn't come, I say we must start again with a new blade. It would have been good to receive the blade that was used by the Eight Stars, but more importantly we must follow them in action, regardless of what blade we use!"

The crowd began to murmur amongst themselves. Pavis found a spot and stood to listen to the debating masters. He looked around. Many of the faces he recognized from his routes as a delivery master and from his more secret wanderings. He gazed out momentarily at the view of the capital. It was unexpectedly beautiful. He was distracted for a moment, then his attention was drawn back to the discussion as one master appealed, "Let us try not to break the chain that started with Master Chibo! Whoever was given the blade and made waiter after the death of the Eight Stars—that is whom we must follow!"

"But he is clearly in hiding!" said another. "We must carry on!"

More grumbling from the crowd commenced.

"I have the blade!" shouted a voice from the entrance. They all looked to see who it was. A second-generation uedin stood, wearing an outfield worker's robe and holding a long object rolled up in a blanket. The crowd immediately fell into complete silence.

"I am Jeber of the western outfields, and I am the waiter!" cried the master. "This is the blade, and no other blade will be needed!"

Pavis felt his heart sink and stir. The waiter had shown up. This balcony was going to be a scene of massive bloodiness. It felt like a whirlpool sucking him in with all the rest of the barren. Their destiny was to die without passing-of-life, and the best prize for a barren was the honor of giving his life for the capital. This was the thinking of hooded masters everywhere these days, and Pavis felt there was truth in it.

Finally one cried out, "Master Jeber! Hail to you! You delayed your appearance all these weeks to give us all a chance to prepare ourselves! We are ready!"

"Master, show us the two-handed blade!" shouted another.

Pavis heard someone beside him say, "Today is our day of glory." He looked at the fitted floorboards at his feet and imagined how the blood of a hundred beheaded uedin might leak through and let fall a rain of blood on the ground two stories below.

"I am going to show you the blade now," yelled Jeber, "but you must hear everything I have to say."

The crowd went silent again as Jeber unwrapped the blanket from around the two-handed blade. He held it up and out for all to see. It was purple-brown with dried blood.

Jeber projected his voice so that all could hear him. "This is the blade that was used by masters whom you are calling the Eight Stars! I was among them the night they died! Master Tono was the waiter who gathered us together! We drew shell pieces to see who would become the new waiter, and I drew the empty shell! I watched Tono die, and then I watched them all take the worm pose one by one to receive the blade, and I . . . " Jeber hesitated, clearly struck with emotion at the memory he was retelling, " . . . I cut the head from the last of the Eight Stars!"

The hooded masters remained silent. Pavis thought about the choice of death that was upon them. It was a choice he had run away from when he had left the temple. Today he would make a different choice. He would not choose to run away. This would be a good way to end his life. He didn't think he would ever feel ready for such a thing, but he was.

Jeber continued. "But masters! Hear me well! This is a day that will be remembered, but not as you imagine! The eighth of the Eight Stars, the one that I killed—he was the last to die by this blade, and he will always be the last! No uedin will ever again die by this blade, or any other!"

Pavis felt a momentary confusion. Had he heard correctly? If no uedin would die by the blade, then what were they there for?

The crowd erupted. "What do you mean?" someone shouted.

"You've all heard about the returned masters who came back from the southeastern desert! I am one of them! That is why I took so long to appear! It wasn't that I was giving you a chance to prepare yourselves for self-extermination! I was gone! But we brought something back to you—something very important!"

"We've heard about the white medicine," shouted someone in the crowd.

"It is more than a medicine!" said Jeber.

"What is it?" called someone else.

"We ourselves did not know what it was! We also thought it was just a special kind of food! But we now know what it is!" Pavis waited with the rest of the crowd as Jeber hesitated, lowered the blade to his side and spoke loudly, "It is the body of Lern Beyana!"

There was rumbling in the crowd and cries of "What?!" as the hooded masters responded to the preposterous claim.

"Lern Beyana has always resided in a place unknown to uedin! What are you saying?"

"The place was unknown to uedin until now!" answered Jeber with certainty.

"Are you saying you have killed Lern Beyana, and you are eating her flesh as a medicine?" cried one of the hooded masters in disbelief. Pavis rarely felt much remnant of his former server identity, but the mention of killing the Soft One gave him a sick and disgusted feeling, and in a flash he remembered his server childhood. He had taken leg in the temple pool, and his connection to server identity was deeper than he realized. The question that the hooded master asked, whether Lern Beyana had been killed for her medicinal flesh, was a shocking one. Certainly that was not the case! Pavis looked to see how Jeber would respond.

"No! We did not know what we were eating! And Lern Beyana is not dead! She has been giving direct communication through the Most High Server at the temple! The whitesponge covers a huge length of space inside a cave at the far side of the desert! There has been a settlement of barren there eating it for many generations! We never knew we were eating the flesh of Lern Beyana! She now tells us through the Most High Server that she demands to be eaten! She says it is critical for the survival of all!"

As the multitude of barren masters murmured in response to this shocking revelation, Pavis thought more about his formative years growing up in the atmosphere of reverent regard for the Soft One. But the Soft One never actually *said* anything. This all sounded outrageous.

"We have always been told that Lern Beyana sleeps," argued Hemi. "Why should we believe what you're saying?"

Serka spoke up. "What Master Jeber says is true. I was in the temple three days ago. Three of us hooded masters were invited to join the high masters for a meal of whitesponge there. The Most High Server spoke to me directly, and I believe it was Lern Beyana speaking. She told us that we must eat whitesponge for our survival!"

"It's crazy talk!" shouted one from the crowd. Pavis, likewise taken aback, knitted his brow to imagine a direct communication from the Soft One happening in the tradition-paralyzed temple. *Was it possible?*

Hemi spoke up again. "We barren are not part of the capital's future," he said. "We have no passing-of-life! Let the non-hooded masters carry out the wishes of Lern Beyana, if that is what she demands!" Pavis thought it was a strange thing to say. It sounded like Hemi didn't care whether or not the Soft One was really communicating her wishes.

"Her demand is that whitesponge be given first to the barren uedin of the capital!" said Jeber. "She said that there is more that is asked of us, and that it is not correct to end our lives!"

"We don't want these lives!" cried one particularly large barren master with a face grown ugly from the syndrome.

"We have come here to die," said another. "If you are the waiter, your role is to lead us in death. Why are you denying us?"

"I also sought death, I tell you! It was my choice to die alone instead of leading a self-extermination—that's why I went to the southeastern desert. But instead of dying, I was found by this uedin!" Jeber pointed to the uedin Pavis had noticed before, the one who appeared small compared to the barren of the capital. He stepped forward and held hands to face.

"I am Daga," he said. "I was once an apprentice with the weavers at Crafting, three novades ago. I never graduated from my apprenticeship because I, like Master Jeber, left the capital and ended up in the southeastern desert where I too was rescued and found a home in the village of the childless. I do not know anything about your Eight Stars or your blade. I don't know about feeding, and I have never worn a hood." Daga briefly turned his head to show that he had no neckstrap. "But I do know that when you eat the whitesponge, your mind will settle, and you will not become deranged, and you will not be driven by worry."

By now, Pavis was completely captivated by the notion that the Soft One, ever considered to be at differing levels of sleep, was *communicating directly* to uedin. He suddenly recalled a brief conversation he and some other young messengers had once had with a senior messenger of the temple, an old ro who always seemed to have a hint of fun and mischief in his manner. Pavis remembered how the ro made a dismissive gesture with his hand when someone voiced concern about so many paper notes being exchanged and messengers scrambling about the temple delivering them. Wasn't it a disturbance to the peaceful slumber of the Soft One? *"Oh, never mind that sort of thinking,"* the ro server had said. "We *are happy to awaken to the Soft One, and the Soft One is happy to awaken to us,"* he had assured them. It was a casual statement at the time, but Pavis remembered those words, and they were the words that came back to him as he listened to this most unexpected revelation.

One of the younger hooded masters called out, "Guard Master Elenn of the hood squadron is one of you who came back—isn't he there? Let's hear what Guard Master Elenn has to say!" Other voices called out, "Master Elenn!" and, "Yes, Master Elenn!"

Pavis watched Elenn come out from the grainhouse doorway where he had been standing and listening in the shadow. His earlier smile was now resolved to a serious look. Jeber, Serka, and Daga stepped aside along with a few other masters who seemed to be part of their group. Elenn stood before everyone and raised hands to face. The crowd greeted him likewise, a mass of hands and elbows coming up in silent respect.

"The is the second time in my life I am speaking to all of you together," said Elenn. "The first was at the hoodstaking ceremony, when I gave you the oath. That oath, it turned out, was as much of a torment to us as it was a help. I had my catheter removed before I left the capital, and Master Jeber destroyed his catheter before he was rescued in the desert. We are living with no draining of skullsap, and we are not suffering derangement. There are uedin living on the far side of the desert, close to the place where whitesponge grows in a cave. The uedin there are all barren, and they also live with no draining of their skullsap, and there is no derangement seen there at all. It is because the whitesponge heals them. And now, . . . Now we finally know that the whitesponge is the flesh of Lern Beyana, and she bids us all to consume it. It is a strange request, but it is our Lern Beyana who makes it."

"Will we not eventually eat it *all*?" asked one of the crowd with indignation. "Will you really encourage us to *eat* Lern Beyana—*completely*?"

"We . . . *must*," said Elenn. Pavis noticed the hesitation in Elenn's voice betraying the fact that he also found it abhorent. "Lern Beyana, speaking through the Most High, tells us that we must do it for our survival, both ours and hers."

Serka raised one hand to face and spoke. "It's true what Master Elenn says. I was there in the temple as a hooded master with an intention to die by the two-handed blade. The Most High spoke to me directly, and I believe it was Lern Beyana speaking through him. We are not supposed to end our lives. Our purpose is to be the keepers of her substance, the whitesponge, and to deliver it to the capital."

"Her substance?" someone asked.

"The whitesponge!" answered Serka with an element of wonder in his voice. Serka himself was still amazed by the news he was now sharing with them.

There was hesitation and discussion in the crowd as they all tried to comprehend the claims they were hearing.

"Masters, hear me!" cried Elenn, and he waited for their attention before speaking again. "When Lern Beyana speaks through the Most High, she refers to uedin as 'dear ones.' She has said that we with the syndrome, we who 'carry no life in our wombs,' are to be the first to receive her substance. We have it with us now." He gestured to Daga. Serka followed Daga through the grainhouse door, and when they came back out, Daga was carrying a basket covered with a cloth, and Serka was carrying a large plyroot bucket, heavy and full with water.

The masters watched in silence. Daga put the basket down and waited. Serka placed the bucket in front of Jeber who still held the double-handed blade in his hands and now raised it in the air. Elenn took the cloth from the basket, revealing its contents of whitesponge carefully cut into uniform small pieces.

"I, Jeber of the Western Outfields, speak to you now as your waiter. You must all decide at this time whether you want to die by the two-handed blade or receive the substance. If you choose to die, you must follow in the same manner given to us by the servers, by Master Chibo, and by the Eight Stars. I am the waiter. You must first cut my head from my body, and whoever follows you will cut yours, until one remains who must then become the new waiter. If you choose to live, you must eat a morsel of the Substance. But let us remember that those who chose death by the blade up to this point did so for the sake of the capital, and they did not know what we now know. When we wash this blade we remember them for their courage and self-sacrifice."

Jeber lowered the blade so that the tip of it, and then the full length of blade dipped into the water. Elenn stepped forward with the cloth that he had taken from the basket and submerged it in the water. He then used the wet cloth to wash the dried blood from the blade as Jeber held it by the handle. When the blade was clean, Elenn wiped it one last time and carefully took hold of the tip. Then Elenn and Jeber, holding the two-handed blade horizontally, stepped forward from the bucket with the blade held between them. Daga took a single piece of the whitesponge and placed it in the middle of the flat blade.

"Any who wants to die, come and place your hand on mine. I will pass the handle to you and kneel in worm position for you to cut my head from my body. Then the blade will be washed again, and you will have to wait for another like yourself to complete your own death. Or, you can choose to receive the Substance. Reach not for the handle, but for the morsel that we place on the blade. Find out how the Substance can sustain you. Make your choice, and come forth!" cried Jeber.

For a long time, nobody moved. Pavis was ready to go up and take the piece of whitesponge from the blade and eat it, but he was reluctant to go first. Then the words of the old messenger server floated through his mind again. Though it had been nearly a novade since he had left the temple, and though he had completely embraced the life of a master in the capital, he strangely felt some part of his server past pressing strongly on his instincts. There was some part of him that unquestioningly dedicated itself to the Soft One on a level that preceded any notion of who he was or how he had experienced life. *"We are happy to awaken to the Soft One, and the Soft One is happy to awaken to us,"* the ro messenger had said. Pavis stepped forward and walked up to the blade held at its two ends by Jeber and Elenn, a small white morsel placed in the middle. Pavis raised hands to face, then took the piece of whitesponge from the blade and put it in his mouth.

There was movement in the crowd as masters stepped aside for Hemi who was now coming forward. The morsel broke into soft shreds in Pavis's mouth as he moved out of the way for Hemi. Two masters followed Hemi nervously. Elenn was placing another morsel of whitesponge on the blade for Hemi to take, but he kept his hand there as if he might need to retrieve the morsel should Hemi reach for the handle. The look on Hemi's face was one of agony. Clearly, he was planning to lay his hand over Jeber's hand and take the handle. Doing that would indicate that he was going to kill and be killed. If that happened, a series of beheadings would take place before all of them in the next moments. As Pavis comprehended this, an anticipatory feeling of disillusionment quickly touched him. It was too simple-minded to assume that all the masters would easily let go of their longing to follow the Eight Stars.

Hemi looked like he was in torment as he faced Jeber. Jeber, looking back at him, had an expression which suggested that he was making peace with his fate. Elenn's hand remained steady as he prepared to pick up the morsel and allow the blade to serve its terrible purpose.

But Hemi couldn't look away from Jeber's eyes. Jeber, showing no sign of anxiety, only looked back at Hemi with kindness. A slight smile, humble and affectionate, crossed his face. He seemed to have accepted that he was about to have to bend to the worm position to have his head cut from his body, and he was reassuring Hemi that it was all right.

Hemi's face conveyed his great confusion. He shouted defiantly, "I am worthy! I am worthy to follow Master Chibo, and the Eight Stars!" but then he threw back his head and cried out in anguish, *"But I am not worthy to eat the body of Lern Beyana!"*

The master who stood behind him reached up and laid a reassuring hand on his shoulder.

Jeber answered calmly, "Let your courage make your choice for you."

Hemi briefly turned around and looked at the master who had agreed to follow him. Then, slightly trembling, he reached out and picked up the morsel. He put it in his mouth and closed his eyes.

Pavis felt great relief as he watched Hemi take the morsel and eat it. He noticed tears streaming down many faces as the masters now started stepping forward to form a line. Pavis scanned their faces. They were all hooded masters, large with the syndrome, exhausted with their lives as barren uedin. But to Pavis, there was something in them that reminded him of his old, fantastic ideas about the poetic masters that he once admired when he was a server. These particular masters had a wisdom born of their suffering that made them great. Behind the scene of their large frames cueing to receive whitesponge, the midday sun was casting a brilliant glow on the walled capital in the distance.

Profound News and Great Rains
Reach the Childless Village

Leci was collecting water from the trickle that ran from one of the caves of the bluff. It was a tedious job, as the water had to be captured in tiny amounts. He repeated the action of waiting for the little wooden ladle to catch a bit of the trickle, then pouring the precious drops into a large deep bowl made of hardened sponge. He pondered the riddle of time presented by the need to do this painstaking chore to get water, even though Great Rains would be there any day.

"Leci, come!" shouted one of his neighbors come to fetch him, "The new one and his group are back! Some masters from the capital are with them—they're wearing white hoods on their heads! They carry gourds!"

More than Great Rains, it was the return of the foursome from the capital that Leci and all the other uedin of the village had been waiting for. It was not surprising that they had brought some capital masters back with them. Leci placed the ladle inside the half-full bowl and carefully carried it as he followed his neighbor back to the dwellings. He looked across at the desert horizon as he walked. It was wavey with heat. Leci noted that the return travelers had chosen to face the heat now rather than wait till after the Great Rains. Of course, gourds for carrying water must have made the return crossing much easier than it had been with nothing but stem cactus to chew on.

When Leci saw the foursome who were back from the capital and the eight or so masters who had come back with them—all wearing finely-crafted protective clothing of woven fabric—it gave him the strangest feeling. What a tremendous gap between the primitive existence in the village on the bluff and the extravagant life afforded to the uedin of the capital! Uedin who had arrived at the village had always come in a state of annihilation. Each new one had arrived like a lost child-uedin, sunburned and dying of thirst. So it had been with Jeber, the last to arrive in that fashion. But even Jeber now seemed less like a "new one" and more like a capital master. Furthermore, none of the accompanying masters who had returned with the foursome were anything like new ones. Leci understood that they were not here to stay.

Jeber was talking loudly enough so that Leci could hear him as he drew nearer. "We will need to speak to everyone together," he was saying.

"Well, we are pleased to see you back at any rate," called out Leci, interrupting as he joined them. "We never knew for certain if you managed to cross the desert and reach the capital. But you made it to the capital, and you made it back again!" Leci wanted to praise Jeber, just as he would encourage any new one.

A familiar voice spoke beside him. "Leci, good to see you." Leci looked and saw that it was Pelto—hardly recognizable in the capital-cloth wrappings he wore.

"What are you all carrying?" Leci asked. "You left with a big cargo, and you've come back with twice as much!"

"It's mostly yamflour," said Pelto. Leci thought it odd that they would bring back a large supply of such a staple when they already subsisted quite well on the staple they had right there.

"Were you able to stop the capital childless from their self-killing?" asked Leci's neighbor.

"Yes, we were," said Jeber. It was Jeber who had told all of them about the self-killing and started the talk about taking whitesponge to the capital.

Leci smiled and nodded, hearing the news. "So the white-sponge had the effect we hoped for?" he asked.

"Yes, it did." This time it was Elenn who answered. "But there's more about it that we need to explain—to everyone at once." It was only a handful of childless who were presently there to greet them. Leci was curious to know what might need explaining, but he waited as word was put out for everyone to come, and he remained patient as the childless showed up one by one till all were present. By the time the last few arrived, the travelers had received water and were rested. Gourds—something that the childless had often wished they could cultivate—were given away, and a remarkable treat of dried peaches was being shared.

Finally Elenn got Pelto, Jeber, and Daga to stand with him and face the crowd. Leci had known Pelto from the time he was the new one, and he knew Elenn in the same context. Jeber was the current new one, and Leci knew him hardly at all, but he felt the normal affection and concern that the villagers always felt for new ones. Those others, though, large and strong and wearing masters' robes and white hoods—he felt no special affection for them. It was hard for him to think of them as even being child-less, though he knew enough to understand that their hoods in-dicated it was so, for Elenn had talked about that.

Elenn spoke loudly for everyone to hear. "We have introduced whitesponge to the childless in the capital, and we've given it also to many regular uedin. Our purpose was to stop the childless mas-ters from their self-extermination practice, and we succeeded." The crowd responded with glad voices. Elenn continued, "I'm afraid what I have to tell you next is not going to be easy for you to hear . . . "

Leci thought he knew what was coming, and he spoke up. "It's all right, Elenn. We understand that we are going to have to share whitesponge with the capital. We know that our life here is going to be different."

"It's not just that," said Elenn gravely.

Leci wondered what other troublesome news there could be. "The regular uedin of the capital, those who are not childless— they also want to eat whitesponge, don't they?" he guessed.

"We will use it up quickly!" interjected someone from the crowd with dismay.

"We learned something about the whitesponge," said Elenn loudly, "We learned what it *is*."

"But, there is no whitesponge in the capital," protested Leci's neighbor. "How could they know anything about it there?"

"It was in the central temple that we learned about whitesponge," said Jeber. "Lern Beyana speaks directly through the Most High Server there now."

"Lern Beyana? The Lern knows about whitesponge?" asked another, incredulously.

"What does Lern Beyana say about whitesponge?" asked Leci.

Jeber and Elenn locked eyes, which made Leci wonder what secret they shared.

"Whitesponge is Lern Beyana's substance," he announced abruptly.

Leci saw the perplexed looks on everyone's face, and he shared their confusion.

"What do you mean, 'her substance'?" demanded Yulig whom Leci now noticed standing there.

"Whitesponge is the physical body of the Lern," responded Pelto. "The location of the Lern has never been known in the capital. It has only been known to us—even though we didn't know that it *was* the Lern."

"Whitesponge is the body . . . of Lern Beyana?!" cried Yulig in disbelief. But Leci saw how Yulig's eyes changed as he considered that it might be true, and Leci himself was feeling the challenge of this bizarre and disturbing allegation.

The stunned crowd was silent. Pelto walked up to Yulig and put his arm on his shoulder.

Yulig looked back at him for a long moment, regained his calm, and spoke. "Pelto, tell us everything. Start from the beginning. You left the village with four great packs of whitesponge. How long did it take you to reach the capital?"

Pelto proceeded to tell them everything that had happened, from the time they had left the bluff until that very day. All the childless of the village listened to the full explanation of all that had transpired, they tried to accept the news with the calm that was their legacy. How strange it felt for Leci to cling to a calm which he now understood to be not just the calm of the white-sponge, but the effect of consuming the substance of the Lern.

Two days later, the Great Rains reached the bluff. Leci was alone in his dwelling, just as most of the villagers had gone into solitude to adjust to the news. Hoping to get his mind off the up-setting revelation, he got out the small sack of yamflour that he had been given. It did attract his interest. Leci had not eaten yam gruel for many generations, and the thought of it was titillating.

By the time he had mixed a gruel, he noticed that heavy clouds were covering the desert and the air was getting heavy.

The yam gruel was strangely delicious—a flavor from so long ago Leci had nearly forgotten it. Leci's first thought that he want-ed to add whitesponge to it, but he hesitated. Whitesponge could never again be thought of in quite the same way. He was pondering his own disappointment about that when the first claps of thunder arrived. When he turned to look at the darkening sky, he saw a familiar face appear at the open side of his dwelling. It was Daga.

"Daga!"

"It looks like the Rains are here!" said Daga, stepping in and raising a hand to face.

"Come in, come in!"

"I thought I would like to watch the arrival of Rains with you . . . Is it all right?"

"Of course! I am having a bit of gruel from that capital yam-flour. I was thinking of adding some whitesponge. Will you have some with me?" He scrutinized Daga's face to gauge how casual his regard for whitesponge would be, given the new knowledge about it.

Daga, however, seemed quite oblivious. "Marvelous!" he exclaimed. "A perfect snack for watching the Rains come in!" Leci was surprised by this comment, and even more surprised when Daga reached around him and stole a little piece of whitesponge and popped it into his mouth. "We ran out, you know . . . " said Daga, "The last few weeks at the capital we were completely without whitesponge. I was so glad to get back!"

"So you went some days with no whitesponge at all? How did it make you feel to be without it?"

"Well I'm more interested in whitesponge than yam gruel, I'll tell you that much."

"Daga, you seem to take it lightly," commented Leci with the first sign of impatience. "How can you not see what is happening . . . We're losing our whitesponge. We knew we would have to share it with the childless ones stranded in the capital, but now that we're sharing it with the whole capital . . . It's going to be gone in a novade. This news about it actually being the substance of Lern Beyana—it's not good news for us."

"I was afraid it might be perceived that way," said Daga.

"Well, how else are we supposed to perceive it?" asked Leci with a shrug. "We will lose the peace of mind that whitesponge has always given us. Without it, what future will we face?"

Daga nodded in understanding. "I know, Leci. I went many days without whitesponge, and I was forced to imagine a future without it. But we have no choice. I try to remember one thing that the Most High Server told us. He said that the Lern's substance will *be enough*."

Leci closed his eyes and shook his head slowly. "It's just so inconceivable that our whitesponge has been the substance of Lern Beyana all this time." He scrunched his face in displeasure.

"Leci, it was the Lern who called the childless to this place from the beginning. It was her will that we should subsist for all these generations by eating whitesponge, *her substance*. But now her will is that it be given to all uedin. We must understand that."

"Yes," said Leci, but he wasn't sure that he understood anything at all.

Later, they sat in desert-watching and observed the advance of the rain. Leci acknowledged to himself that the bowl of gruel and whitesponge had filled his stomach and was now calming his mind. He and Daga didn't make eye contact. The band of rain at the desert's horizon made its way toward them, approaching with a slow steadiness. By the time rain actually fell at the open wall of the dwelling, there was no more visibility of the desert, but the two continued to stare into the falling shower for a long time.

Daga shouted over the drumming of rain, "Now that the Rains have arrived, it will be many days before the caravan can return to the capital with its first load of whitesponge. I'm not planning to go back. But I think you should go with them."

Leci thought about this, but listened to the rain for a few seconds before answering. "Me?" he shouted back, "Why should I go to the capital?"

"All of us who are able must take our turns visiting the capital," said Daga. "I think it's important for us to understand that all uedin are working cooperatively now."

Leci was quiet for a long time, staring again into the rain. Finally he asked, "How long do you think it will be before another caravan comes?"

"It won't take as long now to go and come back, and it won't be as hard. We have gourds for carrying water, and the caravan is going to be making constant trips. Anyway, you have time to think about it."

As Leci continued to gaze into the rainfall, he thought not so much about going to the capital. What mattered more to him was what Daga attributed to the Most High Server at the capital's central temple. The whitesponge, the Most High had said, would *be enough*. That was the promise that everything hung on.

A Generation All Barren

Goril tried to ignore the superstitious talk that had been going around the capital since the Great Rains. Wetuedin had descended, but only into one pool. The hatching pools at Bells, Bramble, Whiteroof—all of them were empty. Only Quarterhouse had received wetuedin, and it appeared there were less than sixty. He sat on a small bench beside Ferin. They were on the feeding platform below the observation deck at the Quarterhouse hatching pool. As Ferin readied the test kit for the next wetuedin, Goril put a mark in a notebook, closed it, and put it under the bench. Master Ferin had insisted that it would be better to do the syndrome testing themselves instead of assigning other medics, and now Goril understood why. The results of the testing were uniform in their indication. Every one of the wetuedin was testing positive for syndrome. It was not an assignment they would have wanted to pass on to other medics—too disturbing. Yet the worrisome implications were somehow less upsetting to Goril than he might have expected. It was because of the effect of the Substance.

The team of caretakers there to assist with catching the wetuedin likewise seemed to maintain calm, even though Ferin and Goril were letting them know results as each was tested, and they were aware that not a single one had yet been found to be unafflicted.

"Ready for another one?" Goril asked.

"Go ahead," said Ferin, prompting two caretakers to step down into the hatching pool and wade to the ends of a net stretched

232

across the pool. Goril stood up to watch them work. Master Benar was directing the other caretakers. Benar was well-known to Goril as well as most of the staff at the infirmary. He had obviously petitioned to oversee this operation, even though his primary role as caretaker to hooded masters usually kept him in other parts of the capital. He didn't seem very well accustomed to the routines of the hatching pool. Goril thought Master Benar looked a little awkward, keeping his robe on while wading in the water. The regular hatching pool caretakers were a humble bunch, deferring to their guest supervisor with great patience and courtesy.

Goril's thought was interrupted by Ferin, who quietly commented on the awful results they were seeing. "When we're done here, we should go directly to Central to report to Master Embal. The council might ask us to put the findings into a medical perspective."

"We're not done yet, Master Ferin," said Goril, trying to sound positive. "We've only tested half of them." It seemed a more suitable thing to say than what he was really thinking. What point was there in trying to come up with a medical perspective, when it was the end of uedin life they were talking about? If the entire generation turned out to be barren, what reason was there to think that the embryo carried by Goril himself was not also going to produce a barren uedin? Capital society still looked upon the hooded masters as an afflicted minority, but in truth, everyone might as well be considered a barren-carrier. They were all looking at the end of their lineage.

Benar was up to his knees in water with his hands on his hips, giving directions. "Move the net a little further over," he called to them. "This end is getting crowded with wetuedin." The net was being used to separate the pre-test and post-test groups of wetuedin. The gentle masters complied, lifting the weighted ends of the net and moving it gradually along to give more of the pool to those already tested while clustering the rest for easier access. "A little more . . . a little more . . . There. Leave it right there. That should be good." Wetuedin swam from both sides to look at one another through the net.

Ferin finally responded, "Well, Master Goril, it's true, we've only tested half. There still could be some fertile wetuedin in there."

As the medic masters watched, four more caretakers stepped down into the pool. The water was about chest high for them. Goril had imagined that the large, developed wetuedin would be difficult to handle, but caretakers were obviously used to doing it. The wetuedin did not race away from them; on the contrary they swam toward them, no doubt expecting to receive a treat. The caretakers handled them with familiarity, gently nudging wetuedin aside as they moved to form a square. They waited for a wetuedin to come to them. "This one looks ready," said one of the caretakers, placing his hands on the two sides of a wetuedin's head, framing its little face.

"Have you got one? Careful you don't scratch!" warned Benar.

The others huddled around the wetuedin. Two placed their hands on its upper torso, and the other two gently placed their hands on its lower torso as it floated cooperatively for them.

"You're a nice little wetty, aren't you?" said one of the caretakers affectionately.

"That one looks a bit smaller . . . Looks like a normal wetuedin to me," said Benar to voice his own hope.

They brought the docile wetuedin in a glide across the surface to the edge, where they then secured their footing on the rocks of the bank and proceeded to lift it up out of the water. The wetuedin wiggled slightly but did not fight to be let go.

"Careful, . . . careful!" said Benar, remaining knee deep as the others rose up out of the pool. The two caretakers who had hold of the lower torso let go, and the other two adjusted their hands to carry it securely. Goril thought that Benar really had no reason to be in the pool at all, since he could just as easily direct the others from the feeding platform, and he looked silly standing there knee-deep with the bottom of his robe in the water. Apparently Benar thought it was an important part of his job to be down there in the pool.

"Here we come! Here we come!" said the same caretaker, talking in the manner used by caretakers when they worked with very young child-uedin. "Now the medic masters are just going to have a little look at you. Nothing to worry about." They carried the wetuedin, wiggling its tail again, over to the small table on the platform, covered with layers of wet towels.

Benar was balancing on a submerged rock, moving his feet in tiny steps to turn and face the platform. "Yes, that one looks very healthy," he said, then added, in the lingo of the hatching pool caretakers, " . . . Cute little *wetty!*'"

The medics wasted no time. Goril held the wetuedin in position with the back of its head in place to expose the bulge that would someday be its skullwomb. Ferin used a small glass instrument to make a tiny incision at the low edge of the bulge. The wetuedin came to life and wiggled with fear and surprise, and it made a raspy, sputtering little cry. The caretakers were immediately ready to quickly return it to the pool, while Ferin squeezed a small piece of cloth around the tip of the instrument to absorb the drop of clear sap he had collected.

"It's all right, that didn't hurt too bad, now, did it?" The caretakers tried to lower it slowly into the post-test section of the pool, but the wetuedin wiggled hard and escaped them before they could manage their gentle release. If flopped into the water with a loud splash, and the surface of the pool broke into big ripples.

"CAREFUL!" cried Benar, and he lost his footing on the rock and slipped right down into the deep water, going completely under.

"Oh, Master Benar!" cried one of the caretakers. They watched to see if he was all right.

Benar came up out of the water, his robe undone and hanging wet and askew on his shoulders. As soon as he got his bearings, he took in a breath and forcefully spit, ejecting a stream of water along with a projectile, a small, dark, wad of something.

Oh my, thought Goril, was that a . . . ? Yes, it was. Master Benar had just spit out a wetuedin's turd that had gotten in his mouth! *Uff . . . How unpleasant!*

Benar had spit out the unwelcome mouthful, but he continued to spit as if there were more to get rid of. "Blegh!" he said, giving his head a shake and making an awful face.

Goril looked around to see if the others had seen what he had seen. They had. Ferin looked embarrassed, his eyes indicating awkward discomfort. One of the hatching pool caregivers looked like he was trying to suppress a smile. Goril spoke up, "Are you all right, Master Benar?"

Benar quickly resumed his expression of supervisory pomposity and sighed impatiently while he adjusted the wet robe on his arms and shoulders. "Oh, I'm just fine," he said. "That rock was very slippery."

Goril quickly discerned that no mention was going to be made of the turd. Master Benar was such a peculiar master.

"Let's see what we have here," said Ferin, redirecting Goril's attention to the small piece of cloth which he had moments earlier let soak up the drop of sap, the wetuedin's sample. He used a tiny straw get a drop of the testing solution from a small cup, and he let it drip over the sample. Goril knew that any hint of metabolized skullsap, the evidence of fertility, would cause the sample to turn yellow when exposed to the testing solution. His eyes hoped for yellow, but the white swab only stayed white. The wetuedin was barren. Another one.

By midday, the testing was complete. Goril and Ferin walked back to the infirmary without speaking. They were both absorbing the fact that all fifty-three wetuedin were barren. It was the smallest generation on record, and there was not one fertile among its members. Goril had started thinking about the depressing implications of a completely barren generation early during the testing, and at this point he was starting to consider another aspect of their reality. He was now pondering the good fortune of having the Substance to lend a sense of calm to a situation of doom. It was that calm that they all relied on now. The time had passed for questioning whether it was prudent to let their minds be sedated. He, along with Ferin and so many distinguished masters of the capital, had struggled with that question and ultimately come to accept the Substance as a gift from Lern Beyana that could not be refused. Who would have known that Lern Beyana would give them her Substance just in time to help them face their extinction with dignity?

Tilke Awakens to a Much-Changed World

For a period that seemed to have no beginning, there was nothing, no thought, not even a sense of being in time. At some point there was dreaming, and he had a flash of awareness—*I am having a dream*. But the dream was stronger than the flicker of self-consciousness, and it swept him along. In it, Tilke sat in a room in the paper mill, having lived his life as a paper master, and inspected two large samples. One was the yellowish white color of the over-bleached server wrappings, and the other was the unmistakable washed-out green of masters who served in the capital guard. He was confused. Was it paper dyed to match the two common colors of cloth, or was he in fact looking at cloth? He heard a voice coming from behind the yellowish-white sheet. It was the voice of the old ro server with whom Tilke had played shell-toss in his early years at the temple. "Haha!" said the old server's voice, full of fun. "There's a root hook at you! Now try to beat that one, young server!" Tilke felt affection grow in him, and it was love for the piece of yellowish-white fabric. "I've got you now!" said the voice, and Tilke felt very happy, amused by the glee in the voice of the old ro. He spoke to the piece of cloth, saying, "Yes you have. You've beaten me."

Then another voice spoke—actually, it yelled. It came from behind the washed-out green sheet. It was the very young voice of an ancient friend, from a time when he was newly-named and hadn't yet entered the temple. The youthful voice yelled, "I'm not joining the servers! I'm going to join the guards at the Flatpools

District station! I've already made my choice—there's nothing you can do about it!" Tilke remembered the name. Elenn. He was angry because Elenn had promised to go with him to the temple. He answered back in anger, "You've rejected the Soft One. Your ideas are terribly twisted. You're the most namely one of all." As soon as he said it, he sensed a deep and immeasurable sadness coming from the piece of green cloth, and he was immediately sorry for his harsh words. "Tilke... you'll be a great server! Tilke, I'm so proud of you!" said the voice through the sorrow of the green.

Then Tilke spoke back to the voice, sympathetically, "Why don't we go in one another's place? I don't care so much about becoming a server, and you want that more than anything else in the world. I'll report to the capital guards and say my name is Elenn. You can report to the temple and say your name is Tilke. We still look so alike, they won't know the difference! It can be an act of unnameliness for us!"

"It's too late for that," said the youthful voice from the green cloth.

"Why?"

"They got you, Tilke. They got you with the root hook."

For a moment, Tilke looked back at the yellowish-white paper. It was silent now, and it was paper. And the washed-out green fabric was turned back into paper as well. A second of confusion served as a reminder that he was dreaming. A feeling of importance suddenly propelled him to consciousness, and he opened his eyes. What had woken him? It was the absurd thought that a game of shell-toss played well after his arrival at the temple had somehow pulled a string through time and retroactively sealed his fate. It was the nonsense of it that jolted him from sleep. As he surmised his location in the Most High residence of the central chamber, his reality came back to him. He looked at the dimly lit ceiling and the corner where it met a bare wall. His body felt terribly stiff and sore. How long had he been lying here? It must have been days! The last thing he remembered was talking to his primary advisor. Then he was struck with a horrible realization. The Soft One—she was gone! The chill of her absence came upon him like a submersion into cold water

He spoke hoarsely, and the rasp of his voice broke the quiet of the room. "The Soft One . . . She is gone," he said. The sound of hurried footsteps came closer, and one of the assistants to the Most High was suddenly looking down at him with great surprise and excitement.

"Most High," said the server, "You're awake!"

Another assistant spoke. "What did he say? The Soft One is gone?"

"Warm some soup of the Substance!" said the assistant standing over him. "I'll go get the primary advisor!"

Tilke quickly decided that he must not be too quick to announce the death the Soft One around these assistants. They were going to get the primary advisor—good. The primary advisor was clever and would know what to do. Tilke so wished he had done a better job of following the primary advisor's suggestion to safeguard his own health. If he had remained strong, surely he would have been able to support the Soft One better and maybe kept her alive . . . He had failed. He had failed as Most High, and the Soft One had perished under his care. He closed his eyes and surrendered to grief and regret.

The primary advisor arrived. Tilke was sipping. from a straw. It was a warm milky liquid that seemed somehow familiar, but he had no clear recollection of where or when he had tasted it before. Tilke looked up at the primary advisor and discerned the look of caution on his face.

"Most High . . . ," said the primary advisor, "Are you . . . ?"

Tilke was weak and in pain from the stiffness. Now he could feel that he seemed to have sores on his body from lying in place. "Primary advisor," he said weakly, "How long have I been lying here?"

The primary advisor's face changed when he heard the question. There was hesitation in his response. "Most High, what do you remember? When is the last time you remember seeing me?"

"I don't know . . . Wasn't it in the vapors chamber? You said the high servers want to announce high rule. Are we in high rule?"

"We were in high rule for some time, Most High. But we are not in high rule now."

"Then has Namestaking already happened?"

"Yes, Most High. Namestaking happened a long time ago, and the Great Rains has come and gone. We are in the first year of the new generation."

Tilke was silent for a long time, considering the length of his coma. He finally spoke, "Primary advisor, I must tell you . . . my communion . . . I'm very sorry, but I feel I must tell you right away. The Soft One . . . she is . . . "

"Gone," supplied the primary advisor in a gentle voice. "We know."

"She is completely gone. I had such a strong communion with her—I can tell that she has died."

"We were aware of her passing away."

"I'm afraid I wasn't persistent enough with my wellness regimen. I'm afraid I have failed as your most high."

"You did not fail, Most High. The Soft One has been speaking through you. Almost the whole time that you can't remember, since we spoke in the vapors chamber—she was speaking through you to us right to the end.

"Speaking through me?"

"Yes. She occupied your body and face, and she borrowed your voice."

"And you're sure it was the Soft One? It wasn't just me in a state of delirium?"

"No, Most High. The Soft One knew things that you do not know."

"Like what?"

"There is a great deal, Most High. The substance of her body was brought to the capital before the Great Rains." The primary advisor spoke slowly, and Tilke wasn't sure he was hearing correctly. "She identified it as her substance, and she instructed us to consume it."

"What? What do you mean?" Surely he was misunderstanding the primary advisor's words.

"Her body, Most High. It was already being harvested before we knew what it was."

"The body of the Soft One was discovered? Where?"

"It was known only to a small colony of uedin with barren syndrome. They have been migrating to the place where it rests, and they've formed a village around it for many generations."

"Did the masters know about it?"

"Shortly before the Great Rains, a group of uedin arrived in the capital who claimed that they had been living in caves on the far side of the eastern desert. They brought something they called 'whitesponge.' It is what you have in your bowl."

"This?!" Tilke looked at his bowl with a mixture of horror and curiosity. Could it be? Could this really come from the physical body of the Soft One? And he was eating it?

"The Soft One spoke—through *you*. She knew that the barren uedin were in the capital with whitesponge, and she asked for one of them, a barren guard master by the name of Elenn. He is one of the ones who came from the unknown village."

"*Elenn*?" Tilke repeated the name in wonder. He had just dreamed of his childhood friend.

"I'm sorry, Most High, it was careless of me to say a master's name . . . "

"No, I don't mind the use of a name. The Soft One isn't here to shrink from it anymore. But you say the master's name was *Elenn*?"

"Yes. I believe he was a guard from the Flatpools District and was renowned in the capital for working closely with barren masters. He was here. He spoke to you . . . or at least to the Soft One, within you."

"Primary advisor, did I—did the Soft One ask for Master Elenn specifically?"

"Well, she asked for the returned master who was a capital guard. Master Elenn was the only one who fit that description."

"And what did the Soft One need to tell Master Elenn?"

"The Soft One told Master Elenn that whitesponge was her 'substance.' That's what she called it."

"Her *substance* . . . " repeated Tilke thoughtfully.

"She said that the purpose of 'dear ones with no lives in their wombs'—that's what she calls the barren—was to be her keepers and to deliver her substance to the capital. She said it must be consumed until it is completely gone."

Tilke was deeply troubled and perplexed by this report. The fact that *Elenn* had been requested made him wonder if everything being described was a product of his own mind, false speech attributed to the One who does not speak. But he had to believe it was true and not a concoction of delirium. He knew that the Soft One had sustained a definite, palpable presence within him. He did not imagine her. Now she was gone—he could feel that, too. And the arrival of the Substance to the capital at the time of the Soft One's passing away was too remarkable for coincidence.

"So the *Substance*," said Tilke, "If it was called whitesponge, is that what it looks like? White sponge?"

"Yes, it is a soft and spongy material. It seems to have a very consistent texture. It doesn't seem to have any kind of lumps or veins in it. It's very strange."

"Is it being delivered as the Soft One instructed?"

"Yes, Most High. Caravans have been practically non-stop. The masters have an enormous appetite for the Substance, and we consume a great deal of it in the temple as well. It has a calming effect on everyone. You are surely experiencing its benefit. We've been giving it to you every day."

"How much is there? Surely it will be consumed very quickly," said Tilke with concern. "Shouldn't we conserve it?"

"Yes, we must," said the primary advisor, and he drew nearer. "There is more to tell you, Most High. The Soft One was communicating, through you, until very recently. The last time she spoke was just days ago. She had me write down her final instructions."

"What are the instructions?"

"I will let you read what I transcribed. I have shown this to nobody." The primary advisor took a scroll from the pocket of his wrappings. He opened it and held it for Tilke to read. It was written in the primary advisor's own hasty but legible handwriting.

Instruction to my dear ones.

I will now sleep, and I will not wake up again. You may remember me when you eat my substance. However, it must be rationed very sparingly from now on, for it must last two novades. When my substance is nearly all harvested, the dear ones who carry no life may come to the deep place of my old organs from when I first developed, and there they may find my Kernel. It is the embryo of my offspring, and my dear ones who carry no life may deliver it to a new home to let it live as I have lived, in closeness with dear ones. Only one dear one who carries life may join, and that is the dear one whom you have called Most High. Together, you may find a place which resembles your home. It must have its own lake and its own high place, and it must be where streams from the lake can reach it, and where my offspring can achieve communion from the high place. Once your new home is found, the first task of the dear ones who carry no life will be to go to the high place, climb to half its height, and there dig a deep hole into the ground. The depth is what you dear ones would measure as one hundred and forty hand-lengths. When the depth is reached, my kernel must be lodged at the very bottom and then the hole filled in. From there the dear ones who carry no life may go to the place in the middle where the lake streams reach, and they may wait for him whom you have called Most High to come into ecstasy. When he whom you have called Most High receives guidance from my offspring for his journey to the lake, you may know that my offspring has awoken and your new Lern will be with you. Our kinds have repeated this cooperative survival for many eons. But nature does not guarantee our survival. The most important thing for all dear ones to remember is that our kinds survive on our mutual love, and if we perish we will at least perish with the comfort of our mutual love. So I say goodbye to you, my dear ones. Thank you for being my dear ones. Great is my hope for our kinds, and great is my comfort in our love. My hope is great, and my comfort is great.

Tilke read it carefully, stopping many times to reread a line or two. He finally finished, and he closed his eyes. "Primary advisor," he said, in practically a whisper, "I cannot be the Most High anymore. The Soft One is gone, and all of this is too much for me. There is nothing I can say to the high servers, or any servers in the temple. I just . . . I . . . "

"It is all right for you to feel that way," said Nekur. "We will all have to find a different way to understand ourselves. We can hardly be servers anymore, with no Soft One to be our center of attention. But you *are* our Most High. And I am your primary advisor."

"What must we do? Who is to see this paper?" When he said the word "paper," he thought of the dream he had had just before waking, the dream of the talking sheets of paper that turned into two different colored fabrics.

"We can share it first with the high servers . . . " Nekur was starting to say, but Tilke's mind had already moved ahead.

"We must call Master Elenn of the capital guards. We will share it first with Master Elenn."

"That can certainly be arranged, Most High."

Tilke paused and then reached for the bowl. He brought it close to his face and directed the straw to his mouth. He took a sip and felt a humility that was like no unnameliness he had ever felt before.

Part 4

A NEW LAKE TO FIND

The Last Generation

Elenn and Nehu were walking through the outvillage of Redrock, heading out to the nearby mudpools to visit Hela's memorial. They passed several longhouses which were alive with the sounds of the young server-masters unpacking.

"I never imagined I would be so glad to smell the smell of uedin urine around Redrock," said Nehu. Elenn knew it meant he was glad to see the outvillage filled with population. Elenn was fascinated by Nehu. He recalled the time when Nehu gave him such discomfort because Elenn was attracted to him, back when Elenn had come to the outvillage the first time, novades ago. Now the attraction was transformed into admiration and respect. Nehu was obviously a leader in the Redrock community, and he bore his rank with great style. Redrock had become a regular training ground and secondary residence for the server-master generation which had grown up in Elenn and Tilke's care.

"Redrock had a big population many novades ago, didn't it?" asked Elenn.

"Our peak was one hundred ninety, many generations ago, long before any of us here took leg. We are used to empty buildings. But now when the server-masters come, the outvillage fills up again. It's something none of us ever imagined."

"They love coming to Redrock. They talk about it all the time, how they miss the mineral springs, how Redrock has the best ballroot pickles . . . They look forward to coming back every year."

"This year is very different for us," said Nehu, "since the server-masters have received names."

"How quickly they've grown up," commented Elenn.

"And they're in hoods!"

"The masters council took our recommendation. Server Tilke and I have been given very wide authority with most matters involving the new generation. Server Tilke's primary advisor has been a great advocate for us."

"And the young server-masters have accepted the wearing of hoods, even though they haven't been given catheters yet?"

"We don't think they'll ever need catheters. They are like the Childless of the bluff. As long as they have the Substance to keep them out of derangement, there should be no need for catheters."

"Why the hoods, then?"

"They wanted to take hood. The hooded masters have mentored them very closely since their taking of leg. They don't take the oath—they just wear the hoods to honor their mentors. They take them off when they practice the exercises, for example."

"I think it's wonderful that this special generation has been raised by masters and servers together. And in the same way that they honor you hooded masters when they wear hoods, we also feel honored when they wear our Redrock robes. We only expect the server-masters to wear them during their mooncycle with us. We want them to know they always have a home here."

Elenn liked the orangish color of the dyed cloth worn in Redrock. "The Redrock robes look very fine on the server-masters."

"We're very thankful to you and High Server Tilke for bringing them to us every year. It has brought life back to Redrock. Even though they only come for a mooncycle, we spend the whole year preparing for them. It was a joy to produce the robes for them . . . fifty-eight of them."

"Well, they seem delighted to wear them."

"Just while they are here," said Nehu, "It is a point of great pride for us to see them wearing our cloth."

"The server-masters are not like the uedin of other generations. I know it has not always been easy to handle them. But now that they have taken name, they are maturing quickly."

"We've loved having them while they were unnamed. Redrock little ones have always been a bit wild compared to the child-uedin at capital domiciles, so we've never felt any trouble. But I agree, they seem very grown up now with their names and their hoods. I'm excited to see a demonstration of that 'laddering' exercise they've taken up. It sounds quite amazing."

Elenn had come back to Redrock many times since they had started bringing the server-master child-uedin there for extended training sessions as soon as they were able to make the trip. The afternoon walk to Hela's memorial happened each time. It was always with great reverence and recollection that they hiked to the mudpools.

"The Great Rains were abundant last year. We've had more greenery around Redrock than I ever remember. Wait till you see how vegetation has grown up around the mudpools. We had to trim around the memorial to keep it from getting overgrown."

Elenn didn't comment on the Great Rains. The capital was lush with greenery as well, but the failure of any wetuedin to arrive was a subject of deep dismay. Uedin history had a few incidences of climate disasters when the season came for Great Rains but hardly any rain fell at all—the infamous "failed novades." But never had there been anything like what had happened at the end of the recent novade. The year after the server-masters took name, rain arrived in horrendous magnitude, causing Great Rains rivers to swell and flood the outfields and turn the northeast marsh into a lake. But not a single wetuedin arrived in the capital. Lern Beyana's Instruction told them that survival was not guaranteed by nature, and the absence of wetuedin at the Great Rains was a frightening reminder of that truth. Despite the hopeful message of the Instruction, there was great doubt in the capital about the future of uedin life.

They walked in silence the remainder of the way until the now familiar scene of the mudpools and memorial came into view. As always, it brought back a flood of memories. The colors of the hot muds were now familiar, but seeing them always gave Elenn the sensation of being back in time. He immediately located the bluish mudpool where he had once taken refuge from wasps with the two Redrock child-uedin under his arms. Not far from it, marking the spot where Hela had died protecting the third child-uedin, stood a small but beautiful memorial of carved redrock and inlaid tin with the inscription: Let Us Remember Hela, Flatpools Guard Master Who Gave Up His Passing To Save Our Child-Uedin.

For some reason, a pang of sadness and love for Master Hela made Elenn think immediately of the Instruction, particularly the last line, *"MY HOPE IS GREAT, AND MY COMFORT IS GREAT."* It was hope and comfort that Elenn clung to, and he saw Hela's death as having served great purpose. Elenn's friendship with Hela was one of the very important friendships of his life. That fateful day had been a turning point for him; it was after that that he had made the choice to accept life as a barren uedin.

He looked around at the mudpools. The paint-like mud produced delayed, blooping bubbles that disturbed the surface with peculiar slowness. Elenn remembered how the hot mud had burned his skin and how he had hugged the two child-uedin tightly as if he might protect them from scalding by wrapping himself around them.

Elenn stood in silence for a long time, remembering Hela and thinking about the dark times uedin now faced. He finally looked up to see that Nehu was respectfully waiting for him to break the silence.

"Redrock has created a beautiful memorial here," Elenn finally said, returning his gaze to the carved and inlaid piece.

"We will never forget Master Hela," said Nehu. "And we will always be grateful to you, too, Master Elenn. The three who were saved that day have grown into fine uedin. All three of them are very dedicated to our work with the server-masters now."

"Yes, I've met them, and they are fine uedin indeed," said Elenn. "They've even come to visit me in the capital."

Elenn spent a long time in somber observation, then finally looked around one more time and said, "Thank you, Master Nehu for walking with me today. I think Server Tilke will be arriving soon. Shall we head back to the meeting house?"

The return walk to the outvillage had a brisker pace, and Elenn's mind shifted back to his immediate supervisory concerns. When they reached the outvillage, they saw that a group of servers were just arriving. A team of server experts in all the various exercises had been invited to lead an extended training session for the server-masters during their Redrock retreat. The team were gathered outside the meeting hall, talking to a small welcoming party of outvillagers and several of the young server-masters. Elenn took notice of the tall and heavy-bodied server-masters in their Redrock garb—how quickly they had grown to such size! They stood with a few normally-statured outvillagers in similar orangish robes and talked with the newly arrived server guests in white. Among the servers stood the small frame of a figure in server garb who looked about the size of a normal child-uedin soon to be named. The small one was Tilke. He was immediately recognizable by his stunted size, a distinction now associated with great respect inside and outside the temple compound.

Nehu, wishing to excuse Elenn to go talk with the servers, raised hands to face in the embellished manner that was customary in the outvillage, and Elenn returned the distinctive Redrock hands-to-face.

"Server Tilke," he called, and smiled broadly as he repeated the special hands-to-face to greet him.

Tilke gazed on Elenn with a smile that lingered long enough to make his own return greeting seem rudely slow. Tilke was in a world of his own, Elenn knew, because of his long communion with Lern Beyana before she passed.

"The server-masters bring their names to Redrock," said Tilke, recognizing their purpose for being there.

"Yes, Server Tilke, and the outvillagers are very excited to have them here."

"We did well to make Redrock part of the server-masters' lives," he said, sounding like a ro.

"And you've brought the exercise teachers from the temple . . . " said, Elenn, inviting Tilke to introduce them.

"These are the servers who've come with me this time; they have great expertise to share." Tilke held up a hand to present them but did not introduce any of them by name. Some server traditions did not go away.

"Except the new *laddering*," said one of the servers. "None of us can coach the server-masters on that."

"*Laddering* is very much a fruit of all the exercises," responded Tilke, "as well as a meditation on the Instruction." Tilke was considerably more at ease about the dangerous new exercise than Elenn was. The assurance of mind that was the gift of the Substance be as it may, Elenn was aware of a great risk of accident whenever he witnessed the laddering exercise, and he could not shake it from his mind. But the hooded masters were passionately enthusiastic in their support of laddering, and Tilke expressed nothing but approval.

"Come," said Nehu to the whole group, "We have milkgrass tea ready for everyone." The group shuffled toward the longhouse. Elenn waited to walk in last with Tilke.

256

In a slow and drawn out voice that reminded Elenn again of ro-uedin, Tilke said ponderingly, "Ah, milkgrass tea. We will have milkgrass tea now. After a very long walk through the salt flats."

The longhouse interior was beset with tiny mirrors on all wall and ceiling surfaces, creating the gorgeous lighting that Elenn so admired. A few server-masters were there to serve tea in their Redrock robes while the elder outvillagers looked on with pride and delight. Nehu sat with Elenn and Tilke.

"How is Master Jeber doing? I thought he and some of the other hooded masters might be coming with the server contingent."

"Master Jeber and the others send their regrets," said Elenn. "They are very busy with the harvesting and caravan."

"The precious Substance," said Tilke, providing an unnecessary reminder, "They harvest it on the bluff of the Childless and bring it to the capital."

"And from the capital we receive it also," said Nehu, demonstrating patience with Tilke's foggy state of mind.

"Yes, you also have the Substance here at Redrock, don't you?" affirmed Tilke.

"We do. We get an annual ration every year when the server-masters come."

"It is a great gift from the Soft One," said Tilke. Elenn was used to hearing Tilke refer to Lern Beyana as the Soft One, and he knew that Nehu understood too.

"As is the Instruction," said Nehu.

"Yes, the Instruction is also a great gift," said Tilke, and he let his head fall forward in surrender to the very thought of it.

"Are any of the Childless living in the capital these days, or have they all returned to the bluff?" asked Nehu.

"Pelto is back and forth. He spends a lot of time at the capital with the server-masters," said Elenn.

"Do the server-masters call him 'Pelto' also?" asked Nehu.

"Yes," said Elenn. "The Childless all go by their plain names to everyone, including the server-masters."

"Speaking of names, have you learned the names of many of the server-masters yet? They are still young and resemble one another. I may have a bit of trouble telling them apart until they get a little older."

"It's a matter of hearing a name many times . . . " said Elenn, and it occurred to him to glance at the server-master who was just pouring tea. "What is one's name, young server-master?" he asked.

In the instant that the youth was about to share his name, Elenn noticed that this was a young server-master whose face, he thought, looked somewhat familiar—suggesting that Elenn had noticed him before. He had a headstrong, enthusiastic look to him.

"I am Wido," said the youth, bringing one hand to face while the other held the teapot. He smiled with no sign of nervousness.

Tilke smiled back thoughtfully. Elenn noticed his nuanced expression and understood that it would always be somewhat awkward for Tilke, as a server, to deal with names.

Nehu repeated the name. "Server-master *Wido*." It seemed to Elenn that Nehu was trying to commit the name to memory. It said a lot that Nehu, a Redrock outvillager who was only going to see the server-masters one moon cycle out of the year, felt already compelled to remember individual names. Yet the server-master generation did seem to win the affection of everyone—capital dweller, Childless of the bluff, or outvillager. Nehu continued with a tender regard, "You all seem to have settled in nicely. And you all look very fine in the robes."

"We're so honored to have these robes," answered Wido.

"I'm looking forward to tomorrow's program," said Nehu, addressing Wido along with the others at his table. "I can't wait to see a laddering exercise."

The disturbing laddering exercise was being mentioned again. Elenn asked, "Are you on the team for tomorrow's laddering, Server-master Wido?"

"Yes. It's my turn to climb tomorrow." Wido smiled with a slightly embarrassed look, anticipating the attention that such a confession would bring.

"You'll be climbing!" said Tilke with awe. Wido laughed with humility.

"I've never made it to the highest rung. Tomorrow I think I will." Wido looked confident. Elenn felt a nagging disapproval. He had seen server-masters fall from the higher rungs before. They were always caught by the spotters on their team, but it always appeared to him that injury was only a matter of time.

"I'll be watching with great interest, Server-master Wido," said Nehu.

Tilke took a noisy sip of the tea. "I love the milkgrass tea here at Redrock," he said, "it's sweeter than what we drink in the compound."

Elenn needed to talk to Tilke sometime soon about the laddering. What was the real impulse behind it? Was it really just a fruit of the all the other exercises?

Elenn and Tilke were awoken before sunrise the next morning by the sound of droning coming from the village center. The droning of the server-master voices had a distinguished quality. It was deeper and rounder than the usual buzz of a dronings from uedin of previous generations. By the time Elenn and Tilke went out to observe them in training, they had finished their droning and were already engaged in shifting exercises. The server-masters would never have the flexibility of the wiry servers who excelled in shifting, but their strength and bulk brought drama to the spectacle of their shiftings, and

Elenn found it very moving to behold. Their muscles bulged and looked about to pop as they forced their large frames into the impossible poses. Elenn was glad to see the server experts praising them heavily for poses which Elenn knew probably would have drawn scorn in regular server training. He and Tilke watched in silence.

Elenn had always known feelings of tenderness toward younger generations. He was now fifth generation. He thought about the Redrock child-uedin whom he and Hela managed to save from death, how he had been overwhelmed with protective love for them. They were of the generation that followed Elenn's own, the one whose newly-named he had come to get acquainted with for the first time when he met first Jutef, then Nula. The generation that followed that one was the one that had many who took leg at the Quarterhouse flatpool where a deranged barren uedin had killed himself. Though Elenn tried not to, he often recalled the fact that some from that generation had eaten the fingers and nose of the dead barren floating in the flatpool. Elenn had had little contact with them during his years of duty with the hood squadron, but now he was learning how they reflected a great change in uedin attitude toward the barren, having one in four of their own numbers in hood. Many of them had spent their apprenticeship period in dedicated service to the new server-master generation, their immediate juniors.

The newly-named server-master generation was, to Elenn, in a category by itself. Elenn felt a fierce protective instinct and love for the server-masters. Of course it was because he and Tilke were given authority in providing for their needs. There was no way to really prepare them for their uncertain destiny, and Elenn often felt lost about how to best nurture and train them. Tilke seemed much more at ease about the whole thing. Elenn looked over to see him watching the server-masters' shifting practice with a look of contentment.

The shifting practice ended, and the server-masters positioned themselves around a space and gazed at the central bit of ground in an imitation of desert-watching as taught by the Childless of the bluff. A group of four server-masters slowly brought the ladder pieces toward the spot in the middle. They had shed their robes and removed their hoods for the exercise. The ladder pieces consisted of two very long poles of sturdy hollowstem into which slots had been carved, and a large net bag of wooden slats. The bag was over the shoulder of one of the server-masters, and two pairs of server-masters brought two poles as they ceremoniously carried the pieces forth.

Elenn quickly picked out Wido from among the four. Wido let go of his end of the pole, as did the server-master holding the bag, and the other two raised the poles to a vertical position and held them close together. The bag-holder crouched a bit off to the side and rested with one hand holding the edge of the bag and the other on a slat. Wido, as climber, stood in silence in front of the two standing poles.

Elenn glanced at Tilke to see his expression. Tilke was clearly enjoying it. Sometimes Elenn felt a bit impatient with Tilke for lacking concern when there was an appropriate reason to *have* concern. His novades in the temple seemed to have given him an indifference to things.

"Remembrance!" shouted the server-master holding the bag, and he tossed one of the slats to Wido. Wido caught the slat and repeated, *"Remembrance!"*

They all watched as Wido placed the slat into the lowest slots of the poles, forming the first rung. He held on to it with his hand and gave it a short forward twist. The slat snapped into place. Wido's shoulder muscles could be seen bulging as he used his strength to hold the locked rung and stabilize the two verticle poles while the server-masters released them. The poles barely swayed. The server-masters kept their hands raised close to the poles to catch them if they should start to fall.

As Wido held the poles in place with his grip on the connecting rung, Elenn understood that all present were expected
to recall the gifts of Lern Beyana. Remembrance was the first of
the many great themes of the Instruction. Elenn, unfortunately,
could think of nothing else but Wido's strain and the tremendous
weight of two verticle poles wanting to lean.

Suddenly the bag-holder shouted, *"Rationing!"* Another slat
was tossed to Wido. He caught it with his free hand and slowly
inserted it into the second slot of the poles, about two and a half
hand-lengths above the first.

"Rationing!" he repeated. The Instruction directed uedin to ration the Substance, and this rung called to mind the importance
of sharing all things regardless of supply or scarcity. Elenn had
seen many server-masters lose their control of the poles when
they had to redistribute their grip with the second rung. That was
in the early days when laddering was first being invented. It was
truly marvelous how the server-masters were now quite adept at
this complex exercise. Wido snapped the second rung into place
then slowly released his grip from the bottom rung and held on
to the top one. He held his free hand up to catch another.

"Kernel!" cried the bag-holder, tossing another slat. Lern Beyana
promised the uedin that they would find the kernel of her offspring
when they finished harvesting the deepest quantities of whitesponge. Elenn still thought of it sometimes as whitesponge, even
though it was now referred to as the Substance, even on the bluff.

"Kernel!" repeated Wido, snapping the slat into place. The
promise of the kernel was also a reminder that the harvesting
of Substance would come to its end. Therefore it was regarded
as a serious matter for contemplation. This step in the laddering seemed to Elenn to be one of the most secure moments in
the exercise. The third rung was just at shoulder height, where
the climber had both feet on the ground and access to full body
strength for holding the ladder in place.

"New Home!" The bag-holder tossed Wido another slat.

"New Home!" answered Wido. He caught the slat, and in one very calculated movement shifted his weight onto one foot and rested the other foot ever so lightly on the bottom rung as he lifted the fourth slat to the slots above his head and snapped it in. The ladder was now held in balance by Wido with only one foot on the ground and leaning slightly backward. At this point, the balancing had to be perfectly maintained. The poles, now connected by three slats, were no longer liable to lean sideways, but the ladder as a whole might easily lean forward or backward, and if balance were not kept just right, the climber would not be able to hold it in place with only one foot on the ground. Elenn scarcely thought about the "new home" spoken of in the Instruction, but he knew that all the server-masters were keenly trying to envision it.

"High Place!"

This was the moment in laddering that always astounded Elenn. Wido caught the slat. A long moment passed during which Elenn appreciated the silence and concentration being focused by the whole assembly of server-masters. He was amazed this time, as he had been when witnessing this maneuver before, as the climber—in this case Wido—pulled back just a little bit and allowed the ladder to lean somewhat forward to balance his weight against the weight of the ladder, and he stepped gingerly up onto the first rung with his other foot.

Wido was commencing with a climb into thin air. The weight of his body and the tilt of the ladder hung in place like a measuring scale. The two anchoring bottom ends of the poles gritted against the rock ground as they bore the weight. The Instruction talked about a "high place" that they would have to find in the vicinity of the "new lake." It was the high place of Lern Beyana's Instruction that the server-masters were to contemplate when the climber reached this critical moment of equilibrium. Elenn felt a mixture of pride and worry that Wido might fumble as he hung on to the balancing ladder. The two server-masters who had initially held up the poles were now standing attentively on either side, with hands in place to catch the ladder should Wido's balance be lost.

Wido held himself in rigid stillness, his feet planted on the first rung, his hand carefully extended to catch the next slat. Here, the bag-holder's skill was important. The slat had to be thrown directly into Wido's hand, because if he should have to thrust out his arm to catch it, the balance would be upset.

"Deep Hole!" shouted the bag-holder, and he sent the slat in a direct toss straight into Wido's hand.

Wido slowly positioned the slat and popped it in. The ladder wobbled slightly. Wido repeated the words, *"Deep Hole!"* and softly stepped up with one foot, and then the other, ever holding the ladder in tension. The name of this rung, Deep Hole, held irony, for it described the digging down into the ground as indicated in the Instruction. Yet while envisioning that downward operation, the climber moved to a higher step on the upward climb. Wido was now holding onto a rung a little above the midpoint of the ladder's height. His feet were only about five hand-lengths above the ground, but he was deeply engaged in the precarious balance.

"Lodging The Kernel," cried the bag-holder, throwing another slat. Wido caught the slat, snapped it into place and moved higher, calling back, *"Lodging the Kernel!"* His feet were now at about eye-level with his observers, and he held the top rung firmly at a height where he might have been picking peaches. The ladder, held upright and into the air, seemed to lean against something invisible.

"Where The Lake Streams Reach!" yelled the bag-holder. Another slat was sent like a projectile directly to Wido's hand. Wido lifted it to the next set of slots.

"Where The Lake Streams Reach!" He was climbing higher, and this was getting to be the level at which Elenn worried about

the danger of a fall. The Instruction said that after lodging the kernel, they would have to form a settlement at the place where the lakestreams reach, a place with the possibility of eventually becoming the new capital. It was a place of potentiality, and its mention did indeed reflect this rung of the laddering exercise. Wido would have to finish building and ascending the ladder in order to come down the other side.

"Wait For Ecstasy!" The next slat sailed to Wido's hand, and he caught it this time by the tip. Elenn felt the need to take a deep breath. Wido was getting very high up. Elenn thought again of a peach tree, and thought that if it were a peach tree he were climbing, he would already be in reach of the top branches. Wido inserted the slat into place to make a new top rung.

"Wait For Ecstasy!" Wido announced. He now held the ladder with less of a strained grip and more of a delicate play of his hands and arms seeking the chancy balance. He eased a foot upward and rested it on a higher rung, constantly redistributing the weight he bore on two feet at different positions. Pulling ever so slightly, he brought the other foot up, and raised his body to the new level. The spotters kept their eyes trained on him and held their arms out in anticipation of needing to catch him.

"New Lern With Us!" The bag-holder maintained cool regularity, for to hesitate might upset the progression. The slat seemed to shoot straight up. Wido caught it, darting his hand out to it like a frog catching an insect with its tongue, instantly. This was the next to the top slot. After this, there would be just one more. Elenn couldn't entertain any such thing as a vision of a new Lern forming in some faraway place. Wido was near the top rung. That is what he had said he hoped to do, and here he was, doing it.

"New Lern With Us!" Wido tried to say it with strength, but his voice betrayed his fear. What a terrifying exercise! Elenn was transfixed and could not think about the legitimacy of the exercise any more than he could think about a new capital. Again,

Wido, ever teasing the ladder to stay in balance, inserted the slat, brought his other hand up to it, and slowly raised one foot and then the other.

There was only one more slat.

"Comfort And Hope!" called out the bag-holder. It was the last message of the Instruction. Catching it, Wido allowed an extra few seconds of contemplation before repeating or making any movement. Elenn also tried to absorb the significance of this final message.

"Comfort And Hope!" cried Wido. His voice reflected both longing and reassurance. Whatever future the Instruction spelled out for them was surely a challenging one, but they would face it with the comfort and hope that Lern Beyana herself had professed before she had expired.

The bag holder took one step back and passed with careful movements to the other side of the ladder, behind Wido. Now positioned oppositely to anticipate Wido's descent, he crouched down to watch his team-mate complete the ascension and transition across the top of the ladder.

This was the most difficult maneuver of all, and Elenn had often seen server-masters practicing it on what they called "half ladders." To cross the top, Wido had to climb up to the top rung which he still clutched with his hands and then balance his body on that top rung while keeping the ladder from wobbling under him. Then he would have to juxtapose one foot, turn his body, and bring the other foot around, all while balancing at the top of the ladder. It had been achieved with the full eleven-rung ladders, but only a few times, and Elenn had never seen it done. Once the transfer to the other side was achieved, the descent could commence with the same strategy and attention with which Wido had ascended.

Wido was doing it. Elenn felt his heart race. He was witnessing such an act of skill and courage that it made him burst with love and pride for the server-master generation. Now he understood why the hooded masters all supported the laddering exercise with such enthusiasm. Wido arched his back and pushed his abdomen forward to concentrate his weight closer to the band of space occupied by the ladder, and he slowly stepped up with one foot, then the other, first hugging the top and then slowly converting the arch of his back to a concave hunch over the top rung.

In an optical illusion, it appeared for a moment that Wido was fixed in space and holding onto a hanging ladder suspended below him. Elenn held his breath. Wido stepped up to the top rung and brought his other foot up. He was perched in a kind of toe-touching position on the ladder's top edge. He simultaneously lifted his arms and moved his buttocks slightly back, keeping the weight of his body in perfect equilibrium. Slowly, slowly, he came up. He was standing erect. The poles of the ladder were like extensions of his legs. How high he was! He turned at the waist and twisted his back to align his hips and spine as much as possible in a side-facing position.

Elenn held his breath as Wido made a quick twist of one ankle to turn one foot to point inward so that his feet were angled in opposite directions. The ladder wobbled slightly. Wido held it still with his awkwardly angled feet and then, in another quick movement, turned the first foot to meet the second facing the other side. He was nearly turned around! He turned his head first, fixed his gaze in the direction that his feet were now pointing, and then slowly swiveled his waist to fully face the direction from which he had climbed.

The assembled server-masters remained absolutely silent, gazing upward from their desert-watching positions. Elenn knew they were focusing to keep their minds calm, and he tried to do the same. Wido now performed a reversal of the series of movements that had gotten him from his toe-touching perch to a standing position. He moved back to the toe-touching perch, now facing the other way. He held on to the top rung, lifted one foot, slowly lowered it to the rung below, and then followed with the other foot. He repeated the sequence of steps again, then again, till the top rung was at chest level. This was going to be a fully successful laddering, thought Elenn; a full ascent, transition across the top, and full descent.

Wido put one hand on the second rung from the top so that he could remove the top rung and toss it back to the bag-holder. He popped it out and tossed it down.

"*Comfort and Hope!*" he called out. Each rung was to be removed and returned with announcement of the messages of the Instruction, this time in reverse order.

The bag-holder caught it, repeated, "*Comfort and Hope!*" and placed it back in the net bag.

In a horrible instant, the ladder wobbled and suddenly seemed to lurch under Wido. The spotters dived to catch him, but Wido's one hand instinctively gripped a rung to hold on, and the careening ladder pulled him across the space and out of the reach of his spotters.

Elenn watched in horror as Wido fell backwards through the air. The ladder, staying mostly intact, whomped to the ground and bounced as Wido landed on his back. He hit rump first, then his head flailed back and struck the rock ground with a terrifying crack. There was a simultaneous shriek of horror from many of the server-masters. For a second or two, the shock of the accident was so stunning that they all just remained there looking at Wido lying face up on the rock, his eyes open and glaring wildly at the sky. Wido tried to move. He lifted his head slightly. A viscous liquid oozed into a thick puddle around his head. He had crushed his skullwomb. Within seconds his brain started to react to the impact, and he began to convulse.

Elenn quickly rushed forward and called for Nehu. While he was stepping through to get closer, he noticed what many of the server-masters, from the looks on their faces, were also noticing. The scent of Wido's skullsap was powerful, strange, and intoxicating.

"Take the server-masters back to the longhouse!" shouted Elenn. Then he addressed the temple experts who had been invited there to coach them. They were stunned and clearly upset. "Servers, get the ladder," shouted Elenn, "We'll use it as a stretcher!"

"He must be given Substance immediately!" said Tilke, finally showing an appropriate sense of alarm.

The servers quickly retrieved the ladder and positioned it beside Wido. Elenn and Nehu bent over Wido.

"Server-master Wido, breathe! Concentrate on breathing! You've been injured, but you're going to be all right. If you can, try to relax."

Wido's face was red as if he were deeply blushing. He looked straight at Elenn with eyes full of fear and surprise. "I—I—am . . . " He tried to speak.

Elenn spoke with the calm that guards practiced for emergencies. "You don't have to say anything. We know what happened. You fell, and you're injured."

In a moment, Wido seemed to comprehend the nature of his injury. He suddenly realized that his skullwomb had been crushed. His face changed to grief, and tears welled in his eyes.

"You're going to all right, Server-master Wido," said Elenn, hoping to console him. "You undertook the laddering exercise with great skill and bravery. We were amazed by your skill. You were very brave."

" . . . but, but . . . " Wido seemed to want to protest. Elenn turned to Nehu who was holding Wido's hand and gently stroking his shoulder.

"We have to pick him up and put him on the ladder," said Elenn.

"I'm worried about the back of his head," said Nehu, "—Look." Nehu gently placed his hand on Wido's forehead to let him know he was going to turn his head a little to the side to show Elenn. "Relax, Server-master, we're just going to have a look here."

Elenn leaned over to see as Nehu tilted Wido's head slightly to show him. Now he could see it. It was a large fragment of the bony skullwomb case completely broken off, attached now only by a miserable little band of skin that clung to it in one corner. The outer skullwomb had not just caved in, it had actually broken open. It seemed to have broken off right at the seam of the ring around the cup of the skullwomb. A chunk remained attached to Wido's head, the piece of skin stretching from it to the broken-off part. Nehu held the bloody piece against Wido's head to keep it from hanging down, and put his other hand under Wido's quivering shoulders. Elenn slid his hands under Wido's lower back and legs. They carefully lifted him onto the ladder.

Elenn managed to ignore the powerful scent of skullsap. They were far from the capital and its infirmary. There was no telling whether they would be able to save Wido's life. Tilke was right. They needed to get Substance into him immediately.

The End of the Harvest

Daga opened the cloth to show Pelto a sample of the most recently harvested section of Substance. It was harder and stringier than any whitesponge they had seen before.

"We can't use shortblades at all anymore," said Daga. "We're using the small saws."

 Pelto had been put in charge of the harvest. He felt a great responsibility for managing the delicate task of harvesting out the last precious pieces of Substance and, supposedly, retrieving the "kernel" that was promised in the Instruction. When speaking with elder Childless, Pelto always spoke of the kernel as a sure thing, but when it came time to find it, he had difficulty imagining it actually showing up. He could concede that the texture and density of the sample brought to him now was like no whitesponge he had ever seen before. He pinched it to see how hard it was. It was as tough as dried whitesponge. It was strangely fibrous. There was nothing about it, however, that made it any easier to imagine finding the "kernel" promised in the Instruction. What seemed most likely to Pelto was that the whitesponge had been so plundered to feed the uedin population of the capital that there was little left of it. It made sense that the soft and moist material that the Childless had harvested in bits across generations was the fresh portion, and this dry and stringy stuff was the stale remains of the oldest section of whitesponge.

"I think we're very close to the end of it," said Pelto. "Don't do any more cutting when I'm not there to direct."

"I think that would be best," said Daga. "The elders wanted to be the ones to do the last harvesting, but they are very nervous. The rationing has been hard on them."

"They had all those novades of fully consuming, and now they have to manage anxiety, something they've never had to do. Anyway, I will be there early in the morning to direct. I don't think we should use the saws though. We'll go slowly, but we have to use the shortblades to work more carefully."

They heard someone coming. Leci appeared at the opening. "A caravan has arrived," said Leci. "Server Tilke is with them."

"Server Tilke? Server Tilke made the trek across the desert?" Pelto knew Server Tilke to be very weak and delicate. How could he have managed the walking?

"A server-master carried Server Tilke all the way on his back," explained Leci. "And here. A letter to you from the masters council." Leci handed the folded letter to Pelto.

Leci and Daga waited as Pelto read the letter. Pelto finally refolded the paper and looked up. "They want us to hurry," he said.

"Is there trouble in the capital?" asked Daga.

"Apparently there is unrest. Rations are only being given to the hooded ones and the server-masters. They get just enough to keep them stable."

"Our harvest of Substance is near its end," said Leci. "How will hurrying help anything?"

"They obviously expect us to find the kernel promised in the Instruction. The letter doesn't come out and say it, but clearly the masters council wants the expedition to begin as soon as it is found."

"Maybe that's why Server Tilke is here," said Daga.

"I don't know, but I'm going now to greet Server Tilke."

When Pelto found Tilke, he saw that the young server-master who accompanied him had some kind of disability. The first thing he noticed about the server-master was what seemed to be his permanent stunned expression. He had the look of someone who was trying to figure something out, but the look persisted and did not vary. When Pelto saw that the server-master's hood sagged in the back where there was obviously no skullwomb, he quickly surmised that the poor uedin had suffered some kind of unfortunate accident.

"Server Tilke, I didn't expect to see you here at the bluff! Welcome!" said Pelto.

In a slow manner of speech that sounded somewhat like the ro-uedin of the capital, Tilke answered, "I came along with Server-master Wido here." Tilke smiled at the shock-faced young uedin. "Server-master Wido, this is Pelto. Pelto is overseeing the harvest of Substance."

Pelto raised hands to face, and as he lowered his eyes as part of the gesture, he noticed the server-master gazing at him with the same perplexed look. Then, as if realizing with a second's delay that it was necessary to respond, the server-master awkwardly brought hands to face. Their eyes met, and Pelto noticed that the server-master's eyes were a little strange. One of his pupils was larger than the other.

"Very pleased to meet you, Server-master Wido," said Pelto.

"Very pleased to meet you," said Wido, and his voice was startling. It sounded like the voice of a child-uedin, high and almost whimper-like.

Tilke continued, "Server-master Wido has come to help here for a while. We hope he can help with the packing of Substance. I'm here to coach him a little . . . he carried me all the way from the capital on his back."

"Well, welcome, both of you, to the bluff. I wasn't sure what prompted your visit," said Pelto.

"I have taken an interest in helping Server-master Wido," said Tilke, nodding to himself as if to affirm this statement. Then he explained, "He had a bad accident at Redrock, and he has some challenges."

Wido stared at Pelto blankly with his uneven eyes. Pelto had heard of the accident. "Yes, I heard about the accident at Redrock," he said with concern. "So you are Server-master Wido. It's good to meet you. You seem to be doing very well."

"Server-master Wido has a hard time concentrating on any task," added Tilke. "His mind wanders."

"Thank you," said Wido, somehow misinterpreting the moment, the same quizzical look on his face.

"Server Tilke, I received a letter from the masters council. They express an urgency. Are things very difficult in the capital now?"

"These are troubling times," answered Tilke.

"Is there trouble because of the rationing? We're finding it very hard here, too."

"Did the letter say anything about the ro-uedin?" asked Tilke, sounding himself like a ro as he asked.

"The ro-uedin? No. Is there a problem with the ro-uedin?"

"The ro-uedin are in distress," said Tilke.

"What's the matter with them?"

"Since the Great Rains yielded no wet-uedin, it is believed that there is something wrong at the Lake of Ceulan."

"They worry about their pilgrimage?"

"They don't want to go." Tilke shook his head sadly. "They live in dread. They don't want to go into ecstasy."

"I heard that only hooded masters and server-masters are receiving rations now in the capital. Perhaps the ro should be included."

"They don't want rations. They want all the Substance to be given to the server-masters. They're counting on the server-masters to carry out the expedition and find the new lake. The masters are convinced that Lake Ceulan is dead. The ro-uedins' only hope is that they might be able to release their embryos into the new lake, if it is found in time."

"I see. Well, the letter from the masters council didn't report any of that, but it did communicate that there is an urgency to complete the harvest."

"Are you any closer?"

"I think we are getting to the end of the harvest of Substance, yes. The Substance that we're collecting now is like nothing I've seen before."

"You hear that, Server-master Wido? Perhaps we will be here when the kernel is reached," said Tilke to his young companion.

"Thank you," said Wido in his weird, high-pitched voice.

That evening, Pelto gazed at the silent gathering of uedin preparing for the partaking of Substance. There were very few open spaces in the Childless village. It was wide open, of course, on top of the bluff, but the village had evolved around the caves that occurred in the steep front that faced the desert. The stretch of flat area where the climbing path reached the dwellings was one of the few spaces where ueden could assemble in a large group. Now that so many from the capital were part of the harvesting and caravanning operations, a larger crowd than Pelto ever recalled seeing there was gathered tightly in the small stretch. All were seated in formal position waiting for the partaking to begin.

Pelto spotted Server Tilke and Server-master Wido sitting amidst the crowd. Tilke was talking to Wido with gentle and patient expressions. Pelto still thought it was remarkable that Server Tilke had actually come to the bluff to coach and guide the disabled server-master. Tilke hardly seemed capable of such a task. Pelto watched Tilke talking to Wido until a wooden clapper was sounded to start the recitation of the Instruction.

Pelto had mixed feelings about the recitation of the Instruction. It was such an obvious replacement of the old recitation of the Names of the Lern. Neither the recitation of the Names nor the Instruction meant a great deal to him. As for the Names, he had not heard them since he was a child-uedin, but he remembered the musicality of the repetitive call and response. The Instruction, on the other hand, consisted only of a chanting in unison, but he had to admit, the Instruction too had a beauty to it, especially when heard in the strong voices of the young server-masters.

"I . . . WILL . . . NOW . . . SLEEP . . . AND . . . I . . . WILL . . . NOT . . . WAKE . . . UP . . . AGAIN . . . YOU . . . MAY . . . REMEM-BER . . . ME . . . WHEN . . . YOU . . . EAT . . . MY . . . SUBSTANCE . . . HOWEVER . . . IT . . . MUST . . . BE . . . RATIONED . . . VERY . . . SPARINGLY . . . FROM . . . NOW . . . ON . . . FOR . . . IT . . . MUST . . . LAST . . . TWO . . . NOVADES . . . " Two novades. Already one had passed, and the generation of server-masters had taken name. Tilke was reporting that the ro-uedin of the capital were in distress and were pinning their hopes on the so-called "new lake." Pelto could never share his concern that expectations were getting too high.

"DEEP . . . PLACE . . . OF . . . MY . . . OLD . . . ORGANS . . . FROM . . . WHEN . . . I . . . FIRST . . . DEVELOPED . . . AND . . . THERE . . . THEY . . . MAY . . . FIND . . . MY . . . KERNEL . . . IT . . . IS . . . THE . . . EMBRYO . . . "

Yes, the first part of the Instruction was already fulfilled—the Substance was rationed and consumed with remembrance. And now they were supposed to be at the point of finding the kernel. Pelto felt a strange mixture of wonder and dread. He didn't like the anxiety that came with supervising the operation.

"OWN . . . LAKE . . . AND . . . ITS . . . OWN . . . HIGH . . . PLACE . . . AND . . . IT . . . MUST . . . BE . . . WHERE . . . STREAMS . . . FROM . . . "

As the Instruction came to this part, and to all the following passages referring to excavation and so forth, Pelto's wonder shifted to concern. The server-masters now practiced in the tin mines of Redrock. But the prospect of doing an excavation at some unknown distant high place was worrisome. It could require equipment and tools that didn't even exist, and everything would have to be transported.

"ONES . . . WHO . . . CARRY . . . NO . . . LIFE . . . MAY . . . GO . . .
TO . . . THE . . . PLACE . . . IN . . . BETWEEN . . . THE . . . LAKE . . .
AND . . . THE . . . HIGH . . . PLACE . . . WHERE . . . THE . . . LAKE-
STREAMS . . . REACH . . . AND . . . THEY . . . MAY . . . WAIT . . .
FOR . . . HIM . . . WHOM . . . YOU . . . HAVE . . . CALLED . . .
MOST . . . HIGH . . . TO . . . COME . . . INTO . . . Ecstasy . . . "

Pelto looked across the crowd at Server Tilke. Tilke was the
"him whom you have called most high" in the Instruction. How
unimaginable. Server Tilke emitted no air of importance at all.
He was diminutive and prematurely aged. It was hard to imagine that something like the Instruction would come out of him.
Following the Instruction meant a crucial role for Server Tilke
himself. Is that where it would all come apart?

Then Pelto felt aggravation at listening to the chanting of the
Instruction. Thank goodness the Childless had collectively chosen to *listen* when the Instruction was chanted and didn't have to
join in the chanting. A good desert watching was what Pelto really
longed for. How lucky were the elder Childless who died in the
calm of whitesponge before it was ever known to be the Substance.

"HOPE . . . IS . . . GREAT . . . AND . . . MY . . . COMFORT . . .
IS . . . GREAT." The recitation of the Instruction was over. Pelto was suddenly in a slightly better mood, anticipating the partaking of Substance. Partaking of Substance, especially now that
such rationing was in place, was completely unlike the eating
of whitesponge that Pelto had once taken for granted. He gazed
across the crowded ledge, many heads covered with hoods and
many uncovered, but all barren, except for Server Tilke.

The consumption of Substance did not always take place with
reminiscences of the first communal partaking by the hooded
masters at Murro, but sometimes it did so, and Pelto remembered the event clearly. The appearance of a two-handed blade
at a partaking was a reminder of the suffering and lostness of the
hooded masters before Substance was brought to them. It cer-

tainly seemed to mean a lot to the hooded masters. Pelto didn't mind the trappings and ceremony of the two-handed blade as long as he got a nice big morsel.

Four days later, Pelto was reaching a state of emotional exhaustion as he labored in the cave of the whitesponge. Ever since capital contact, lamplight was employed in the harvesting. It made movement in and out of the cave much faster, and the cutting and taking away of Substance was likewise expedited. Pelto often felt that the light changed everything, just as everything was changed by the idea that whitesponge was the Substance of Lern Beyana. Yet there was no merit in longing for those days of innocence, and no point in nostalgia for the dark cave. There was a new job to do, and it was an important one. It was so important, in fact, that it burdened Pelto, and he tried to banish thoughts of finding no kernel at all, but only coming to the end of the Substance. It was a fear that aggravated him. He told himself it was partly anxiety arising because of the rationing.

Shortly after he had arrived at the cave that morning, as he was lighting lamps and entering with a small team of elder Childless, Pelto wondered how much everyone present anticipated actually finding the kernel. It was tempting to come right out and ask them, but Pelto knew that no benefit would come from such a conversation. Better to work quietly with them and say nothing. Leci and Daga were there with him, along with other old familiar faces, uedin who had been around for as long as Pelto had been at the bluff. They were of various generations, but they were all friends to him. They were the kind and gentle souls who had once rescued him and made him their new one. He loved them all. He did not want to burden them with his doubts.

The hours seemed only to grow longer and more tedious as Pelto worked through the morning. The team labored away using only knives, and the hardened and tough Substance proved dreadfully difficult to cut through. Like no whitesponge any of them had ever encountered before, this Substance was dense, fibrous, and seemed to defy their blades. It was hard to imagine that the hard, woody substance they were cutting away at was even consumable. It would have to be shaved into tiny bits and cooked with water for a very long time. It didn't matter. Though they were all veterans of the bluff, Pelto was sure that none of them was thinking about the material they were cutting away at in the same way that they once regarded whitesponge. They talked about the "final harvest," but it hardly felt like a harvest at all—any sense of that had ended mooncycles ago. It was more of a search.

Pelto tried to ignore the pesky thoughts of Server Tilke that kept popping back in his head. Server Tilke seemed absent-minded, docile, and much like a rouedin in his behavior. Was it possible that Server Tilke, in his doddering, had invented the death of the Lern and the Instruction that followed? Might it not be a fool's errand, racing to the end of the whitesponge in search of a "kernel" that did not exist? Pelto, as supervisor of the final harvest, would have to explain to the masters council that the harvest had been completed and that no kernel was found.

"Pelto, look at this," said Daga. He was holding his lantern up to a concave section of Substance that he had been cutting away at. To Pelto, it looked like nothing but more of the same gnarley whitesponge that they had been encountering for the past few days.

"What about it?"

"It looks like these strands are drawing together . . . See?"

Pelto looked more closely. "I don't see it."

"Come and stand where I'm standing, and hold your lantern right about here," beckoned Daga.

Pelto switched places with Daga, held his lantern at chest height, and looked at the carved up surface of the wall of Substance. Yes. He could see something. "I see what you mean . . . especially around the edges, here and here," he said, pointing at two spots, one at shoulder height and another at knee level.

Leci and the others were now gathering around them, holding their lanterns up to see.

"I don't see anything," said Leci.

"These strands here," said Pelto, "They do seem to be drawing inward toward something. Go ahead and keep cutting into that mid section. I'll watch while you cut."

"Oh yes, I see it now," said Leci.

They all watched silently as Daga continued to cut away at the tough, fibrous material. Indeed it was appearing to be made of hundreds of strands that were converging tightly into a core. As the pattern became more evident, Pelto's interest was peaked.

Daga started removing discrete pieces that separated easily, breaking off with the grain of the strands. Pelto resisted the urge to take over. Daga had discovered the pattern, and it seemed fair that he be allowed to carry on, as long as he wasn't getting tired.

He worked on for the next few hours until it was getting to the time when they ordinarily would be quitting the harvest for the day. The strands themselves were just starting to vary in thickness, and some were appearing to be hollow, like petrified veins.

"I believe we are close to our normal quit time," said Leci, "but it seems a shame to quit."

"We can stay and work a while longer, but I think Daga must be getting tired," said Pelto.

"I am a little tired, but I hate to stop," said Daga.

"Let me take over for a bit?" asked Pelto.

Daga moved out of the way and put his shortblade into its holder on his belt. Pelto took out his shortblade and began to cut. He worked with fresh strength and cut chunks away with deftness.

The lamp flame was starting to shrink when a large, round, rope-like strand appeared. Daga stopped working and just looked at it for a while.

"There's no way to cut around it," he said. "I'll have to keep cutting it off to find out what it's connected to. But perhaps we should come back tomorrow. The lamp is getting low."

"Oh, we don't need that lamp!" said Leci. "We've always worked in the dark in here!"

"But will we cause everyone to worry if we're gone for too long?" asked Daga.

Pelto felt that they probably would create worry, but let that be blamed on the rationing! Leci was right. They had always harvested in darkness. He didn't want to quit.

All looked on and said very little as more of the ropey strands were discovered. The lamp burned low until there was barely a separation of light and shadows, and finally one of the elders watching from behind said, "I will need you to tell me what you're finding. The light is too weak now."

"All right," said Pelto. "Well, four of those thick strings are leading into the middle. It's a little harder to cut now because everything I'm cutting at is against the grain."

"We don't mind waiting while you work," said Leci. "Just let us know if you find anything more."

Before long, they were in complete darkness, and it felt like a familiar darkness, being what they had always harvested in before the caravans started. Of course that was a simple job, and this was a very intense one. Pelto tried to maintain his attitude of wait-and-see, but they certainly seemed to be on to something very unusual. He had to use both hands now, cutting slowly and cautiously while feeling about with his other hand, ever careful not to cut his own fingers.

"I've reached a kind of hollow pocket," he reported to those standing behind him. "It's very strange. It has a smooth lining inside."

"You think it might be an organ?" asked Daga. It was the first time anyone mentioned anything to remind them that it was supposedly the body of Lern Beyana that they were cutting away at.

Pelto hesitated before answering. He had to admit that it was, indeed, the first thing resembling an organ that they had encountered. "It could be," he said. Were they actually going to find some kind of kernel? Server Tilke floated back into Pelto's mind, wearing that vacuous smile. Before long, he reached something else. It was a smooth mass with a sharp rim.

"I've reached some kind of smooth lump," he told the others. "It's very smooth. It's even smoother than the skin of regular whitesponge.

"You don't think that's the kernel, do you?" asked one of the elders.

"No, I don't think this is any kind of kernel. It's too flat."

"Another organ?"

"I suppose. It feels like it could bend, but it's very dense. Let me see if I can cut into it." Pelto attempted to cut into the mass, but it was so dense that cutting it was slow and painstaking. As he cut, he paused periodically to say, "Still cutting through that lump." After a long time of cutting, he got to the other side of the mass, finding nothing inside.

"I've cut through the lump. It didn't really have anything inside. But I'm noticing something else. The substance isn't stringy here, it's coming off in little clumps of tiny segments. And those fat strings are splitting into little branches."

"The Instruction described what you are finding now," said Leci.

"Yes," agreed Daga, "Lern Beyana's old organs."

Pelto made the slightest gasps as he worked away to cut through the now corklike Substance. "Yes, the Instruction . . . " responded Pelto between gasps, "It would seem to be so."

Suddenly Pelto reached something very hard. It felt like rock under his blade. His first thought was that he had reached the cave wall.

"I've struck stone," he reported.

"Oh . . . maybe it's the wall," said Daga. "Do you think you've reached the wall?"

"It doesn't feel that solid. It has a bit of give to it. I think it might be a piece of stone that's just embedded." It was hard to imagine a piece of stone being embedded inside the Substance, but when Pelto pushed on it, it had a little give to it. After much cutting, it turned out to be some kind of plate, and he was able to lift it out.

"It's like a plate, and it's coming out." Pelto lifted the rock plate out of its crevice and held it forward to find Leci's hands. "Here, I'll pass it around."

"It's definitely rock," said Leci.

"Are you sure it's not the kernel?" asked Daga.

"Feel it . . . what do you think?"

"It's rock," said Daga, now feeling it. He passed it on, and each elder held it and agreed that it was rock.

"Shall we keep cutting?" asked Pelto. He didn't want to make the others stay there longer than they wanted to.

"You can't stop now," said Daga.

In short order, Pelto found more of the flat stone plates embedded in the substance. They were all exactly the same shape, all spaced a bit apart like little shields. Behind them was a second layer of smaller ones. Pelto described everything as he lifted them away one by one and passed the stone platelets around for everyone to feel. They made a clink like pieces of pottery when they were placed in a pile.

Pelto had somehow prepared himself, and he remained calm when he reached the kernel.

"I think this is it," he said.

"The kernel?" asked Daga.

"Yes, I think I've reached it."

"What does it feel like?"

"It's pretty round. About the size of a small melon. Feels like wood. It has a ribbed surface—very peculiar. It's going to come out pretty easily."

"Be careful with it!" said Leci.

"It might not be the kernel, but I think it is. We'll need to cut everything else away before we know for sure."

"Lern Beyana's kernel!" exclaimed Daga, trying to control his excitement.

Pelto made a few more small cuts in the Substance that surrounded it, slipped his fingers around the edge of it, and lifted it out of its cavity. It had wavy ridges on it and deep seams going up both sides. He held it in his hands for a few moments, feeling its weight and the texture of its surface.

"Daga, hold out your hands. I'll let you hold it."

"Don't drop it!" said Leci.

Pelto held the kernel forward and passed it into Daga's hands.

"It's marvelous!" said Daga.

The kernel was passed with utmost care from the hands of one to the other until all the elders had held it. Then it was placed in a large sack which was wrapped around it and put into another sack.

"We'll come back tomorrow to finish cutting through the rest of this," said Pelto, "but I'm pretty sure we have found our kernel."

"The Instruction is true," said Leci.

"Yes," said Pelto, "I must admit I had much doubt, but I think the Instruction must be true."

"Isn't it wonderful that the Most High is here at the bluff just in time for us to find the kernel?" said Daga with glee.

"I think you're right, Daga," said Pelto. "I think it is wonderful." Server Tilke, in Pelto's mind the most unlikely candidate, had led them to this great finding. If the Instruction was really true, that meant that there was a great deal more to follow.

A Plague of Mice

Pavis knew every street of the capital and walked automatically through Crafting, entirely distracted by his thoughts. Jutef was on his mind. Who would befriend Jutef after Pavis was gone? Jutef was highly regarded in the capital because he never let his blindness get in his way, and he was brave—living out there in the caretaker hut all alone! Pavis felt sure that he was a great asset to the masters council, now that he was given that honor. But only Pavis knew how Jutef secretly suffered. Pavis was going to have to leave him behind when he left with the expedition. Maybe Yenca could become a closer friend to Jutef. Yenca was a generation older, but the two of them had been through much together. Perhaps Pavis would make a visit to Yenca's hut and find a way to share his concern about Jutef. He made a mental note of it as he turned the corner on the street that ran parallel to the capital wall, that street that had all the warehouses on it.

A great many of the bales of Substance had been wrapped and waxed for taking along on the expedition, but hundreds of bales were still stored in Crafting warehouses for slow rationing among the non-barren masters and servers who would be remaining in the capital. Pavis was one of the delivery masters given the honor of transporting bales to approved locations, and that morning he had received instructions to deliver one bale to the Southgate District guard station where some masters council representatives were overseeing distribution.

He found the designated warehouse by checking the number on its signage and undid the heavy latch on the door. Before he saw anything, he could hear the strange nibbling sounds coming from inside. He swung the door open to let in a stream of light.

He took a step inside and actually heard the noise before he saw anything. It was the sound of hundreds of mice exploding into movement, racing from the sun's glare into the dark back end of the warehouse. The noise startled him, and the picture he saw filled him with horror. Mice by the hundreds scurried away from the light. A few ran chaotically toward his own feet, and Pavis jumped backward. He had indeed seen mice and their droppings a few times recently, but he never imagined encountering an infestation like this! Clearly this warehouse had not been checked for some time! He propped the door open with a loose cobblestone and reentered. The window-covers would have to be opened, and many of them were behind stacks of baled Substance. As he moved some of the bales to get to the windows, he had to bat away stray mice that scampered across the tops of the bales. Pavis was sure that much of the Substance was ruined or eaten. What a disaster! He needed to call a guard. Before going any further to get the windows open, he decided to see if there was anyone on the street whom he could send for help.

He went back to the door, stepped out and looked up and down in both directions. There was someone walking away in the other direction.

"Hello! Can you help me please!" Pavis shouted.

The uedin wore a robe from Quarterhouse, but it was unmarked as far as belonging to any particular contingent, teacher, caretaker, or otherwise. The uedin turned around, looked at Pavis, and called, "Are you speaking to me?"

"Yes!" shouted Pavis, "I need your help! Come quickly!" As the master hurried over, Pavis was a little surprised to see that he was clearly a barren master, but unhooded and a little smaller than what he was used to seeing. The uedin came closer, and Pavis understood. He was one of the Childless from the bluff.

"What's wrong?" asked the uedin, eager to assist.

"There's Substance stored in here, and it's been infested with mice!"

"Oh no!" The uedin's face was genuinely horrified.

"I'm going to start moving bales out into the street. Can you go find a guard? Let them know we have an emergency?"

"Yes, right away!" The Childless took off running. It occurred then to Pavis that the uedin looked to be at least sixth generation, and yet he ran like any apprentice messenger. Pavis turned his attention back to the warehouse, went in, and started dragging bales out from in front of the window covers. He knew that there were mice nestled in the substance behind the heavy cloth that wrapped the bales, but he had no blade to cut the cloth away.

As he got the window covers all open, he could see mice escaping out of holes in the back wall. That was where they had gotten in. He looked around to assess the haphazard stacks of bales he had moved. All these bales had to be taken out into the street. He took hold of one and started dragging it out. Just then, he heard the sound of running feet, and in a few seconds the Childless and a guard appeared.

"Mice is it?" shouted the guard, and he looked up at Pavis. "More guards are on the way!" Pavis knew him. It was Master Ribol from Flatpools District.

"This Substance has been completely infested! Do you have a blade? There are mice inside these bales! We need to cut the cloth covers off!"

Ribol immediately withdrew a blade from his belt and started cutting the cloth away from a bale. As he peeled it away, mice jumped out, and nests of pink baby mice were likewise exposed. Some fell on the cobblestones and squirmed there. They were awful to look at. Pavis and the Childless kept moving, dragging more bales into the light of day. Most of the mice had run away by this point, but as they picked up bales, more of them skittered away from their feet.

"There are so many!" said the Childless. Pavis thought his face to be strangely young and old at once.

"You should have seen how many there were when I opened this door! I think hundreds!"

"Where did they come from?!"

"We started seeing them last warm season when we were having a drought. They've been getting worse ever since. How long have you been in the capital?"

"Oh, you could tell I'm from the bluff?"

Pavis hoped this stranger wasn't insulted. "Well, the fact that you're wearing a robe with no insignia gives a clue. And the Childless have a very healthy look. You shouldn't mind being identified as one."

"This is my fourth caravan to the capital," said the stranger. Pavis wondered what his name was, but one of the habits of his early upbringing was to never ask for a name. They carried another bale out onto the street where Master Ribol was still cutting covers from the bales.

"Here comes someone now," said Ribol.

A small group of guards came running, two with Crafting guard's garb and one with a Flatpools garb. Pavis had to stop and look. The Flatpools guard looked like Master Elenn . . . It *was* him. Pavis hadn't seen him since the day Substance was introduced to the hooded masters at Murro. Master Elenn immediately drew his blade and started helping Ribol cut covers off the bales. He looked up, saw Pavis, and made an abbreviated hands to face with the hand that wasn't holding a blade. But he spoke no salutation, instead addressing the infestation. "Whatever Substance remains in the capital is going to have to be stored in clay urns," he said, pulling the cover from a bale.

"Master Elenn, it's been a long time," said Pavis. "You were at the Crafting guard station?"

"Stopped to say hello to Master Huma . . . Master Leci came running—said there was an emergency."

Ribol looked up from the covered bale he was working on. He had a strange look like he had just thought of something. Ribol and Elenn exchanged a long glance.

Pavis, thinking that whatever it was was none of his business, turned to go back in the warehouse. There were still more bales to move out. The Childless followed him in. As they dragged a couple of the remaining bales toward the warehouse door, Pavis could hear Ribol and Elenn discussing something.

"Leci, come out here," called Elenn.

Pavis paused to let the Childless go out ahead of him with his bale in tow. He then followed, dragging his own bale.

"Leci, do you remember when I told you that there was a ue-din in the capital who remembered you from when he was un-named?"

The Childless looked at Elenn, a bit mystified. "Why, yes, I do remember when you told me that . . . " he said.

"Leci, this is Guard Master Ribol of Flatpools. He's the one who told me that he had a teacher named Leci who disappeared before he received name."

Ribol stood with his head slightly down, looking very shy and humble.

"Master Ribol," said the Childless, raising hands to face, "You actually remembered me? From childhood?" He looked at Ribol with earnest curiosity.

Ribol nodded, eyes cast downward. "You were kind to me," he said.

"I would have just been an apprentice, not a teacher. But I'm amazed that you remembered my name."

"I missed you greatly after you left," said Ribol.

"Thank you, Master Ribol . . . I don't know what to say. I never think that anything good happened during that time of my life. It was a very difficult time for me."

"I'm sure it was, Master Leci," said Ribol.

Pavis was fascinated. So this Childless had been a tutor at one of the domiciles. But the Childless looked younger than Ribol! How was it possible?

"What do you remember about me?" asked Childless.

"You taught us how to put on our clothes," said Ribol. "I had trouble with it."

Leci chuckled. "I remember teaching that to the unnamed!"

"You were very patient with me," said Ribol. "I have thought of you many times."

"I'm honored that I was able to help you with something. I rarely think about those days, and when I do, it's with mostly unpleasant memories."

"I thought you died," said Ribol. "I'm glad you didn't die."

"Thank you, Master Ribol. I'm very grateful that you remembered me."

There was an awkward moment of silence, followed by a quick return to the bales of Substance.

"Perhaps the two of you can share yeastdrink before the expedition leaves," suggested Elenn, as they moved to carry on with their efforts.

"That would be very nice! I do enjoy yeastdrink here in the capital!" said the Childless. Ribol nodded, and Pavis went back in to get another bale. He knew that all the Childless were barren uedin who had found their way to the southeastern bluff, but he never thought much about the fact that they all had lived their early days in the capital.

That evening, Pavis went to the caretaker hut to tell Jutef about finding the mice.

"The Substance will all have to be stored in clay urns and sealed with wax," commented Jutef.

"That's what Master Elenn said," answered Pavis.

"Master Elenn was there?"

"Yes, he was visiting Crafting station today, and he came with one of the other Crafting guards."

"How much did you save?"

"Most of it is fine. The mice only ate a little."

"This could effect plans for the departure," commented Jutef.

"The expedition rations are all sealed up in wax. I don't think mice will get to them."

"Wax might help keep out moisture, but it won't keep out mice," said Jutef, "The masters council is arguing about whether to let a select group of rouedin follow the expedition, and we aren't going to have time to come to a good agreement. The departure should probably happen in the next few days."

"Rouedin want to follow the expedition?"

"It's a terrible situation. We have eleventh and twelfth generation uedin with no place to go. They were refusing their rations, but we've asked them to resume. As long as they consume a ration of Substance they don't go into their ecstasy. We know there's something wrong with Lake Ceulan. The new lake that the Instruction promises is their only hope."

"I don't see why they couldn't follow us," said Pavis. "If they're not going to have passing-of-life at Lake Ceulan, what difference does it make if they try to follow us?"

"That's what many on the masters council are saying. But the Instruction is very clear about it. Only uedin who have no embryo may join the expedition to find a new lake, with the single exception being the Most High, and that is Server Tilke."

"So you don't think they should be allowed to follow us?"

"Their fate is not an easy one. But how can we ignore something clearly stated in the Instruction?"

Pavis thought about this with uneasy feelings. It was one thing to follow the Instruction closely for the sake of finding a new lake and a proper location for putting the kernel into the ground. But when it came to letting a rouedin follow the expedition so that he could at least try to have his passing-of-life, Pavis thought it was the only decent thing to do. "I must disagree," said Pavis, finally. "Who is to tell a rouedin who is allowed to leave for his pilgrimage whenever he is ready that he cannot now leave to follow the expedition? The rouedin would prefer to die on their way to *something*, even if they never reach it."

"Master Pavis, all uedin are facing extinction. Our individual rights must be sacrificed."

"No," said Pavis. "If we are uedin, we must be true to uedin understanding."

"And disregard the understanding of Lern Beyana who has given us the Instruction?"

Pavis felt sickened by this response. The Instruction was not to be dismissed, but in this case it made no sense to him. Sometimes his server upbringing seemed to bestow a special feeling toward Lern Beyana, but here it seemed rather to give Pavis distance and disconnect. Uedin, it seemed to him, should always follow uedin instincts regardless of whatever help they received from Lern Beyana.

"There is too much at stake," said Jutef. He seemed cold in his resolve.

Pavis knew that Jutef had great anxiety about ever completing a pilgrimage to passing-of-life. Maybe he had diminished sympathy about the loss of passing because of his own fears.

Jutef continued, "You hooded masters are going on the expedition to follow the Instruction. You go with no passing-of-life ahead of you. The rouedin will accept their fate. But first the masters council must come to consensus. The Substance is all harvested, and we've obtained the kernel. Now with mouse infestation, we just have to move more quickly."

Pavis decided to change the subject. "When we were dealing with the mice, Master Elenn called the Childless outside to speak with them. Master Elenn knew him—called him by the name of 'Leci.' He called him over and introduced him to Master Ribol, the Flatpools guard. Master Ribol claims to remember him from when he was an apprentice, before Ribol even had name. Can you imagine that?"

"It's not unusual," said Jutef, reaching for cups. "I remember the names of my caretakers at Bells."

Indeed there probably was nothing unusual about it. Pavis as a child-uedin in the temple had never been exposed to names, but in the rest of the capital it was probably to be expected.

Jutef filled two cups with plain water. He handed one to Pavis. "Of course they all remember me, too. I was their blind child-uedin."

"Master Ribol not only remembered the Childless, he remembered him with great fondness."

"It's a shame they will not be able to form a friendship. The Childless will be going with you on the expedition. Master Ribol will be staying in the capital."

"We will return, you know, Master Jutef. We'll be back when we have completed what the Instruction requires. And then we will all be moving to a new land together. I imagine Master Ribol and the Childless Leci will have their chance to form a friendship, just as I imagine that you and I will continue in our own friendship."

"That is the hope of all of us," said Jutef as he brought the cup of water to his mouth.

Departure's Eve

Benar's formal Quarterhouse caretaker robe with Alliance insignia was washed and dried flat. He had bathed. Everything was put away in his hut, and he had nothing to do but wait for Master Elenn to drop in to bid him farewell. It had taken him a long time to forgive Elenn for not telling him when he left the capital and found the Childless village. Benar was confident that nothing like that would ever happen again. Guard master Elenn had visited a number of times since his return. Benar was happy to think about Elenn, as important as he was, taking the time to stop occasionally and say hello. Elenn would be there any minute now, and Benar had some fresh milkgrass ready to make tea.

While he was waiting, he decided to try the desert exercise. Some Quarterhouse teachers had invited the Childless Daga to come and teach them about a kind of desert exercise that they do in their village. Benar had been attending the sessions. He had an idea how to do it. He brought a stool out to the yard of his hut and looked around for something to watch, since the exercise primarily involved *watching* something. There—the little corner of Quarterhouse with its eave extending way out—that would do nicely. Benar sat, folded his hands on his lap, and started watching the eave. Behind it, some trees formed a background. The eave stood out, being much darker than the sunlit trees. Benar looked at it and tried to slow his breath, just as the Childless Daga had explained to them. The slow breathing did help one focus on the exercise. But he kept thinking of other things. The memory of Master Elenn apologizing, and of how the apology made him feel. How wonderful Master Elenn, one of his first counselees, had turned out to be! The masters at Quarterhouse seemed to recognize that Benar, as counselor, deserved some credit for guiding Master Elenn to become one of the most important masters in the capital. He just hoped the masters of the Alliance likewise gave him credit for that. But then Benar caught himself, sighed briefly, and refocused on the eave and his breath. This was already making him weary.

Breathe in slowly, hold the breath just a moment, and then breathe out. Benar was thankful that the Quarterhouse masters admired and didn't resent his wearing the Alliance insignia. It certainly didn't take long for the bench to start feeling uncomfortable. Benar squeezed his eyes shut a moment and then kept looking at the eave.

He just looked at it. The little slice of view that gave him that peek at Quarterhouse was one of the things he liked about his hut. It was nice to see it there every day. But it made him tired to hold his neck in one position and keep looking at it for such a long time. Sometimes he thought the Childless exercise worked much better at their bluff, where the desert was wide and they probably didn't have to hold their necks in place like that.

Maybe if he took deeper, slower breaths . . . Benar really only wanted one thing out of the exercise, and that was the knowledge that he was doing it properly. Supposedly, if you did do it properly, you found it very satisfying. That being the case, Benar had a stubborn sense that he was not doing it properly at all.

After all, most of the Quarterhouse masters attending the sessions were tutors. Benar was a caretaker. Maybe he wasn't clever enough to learn how to do the desert exercise. If that was the case, he certainly wasn't going to let on to the group that he couldn't keep up.

Why not let his mind wander? What harm did it do? Wouldn't it be nice if Master Elenn showed up right while he was sitting there doing the desert exercise. That would impress Master Elenn. But he had better show up soon if that was going to happen . . . Benar didn't feel quite up to a long desert exercise.

Eventually his patience wore out and he got up, put the stool away, and went back into his hut. Where *was* Master Elenn? Benar had already gotten through the morning telling himself that Master Elenn would be there in the afternoon, and then had spent the afternoon telling himself that he would show up in the evening. Now it was almost evening, and Benar was getting aggravated. He deserved to have a little more priority in Master Elenn's schedule. He had been his faithful counselor through how many, was it three novades? Would it have been too much trouble to at least send a little note to let Benar know when he might stop by? All he had was the unspoken understanding that Master Elenn would not ever again leave the capital without bidding him farewell.

An hour later, Benar fiddled with a string puzzle and considered going to bed. Master Elenn apparently wasn't coming. Fine. He would get up early and use the fresh milkgrass to make himself a nice cup of tea. It shouldn't be wasted. Then he would put on his Quarterhouse robe with the Alliance insignia and walk to Northgate where the uedin of all the syndrome communities were going to take their leave. Benar had heard that they were planning to follow the Chalk Road as far as it would take them and then go on through the hill country. It made sense that the hill country was likely to lead to high places and possibly another lake. If anyone asked him, he would say that Master Elenn had certainly stopped and bid him farewell. It was a lie, and it made Benar feel rather unpleasant, but it was necessary. He wasn't about to reveal his disappointment. He put the packet of milkgrass on the shelf beside his mismatched collection of cups and bowls, then tossed the string puzzle there too. He had no patience for it tonight.

Benar was unfolding his sleep mat when he heard Elenn tapping on the door tarp. He felt a momentary thrill, but he decided not to be too happy. He wanted to let Elenn know he was displeased with his tardiness. He deliberately finished preparing his bedding and even took off his robe to give the impression that he had already gone to bed. Then he picked up the lamp and walked over to the door.

"Who's coming at this hour?" he called, trying to get the right note of impatience in his voice.

"Master Benar, it's me, Elenn. I'm sorry to come so late."

"Come on in, Master Elenn," said Benar. He rubbed his eyes to appear sleepy.

"I came from Crafting. The silkmasters wanted to give us a carrier they had made for the kernel, and they insisted on serving tea."

"Well then you won't mind if I don't serve you any," said Benar. Master Elenn might as well know that he was a little bit upset with him.

"Oh, that's quite all right, Master Benar. I hesitated to come at this late hour, but I wanted to see you one last time."

"I would have seen you at Northgate, I suppose," said Benar.

"Well, yes . . . " Elenn looked sufficiently contrite. Benar decided to forgive him.

"So the silkmasters made a carrier for the kernel. I'm sure it's very nice," said Benar.

"It's beautiful. I have it with me. Would you like to see it?"

Benar then saw that Elenn had a bundle in his hand, something wrapped in bleached cloth. "Yes," he said, and he adjusted his lamp to make it brighter. "Bring it over to the table."

Elenn unwrapped it. It was a quilted black silk bag with green embroidering in a delicate wavy pattern. Attached to it were two long straps with metal buckles.

"Server Tilke will carry it," said Elenn.

"It's very beautiful," agreed Benar. He ran his fingers over the silk embroidering to feel its texture. "The silk masters did a wonderful job."

"It is a strange and powerful feeling to hold the kernel in one's hands," said Elenn. "It's not particularly heavy, but the knowledge of what it is makes up for its lightness. I'm glad Server Tilke agreed to carry it. I don't think I would be able to relax at all if I were carrying it."

"Ew!" said Benar, "I wouldn't want to touch it!" Immediately after saying this, he felt that that response was probably not the right one. "What I mean is, how awful it would be to accidentally drop it!"

Elenn chuckled, and Benar remembered why he liked him so well. Elenn had once been the most self-pitying of all his counselees, but somehow he had grown to be this clever uedin with an easy chuckle. Elenn's little chuckle made Benar feel completely accepted. He was suddenly very thankful that Elenn had bothered to come, and it didn't matter at all that he had arrived late.

"Everything is all ready to go tomorrow morning?" Benar asked, his tone a bit warmer.

"Yes, more or less," answered Elenn, smiling politely.

"I can't imagine carrying such a massive cargo of food and Substance as you go," said Benar.

"The hooded masters of the caravan have become quite adept at transporting large quantities. They are taking charge of those matters."

"I think the decision to leave on the Chalk Road is a good one. I know there was little time to discuss the plan," said Benar. Master Elenn might not know it, but Benar kept himself quite informed. He had a few friends on the masters council.

"Yes, we've had to rush a bit. The mouse infestation is only getting worse," said Elenn.

"Well it's too bad about Master Obu. He left, you know." Master Obu was a Quarterhouse teacher of twelve generations. He was one of the ones that were hoping to follow the expedition.

But Elenn's look changed in an instant, and Benar regretted mentioning the rouedin. Elenn apparently felt guilty about their fate.

"Master Elenn, you should not be too unhappy about the rouedin," said Benar. He was, after all, Master Elenn's counselor, and he was quite within his place to say this. "They have the same chance they would have if there were no expedition going off. They can go to Lake Ceulan like every other uedin up until now. Just because we had one failed generation doesn't mean our Lake Ceulan is dead. I don't believe any of that."

"Well, that's true," said Elenn softly, "We don't know for sure that it's dead."

"That's right, we don't," affirmed Benar. He felt good about giving Master Elenn some sound advice even after all these novades. There was no reason for a master with barren syndrome to feel bad about those rouedin having no guarantee of a good passing-of-life. "You and Server Tilke have enough responsibility directing the expedition. You mustn't worry about things that can't be helped."

"You are right about that, Master Benar. Thank you."

Benar liked nothing better than being thanked by a counselee who was doing well.

Pavis's Scheme

When the barren all came together at Northgate the next morning, there were rumors that an exodus of some sixteen rouedin had taken place the night before. The thought of encountering them on the way through the hill country made Elenn feel very ill at ease. He managed to put it out of his mind by watching the caravan masters help one another with loading up their packs. He noticed Master Serka among them and went up to greet him. Serka was beaming.

"Good morning, Master Serka. Can you believe it? The day has come!"

"Indeed it has, Guardmaster Elenn! I can't wait to see what's on the other side of the hill country!" Serka's innocent enthusiasm reminded Elenn of the first time Nula and he had met the young Serka pulling a cart right there in the Northgate District. Serka had always been passionate about one thing or another, including a commitment to self-extermination at one time. Now he fully embraced the Instruction and couldn't wait to leave with the expedition.

"In a week or two we will all see what's there," answered Elenn. Out of the corner of his eye he saw Benar in his formal robe talking with some other Quarterhouse masters. The robe had the Alliance insignia proudly attached. Benar, smiling, looked up at Elenn and gave him a little hands-to-face and then turned back to his conversation. All the capital was coming to see them off, and they needed to at least move outside the gate to accommodate the crowd.

Tilke arrived in the company of Server-master Wido. Over unbleached heavy wrappings, the black silk carrier was strapped to his chest.

"We have full attendance," said Tilke. "Shall we move out?"

"Yes, we better get outside the gate at least," said Elenn. "The crowd will soon be pressing on us." Then he shouted to the caravan masters, *"Let's move outside the gate! Once we're all out, we'll stop and do one last check for mice!"*

The crowd followed the expedition caravan and circled around them in the small rocky field just outside the gate. Directly ahead was the North Route Bridge. They would cross the bridge, follow the North Route till they got to the Chalk Road, and it was the Chalk Road that would lead them past the lichens fields and into the hill country. It was strange to see so many of his fellow barren coming together. Just looking around he could see Umat and Cebik from the original hood squadron, as well as Pavis and Leol, all carrying cargo. Pelto and Daga were there, both with great packs on their backs. The whole population of the capital was there to see them off. Elenn searched the crowd for Jutef. His one regret was that Jutef had declined to meet with him in recent days, claiming that he was very busy with a project. Elenn thought that they had long since made amends. Perhaps Jutef still harbored resentment about the horrible injury Elenn had done to him at Murro. If only he could raise hands to face and bid him a heartfelt farewell. But he didn't see Jutef anywhere.

It was noisy, and the time for speeches and formalities was past. Finally their check for mice was complete, and Elenn gave a nod to Tilke. Tilke bowed slightly and made a hands-to-face gesture to Wido who presently went down on one knee to let Tilke climb onto his back. A small seat of basketwork was attached to Wido's back, and Tilke comfortably settled into it. Jutef had conceived and woven it, and it worked very well. It carried Tilke high and allowed him to look over Wido's shoulders.

"Let's go!" called Elenn.

First it was just the crowd there to see them off who started chanting the Instruction, but soon the entire expedition party joined in. The chant continued as they headed across the North Route Bridge. *"THERE . . . THEY . . . MAY . . . FIND . . . MY . . . KERNEL . . . IT . . . IS . . . THE . . . EMBRYO . . . OF . . . MY . . . OFFSPRING . . . AND . . . MY . . . DEAR . . . ONES . . . WHO . . . CARRY . . . NO . . . LIFE . . . MAY . . . DELIVER . . . IT . . . TO . . . A . . . NEW . . . HOME . . . TO . . . LET . . . IT . . . LIVE . . . AS . . . I . . . HAVE . . . LIVED . . . IN . . . CLOSENESS . . . WITH . . . DEAR . . . ONES . . . "*

It was mid-morning when they neared the lichen field, and Elenn thought about the fact that he hadn't seen it since his days on the hood squadron. But as the red lichen came into view, Elenn quickly saw that there were uedin there, and his heart sank. It was a group of rouedin, their robes bulging with extra pockets sewn on to hold gourds and sweetbuns for a long journey to passing-of-life. There were about twenty of them, including one in server wrappings, huddled and waiting at the spot where the Chalk Road reached the edge of the lichen-covered rock ground.

"Look! There are other travelers coming through here today," said Tilke from his perch on Wido's shoulders. Elenn was annoyed by his unconcerned tone. Tilke had to know that these were rouedin, and that encountering them was going to be a problem.

Elenn gave a shout for the caravan to stop, and then called to Tilke, "You should come down, Server Tilke. We have to speak with them." Tilke bent over and spoke into Wido's ear, and Wido knelt to let Tilke get down. Tilke kept his hand on the quilted bag over his chest that held the precious kernel as he walked with Elenn over to the rouedin. The rouedin regarded them with wide-eyes, looking as though they expected to be sternly scolded, and their innocence made Elenn feel worse. They had been told that they would not be allowed to follow the expedition and that they should stop consuming Substance so that their ecstasy could be hastened. Elenn wondered how much they were into their ecstasy. It was irregular, though, that they should be traveling in a group. Departure for pilgrimage was always an individual and solitary event. Elenn noticed Master Obu of Quarterhouse among them.

"Master Obu, we are surprised to see you all together," said Elenn. Obu looked back at him with a rather confused look. "Where are you going?" asked Elenn.

"Well, . . . " Obu looked around, clearly uncertain about what to say. "Well, we are going to the Lake, of course. Yes, that's right, isn't it, Master Linop?"

The rouedin Linop looked at Obu and looked back at Elenn. "Yes, that's right. That's just where we're going. We're going to the lake," he said with a nod, "Master Obu is quite right."

"All together? To the Lake of Ceulan?" asked Elenn.

The two rouedin looked at each other questioningly. Another rouedin master standing behind them interjected in a weird voice, "No, not the Lake of Ceulan. The Lake of Ceulan is dead."

"Shhhh!" Obu turned and hushed the other rouedin. "No, no, no!"

Elenn looked at Tilke. Was Tilke aware that there appeared to be a problem here? Tilke had a vacant look on his face. Perhaps he was too preoccupied with the task of carrying the kernel to help him sort out this awkward situation. Elenn would have to manage it on his own. "Who told you that the Lake of Ceulan is dead?" The rouedin did not answer. "Has anyone in the capital ever been to the Lake of Ceulan?" he asked them.

The rouedin looked back at him with wide eyes. "No," said Obu, "No one has ever been to the Lake of Ceulan. It's true, isn't it, Master Linop?"

"It is true. No one has ever been to the Lake of Ceulan."

"So we don't know for sure that it is dead, do we?" said Elenn.

Obu's face reflected a kind of obedient passivity. "You're right, Master," said Obu. "We don't know for sure."

"But the capital doesn't get any more wetuedin," objected Linop.

Elenn had to convince them that they should make an ordinary pilgrimage, even if he had his own grave doubts. "One absent generation doesn't mean that the Lake of Ceulan is dead," he said, "Does it?"

"It might *not* be dead!" said Obu. It was hard to know if he was being obediently agreeable or was actually being persuaded.

"Let's hope it is not," said Elenn, "because Lake Ceulan is the only lake that you can go to. You understand that, don't you?"

"But can't we follow you to the new lake?" asked Linop. "Just in case Lake Ceulan is dead?"

"The Lake of Ceulan is dead!" repeated the rouedin in the back.

"No, I'm sorry," said Elenn. "You can't follow us. Let's hope the Lake Ceulan is not dead. That's what you must hope for," said Elenn.

Linop turned toward Obu with disappointment. "You said we could follow the expedition if we met them at the lichen fields."

"I'm sorry," said Obu. "It was a mistake. We cannot."

"Why did you say we could?" asked Linop.

"Because Master Pavis told me we could," said Obu. "Maybe he didn't know any better."

"Who is Master Pavis?" asked Tilke, "Someone on the masters council?"

"No," said Elenn, "Master Pavis is not on the masters council." He felt an intense rush of aggravation, immediately understanding the mischief that Pavis was up to. He looked around and saw Umat. "Master Umat," he called, "We need to find Master Pavis. You know him?"

"Yes, Pavis the delivery master," said Umat, "I'll find him." He took off his pack and ran toward the back of the caravan to find Pavis.

"Master Obu, there may have been a misunderstanding. You understand that the Instruction is clear about this. Other than the Most High Server, only barren uedin are making this expedition. But you mustn't despair about the Lake of Ceulan. It is only rumor that says it is dead."

"You're right, young master," said Obu, trying to be cooperative. "One failed generation doesn't mean our lake is dead. There have been failed novades before."

"Like the failed novades leading up to the Claybridge Period!" offered Linop.

"Yes, that's right, Master Linop," said Obu with a big smile, "Very clever, very clever!"

The comparison was not quite accurate. The failed novades of the Claybridge Period were caused by draught when the Great Rains never came. The recent failure was caused by something else; the rains had arrived normally but no wetuedin descended from the lake. Elenn chose not to point out the difference.

They waited until Umat returned with Pavis. Pavis looked a little too calm, as if he weren't even worried about why he was being called.

"Master Pavis!" said Obu, "Guard Master Elenn says that there may have been a misunderstanding. We can't follow the expedition. But we are hopeful again about Lake Ceulan!"

"Master Pavis," said Elenn, "did you tell Master Obu that he and other rouedin would be free to follow the expedition?"

Pavis was unperturbed. "Once departed for their pilgrimage, they are free to go in whatever direction they like, are they not?"

Elenn suppressed his anger. He wished he could yell that he, too, felt terrible about having to refuse the rouedin, but that he had no choice. With the rouedin standing right there, he could by no means speak openly. Pavis certainly knew that, and that aggravated Elenn even more.

"The only reason the expedition is happening is because the Instruction directs us. We must comply with it."

Pavis's affectation of self-assuredness gave way to protest. "We are uedin! We can't just let them go to perish with no passing-of-life! Just because we ourselves are barren—"

Elenn interrupted, "Master Pavis, please don't make things worse!"

Tilke spoke up, "Even if we say that the rouedin are free to follow us, I don't think they would be able to keep up with the caravan."

"It's true," said Umat, "We are larger than them, and the caravan moves quickly."

"We can easily carry them!" argued Pavis, "Just like the Most High Server is being carried!"

Elenn shook his head miserably, "We cannot violate the Instruction."

"Even if they tried to follow," said Tilke, "I'm afraid they would not keep up."

Pavis sighed with dissatisfaction. He understood that the rouedin would not argue on their own behalf and that his idea for a last-minute appeal was not going to succeed. Abandoning his argument, he turned to Obu and spoke, "Then you rouedin must return to the capital. I'm sorry I misled you."

Obu smiled cluelessly. "Oh, but now we are all ready to go to Lake Ceulan."

"But you're not really in ecstasy. You won't have the instinct to lead you until you go into ecstasy."

Elenn wondered why he hadn't noticed this until now. These rouedin were not quite at the state of raving that he had observed in departing pilgrims to passing-of-life in the past. He thought of

Master Domas who had been largely incoherent at the time of his departure from the capital.

"It's because we were eating Substance," said Obu. "But some of us have not eaten it for many days, and they're getting into their raving now. They have the instinct. The rest of us will follow them." Obu looked around at his fellow rouedin, and Elenn likewise perused their faces to see who might have the appearance of raving. They had a dazed look about them, but none looked to be deeply into their raving.

"I must agree with Master Pavis in this case," said Elenn, "It would be better if you returned to the capital to wait until you're really ready, one at a time."

Linop shook his head, "I've said my goodbyes. I'm not going back." Several other rouedin murmured their agreement.

"We'll follow each other," said Obu. "Lake Ceulan! Lake Ceulan!"

Elenn understood the problem. These rouedin were not sufficiently into raving for pilgrimage, but too confused to take sound advice.

"They've said their goodbyes, Master Elenn," said Tilke. "We understand that, don't we?" Tilke looked at Elenn as though this were the simplest thing imaginable. "As Master Pavis said, these rouedin have departed the capital for their pilgrimage, and they are free to go in whatever direction they like. We wouldn't try to stop them, would we?"

Elenn looked at Tilke and looked at the carrier on his chest which held the kernel. He was afraid that Tilke's past life of seclusion in the temple and the ordeals associated with having been Most High rendered him slow to grasp the reality of a situation. But at times like this, he needed to put a little more trust in Tilke to share the burden of a difficult decision. "We wouldn't stop them, no . . . " he answered. He was left with the unpleasantness of lying, the guilt of sending rouedin to a likely dead lake, and the frustration of not being able to express his complex feelings.

"We will go to the Lake of Ceulan—it's what we all wanted to do all along!" announced Obu, and other rouedin responded with "Yes!" and "We never wanted to go anywhere else!"

"Master Pavis, you've been very kind, and we hope you aren't disappointed that we aren't going to follow the expedition . . . "

Pavis said nothing but raised hands to face to Obu and the others.

Obu continued, "This is as it should be. As the Instruction says, *'My hope is great, and my comfort is great.'*" Elenn felt a strange chill on his back hearing the final words of the Instruction quoted in this situation.

The rouedin bowed and raised hands to face as the expedition caravan once again moved into formation and started off. Tilke had a look of calm acceptance as Wido knelt for him to climb up to his seat behind the server-master's broad shoulders.

Elenn heard Wido speak to Tilke, saying, "Hill country?"

"Yes, Server-master Wido," said Tilke with a ring of praise in his voice, "That's right! We're going on to the hill country now!"

When they were a mere half hour's march out of the lichen fields, Elenn looked back to see if there was any sign of the rouedin travelers. They were nowhere to be seen.

Thirst

Elenn had once before had the feeling of being in a different world, and that had been at the bluff. But this time, the feeling was intensified by the fact that they were together in a place that was entirely foreign and unknown to all of them. The two days of westward movement had brought them through a stange landscape of windswept grass-covered hills that rolled on and on. Elenn was growing accustomed to the buffeting wind and dust in his face.

When they reached a wide drystream on the third day, elation was quickly tempered when they saw that there was no moisture in it—only patches of grass and shrubs that grew here and there along its trail of boulders and cracked mud. Drystreams only carry water during a Great Rains and the smaller rainy seasons that follow for the first few years of a novade. There been a few rainy days that year, but the drystream near the capital had not presented any flow, and neither, apparently, did this one. Nonetheless, hills rose around the streambed forming a valley, it offered a welcome retreat from the wind and sun, so the caravan stopped there to camp.

By late afternoon, a few of them were tending little fires to make soup from remaining gourd water and Substance. The silence that predominated during the caravan's movement gave way to the social sounds of laughter and conversation. Elenn could hear Pavis's woodflute playing a lively tune to the beat of clapping hands. The camp seemed almost like a village to him—populated by all the different groups and generations of barren uedin who had come together for the expedition. There were hooded masters of his own generation, such as Pavis and the masters of the original hooded guard. Then there was Nula's generation, out of which the threesome of workermasters of the western outfields were particular friends to Elenn. He knew hardly anyone from the generation that followed. They were the ones who were the unnamed during Nula's brief career as a caretaker at Bramble— hard to believe they were now third generation, having lived through two Great Rains since taking leg. One in four of that generation was barren, and they were amply represented. The youngest uedin there, of course, were the server-masters. Their orangish robes had originally only been intended for wearing at Redrock but had long since become their official garb, and the robes seemed to announce their brash and unpredictable reputation. The robes Elenn was looking for, however, were harder to pick out—the gray robes that the Childless took to wearing after their village reconnected with the capital.

Elenn scouted the crowd but saw none of the Childless. He hesitated to leave Server Tilke alone with no one but Wido to look after him. Though Tilke never complained, Elenn knew that carrying the kernel was exhausting, not because of its weight but because of its fearsome importance.

"Server Tilke, is it all right if I go look for the Childless? I haven't spoken with any of them since we left the capital."

"Server-master Wido and I will be fine here," said Tilke, "Go right on and have a visit."

Elenn was greeted everywhere he walked but avoided being drawn into conversations. Finally he did find the Childless, camping together a little ways down the streambed. He encountered Daga first.

"Hello, Elenn!" said Daga.

"Hello, Daga. It's nice and quiet down here."

"We prefer a little quiet," said Daga.

"Is Pelto around?"

"No—you might have passed him. He's concerned about the server-masters. He thinks they'll drink all the water in their gourds and won't have any left."

Elenn took this bit of news with great interest. That was exactly the concern he was looking to discuss. Too bad they had missed each other.

"Pelto will get them all to wake up and pay attention to their water supply," said Daga, then added the comment, "Those young server-masters have never lacked for anything in their lives."

Elenn wanted to talk about water, not the server-masters. "This is the first streambed we've come to since leaving the capital, but it has nothing but dry mud."

"It has succulents," said Daga. "Didn't you notice them?" He pointed to a few riverweeds that had swollen little leaves.

"Not enough for our needs. There are nearly two hundred fifty of us in this caravan."

"It's difficult not to worry when we are limited to small rations of Substance," said Daga, "but worry will not help us."

This was why Elenn had wanted to speak to Pelto specifically. Pelto was a little more capable of recognizing an urgent situation without dismissing it as needless worry. "It's thirst I'm worried about," said Elenn. "I figured that the childless would have a better appreciation for a water shortage. Those of us who crossed the southeastern desert remember what thirst is."

Daga looked unimpressed. "Ah yes, we remember that misery. The memory of it doesn't provide us any water."

Elenn was unsure how to respond. No matter how carefully they might conserve their remaining water, it would not last more than a few more days. "We will see how much we can hydrate ourselves with succulents," he finally conceded, primarily interested in extending politeness to Daga.

"Perhaps we should follow this streambed and go north," suggested Daga.

In fact, Elenn had considered this. The problem, however, was that it would go against the very basic intention of the expedition. The drystreams that ran north and south were understood to be sourced at the Lake of Ceulan. The whole point of the westward course was to bypass it and seek another lake.

"This drystream would probably take us toward Ceulan, you know."

"And you think we'll just be lucky enough to find water if we continue westward?" asked Daga.

"It's true, we don't know what lies to the west. But following the drystream doesn't promise us water either. Who knows how far we might go before an actual stream of water appears. It could meander endlessly, and we would follow it for days without getting close to lakewater."

Again, Daga shrugged. "Why not play a shell-toss to decide?"

Elenn looked at the elder Childless. Like his counterparts from the bluff, Daga had the look of a uedin who had escaped the effects of age; it would be hard to guess his generation. Was he serious now, suggesting a shell-toss to determine the course of the expedition caravan?

Daga saw Elenn's surprised look and laughed. "Do you think that's outrageous? Wasn't it a shell-toss piece that brought Jeber to us, the last of the new ones? It was his report about the self-exterminations that set all of this in motion."

Just then, they saw Pelto approaching. Perhaps Pelto would be more inclined to consider their dilemma without passing it off as something to decide by shell-toss.

"Elenn!" said Pelto, "How is everything going with Server Tilke? Is the carrier bag working out for the kernel?"

"It's perfect," said Elenn.

"I've just circled the whole camp warning everyone to conserve their water," said Pelto.

"Yes, Daga told me you were doing that. I want to talk to you about our water situation. We will be in trouble if we don't reach water in the next few days, but if we change our course and travel up the drystream we'll be heading for Lake Ceulan instead of new territory."

"It might be our best option."

Elenn felt a strong instinct that they should *not* go to Lake Ceulan. There was superstition that was a deep part of uedin culture—Lake Ceulan had always been the destination for pilgrims to passing-of-life, and for them alone. It felt very wrong to go there with the expedition when the Instruction directed them to find a new lake. "Say we follow the drystream and find water to fill our gourds and drink what we can," he said, "We will still have to leave it behind and venture westward again, and we will be exactly where we are right now."

"It's a hard choice," said Pelto. "The caravan will go wherever you say to go."

"So I suggested shell-toss," said Daga.

It seemed to Elenn that Pelto had a look of disapproval, but then Pelto said, "There are times when wild luck is the only strategy one can have. Perhaps this is one of those times."

Very well. A shell-toss would determine their course. Elenn bent and picked up a pebble. It was smooth on one side and had a ridge on the other side. "We don't have proper shell pieces, so I'll use this stone. If it lands with the smooth side up, we'll continue westward. If it lands with the bump showing, we'll follow the drystream." He gave it the kind of spinning toss that was used in the game. The stone spun a few times in the air and landed on the flat dried mud. The ridge side was up.

They were going to follow the drystream. This development solicited neither gladness nor disappointment, but Pelto took the opportunity to pick a bit of the succulent riverweed and put a few of the swollen leaves in his mouth. "This riverweed might sustain us if our gourds are empty before we reach water. We better get used to the taste of it," he said.

They were four days following the drystream, but instead of getting used to the taste of the succulent, Elenn found it more and more disagreeable. Word quickly spread through the caravan that thirst should be dealt with by chewing on the riverweeds, and that the water in gourds should be used only for mixing with Substance. As they traversed north, the riverweed became more abundant in the streambed, so there was plenty enough. But as the riverweed became ample enough to provide hydration for everyone in the caravan, its flavor grew more unpleasant, and there seemed to be no relief from its lingering aftertaste. Complaints were not voiced, but the misery of the situation was apparent, especially for the server-masters.

By the time wet mud appeared under their feet, the entire stream bed was thick and crawling with the plump-needled riverweeds. The front of the caravan was able to traipse over them with little difficulty, but for those in the back, the ground was so slick from the slime of the crushed succulents that walking on it became difficult. The combination of disgust at the taste and trouble with walking resulted in a general revulsion toward the plant. Eventually the caravan gave up on walking along the floor of the streambed and moved up to follow along its bank.

Elenn looked around at hills of grass and rock. They seemed to go on forever. The grass was brown from drought and made a stark contrast to the bed of swollen riverweeds that seemed to make a river of green in the streambed. It was Tilke, with an advantaged view from his position on Wido's shoulders, who first spied the connecting river when they reached a high section of the bank.

"Master Elenn, look there!" said Tilke.

They were at the front of the caravan, with only a handful of eager server-masters ahead of them, and the view was clear. The path of green that they were following clearly converged with another drystream! And most importantly, the larger stream and the other tributary were connected by a mud-lined rivulet! The server-masters saw it too, and at first came to a stop at seeing the view, but then immediately started running. Elenn felt that they really should be waiting for a caravan consensus, but they were the server-masters, they had learned much mischief from the third generation, and had been spoiled by everyone in the capital. Perhaps this bold behavior was a strength.

"They will be so glad to stop eating that riverweed," said Elenn.

"It's become rather unpleasant, hasn't it?" said Tilke, simply making the observation.

They didn't jog after the band of running server-masters, but they did keep walking. Behind them, the next bunch of caravan walkers stopped to take in the view and its significance. Elenn, Tilke, and Wido continued down the slope, and the view of the confluence disappeared behind another section of the bank. The rivulet was out of view, but they were determined to reach water. What they felt at this point was thirst, but not just a thirst for hydration; it was a thirst for *real* water instead of that unpleasant riverweed. Elenn would be happy if he never had to taste that again!

Server-master Wido, gentle as he was, suddenly spoke in a rare show of excitement, "Can we go faster?" he asked Tilke.

Tilke looked at Elenn and asked, "Master Elenn, is it all right if we pick up the pace?"

"Certainly," said Elenn, and before he knew it, they were jogging after the server-masters. Elenn kept up with Wido, Tilke bouncing on his perch hanging on to Wido's shoulders.

They were all huffing and puffing when they reached it. At first it looked like there was nothing there but mud, but more careful observation revealed a trickle running through it. It didn't surprise Elenn too much when one of the server-masters waded straightaway into the deep mud holding his empty gourd up high in his hand. Elenn remembered times when marsh formed above the northeastern corner of the capital, and he knew that deep mud could be extremely dangerous. Fortunately, the server-master didn't sink in any more than knee depth. He may get stuck, but he wouldn't get swallowed. Another server-master followed right after him. They held their gourds carefully in the stream to let them slowly fill up with the water that ran in a delicate trickle through the mud. Elenn followed the Tilke-carrying Wido down to the muddy bank. He watched the faces of the two server-masters as they tasted the water from their gourds. They both looked at each other in shock.

"What's wrong?" shouted one of the other servermasters just stepping into the mud with his gourd in hand.

"It's bad!" yelled the two server-masters in unison.

"What?" said the other, insisting on holding his gourd to catch some of the water.

"It tastes just like the riverweed!"

Unfortunately it made perfect sense to Elenn. It was probably the foul water that caused the riverweed to taste so bad in the first place. His heart sank with disappointment.

Tilke actually laughed, which probably seemed almost cruel to the devastated server-masters. But Elenn had to admire his unnameliness. The riverweed provided hydration and didn't kill them, and hopefully this water would do the same, even if it was not as fresh as they had all been hoping it would be.

"Stay right where you are, Server-masters!" shouted Elenn, "We're going to send you our gourds and you'll refill them. All right?"

The server-masters seemed to find their bearings. "All right!" answered the first one who had tasted the water, duty in his voice.

It took many hours and numerous server-master volunteers to relay the long line of gourds for filling for the entire many members of the caravan. The server-masters switched places a few times so the job could continue even as some in the waiting crowd drank up the water, failed to vomit, and sent their gourds back for more. Elenn gradually adopted a wry amusement at the fact that they had longed to be rid of the taste of the riverweed only to get to water which tasted just like it!

They camped beside the bank that night. There was little levity, little chattering, no woodflute. Despite the taste of the water, it did not have any ill effect on Elenn, or apparently anyone else. He slept well.

The Dead Ceulan

"Guard Master Elenn! I'm sorry to wake you!" It was a server-master's young voice.

"What? Is anything wrong?" Elenn sat up, his camp blanket around him. It was barely dusk. The larger moon was still clear.

"I'm sorry to wake you, but I've been waiting all night to show you. We found this on the other bank!"

Elenn got up, folded the blanket over one time and dropped it to the ground. Then he reached for the empty gourd that the server-master held out. It was an etched gourd, different from the ones they carried, and had a small inscription in it, *Lerna Beyana ulrana uedina*.

Elenn immediately called over to Tilke. "Server Tilke, are you awake?"

Tilke sat up quite unfazed as if he hadn't even been sleeping.

"Good morning Server-master," said Tilke, "Good morning Master Elenn."

"Server Tilke, do you recognize this? Is it from the temple?"

Tilke took the gourd and looked at it. "Yes," he said, "Now how could that have gotten here? I didn't bring it. There are no other temple servers in the expedition."

"It's not from the expedition," said Elenn, "They say they found it on the other bank."

The server-master explained, "Some of us went across to explore a bit just before the sun went down. We found a trail of footprints in the mud. We followed it a long time, and we found that gourd."

"You got back late?" asked Elenn.

"Yes, everyone was asleep. I waited till morning to wake you."

Elenn remembered that there had been a server among the rouedin that they had met at the end of the Chalk Road. How could the group have possibly reached this point in their condition? But then it started to make sense. The newly appearing streamed that the caravan had just joined up with was probably one and the same with the drystream that ran north of the capital. The rouedin had followed it to this very place. Given the pace of the caravan, the stream that the rouedin followed up must have been much more direct, or they would never have arrived there first.

Later in the morning, Elenn brought together a meeting of elder barren including Tilke, Pavis, members of the hooded guard, and many of the Childless, and reported what had been found.

"I say we follow the tracks," said Pavis.

"We don't have sufficient reason to follow them," said Elenn, "What is our purpose? Lake Ceulan is their destination, but it is not ours."

"But, Master Elenn, we must admit we have little to direct us but the general idea that more lakes like Lake Ceulan will be found at the higher altitudes of the hill country. That's the only reason we're heading west."

"It may be only an idea, but it was decided upon with input from the masters council, and we should not abandon it. This detour was only necessary because we needed water."

"This water is foul. It's foul because Lake Ceulan is dead. We must catch up with the rouedin and stop them before they and their offspring perish there!"

"Pavis, what if we catch up with the rouedin? What are we going to tell them? That now they can follow us? They can't!"

"Why not?" insisted Pavis. "If we find a new lake—and we must hope that we will—why shouldn't we let the rouedin make their passing-of-life there?" He looked around to see if his argument was convincing anyone, and when he saw no change in the others' reluctance, he said, "Please, wait right here one moment—I'll be right back! I want to show you something!"

Elenn and the others exchanged curious glances having no idea what Pavis had to show them. He returned shortly with the large wrapped pack of bundled Substance and supplies that comprised his personal caravan load. Elenn's first thought was that Pavis was announcing his intention to share his food and Substance with the rouedin, but it wouldn't have been necessary to bring his pack there to show them.

"I've brought something that you don't know about," said Pavis. "It might make a difference." He then removed a partial bale of Substance from the side of the pack and pulled out an item of woven reeds. It looked like Jutef's work.

Tilke understood right away. "It's just like my seat," he said.

"I have eighteen of them," announced Pavis. "Master Jutef asked me to bring them."

"Eighteen?" asked Elenn, "You have eighteen of these?"

"Master Jutef was very busy making them in the last few days before we left the capital."

Elenn was shocked and deeply moved. Jutef was part of this conspiracy to make the expedition take the rouedin with them.

"Did Jutef encourage you to organize the rouedin and have them meet us at the end of the Chalk Road?"

Pavis looked back with defiance in his eyes. "At first he was against it," he said. "He was afraid, like you are, of disregarding the Instruction. But as the departure date got closer, he changed his mind, and in the end he worked very hard to make these seats."

Elenn loved Jutef very much, and could never forgive himself for the violence he had once done to him. Even though Jutef had insisted that Elenn was forgiven and should put it out of his mind, there would never be an end to the shame Elenn felt about having harmed his dear friend.

Posha of the hooded guards spoke up. "We still don't know that the Lake of Ceulan is dead! Just because this water is foul doesn't mean that the whole Lake is foul."

Elenn was unable to go along with the ruse this time. "Master Posha, we must be realistic. Think about the last Great Rains. There was no descent of wetuedin at all—none. Something is wrong with Lake Ceulan."

"We can catch the rouedin!" cried Pavis. "Most of them are not into their advanced ecstasy because they left the capital early!"

Pelto, who had grown in his trust of the Instruction since finding the kernel, brought up the essential dilemma. "We cannot dismiss what the Instruction says," he reminded them. "Only the Most High--"

Pavis resisted. "The Instruction says that in the end, Lern Beyana had comfort and hope! That's all we have too! We have the comfort of each other and the hope of finding the new lake! The Instruction guarantees us nothing!"

Pavis's words reminded Elenn of the ro-master Obu. Those words about hope and comfort had been the last words Elenn had heard spoken by the rouedin Obu when they left them all in the lichen fields. But it was really the thought of Jutef working on those woven seats that stirred his heart. He looked to Tilke's face for some suggestion of what to do. Tilke looked concerned about Pavis and had a sympathetic frown, but Elenn suspected that he was reacting to Pavis's desperation more than thinking about the rouedin.

"Pelto, what do you think? Should we go after the rouedin?"

Pelto looked back at Elenn with concern. "Do you agree with Master Pavis?" he asked. "Do you think we should not worry about following the Instruction?"

"It's true that the Instruction guarantees us nothing," said Elenn.

Pelto sighed. "We need to decide together." Pelto looked around at the barren elders gathered there. "So let us have a show of hands. Who thinks we should go after the rouedin?"

Pavis's hand shot up with urgency. At this point, Elenn knew that he was going to side with Pavis, but he waited to see who else was leaning that way. Wido happily raised his hand as if playing a game. Tilke looked at Wido, surprised. He then got a little smile on his face and, seemingly making a quick mental calculation, put up a hand to go along with Wido. After that, hands went up quickly. When Elenn finally held up his own hand, he imagined Jutef looking up from his weaving with a smile.

Pelto finally bowed his head slightly and raised his own hand. "I am not feeling so much comfort right now," he said, "but I will hold on to hope."

Soon afterward, the word was spread that they would be following the muddy stream and heading north. On the opposite bank, Elenn waited while the rest of the caravan came across and cleaned mud from their legs and footwear. He and Pelto surveyed the trail of footprints apparently made by the rouedin.

"It looks to me like this is an established trail, and not just footprints from the rouedin we met at the lichen fields," said Pelto. "We could be looking at a migration trail that pilgrims to passing-of-life have walked for generations."

"How far do you think we are from the lake?" asked Elenn.

"It can't be far," said Pelto.

"That's what I was thinking. It's amazing that rouedin walk this far from the capital, and I can't imagine them walking much further."

It was late afternoon when Elenn was walking at the front of the caravan with Pelto, and Serka came jogging up from behind. He carried a half-filled gourd that sloshed as he approached. Elenn turned around to see him coming. He looked like he had bad news.

"Master Serka, what's wrong?" asked Elenn. He and Pelto stopped walking.

"The water," said Serka, "It's worse. We can't drink it." He handed Elenn the gourd. Elenn took it and smelled it. I did smell worse. He braced himself to try the disgusting sour taste that he was by now quite familiar with. It was indeed worse . . . much worse. He spat it out immediately.

"What are we going to do?" asked Serka. "There's hardly any riverweed in this streambed." Elenn looked at the muddy stream. It was true; the muddy channel was wider and the trickle that ran through it seemed larger, but the banks were void of the succulent.

"Let me see that," said Pelto. Elenn handed the gourd to him. Pelto smelled it, let a drop touch his tongue, and spit on the ground.

"We can't drink it," said Elenn.

"We've come this far," said Pelto. "I don't see how we can turn back now."

"How far do you think we can go without drinking water?"

"We are already dehydrated," said Pelto, "Maybe one day."

"We need to allow for the possibility that we'll have to walk back downstream to the confluence where there's riverweed," said Elenn.

"Let's hope we catch up with the rouedin by nightfall," said Pelto.

Elenn knew that Pelto would probably prefer to turn around and go back without the rouedin. He looked back to see if Tilke and Wido were far behind. He wanted to let Tilke know that they were facing a more serious water situation. Indeed Tilke and Wido were not far behind, walking with a few other young server-masters. Elenn waited with Pelto and Serka as Tilke and the server-masters approached. As they got closer, Elenn overheard their conversation, found it interesting, and decided not to immediately interrupt.

" . . . every one of us, I suppose," Tilke was saying from his position on Wido's shoulders, "on a Great Rains river through this very streambed."

"How do wetuedin know which stream to follow when the drystream divides into branches, like it did back there where we camped last night?" asked one of the server-masters.

"Maybe something guides them," said another one of the server-masters, "Some traces of something in the mud and silt on the bottom of the stream perhaps."

"Living in the temple, I was always told that the Soft One guided wetuedin to the capital," said Tilke wistfully.

Tilke then looked up, saw Elenn and the others, and saw that they were waiting to speak with him.

"Server Tilke, our situation is worse than we thought. This server-master just brought me a sample of the water from the stream."

"Yes, we noticed him running ahead to you," said Tilke. "What's wrong with the water? We already know it's foul-tasting."

"It's entirely undrinkable now. We know it's flowing from the lake, so that means the lakewater will not be drinkable."

"Are we close?"

"We must be. It's already incredible that the rouedin made it this far. Perhaps it is raving that has propelled them onward. But we may have to make a very difficult decision whether to keep going or turn around."

"Turn around?"

"To go back to the other stream with the riverweed," said Elenn.

Tilke looked around. "Not much riverweed here," he observed.

"We'll continue through tonight. Tomorrow we'll need to decide whether to go any further. Serka, stay here as everybody comes through, and tell them that the water in the stream is undrinkable and they will have to manage on whatever they have in their gourds. Riverweed is scarce now, so if they see any, please share it."

Serka quickly raised hands to face, acknowledging his task.

"We're going on ahead, Master Wido," said Tilke to his companion who bore him on his shoulders. Elenn and Pelto walked alongside them as they ventured on.

Within hours they noticed the streambed widening and the mud banks expanding into large muddy pockets that reminded Elenn of the marshy area outside the capital's northeast corner. The path seemed to follow a ridge of firm ground that rose out of the flats. By late afternoon they realized that they would have to either stop to camp soon or they would be surrounded by mudflats with no solid ground on which to camp other than the trail itself. Thirst was becoming oppressive, and the idea of following the rouedin all the way to the lake was beginning to feel like a bad idea. Elenn felt discouraged. Perhaps Jutef's efforts, as convincing as they were, were all for naught.

The landscape was turning into a field of mud with little growing in it but sparse grass. The stream separated from the trail and seemed to divide up ahead in the distance. At least the trail remained solid. Distinct footprints could be seen on the trail's mud edges here and there, but the ridge of ground held up. With their numbers, the expedition would not be able to follow it if it turned to soft mud. After more consideration of the possibility of having to turn around, Elenn summoned all the elder barren to the front of the caravan. Any decision would need their unanimous acceptance. Elenn couldn't help thinking about the extreme contrast between the idyllic images of the Lake of Ceulan he entertained as a child-uedin and the ugly reality of this muddy place.

That evening, however, when they finally reached the lake proper, its magnificence did not fail to astound them all. The trail kept them out of the mud as noodling pools of water resolved finally into an expansive, glassy lake surface. Knowing, as they all did, that the water was undrinkable did not diminish the beauty of the brilliant reflection of evening sun on the shimmering mirror surface. The whole caravan came to an uncommanded spontaneous halt.

"There they are!" yelled a server-master.

Elenn looked at where he was pointing. The rouedin were huddled together at the lake's edge not far from where the caravan was stopped. In fact, when the server-master shouted, Elenn could see a few of the rouedin turn their heads to look. It took only a second for Elenn to turn his attention from the beauty of the lake to the urgent situation at hand.

Now the rouedin were all standing and appeared to be looking back at them. But they did not move.

"Master Serka, make sure no one ventures from this spot," said Elenn, and he beckoned the rest of the elder barren with his hand. "Let's go."

As they got closer to the place where the rouedin stood, Elenn could see why they hadn't moved from the spot. One of the rouedin was lying down. He was wearing wrappings—it was the server.

Pavis ran a few paces ahead and called out, "We found you! Are you all right?"

There was no answer. Obu looked up for a moment and then looked back down at the uedin on the ground. When they got a bit closer they could see what the rouedin were looking at.

The server rouedin was sprawled out on the mud, his head turned to the side, dead. In the shallow water by his head floated a whitish fish-like wetuedin, barely a hand-length long, in a pre-developed state that none of them had ever seen before. It was motionless, but then it wiggled slightly in the water, obviously in distress. The rouedin had been watching to see if it would survive.

Quickly ascertaining the somber occasion, Elenn maintained silence, and the others followed suit. They stood quietly beside the rouedin and observed the tiny wetuedin as it alternately floated, flittered, and sank. It was dying.

Obu finally looked up and spoke. "Master Pavis," he said, "It was a mistake to come here. We left too early. We're not far enough into our raving—only the server . . . " There was a great sadness in his face and in his voice.

"We're taking you all away from here!" said Pavis, "We're going to carry you! Like that!" Pavis pointed to Tilke who was looking down from his seat on Wido's shoulders.

Obu looked up at Tilke curiously, but the none of what Pavis said seemed to penetrate his despair. Elenn tried to imagine what it must feel like to be there as a pilgrim to passing-of-life, too early to release one's embryo, and too coherent to avoid the knowledge that the lake was dead and that one's embryo would die as well, once released. Obu continued to stare at them vacantly, but one of the other rouedin finally spoke, "Do you have water?"

"You are welcome to share what we have," said Elenn. "We also have yamcakes . . . and Substance."

They waited until the tiny wetuedin stopped moving completely and floated on its side at the surface right beside the deceased ro server's head.

As they led the group of limping rouedin back to the caravan, Elenn thought about the dire predicament the rouedin were in. In all likelihood, they were either too early or too late for a proper passing-of-life. It was true; they had come to Ceulan too early for their own passing. But heading westward with the caravan by no means ensured that they would reach the so-called "new lake" in time for their real ecstasy. This was on his mind when he heard a crunch under his foot and looked down. He had stepped on a half-buried skull, apparently in such a crumbling state that it crushed like dried clay under his boot. He glanced down at it and then looked back at the body of the server lying dead in the mud on the lakeshore. That poor server had come all this way for a passing-of-life that ended very sadly. They had left it there with no recognition or formality. But there was no time to linger at the lakeside. The server-masters would be recruited to carry the rouedin. Packs would have to be redistributed. Lake Ceulan was better forgotten.

Mud

In the wee hours of the morning, Wido dropped Tilke into the mud. Pelto had thought that he had seen Wido's walk getting a little uneven, but it was dark and he didn't think to intervene. They were hiking back to the confluence for its riverweed and drinkable water, and everyone was tired from a sleepless night. When Tilke got tipped sideways out of his seat and fell down into the mud of the drystream, Wido let out a single loud shriek of horror which got everyone's attention. It was clear that Tilke was not injured because he pulled himself out of the mud and immediately began to laugh. Wido himself started laughing in response, and he laughed in great guffaws. Everyone who was close enough to see what had happened and hear the funny sound of Wido's goofy laugh was likewise moved to laughter.

Pelto did not laugh. "Is the kernel still safe in its carrier, Server Tilke?"

It was still dark, but he could see Tilke feeling his chest, and it seemed that his response was taking too long.

"Server Tilke, the kernel—it's all right, isn't it?"

"It's . . . It's . . . " Tilke let out a short scream. It was completely unsettling to hear a scream come from the lips of Server Tilke. The shock of realization came to Pelto quickly—the kernel had somehow slipped out of its carrier and was somewhere in the mud. He looked down into the mud creek. He could see nothing there but total black darkness. The horror sank in.

Pelto didn't know many of the hooded guards other than Elenn, and he had only a vague sense that they had once been a very proud unit. Now, as he watched them spring into action, he was a little ashamed of himself for having thought of them as no longer relevant.

"No one move!" said Elenn. "Jeber, get Master Posha! He's not far back!" Everyone halted. Some of the server-masters who were walking ahead turned around when they heard Elenn's command. The group that had been following them caught up and started mumbling about what was going on. Jeber ran past them to find Posha.

A moment later, Posha came running with Onnek.

"We sent word to Masters Umat and Cebik! They should be here shortly! What's happening?"

"Server Tilke accidentally fell into the mud, and the kernel is in there somewhere!"

"Where?"

"Just right in this area," said Elenn.

"I can't see a thing," said Posha, "Can't even see where the mud is!"

Elenn got Pelto's attention. "Pelto, there's a lamp in my pack! Get it!"

Pelto was roused from his stunned mental state. He immediately rushed over to the spot where Elenn had dropped his pack. He rummaged through the side pockets until he found a small wax lamp along with a flame-maker in a box with some powder. He got the flame-maker going and lit the lamp. It wasn't bright but it would be better than nothing. He quickly took it to Elenn. Elenn held the lamp in front of him to see the edge of the stream bank leading down to mud.

"Server Tilke, is this about where you fell in?" The other pair of hooded guards came running.

Tilke answered in a desperate voice, "Just a little more that way . . . Yes, I think right about there!"

Posha stepped over to explain the situation to the other guards. The caravan was stopped by now, and everyone was crowding around to see what was happening. Elenn held the lamp over the edge of the mud creek once more. "It was right here," he said, "I can see where you dragged mud with you when you got out here."

"Master Elenn," said one of the newly arrived hooded guards, "I have an idea."

"Listening," said Elenn.

"Instead of poking around in the mud in that area, we should get two groups to wade in. One group will go over there, a little ways up from where Server Tilke fell in, and the other group will go in a few paces below it. Then the groups can work their way toward the middle and try to feel for it without it slipping past them."

"Let's try it!" said Elenn.

Elenn handed the lamp to Tilke, who stood there covered in mud, shock still on his face. There were just five hooded guards, so some other uedin stepped forward to help. Pelto usually felt reticent among capital uedin, but this time he was overwhelmed with concern about the kernel, and he immediately stepped forward to join the effort. He took off his robe and followed a couple server-masters who had volunteered. They were directed to a point below the key spot, while the hooded guards were going in above it.

Pelto's foot sank deep into the soft bottom of the mud stream, stopping only when the mud density was firm enough to support his weight. The mud came up to his waist. It was not going to be easy to maneuver in it, and the darkness was disorienting, though the lamp helped a little.

He held his breath and tried not to think that the groups would probably come together in the middle without finding the kernel. Of course he could not claim the right to care about the kernel more than anyone else, just because it was he who had been the first to hold it in his hands when they had harvested it at the bluff.

The server-master in front of him moved very slowly to get across to the other side of the mud stream, and Pelto looked up to see that the hooded guards were also moving with incredible slowness over on the other side. When he started across to get into his position, he understood why movement was so slow. It was very hard to move against the resistance of the thick mud.

"Position yourselves shoulder to shoulder!" yelled Posha, "Try to get your hips and legs together . . . make a wall with your bodies!"

The groups slowly came into position in two tight rows facing inward.

"Stay tight!" yelled Elenn, "Edge forward together—slowly!"

When Pelto pushed his frame forward to advance, he felt the resistance increase from the pressure of their combined bodies pressing against the mud. They tried to press against each other side to side. Mud squished through his legs and through the spaces between him and the bodies of the server-masters on his left and on his right. The kernel would slip through if they didn't press together tightly.

The two rows of uedin slowly commenced to move toward the middle. The awkwardness of pressing one foot forward and pulling the other foot up made it very difficult to stay together. Pelto quickly understood how easy it would be for the kernel to get past them. Given the thickness of the mud, the kernel would not have sunk all the way to the bottom. It was probably lodged somewhere in there at about mid-thigh depth. The server-masters on both sides of him were, of course, larger and taller. His thighs rubbed their knees. He tried to pay attention to the small gaps between them to keep them from widening. He tried positioning his knees just right to make sure nothing got through any of the worrisome spaces.

They were almost at the middle when the server-master on his left stepped forward and Pelto's own foot slipped into the hole left by the extracted foot. It threw him off balance, and he almost slid sideways. To catch his balance, he reflexively pushed his hand down to steady himself. The mud was not solid enough for him to steady himself, but he managed to get a foothold and avoid going down. As he pulled his hand out, he felt his fingertips touch something solid. He tried to grasp at it, but it slipped from his fingers. Then he plunged both hands into the mud and managed to locate it and get a firm grip. He had found the kernel! Its wavy ridges were unmistakable!

"I have it! I have it!" he cried.

Voices in the crowd hollered out, "Someone found it!" and "One of the Childless found it!" until there was a general crescendo into loud cheering.

Pelto heard Elenn yell out, "Careful you don't drop it!"

Pelto looked around and saw all eyes on him. Very few of them had any idea that it was he who had found the kernel buried in the Substance in the cave at the bluff. He had found it again, this time here in the mud stream that led to Lake Ceulan. It didn't matter. All that mattered as that the kernel was not lost. He looked at Server Tilke who was staring at him wide-eyed, still stunned by what had happened. Tilke, being so small, stretched his arm high and held the lamp up to let the light shine on Pelto. Pelto held the kernel up and looked to Elenn who was now emerging from the mud.

"Pass it over—carefully!" said Elenn.

Pelto held the kernel for the server-master on his right to take. The server-master took it with both hands and passed it to the uedin on his right. The crowd was silent as the kernel was passed across the row and handed up to Elenn, who then took it to Tilke. Tilke gave the lamp to Wido and took the kernel into his hands. He looked up at Elenn. "Should we rinse the mud off?"

"We can't waste the water," said Elenn. "Just put it in the carrier like that. We'll clean it in the daylight tomorrow."

Tilke ran his hand over the outside of the kernel to get just a bit of the mud off, then peeled open the mud-caked carrier on his chest and carefully put the kernel inside. He kept his eyes downcast, and it seemed to Pelto that he was ashamed of having caused such a scare.

"I'm sorry I dropped you, Server Tilke," said Wido.

"You didn't drop me," said Tilke, "I fell asleep and fell out of my seat."

"Let's keep moving!" yelled Elenn. "We'll reach the drinkable water by morning!"

Wido put out the lamp, and they started walking again. Pelto stood to the side and waited for the Childless who generally followed at the end of the caravan. He watched the parade of uedin walking in single file under the dark sky. Among them were those who now carried rouedin. He was glad to see that the rouedin were secured with ropes and in no danger of falling into the mud stream. Pelto had felt uneasy about the decision to take them along on the expedition until he had seen them up close at the lake. They had presented a heartbreaking picture there— starved, weakened, and lost in their hopelessness. Now it was as if his mind had been washed of all its pettiness by the near disaster with the kernel, and Pelto felt no objection to their presence.

When the tail of the caravan came along, the Childless had no idea what had transpired.

"Pelto! What happened? You're covered in mud!" said Leci.

"You won't believe it!" said Pelto. He took some pleasure in telling them all how Server Tilke had fallen in the mud and the kernel had to be retrieved.

Reunion of the Hood Squadron

Back at the confluence of the two drystreams, where there was both riverweed and drinkable water, the great expedition again formed a temporary village right where they had done so before. The fire pits and the dug-out toilets were still there from two days earlier, though it was hard to believe they'd hiked all the way to Ceulan and come back with the rouedin in just two days. Elenn found it remarkable how such a large number of uedin could self-organize with little administrative direction. The plan was to camp there for however long it took to determine their course. They knew they wanted to go west. The most critical issue was water. The caravan could not move until water was found somewhere in the hill country, somewhere well apart from Lake Ceulan and the drystreams that formed when it flooded.

Water was much more critical than food supply, given that they carried enormous packs that non-barren uedin could never have lifted. The packs contained equal portions of Substance and dry-preserved foods from the capital. They had packed as much as they could carry, and they had no choice but to simply hope that it would suffice. Elenn remembered when Tilke, speaking for Lern Beyana, assured them that the amount of her Substance would "be enough." He felt best when he practiced telling himself that there would be enough Substance, *and* food, *and* water. But water was heavy, and only a minimal amount could be carried. So it was water that would determine where to take the caravan next, and the expedition would need to remain right there while smaller search parties were sent to find it. Elenn was meeting with the hooded guards to plan the search.

It felt like old times to meet with the hooded guards. Elenn thought about their days of pride and high regard in the capital. Those were happy times for Elenn, back when Nula was still living. Nula's death had marked the end of all that. And then the feeding crisis got so bad, and the hooded guards themselves had to give up their posts. None of them had anticipated that they would operate as a squadron again during the expedition. The emergency with the kernel had certainly reminded them how to respond as guards. The Instruction was reuniting them with new authority.

"I think we should split up," said Umat. "We can go in five separate parties and comb that whole region to the northwest. We can each take three or four volunteers with us."

"The server-masters are eager to do anything," said Posha, "They'll be jumping at the chance to go. But they're so young. I don't want to be a care-taker to them." Elenn understood the sentiment. The server-master generation had produced the largest, the strongest, and the most physically adept uedin that the capital had ever seen, but they were also undisciplined and naïve.

Onnek agreed. "I'm going to stick with at least third-gen."

"That makes sense," said Elenn. "We can tell the server-masters we want them to keep an eye on things while we're away."

"I've been talking with some third-gen hooded masters from Quarterhouse," said Cebik. "We can go ahead and recruit whoever we want, right?"

"That should work fine," said Elenn. He knew already that he wanted to take the outfield workers with him. "How long should we give ourselves? Three days?"

"Let's say four," said Cebik. "Two out and two back, then meet back here."

"Then, if we don't find water in four days, we'll try again with a six day search," suggested Onnek.

So it was decided. The next morning they all filled their gourds with the water from the mud stream, foul-tasting but drinkable. Serka, Leol, and Jeber were excited to join Elenn, and they were the first group to leave, heading as closely as possible in a due westward direction. The other groups would all branch out in various degrees to the north.

The first day out, Elenn and the three talked non-stop. The landscape they encountered as they hiked directly west was one of monotonous grassy hills with small stands of shrub and bush. The blowing wind made them shout their conversation to one another.

"Master Elenn, what do you think about the rouedin being with the expedition?" asked Serka.

Elenn suspected that Serka disapproved. Serka was as zealous about the Instruction as he had once been about the Eight Stars.

"We had to do what was right," said Elenn. It was not a very complete answer, but it was the point Elenn most wanted to make for Serka. "Does it bother you—any of you—that the rouedin are with us?"

"It doesn't bother me," said Leol, "It bothered me more when we left them behind at the end of the Chalk Road."

"Master Leol!" scolded Serka, " . . . the *Instruction*."

"I'm not saying we shouldn't follow the Instruction," answered Leol. "Master Elenn asked if it bothered us. I'm answering truthfully."

"Well it bothers me a little," said Serka. "It makes me worry what could go wrong from disregarding the Instruction."

"We are uedin first," said Elenn. "Our dedication to Lern Beyana's Instruction is very strong, but we are uedin first."

Jeber spoke up. "I'm glad, at least, that the rouedin are coming back to life so quickly. They really responded to the Substance."

"Other than the server who made passing-of-life at Lake Ceulan, none of them seems to have gone into full-blown ecstasy," said Elenn, "I hope the Substance will keep them out of raving as long as they keep eating it."

"Yes it would be dreadful if they went into ecstasy during the expedition," commented Leol. "Have you ever seen a rouedin in full-blown ecstasy, Master Elenn?" he asked.

"Oh yes, I have," said Elenn. He thought of Master Domas. He hadn't thought about him for a long time. "I had a tutor when I was growing up at Quarterhouse, and sometimes I sought his advice after taking name. He had an early ecstasy, and I remember it well."

"Isn't it odd how the server-masters all wanted to carry the rouedin?" said Jeber.

"Lighter load," said Serka. "They want to trade their heavy packs for a rouedin . . . Who wouldn't?"

"I don't think that's it," said Elenn. "I think they've been admiring how Server-master Wido carries Server Tilke. They want to try it."

"Server Tilke is so small," said Serka, "He's small for a uedin, and we're large, so he must be easy to carry."

"Server Tilke makes me laugh sometimes—when he's not trying to be funny," said Leol.

"I imagine the servers greatly miss their Most High Server," said Jeber.

"Do you think they miss *us*?" asked Leol. "Do you think the uedin at the capital miss us hooded ones and all the other barren?"

"I suppose they do," said Elenn, "especially those who had strong friendships with us."

"I think Master Yinat misses us," said Leol.

"That old grouch!" said Serka, "I don't miss *him*!"

"It must be different in the capital without us," said Jeber.

"Besides missing us, it's a time of waiting for them," said Elenn. "Waiting in a capital that's going to move to a new place, if we succeed."

"I don't like to think about leaving the old capital behind," said Leol.

"All the uedin in the capital have to live there day after day, knowing they are going to leave it," said Serka, "It must feel strange to them."

"I can't imagine bringing the entire population of the capital all this way," said Jeber, "It's hard enough for our caravan to move."

"We will have to move the capital in phases," said Elenn. "And in the meantime, we'll need to plant many fields in our new location."

"We think about that constantly," said Serka. "Our packs look small, but they're heavy with yam seeds and fieldpear seeds. The server-masters have no idea how heavy our packs are."

"Why don't you ask a server-master to switch packs with you sometimes?" asked Elenn.

"What do you outfield workers think of that idea?" Serka asked his comrades.

"I'm fine carrying my own pack," said Jeber. "It's heavy, but I can handle it."

"I'm fine with mine, too," said Leol.

"Me too," said Serka.

Elenn smiled. They were proud of being outfield workers, and proud they should be.

"The capital seems so far away now, doesn't it?" said Leol. "We've seen Lake Ceulan—something no one from the capital has ever seen."

"That's very true," said Elenn. " . . . Unless you believe that Alka went there."

"Alka? Isn't Alka a constellation?" asked Jeber.

"Don't you three know about Alka?" said Elenn with surprise.

"No. Tell us about Alka," said Serka.

"Very well, I will," said Elenn. He proceeded to tell them all about the historical Alka who wrote down the ancient codes, and also about the mythical Alka who followed the "broken box" constellation to the Lake of Ceulan.

Dusk came, and they stopped to camp, collected shrub sticks, and made a fire with expert efficiency. The second day they hiked on with much less talking and kept their eyes focused for water.

But by evening they had found none, and the next morning they headed back. Hopefully one of the other groups found water. If not, it was going to take a second, longer search.

It was evening when they got back to the expedition caravan at the confluence of the drystreams, having been gone four days. They didn't expect to be the first group back, but indeed they were. Serka, Leol, and Jeber remained at the edge of the camp with Elenn to watch for the arrival of the next group to return. They were anxious to find out if water had been found. One by one the groups returned, Onnek's group, then Posha's, then Umat's. No water had been found. Cebik's group was still out. When it got very late, the outfield workers, along with the other returned water-scouting volunteers, excused themselves to go sleep. They were naturally exhausted from four days of hiking the hill country. The hooded guards were tired too, but they stayed awake to wait for Cebik and his group. By this time, they were beginning to worry.

All the next day, they continued waiting for them. They stood at the edge of the camp and watched. Cebik had recruited Quarterhouse masters, and now their Quarterhouse friends were also worried, and joined the hood squad guards, standing and watching. Dreadful long hours passed with no sign of Cebik's group. The guards considered going to look for them, but given the number of days that had passed and the vast area they had attempted to explore, it would be impossible to try to track them.

It was on the sixth day, two days late, when the missing group was spotted approaching. They were dragging themselves back to the camp and appeared to be injured. When Elenn saw them coming, he was confused for a moment. One of them seemed to be carrying a large pack, and he knew that they had only taken shoulder bags with them. They ran to meet the group, and Elenn saw quickly that it was not a pack but a uedin being carried. They were all struggling to walk and appeared to be bloody.

It turned out to be Master Cebik who was being carried.

"We encountered wild dogs. They were vicious!" cried one of the Quarterhouse masters.

"Vicious?" That was odd. Wild dogs usually did nothing but root for grubs, at least the ones that lived near the capital.

"They looked different from the wild dogs we're used to seeing," said another, his hand wrapped in a blood-soaked cloth. "They had huge teeth! They came after us! Master Cebik is clinging to life!"

It was true. Cebik was seriously injured, completely unconscious and covered with blood.

"We found water," said the first master, holding up a gourd. It was the last thing Elenn expected to hear.

"You did? Is it good?" asked Elenn.

"Taste it." The server-master handed the gourd to Elenn. He tasted the water. It was pure. "It's warm now," said the Quarterhouse master, "but it was very cold when we filled the gourd. It's a beautiful stream, nothing like the mud stream back here."

The discovery of water was important, but there could be no celebrating. Cebik's injuries were grim. Leci took charge of trying to care for his wounds, but he did not express confidence. Cebik had lost too much blood.

When Elenn went later to check on him, he found Umat sitting beside the unconscious Cebik. Umat and Cebik had been partners since the hood squad had formed, the same time he had met Nula. During the worst times of the feeding crisis, Umat and Cebik had worked apart, but they had always remained close companions.

"Leci, how is he doing?" asked Elenn.

"At the bluff, we treated everything with whitesponge," said Leci, "but it doesn't seem to be working for poor Master Cebik. He can swallow, but he's not responding to it at all."

"How are the others doing?" Umat asked Elenn.

"One of them has a bad hand wound, but he's going to be fine," answered Elenn. Then he added, "The other two are going to lead me and Masters Posha and Onnek back to where they found the water. We need to assess the route before we move the whole caravan. But you don't need to go with us."

"What if you run into those wild dogs again?"

"We have our guard's blades," said Elenn, "and we'll find blades for the Quarterhouse masters."

"Are you sure you don't need me?"

"You should stay here with Master Cebik . . . make sure he pulls through." When Elenn said this, Leci looked up at Elenn for a second, and Elenn knew that Leci had doubts about Cebik's survival.

"Bring back more fresh water when you return," said Leci, "I don't want to give Master Cebik any of that foul water from the mud stream if I can help it."

"Have you used up what they brought back?"

"Most of it. There's just a little bit left."

Umat said nothing. Elenn knew little about the partner guard relationship between Umat and Cebik. He knew more, of course, about the partnership between Onnek and Posha. Onnek was the one who had suggested the employment of unhooded guards when the feeding crisis had overwhelmed him, and it was a little easier to imagine how those two had struggled in the time leading up to that. Umat and Cebik were more of a mystery. They were both quiet and reserved.

The next morning Elenn, Onnek, and Posha followed the two Quarterhouse hooded masters into the hills to retrace their steps. They had taken the northernmost trajectory. After two days of hiking they came into a higher area of hill country than what Elenn and the others had seen up to that point. There was little conversation. Cebik and the question of his survival was on everyone's mind, and it wasn't a time for easy conversation. They were constantly vigilant for the wild dogs, but they didn't see them at all. When they reached the stream, it was indeed completely unlike the mud stream or any of the drystreams they had encountered before. The water was bitingly cold and clear, running over a bed of beautiful speckled rocks. Confident that they could lead the caravan there in the coming days, they filled their gourds and started back to the camp.

As soon as they got back, they immediately went to check on Cebik.

They found him conscious. He even smiled and greeted them.

"He's recovering well," said Leci, "We're so relieved!"

"Where is Master Umat?" asked Elenn.

"He's gone to get water."

"From the mud stream? We have good water here for Master Cebik." Elenn held up a gourd.

"It's the strangest thing!" said Leci, "When we ran out and started using the mud stream water, Master Cebik made a quick recovery!"

"That water is foul," said Posha, "Do you think it's coincidence?"

"I don't think so," said Leci, "It was remarkable how he got life back after drinking it."

"Maybe the awful taste woke him up," said Elenn in jest.

"Well, it wouldn't hurt to keep a few gourds full of that stuff in case we need it again sometime," said Leci.

A few days later, when Cebik was strong enough to walk, word was circulated to prepare to leave, and the caravan was reorganized for movement. This time, they were on their way to a new stream of cold, clear water.

Elenn was glad that he, Posha, and Onnek had gone to check the route so that they could lead the caravan with a good idea of where they were going. Everyone watched for wild dogs as they traversed the hill country, but there were no sightings.

They reached the cold stream the second day, and everyone drank and filled their gourds with great pleasure. It was as pure and satisfying as anything they had ever drunk from the capital wells. It was decided that they would only stay there through the night and travel upstream the next day. Perhaps the stream would lead them to their new lake, just as the drystreams had led to Lake Ceulan.

Into the High Hills

In the dark shadows of dense needle-leaf trees, the hundreds of packs and tightly placed bedding of the expedition caravan hugged the stream bank for a night's rest. There was no room to form the camping village that they had achieved on other nights, with a large central campfire and easy communication. Instead there were multiple small fires, and groups making noise at distant points that Elenn could not see. On top of the gurgling of the stream, Pavis's woodflute could be heard in the distance, as well as other sudden rises of laughter in the night.

Elenn and the hood squadron guards had arranged their bedding around Tilke and the rouedin. Their campfire was nearly burned out. There was no proper spot for lying face down, so Elenn lay on his side, his bedding tucked around him, and stared into the delicate flames of the diminishing fire. He thought about the uedin he had left behind in the capital. When would he see them again? When would he drink milkgrass tea with Master Benar or talk with Jutef about what was happening with the masters council? As much as he clung to the promises of the Instruction, he had a sinking feeling when he thought about the expedition traveling on without knowing where they were going.

They had been following this cold water stream for half a moon-cycle. They had no lack of water now, but they could all feel their loads getting lighter from the consumption of their food supply. It was a race against time. Elenn was so tired of repeating the lines of the Instruction and pondering the layout of the destination they hoped to find. It was supposed to be a place that resembled the capital, and that meant a place of low fields. This rugged land of constant wind and endless needle-leaf trees was nothing like that. Maybe it had been a mistake to think that they would find their new lake by crossing the hill country. The Lake of Ceulan had been associated with the hill country, and the masters council had recommended that it would be the best direction to search for another lake. But maybe they should have gone south . . .

Sleep came quickly.

Then, in the middle of the night, Elenn was awakened by screams and shouting. He jumped from his bedding and quickly fastened the belt of his guard's garb. The other guards were reacting simultaneously. They ran in the direction of the noise. Elenn knew it had to be wild dogs. They had been hearing them howling at a distance in previous days, though somehow none had actually been spotted. They knew from Cebik's near-fatal injuries what a danger the wild dogs could be.

They had to step around the uedin tightly bedded down along the streambank. Many were sitting up and looking toward where the noise was coming from. In a short stretch, the guards reached the shouting figures. Elenn was right—it was wild dogs! Their growling and yelps could now be heard.

Elenn leapt into the fray with his blade in hand. It was dark, but he could tell on account of their largeness that the uedin under attack were a group of server-masters. He saw one of them stab some kind of sharp object into the side of a wild dog and heard it yelp. How did the server-masters have blades? In any case, he then noticed another wild dog, crouching in the shadows of the needle-leaf trees ready to lunge. Just as he turned to face it, another wild dog, unseen, leapt at him from the side. He felt its paw hit his nose first, and then its body slammed against him, and its razor teeth sank into the side of his head and bit deeply around his ear. He reflexively swung his hand up and buried his blade into the wild dog's neck, but it was too late. The wild dog had ripped Elenn's ear from his head. As he got in another hard thrust with his blade and saw the animal drop, blood streamed from the side of his head where the ear was severed. He pressed his hand against the fresh wound. It took a few seconds for the pain to strike, but it soon grew horrendous. Close by, another one of the guards was wrestling with a wild dog, but within minutes the attack was over. The remaining wild dogs ran off. Someone lit a lamp. One dying wild dog twitched its legs and rolled its eyes under the lamplight.

"Is everyone all right?" shouted a voice. It was Onnek. Elenn waited a second to hear if anyone else would respond.

"One of them got my shoulder pretty good," said someone.

"I've lost an ear!" yelled Elenn. "I'm bleeding pretty badly!"

More lamps were lit, and someone approached Elenn and held up light. It was Posha. He looked at Elenn. Elenn pressed his hand tightly against the wound on the side of his head. Posha put down the lamp and lifted the edge of his robe. He took hold of his upper undergarment and tore a piece of it off. Then he gently held Elenn's wrist and guided his hand away. When Elenn lifted his hand, he felt trickles of blood streaming down his neck. Posha put the piece of cloth over Elenn's ear hole and placed his hand there again.

"Hold it as tight as you can," said Posha. Elenn let him lead him back to the place where the guards had put down their bedding. Tilke and the Childless had lamps lit, and they were sitting up, waiting for the guards to return.

"Master Elenn's been wounded . . . lost an ear," said Posha.

"Here. Put him back in his bedding," said Daga. Elenn lay down, his hand still pressed to his ear. The pain was increasing to a burning blistering pain. His whole head throbbed.

"Are the others all right?" asked Pelto.

"As far as I know, nobody was injured worse than this," answered Posha.

Daga looked down at him with confident kindness. "You'll be all right, Elenn," he said. Elenn felt no reassurance; the pain was too much. He became dizzy from the pain, and finally fainted.

When he awoke the next morning, his head was thoroughly bandaged with a length of cloth wrapped completely around his head and tied under his neck. The pain was still great, but he was able to stay calm and sit up.

Onnek and Posha were both there checking on him, and Daga was holding a bowl of minced Substance in warm water to feed him.

"Eat a little bit of this," said Daga, "Do you want me to hold it to your mouth?"

"I can hold it," said Elenn, and he sat up straighter, took the bowl, and had a sip.

"That wild dog got you, but you got it back, didn't you!" said Posha.

"Ach, this hurts so bad!" said Elenn.

"It's going to hurt for a few days," said Daga. "Drink this. Leci kept a gourdful of that water from the mudstream. He thinks it helped Master Cebik."

Elenn took the gourd and drank a few swallows. It was the familiar foul taste. "Where's Server Tilke?" he asked.

"He and Server-master Wido went to look at the dead animals."

"Are there many?"

"We killed eight of them."

"Just the guards?"

"No, the server-masters got most of them with sharpened sticks. You're the only guard who killed one."

"I was wondering how they all got blades . . . " said Elenn. He took a gulp of the minced Substance to rid his mouth off the taste of the foul water. The flavor of the Substance was comforting. "I don't know if I'll be able to carry a pack for a while," he said.

"Relax, Master Elenn," said Onnek. "The caravan is going to stay right here for a day or two until you're ready to walk."

Elenn looked across at the thick pine-needle trees on the opposite bank of the cold water stream. Maybe it was the pain that discouraged him. He had a feeling that they were following that cold water stream in vain. He didn't think it was going to lead them to any lake.

Wrong Lakes and Wooden Blades

Day after day, the caravan followed the cold water stream further into the high hills. The broad stride afforded by their large size enabled the barren to step easily over fallen trees and bound over gullies and gorges. They traveled at a pace that regular uedin, being smaller and more delicate, could never have achieved. The server-masters vied for the chance to carry rouedin. They took turns fastening Jutef's woven seats to their shoulders and helping them up. Tilke and the rouedin watched from their raised positions for wild dogs while the uedin carrying them kept their eyes down to watch where they were treading.

It was the rouedin Obu who first spotted the lake from his high position on the shoulders of a server-master. "I see water!" he shouted. "I see . . . a lake!"

Elenn was rubbing his ear scab, which itched with healing. He looked up, along with everyone else, and the caravan came to a confounded stop. At first, few had a view of what Obu was talking about.

"I see it," said Tilke, who was right beside Elenn. "Let's go!" Wido started jogging ahead and Elenn ran after them. Soon there was a mad rush as the caravan crowded the shore. It was the thing that Elenn thought they would never reach—a lake! He stood with Tilke and looked at the rippling surface. It was a strange little lake of dark, bluish-gray water, occupying a depression in the hills.

A few server-masters audaciously threw off their packs and sprinted to the water. As soon as they jumped in, they came hopping right back out.

"Ho! The water is *biting* cold!" cried one.

"Cold! Cold!" cried another. They sheepishly withdrew themselves from the water.

Tilke, who had climbed down from Wido's shoulders, planted his foot on a rock and bent down to dip his fingers in the water. "It's as cold as the stream," he said, "as one would expect."

Hearing the mention of the water's cold temperature, Elenn felt the first stirrings of doubt about whether this had the potential to be *the* lake. The cold water stream that they had been following ran directly out of the lake. It was a heavy gushing stream of water that made noise when it rushed over rocks, essentially spilling from the lake. How could this be suitable for uedin to complete passing-of-life? Wetuedin usually lived their early stage in a lake that held them and allowed them to grow and develop until the Great Rains came to flood it. Wetuedin in this lake would be swept down the stream before developing at all.

Despite the two server-masters announcing that the water was biting cold, a celebratory attitude was quickly overtaking the whole crowd of the expedition. Seeing this, Elenn had the feeling that the elders had better meet as soon as possible to figure out whether this lake could be the "new lake" of the Instruction.

Within hours, the expedition tribe had formed a string of camps along the lakeshore. It reminded Elenn of the makeshift village they had formed at the convergence of drystreams below Lake Ceulan. This time, uedin kept close to their fires, the air being much colder than it had been at the other place. Elenn and the squadron guards met with Tilke, Pavis, and a few of the Childless. They distanced themselves from the noise and activity at a quiet spot further along the lake shore.

Elenn brought up his concern right away. "The capital always received its wetuedin with the Great Rains when the drystreams flooded. There are no drystreams here. Only a flowing cold water stream. If wetuedin are born into this lake, we will have to stop them from swimming down the cold water stream before they develop. We'll have to place a net where the cold water stream runs out of the lake." He looked around. Some were nodding, others just looked worried. Tilke, in particular, wore a rare expression of dismay.

"Uedin have never done anything like that before," said Pelto. "What if the nets didn't last long enough?"

"This will be a concern of the new capital," said Elenn. "An outvillage will have to be established here just to maintain the nets. Otherwise we will have no wetuedin."

"And when the Great Rains come, the outvillagers will release the wetuedin?" asked Tilke.

"Something like that. Nets will have to be put in place and taken away."

"Does that mean the new capital will have to be built somewhere along the path of the cold water stream, somewhere in the hill country?" asked Posha.

"But we need fertile lowlands," said Cebik. "We must grow crops."

"I don't know about any of the that," said Elenn. "But this lake is the only lake we've found. And we are getting low on food and Substance."

"We need to explore more," said Posha. "Tomorrow, we guards can circle the lake and get a better idea of the area. We'll meet again when we get back."

The next day the hood squadron explored the shoreline of the small lake. They found another cold water stream feeding into the lake on the far shore, and when they followed it, it led to two other lakes. One lake, it seemed, fed into the next. It was not one lake they had come upon, but actually a series of three. They talked as they walked back to the camp.

"Might future uedin come for passing-of-life to all three lakes?" asked Onnek.

"But the way the streams gush from one lake to the next, they will all end up at the bottom," said Posha.

"They will all be constantly dragged toward the net by the rush of water," added Elenn. "But netting in the wetuedin is the only solution I can think of. Let's see what Server Tilke and the others have to say."

Having circled the lake, the guards returned on the opposite side of the camp. Walking back, they saw something strange. There, in the weeds, lay the dead body of a wild dog that had been killed the night before. The dead animal had lain there and gotten stiff and gray-eyed. The wind blew against its blood-matted fur.

"One of the Bells masters killed it," explained Posha.

"A Bells master. I wouldn't have expected that," commented Elenn. Everyone in the caravan carried sharp wooden spikes now, all except Server Tilke and the rouedin. The few metal blades that had been brought from the capital were used to carve spikes from needle-leaf wood, which proved dense enough to hold a good, sharp tip.

No one had anticipated that the expedition would encounter danger in the form of a hostile animal. The idea of such a thing had never occurred in uedin history or lore. Animals could be a nuisance, like biting bugs, or they could be intrusive like mice. The presence of wild dogs that had to be feared was bizarre and unsettling. Yet, to Elenn's surprise, many of the hooded masters seemed quite emotionally prepared to confront them. After the group that discovered the cold water stream was attacked, and Cebik was almost killed, they understood that the wild dogs were a serious danger. Then, after the second encounter, when Elenn had lost his ear, it was understood that vigilance would be absolutely necessary, but that the animals could be repelled. The masters were getting quite adept at repelling them. The dead carcass on the lakeshore was a reminder that uedin could certainly defend themselves as needed. Some of the masters seemed at the point of being able to kill a wild dog with very little struggle.

Tilke, Pavis, Pelto, and Daga were waiting for the guards when they got back. Elenn described the three lakes and the cold water streams that connected them.

"There's something else we need to discuss," said Pavis. "The rouedin. They think they have come to their passing-of-life here. They've stopped eating Substance—they say they had to stop eating it or they would never come into their ecstasy. But we can't let them complete passing-of-life until we have nets—or whatever we plan to do."

There was a long pause as they waited for Elenn to provide leadership on the subject. Elenn considered that they might use branches from the needle-leaf trees to build a mesh across the stream that spilled from the lake, but it would hardly be a proper net. He rubbed his itching earhole as he thought about it. The scab was healing nicely. Daga had looked at it closely and announced that Elenn's ear was going to grow back. As he softly rubbed the itch, he thought about how a mesh of needle-leaf branches might serve as a barrier to keep wetuedin from getting flushed out of the lake by the stream. All he could picture was a horrible scene of small wetuedin trapped in the branches as water rushed against them.

"We are in the wrong place," said Tilke suddenly.

"What do you mean, Server Tilke? What other place is there?" asked Elenn.

"I hope there is another place. This can't be our new lake." Tilke shook his head with disapproval. "This just won't do."

"Server Tilke is right," said Pelto. "The Instruction tells us to find a place that resembles our old home, with its own lake and its own high place like the bluff. None of this is anything like what we've known as home for uedin."

"This lake looks nothing like Ceulan, that's for sure," said Onnek.

"We had no idea what Lake Ceulan would look like," said Elenn, "and I highly doubt that we will ever find any place like that again."

"True," said Tilke, "But passing-of-life cannot take place here."

As Elenn looked around, he also felt that the lake was not right. They had to keep looking. He rubbed the itchy area around his ear and stood up. "Then we will keep going. Straight past the lakes in the same direction we've been traveling. We need to get across the hill country to whatever lies on the other side."

"Master Pavis, can you speak to the rouedin? They will surely be disappointed."

"I will speak to them," said Pavis. "They will understand."

Elenn got back to his pack and picked it up to untie the rolled bedding that was fastened to the back of it. How light his pack had gotten. It was disturbing to think about it. He mentioned it to Tilke.

"Server Tilke, you don't carry a pack, but if you did you would notice that we are running out of food and Substance."

"I do notice," said Tilke. "I don't carry one, but I can see how they have gotten much smaller on everyone."

"There was never any question of returning to the capital without fulfilling the purpose of the expedition," said Elenn, "But that wouldn't even be possible anymore. We don't have enough food. If we tried to go back, we would starve on our way."

"Master Elenn, do you think we will find another lake when we get out of the hill country? Do you think we will find good lowlands?"

"We must," said Elenn. "We must find another lake, and good lowlands." He looked at the carrier on Tilke's chest and thought of the kernel. After every other requirement of the Instruction was properly met, they must also find a perfect high place to bury the kernel. He did not feel great hope, and he did not feel great comfort, but he understood that there was nothing to do but carry on.

Only Great Misfortune

It was the second time the rain was changing into something different. The first time had been just a few days after they had left the lakes. That had been a great distance back, at a lower place where there were still trees. It had happened just like this. The strange watery grains had fallen like bits of wet salt against Elenn's face. He could not pick them up with his fingertips; they melted instantly. Gradually the strange rain had turned into a kind of water dust that appeared white, but instantly melted when one touched it. This time the grainy stuff was again falling like wet salt, and Elenn wasn't sure if it would turn into the light water dust like it did before.

When it happened before, the water dust had made them so cold and wet that they had taken refuge under the needle-leaf trees, and that was the night all the trouble had started. The Quarterhouse masters had gotten in a terrible quarrel amongst themselves. Some of them had apparently cut muscles from wild dogs they had killed, and they had eaten the muscles. Some of the Quarterhouse masters defended the action, while others were appalled. The quarrel within their group was putting the whole expedition into a mood of worry and fear.

Everyone expected Elenn to make some pronouncement about it, one way or the other. He privately found it very disturbing, but so far he had said nothing because he wasn't sure what to say. Elenn remembered the time when he was very young, just after taking name, when he had seen a barren uedin in derangement eating a wild dog. The experience had deeply upset him. It was a horrible memory which had haunted him from time to time through his life. Whenever he thought of it, he tried to remind himself how Guardmaster Deben had helped him through that difficult time. But the memory, he knew, made him feel involuntary shame and disgust when he thought about the fact that there were hooded masters who were eating dog muscles—hooded masters from his own Quarterhouse!

Now they were here in this treeless place. There was nothing here but rock, scrub brush, and ceaseless wind. They seemed to be getting into very high regions of the hill country. Wind whipped at their garb and peeled away corners of the stitching on their packs. Elenn paused to touch his cheek and see if he could pinch a grain of the gritty rain between his fingers before it melted. He couldn't resist reaching up and giving his itchy ear a rub. Most of the scab had already come off. The tender new ear was a smaller version of the other. At the moment, both ears felt numb from the cold. He turned around to see if others were taking notice of the gritty rain.

His heart sank at the look of the young server-masters walking behind him. They were gaunt. Their eyes looked back and forth at the visible precipitation, but they were too weak to react. They never once complained about their rations or asked for more. He felt pretty sure that the server-masters would not be going after dog muscles like his Quarterhouse juniors. The expedition had to get out of the hill country and into someplace where they could look for tubers or anything edible. It was fortunate, at least, that the packs were made of good waxcloth. The Substance was safe from the rain. The Substance could last for a long time, as long as rations were kept small.

In a short while, the gritty rain did turn into light water dust that melted straightaway into wetness when it reached their skin, but did not melt when it landed on rocks, collecting instead like sifted yamflour on a tabletop. Elenn delayed stopping as long as possible with hopes that they would find some ledge or crevasse, but there was no place where the terrain provided any kind of wind break or shelter from the weird precipitation. Finally, after checking with Pelto and a couple of the squadron guards, he determined that they would just have to stop and try to endure the night in full exposure.

A miserable night it was. They spent it lying on the ground, their blankets pulled around them, pressed against one another to conserve body heat. Late in the night Elenn heard what was becoming a common disruption. Wild dogs were being spotted and killed. Elenn woke momentarily when he heard the yelp of a wild dog meeting the end of one of those wood spikes. In his mind, he pictured masters in Quarterhouse robes ripping the animal's fur away to eat its muscles. The thought of it made him sigh in disgust, but he quickly fell back to sleep.

When morning came, there was a white blanket of water dust all around them with more of it still falling. There could be no fires built because there were no trees from which to collect dead branches. They huddled together and waited for the precipitation to stop.

A thin figure carrying a very large pack came trudging up to them. It had been some time since Elenn had seen anyone carrying such a pack; most of them had dwindled to such a small size that the server-masters who carried rouedin now had the heavier loads. Who was this coming?

"Master Elenn, may I speak with you?"

It wasn't until he heard the voice that Elenn recognized the outfield worker's robe. It was Leol. His face was so changed by weight loss that he was practically unrecognizable.

"Master Leol! Why are you carrying that huge pack all by yourself?"

"It's the same pack I've been carrying all along," said Leol, "I can manage it."

"Come, come here!" said Elenn, "Take your pack off." Elenn beckoned him, and Leol took his pack off and sat close to Elenn.

Elenn put his arm around Leol and rubbed his shoulder hard to warm him. "How are Masters Jeber and Serka? Are they holding up all right?"

"That's what I want to talk to you about," said Leol. "It's Master Serka. He's getting very weak."

"Is Master Serka also carrying his original pack? Your packs are too heavy!"

"We don't want to let anyone else carry them," said Leol. "The seeds are our responsibility."

"Well, if Master Serka is too weak to carry his pack, holding on to it will do no one any good."

"Master Jeber and I have been eating wild dog muscles," said Leol abruptly.

Elenn looked to see if Tilke heard. He wasn't sure if Tilke knew about the dog muscles.

Tilke looked straight at Elenn. He had heard. "Master Elenn, I already know that some masters are eating wild dog muscles," he said. "The Childless Pelto told me about it."

Elenn would save discussion with Tilke for another time. He kept his attention on Leol. "And what about Master Serka? Is he angry with you?"

"He is too weak to be angry. That's why I need your help."

"What do you want me to do?"

"Master Serka won't eat the wild dog muscles because he thinks it is too dishonorable. But if you tell him to do it, he will eat. We know he will. He has such respect for you."

Elenn was silent. How could he tell a uedin to eat the muscles of an animal as if they were yams or fieldpears?

"Master Serka thinks that it is a great wrong. He says it would be better to eat our seeds. But of course we cannot eat our seeds— we will need them for the new capital. And the rations are so small now. I'm worried that Master Serka may not survive."

For a moment, Elenn felt immensely proud of Serka. He was willing to die for uedin decency.

But then, Tilke said, "Eating wild dog muscles is not so much a great wrong. It is only a great misfortune."

Hearing this made Elenn look away. He wasn't quite sure how he felt about it. He looked up at the hill above them, white with water dust. The water dust had stopped raining down. Uedin were starting to stir around him. Elenn could not rid himself of the memory of the wretched barren uedin standing in the spring near the lichen fields, eating the brains of a wild dog, any more than he could rid himself of the memory of how he had let feeding take over his life after Nula's death, or when he had broken Jutef's arms. They had always seemed like great wrongs. Were they, perhaps, only great misfortunes?

"I'll go with you to speak to Master Serka," said Elenn.

"Thank you, Master Elenn!" said Leol with tears in his eyes. "I know he will listen to you!"

When Elenn and Leol reached him, Serka was on his side, half propped up with his pack under his arm. Two Quarterhouse masters were there with Jeber sitting beside him. Unmelted water dust clung to his outfield worker's robe.

The Quarterhouse masters immediately rose to their feet and raised hands to face. They stepped back like they were going to leave.

"Stay here with us," said Elenn.

Serka looked up. Elenn saw his sunken eyes and understood the danger.

"Don't worry, Master Elenn," said Serka, "I refuse to eat it."

Despite the fact that Serka might be dying, Elenn couldn't help feeling proud of him. Serka was a true uedin, for better or worse. But Elenn couldn't let him die. "Master Serka, you are needed for this expedition, and for the outfields of the new capital to come. We cannot lose you."

"I will be fine, Master Elenn. I'm going to have my ration of Substance soon."

"It's not enough, Master. You are under-nourished. You won't be able to walk if you don't eat something." Elenn looked at the Quarterhouse guards. "Do you have any with you right now?" he asked them.

One of the Quarterhouse masters looked at Elenn with dumb surprise. All the uedin in the expedition were aware of the controversy, but this master was still under the impression that it was a secret. With a guilty look on his face, he dropped his shoulder bag, opened it up, and took out a section of skinned carcass. It was mutilated in one section where they had used their wooden spikes to rip away bits of flesh.

Jeber saw what Elenn was doing and spoke assertively to Serka. "I told you, Master Serka! I told you this was the best choice you have!"

"Master Elenn, no!" said Serka, "I'd rather eat the seeds that I've carried than eat animal muscles! It's an offense to the Lern!"

"Master Serka, Lern Beyana has gone to sleep, never to wake again. We have no Lern but the kernel in Server Tilke's bag." Elenn took his shortblade from his belt. He reached out and took the carcass section into his hand. "We Quarterhouse masters know when the time has come to do something like this. Isn't that right, Masters?" Elenn noticed their faces show some relief when he said this. He could imagine how they must feel. They were the ones who had been teased for eating the lips and fingertips from the uedin who had cut his own throat in their hatching pool, and now they were the ones who were eating wild dog muscles.

He used his blade to cut a small piece.

"Master Elenn, I don't want to . . . " said Serka, shaking his head.

"Master Serka! Watch me!" said Elenn. Serka looked up. Elenn deliberately held his head high and assumed the posture of a proud Flatpools guard, knowing that that would be important for Serka to see. He put the scrap of wild dog muscle in his mouth, chewed it, and swallowed. The texture was unpleasant, but the taste was indistinct. He was able to swallow it without showing any sign of repulsion.

Serka watched him in astonishment. Elenn cut another piece and did it again. "Do you know why you have to do this?" he asked Serka.

"Why?" asked Serka.

"So that future uedin of the new capital will never have to. You have to survive to plant the outfields."

Serka slowly held out his hand. Leol, Jeber, and the Quarterhouse masters watched in respectful silence. Elenn cut a small piece of the dog muscle and used the tip of his blade to gently pass it into Serka's fingers. He looked at it for a moment, and then, keeping his eyes cast downward, put it in his mouth and chewed.

"Will we all be required to do this?" he asked Elenn.

"I hope not. I hope that Server Tilke and the rouedin, at least, will not have to do it. They are carrying offspring."

"We must keep their rations bigger," said Serka.

"Yes," agreed Elenn, "we will."

Onward Through the Lowlands

The childless had settled into the habit of traveling at the tail end of the caravan, and the path they walked always reflected the traffic of the two hundred or so uedin who walked ahead of them. Sometimes that meant they had to slog over the muddy tracks of the caravan's advance through wet ground. Other times it meant a nicely cleared way that was more or less rid of thorny plants and sharp rocks—or in this case, tall grass in need of trampling down. Four days after they had reached the base of the hill country, Leci noticed the path changing. The ground was soft under his feet.

Leci pondered the mild aggravation he felt about Elenn's decision to head straightaway into the lowlands instead of following along the hills to get a better idea of the lay of the land. Pelto had given only the mere suggestion that they follow the hills, and he had been far from insistent about it. When Elenn gave a sensible explanation that a direct entry into the lowlands was more likely to lead to a lake, Pelto had quickly accepted it. So why did Leci care? It was certainly not because he thought it important to stay at a higher altitude for the sake of surveying the land. Rather, it had to do with the fact that Pelto had been Elenn's direct senior at the bluff. There was a customary relationship between a new one and his predecessor. The new ones had always received a privileged authority in the childless village, but each had always acted humbly, usually with eager solicitation of advice from the previous new one. So it had been with Jeber when he proposed taking whitesponge to the capital only after earnest conversation with Elenn. Elenn's experience with the guards and close ties with Server Tilke were fair reasons for his leadership in the expedition, but Leci found it regrettable that he did not act like a new one these days. On the bluff, when you were a new one, you had authority over every childless who had arrived prior. And when another new came, you gave your authority to him, and you could expect him to respond with deep respect. When Daga had come as new one, Leci had given him authority, and Daga had always shown him great respect in return. Was Elenn discarding his association with the childless? Leci was silently contemplating this regret as he walked with the childless contingent at the back of the caravan.

"Look over there," said Yulig suddenly. It was a stand of trees. They had been traveling through a vast and uninterrupted grassland since leaving the hill country, and these trees were strange looking broadleaf trees with trunks peculiarly wide at the bottom. They were nothing like any trees Leci had seen in the capital or in the hill country. Two hooded masters had separated from the caravan and were under the spectacular trees, investigating.

"What do you think those masters are doing?" asked Leci.

"Maybe they're checking to see if they might be fruit-bearing trees," said Yulig.

"That would be wonderful," said Leci. But no sooner did he let his imagination touch on the idea of fruit, than the masters turned and shook their heads—there was apparently no fruit. Still, the trees were beautiful, and Leci was encouraged by the thought that they might get through this interminable grassland.

It wasn't long before they came to another—larger—stand of similar trees. By this time the sun was at mid-afternoon, and the caravan came to a decisive halt. No communication was necessary; it was clear that they were going to camp there. Leci noticed even more the softness of the ground. It was spongey. The space under the trees had a coziness to it that reminded Leci of the bluff dwellings that were open to the desert as this space was open to the plain. The childless formed their usual edge camp, mindfully spacing out their packs. They formed a distinct clique within the expedition, and Leci hoped that they were not seen as separatist by the groups that traveled ahead of them in the caravan. Rouedin, hooded masters, and server-masters all interacted freely with one another, and only the childless kept more or less to themselves. It wasn't intentional. The childless were so habituated to their own quiet interaction that they just naturally withdrew into it. Yulig, for example, was an indispensable companion to Leci. Many novades ago, Yulig had been the new one when Leci had reached the bluff and traded lives. During Leci's period as new one, he had come to know Yulig as an invaluable confidant. As usual, he opened his pack and prepared to lay out his gear and sleeping mat next to Yulig's.

Their packs were half the size they had been when they had left the capital, most of the non-Substance foodstuffs having been consumed. Leci's pack contained, in addition to various tools and personal items, the remnants of a bale of Substance which he had transferred to a sack, along with one full and unopened bale, still sealed and intended to last for the remainder of the expedition. He also carried water gourds, half of which were empty. He noticed that Yulig's pack was nearly identical in its contents.

"How's your water supply?" he asked Yulig.

"I have enough for another couple days," said Yulig, "but I'm only using it with whitesponge."

"What about the yamflour?"

"I still have some . . . Do you want some yam gruel?"

Leci realized that Yulig planned to use his water for Substance, and did not intend to use it with anything else.

"No, thank you. I am glad to have Substance."

"I am accustomed to the small portions these days. A day's ration satisfies me. But we can certainly mix some gruel . . . "

"No, a small portion of Substance sounds just right."

Some time later, tiny fires burned under small cooking pots all around, and Yulig was tending one beside Leci. Larger fires and communal cooking pots were no longer used much, as the members of the expedition had gradually taken responsibility for their own rationing. Only the servermasters, who walked at the front of the caravan, still had big fires and cooking pots, and Leci could see one of their fires in the distance. The caravan camp was stretched all along the stand of trees, taking advantage of the shade. To Leci, as the sun set over the plain, the darkness under the trees was just like at the dwellings of the bluff.

"Hope you don't mind if it's a bit thick," said Yulig.

"That's fine. Save water," said Leci.

Insects were starting to chirp, and it seemed to Leci that they had not been heard anywhere on the expedition until then.

Yulig divided the barely warmed white mixture into Leci's and his bowls. Leci raised a hand to face and took his bowl. It weighed very little. There wasn't much in it.

They sat on top of their bedding with their bowls. Yulig ate by dabbing his finger into the thick mixture and tasting a bit at a time. He did this slowly and methodically, and Leci tried to slow down and exercise remembrance. Surely that was why Yulig ate so carefully—he was contemplating the meaning of the Substance. Leci was afraid to interrupt, so he didn't try to make conversation. But then, suddenly, Yulig looked up and asked him, "Are you sure you don't want some yam gruel?"

"Oh no, this is fine," answered Leci. Though he tried to eat slowly, he finished his bowl in a very short time.

"I'm afraid that is our ration for today," said Yulig. Leci worried that he looked dissatisfied. He didn't want Yulig to know how much he really longed for more.

He shook his head and smiled, "It's enough. My problem is that I don't practice remembrance enough."

"Remembrance?" said Yulig, "You're referring to the Instruction?"

"Well, yes. If I could concentrate more on remembrance, I think I would not feel like I need more."

"Oh," said Yulig. "If you feel that way, I hope you will learn to do it more."

Leci was a bit surprised. "What do you think about when you're eating Substance? Not the Instruction?"

Yulig chuckled with defeat. "It's true," he said, "I don't think much about the Instruction when I'm eating Substance."

"But the way you eat it, you look like you're thinking about something. What are you thinking about?"

Yulig looked down at his bowl, still half full. He looked back with a puzzled expression. "I don't know what I'm eating," he said.

Leci didn't understand at first, but then Yulig clarified, "I don't know whether it's *Substance*—or just whitesponge, as it has always been for us."

"I agree with you," said Leci. "It is hard to forget our old regard for whitesponge."

"Nobody knows if Substance is really what we say it is. That's what I think about when I eat it. I think about the fact that I don't know what I'm eating."

"I believe in the Instruction," said Leci, "but it doesn't help me eat slowly and be easily satisfied."

"You say you believe, but there's no way to know. Even Server Tilke who delivered the Instruction doesn't know."

"Do you think Server Tilke may even have doubts from time to time?"

"I'm sure he does. And I think he would admit to it if he were asked directly."

Without thinking, Leci said, "Well then you should ask him directly!" He was half joking, but he noticed immediately by the expression on Yulig's face that it was being received as the request of a new one.

"All right," Yulig nodded with serious, downcast eyes. "It means I will have to befriend him."

Leci was a bit stunned that his facetious suggestion was being taken as direction. "I was only speaking in jest," he said. "I don't mean to tell you that you must question Server Tilke."

"It's a good suggestion, Leci. Don't retract it. I will befriend Server Tilke, and someday I will ask him if he ever doubts the Instruction."

Leci raised hands to face. This is the way it usually went with Yulig, and all the elder childless. They took him seriously, even when he did not demand it.

Before first light, Leci lay in his bedding and dreamt. He was back at the capital, walking through the Crafting district. He knew he was dreaming, and he knew that he couldn't be back at the capital because the capital was far away, but the dream felt very real, and he could feel the sun on his face. He heard some shouting and turned around. Master Pavis was calling for help. He ran to see what he needed.

"There's Substance stored here, and mice have gotten in it! Please go get the capital guards!"

Leci turned and started running through the streets of the capital, but he couldn't remember his way to any guard station. He looked for someone to ask, but the streets were empty. He ran about in a panic, not knowing where to go.

Finally he arrived at Quarterhouse. He entered and saw a bunch of unnamed child-uedin. Now, in his dream, he was young, newly-named. He was an apprentice caretaker to the unnamed, and it was a time before he had crossed the desert.

A small unnamed came up to him with tears in his eyes. He was undressed, and he needed help getting his undergarment on.

"That's all right, little one, I'll help you," said Leci. He let the child-uedin hold on to his shoulder and helped him put on the little undergarment. That's when he noticed that the garment, instead of being white like an unnamed's, was made of the dyed green cloth of the capital guards. He looked into the face of the unnamed and saw that it was the child-uedin face of Guardmaster Ribol, the one he first met when he went to get help for Master Pavis at the warehouse.

"There's an emergency!" he told the unnamed child-uedin Ribol. "Mice have gotten into the Substance!"

The child-uedin looked back at him sadly. "It's too late," said the unnamed. "All the capital is lost." The look in the child-uedin's eyes was of tremendous sorrow, the kind of sorrow that an unnamed should never have.

A terrible feeling swept over Leci, but then, for some reason, he reached into his pocket. His fingers touched a small piece of fresh whitesponge, still moist.

"Here," he said, "This will help." He gave the piece of whitesponge to the unnamed.

"Is it Substance, or is it whitesponge?" asked the unnamed.

"Yes, it's both," said Leci.

The child-uedin took it, bit off a corner, chewed, and swallowed.

Leci knew again that he was dreaming, because he knew that he couldn't have had whitesponge when he was an apprentice. That was before he had even crossed the desert, a time when he hadn't even known about the existence of whitesponge. Aware of the discrepancy, he felt his dream interrupted and woke up. There was silence but for distant insect chirping, and the lesser moon was over the plain. It had been a very strange dream. He had a little trouble getting back to sleep. He couldn't rid his mind of the look of despair on the child-uedin's face in his dream.

Tilke's Lake

"What's another word for repeat?" said Wido. It was a joke he never tired of. One of the server-masters had taught it to him.

"Say again," answered Tilke. He could play along for a very long while.

"Ha, ha, ha!" Wido laughed bizzarely. "What's another word for repeat?"

Tilke chuckled at Wido's silliness. "Say again," he answered. Wido laughed more. They were entering an area where the wide-bottomed trees formed a definite kind of forest around them. It was much more sunlit than the forest in the hill country, for the trees were very much spaced apart. The ground they walked on was mushy. Elenn had told Tilke that it reminded him of the marsh at the northwest corner of the capital during the dry years at the end of a novade. Tilke had never seen the marsh, dry season or otherwise.

"Oh! Bug!" said Wido suddenly, pointing into the air. Tilke didn't see anything.

"What did you see? A flying bug?" Tilke looked around from his seat on Wido's shoulders. Elenn, the young Master Serka, and the childless Pelto were walking close by; otherwise the front of the caravan was headed by the server-masters.

"A flying bug?" said Wido, mimicking in response, as he sometimes did.

"Oh. Do you think it was a butterfly?"

"I don't know," said Wido.

Suddenly there was commotion from the server-masters at the very front. Tilke looked up. His position at higher than head-height of everyone else gave him a distinct vantage point for looking at what was up ahead. What he saw was astounding.

In the distance, somewhat to the left of the path they were on, there was a separation between trees that revealed a patch of what looked like a lake. He could see it clearly. The trees on the far shore appeared very small, suggesting that the water covered a large area. The trees were of the same type that surrounded them now, but they appeared to be denser on the other side.

Tilke noticed Elenn, Serka, and Pelto looking ahead with urgent interest. They could not see what he could see. He took a breath to speak, but he suddenly felt unable to make a sound. It was so amazing to him that he stuttered. "I, . . . It . . . " he said.

"Server Tilke, can you see anything?" shouted Elenn.

Tilke took a deep breath. He tried to announce what he was seeing, but he choked on his words and was unable to make a sound.

"*A lake!*" shouted one of the server-masters up ahead.

Elenn, Pelto, and Serka broke into a jog. Wido quickly followed, and Tilke bounced on his seat, holding on. But the ground soon turned to mud under their feet, and they had to trudge slowly.

As they got closer, they came out of the trees into the open lake area and entered a section of tall water grass, brilliantly green. It quickly became apparent that the server-masters up front were encountering deep mud and could not advance all the way to the water's edge.

This lake was flush with life, with birds darting about above its surface to catch flying insects. Its water surface was still and glass-like except for beautiful rippling and ruffling made by little breezes and gusts. As Tilke took in the sight, he felt a need for caution. Could he dare to say it—that this was the lake of the Instruction? He tried, instead, to simply behold its beauty without taking anything about it for granted.

"Another one!" said Wido, pointing to a dragonfly. Tilke watched it momentarily. It hovered in front of them for what seemed like an oddly long moment. Tilke felt a great humility. He felt that he was a creature of the lake, no better or worse, no more or less, than this dragonfly. He had a sudden wish he would never have to leave the lake. But, he thought, putting his hand on the quilted carrier that held the kernel, this was not the end of the journey—not yet.

"It's a dragonfly," said Tilke to Wido, as the creature rose and zipped away skyward.

"Dragonfly," repeated Wido.

The sound of water lapping against the tall grass had a beautiful and peaceful quality in Tilke's ear. He smiled at Wido, but did not engage him in any more talking. He just wanted to listen to the sounds of the water and wind in the grass.

It felt like a rude interruption when commands were given to lead the caravan back to a stretch of solid ground where they could camp. Some chatter began as the entire caravan prepared to back up. It required a wait while word reached the childless who would need to turn and lead them back a distance to solid ground. Finally there was movement, and the caravan was headed out from the lakeshore. In a short while, they made their way back to an area of solid ground that was suitable for setting up a long-term camp. It made sense that they should do so, for they were likely to remain there for some days.

As the expedition party settled in, Tilke was keenly and uncomfortably aware of tremendous respect and regard being shown to him. It was because they were evidently at the lake that they had all been seeking specifically for *his own* passing-of-life, in keeping with the Instruction. The attention reminded him of the awkwardness of being Most High in the temple, back in the early days before he achieved full communion. It was particularly unpleasant to receive such attention when one was attracted to unnameliness. He escaped the gaze of admirers that evening by walking with Elenn back to the lakeshore, as far as the mud would allow them to reasonably go. While they walked, Tilke tried to discuss mundane matters, anything but the fact of where they were or what they were looking at. Peering across the lake, Tilke rambled about the marshflower root they had given him since crossing the lowlands. They didn't want him or the rouedin to eat the wild dog muscles.

"It's stringy compared to yams, but I don't mind it," said Tilke.

Elenn looked at him, a little worried. "I'm glad you can digest it," he said and looked back over the water.

Suddenly there was a big splash at the edge of the lake. "What was that?!" said Tilke.

They ventured a little further toward the water.

A number of rock-like lumps were protruding from the surface where the grass met the water. When one of them leapt high, revealing its huge fat body, they both immediately recognized it as a frog, though they had never imagined such a large one. Another one jumped and dove. Tilke was astounded—it was as big as he was!

When he looked at Elenn, he saw the troubled look and quickly discerned Elenn's concern. The frogs could be a danger to future wetuedin.

"Let us hope that they eat only insects and water plants," said Tilke.

"I wonder if they are all over the lake," said Elenn, clearly troubled by the discovery.

Tilke understood that Elenn saw this as a potential disaster, but at a deep level he had already adopted the lake as his passing-of-life destiny, and he knew that there would be no further search for a more perfect lake, regardless of such an element of danger. They had to just accept the risk that came with this lake. "Until we know that to be the case, let's not be discouraged," he said.

Before Elenn could respond, another of the mammoth frogs dove and swam away. They silently made their way back to the camp. Tilke waited to see how Elenn would report the matter to the others. Interestingly, Elenn said nothing to anyone about the frogs.

On the second day there, a team of scouts returned with reports of having located a mudstream on the opposite shore, one that was sure to turn into a drystream further out. The existence of a stream was confirmation that they had arrived at a lake where passing-of-life could take place and wetuedin could make their way to hatching pools at some distant location. Some server-masters spoke about having seen some big frogs in the lake, but they did not seem to recognize the danger there, and Tilke did not comment. He heard no more said about it, and decided that as long as the subject did not present itself as a matter of concern to the expedition, he would refrain from mentioning it. The lake was beautiful and it filled him with a sense of belonging. He recalled his server training to dismiss fear about the frogs and treat it as a case of futile spiraling. He was glad that Elenn also remained quiet about it.

With the news of a drystream being found on the far shore, the mood of the expedition changed from the wonder of discovery to celebration. Tilke could think no more about the frogs, as he was suddenly made the center of attention—which was never a pleasant position for him to be in. He marveled at the fulfillment of the Instruction, but at the same time felt an urge to shrink from his own role in it. No sooner did the news of the discovery of the stream arrive than some nearby server-masters, in their enthusiasm, began to chant, *"Tilke's Lake! Tilke's Lake!"*

They looked at Tilke with celebration in their eyes, and he knew that it would not be suitable to reveal the discomfort it caused him to hear them chant his name like that. Hearing it, more server-masters and hooded masters gathered around and joined in the chanting. It nearly sickened him, but he forced a smile. It helped to turn and face Wido, who seemed a little perplexed by it all. Wido's appropriate innocence was tremendously comforting, and it allowed him to dissolve his fake smile into a real one.

The expedition party decided to stay at the lake for another four days to rest and reorganize. Those who had adopted skills in searching out and killing wild dogs were bringing back water-dwelling rodents instead of wild dogs. One afternoon, Tilke noticed server-masters cutting and collecting branches in a very selective manner. They were paying careful attention to the thickness and straightness of the branches, and Tilke became very curious about what they were up to. He happened to see Master Jeber helping them, and he approached him. "Master Jeber, what are you all working on?"

Jeber put down the shortblade he was using to carve something into a straight length of branch, and raised hands to face. "Hello Server Tilke," he said. "I'm helping the server-masters a bit here. They always used hollowstem back at the capital, but they're trying to make their laddering pieces with these wooden branches."

"Laddering? They want to do a laddering exercise?"

"Yes, they want to see if they can do it with branches from these trees."

"They want to do it *here*?"

"The ground is soft," said Jeber. "That's why they want to try it here."

"Very interesting," said Tilke. "How long do you think it will take them to get the pieces made?"

"It's just one set. It won't take long."

"I never would have imagined that they would want to do a laddering here . . . " said Tilke.

"It's just to celebrate," said Jeber, "just a little fun before the caravan moves again."

That evening, fires were built high, and the server-masters assembled all the pieces needed for a laddering exercise. Everyone watched as they made their awkward attempts with the makeshift pieces and quickly found them too uneven. Since the poles weren't going to work for any serious attempt at laddering, they festively played out a comic version of a laddering by holding the side poles for the whole duration while a server-master put in slats one at a time for a ludicrously easy climb to the top. Instead of the usual breath-holding and watchfulness, the exercise was performed with shouting and cheering.

"REMEMBRANCE!" shouted the server-master doing the climbing. He shouted it to everyone present.

"REMEMBRANCE!" echoed the crowd as he stepped up on the first rung. They whistled and cheered.

"RATIONING!" shouted the server-master.

"BOO!" some of them shouted, eliciting laughter from the crowd.

Tilke looked around at the joyful faces of the server-masters lit by sunset and firelight. Then, he looked across at Wido, who had a strange look on his face, one of sadness and confusion. Tilke went over to him.

"They are playing. It's not a real laddering."

"I don't want to play," said Wido.

Tilke felt a pang of sadness for Wido. He comprehended that they were acting out a play version of the laddering, but the association of his own accident must have occurred to him. He looked like he was about to cry.

"Don't be sad, Server-master Wido. They are celebrating because we have arrived at this lake. Do you know what lake this is?"

"I don't know," said Wido.

"It's Tilke's Lake," said Tilke with a smile.

"That's you!" said Wido with recognition, "You're Server Tilke!"

"Yes, I am," said Tilke. He nodded and smiled to Wido.

New Home

The caravan followed the winding drystream from Tilke's Lake for four days. The plan had been to follow the drystream until open fields were reached. Then, they could go off in search of a high place, and after burying the kernel, they would return to the open fields to establish a new capital. The problem was that they never reached open fields. There had been plentiful open fields on the other side of the lake, but no drystream ran there. The drystream had formed on the side of the lake which led only through endless forest. It finally split into separate streams going in two directions. The caravan set camp there at the split to consider all options. The hooded guards were quite prepared to let Elenn decide the issue with Tilke, but Pavis and Pelto were both wanting their opinions to be heard on the matter, and it was between the two of them that an argument developed.

Elenn led them away from the camp to a small clearing in the forest where sunlight penetrated the canopy, and there he heard their arguments. Pavis felt that the new capital should be built right at the split, where a single larger drystream could be followed directly back to the lake. That way, the rouedin would easily find their way for their passing-of-life. Back at the lake, it had been decided that the rouedin would stay with the caravan until all the conditions of the Instruction were met, and Pavis had been the one to deliver this news to them. Of course they had been disappointed, for they had hoped that they would be allowed to stay right there at Tilke's Lake, cease eating Substance, and wait for their passing-of-life. Pavis carried the burden of looking after them and reassuring them, and he didn't want to tell them that they would have to travel a lengthy and potentially confusing course in their ecstasy mind.

Pelto, on the other hand, wanted to pursue one of the branches. Since there had been two branches of the mudstream that led from Lake Ceulan, and only one of them led to the old capital, he believed that future wetuedin would find their way just as all generations had always found their way to the old capital. He felt that they should go further in hopes of getting closer to another range of hills, or *some* sort of high place, whatever it might be.

Elenn was unsure. But with dense forest all around the place where the drystream split, the clearing of land for agriculture was going to be a horrendous task if they decided to establish the capital right there.

"The Instruction tells us all we need to know," said Pelto, "It tells us, '*Together, you may find a place which resembles your home . . .*'"

"Yes, and it must have its own lake," interrupted Pavis, "Believe me, Pelto, we know what the Instruction says. But it is only our guide, and it even *says* it guarantees us nothing."

"Well I'm thinking of the important part of that piece of the Instruction. Where it says, '*where my offspring can achieve communion from the high place.*' We can't establish the capital until we know where our high place is going to be. We could clear land here and have more confidence that rouedin will have an easy pilgrimage to the lake, but then we might as well have left the kernel in the mud when it was dropped."

"So you want to keep going—where? Which branch would you follow?" asked Pavis.

Pelto looked a bit stumped. He looked to Elenn to see if Elenn had thought about which branch to follow. "We have to go further, regardless of which stream we follow," he said.

"We also have to consider how much clearing is going to be necessary if we—"

Suddenly Pavis interrupted, "What is that?"

Elenn turned around and looked. She saw nothing. "What did you see?" she asked.

"It looked like . . . a bird, a very large bird . . . " said Pavis. "It's gone."

"Did you see it?" Elenn asked Pelto.

"No, I didn't see anything," said Pelto.

Pavis continued looking there for a moment, and then said, "Ah well, whatever it was, it's gone now."

"There are bound to be creatures living here that we don't see around the capital . . . Like the wild dogs in the high hills are different from the wild dogs that we used to see in the slopes."

"Anyhow, Master Pavis, do you understand that we need to follow one of these drystream branches to a further location? Pelto is right. We've come too far from the hill country—we can't explore high places back there. We have no choice but to see where the drystream leads us. "

"As long as we don't go too far from the lake," said Pavis. "It's not just our current rouedin we need to think about. We have to think about future uedin who will be going to the new lake for their pilgrimage."

When the three got back to the camp, Elenn sought out Tilke. "We have decided we must go further until we know there is a high place to take the kernel."

Tilke nodded and self-consciously raised his hand to touch the carrier on his chest. It was hardly recognizable as the beautiful quilted item Elenn had received from the silk masters. It was covered with traces of mud and dust from all it had endured.

"Let us follow the larger stream," Tilke said. "Wetuedin will someday go wherever we are going, and they will more likely follow the larger."

Elenn nodded. "We may have to come back and place nets someday, like we talked about doing at the cold lakes in the hills."

News of the final decision spread through the expedition party, and there was no objection. As they followed the branch for the next few days, they stopped often to search the horizon for hills. To do this, it was necessary to climb to the tops of tall trees where an unimpeded view could be gained. They hoped to see a prominent high place with a steep rise in altitude, like at the bluff, or even at the Haka Cliffs. But the most they ever saw were gently rising tree-covered hills. Finally, when they were more than ten days from Tilke's Lake, Pavis could acquiesce no more. The rouedin, he reported, were getting very anxious—going any further would make a rouedin's pilgrimage too arduous. They had to stop there and seek out a high place the best they could, even if no sign was evident.

Elenn sent Daga to the top of a tree to look for hills. The Childless were smaller than the barren of the capital, and Daga was small even by Childless standards. Daga carried a clingstone compass with him to get a good direction. After coming down out of the tree, he immediately looked at the clingstone to reestablish orientation.

"Just tree-covered hills?" asked Elenn.

"That's all I could see," said Daga, "But I picked out the highest one. It's at north northeast."

Elenn considered their few options. "We will find a place nearby for a permanent camp," he said, "and then we'll go where your clingstone tells us to go. Did you see any areas of open field?" asked Elenn.

"Nothing," said Daga, sharing the frustration. "We're going to have to clear land." The clearing of land would be a formidable task indeed, for the permanent camp would someday become the new capital, and the forest was thick around them.

The clearing of land was yet to begin when Elenn prepared to depart with a team of twenty to seek a suitable high place for the kernel. After some discussion, Tilke decided he would stay behind and help Pavis look after the rouedin. He worried that if he were to go along on Wido's shoulders, they would only slow down the excursion.

Elenn consented. The group leaving to search for a high place needed to be small and fast-moving. "Then shall I carry the kernel the rest of the way?" he asked. He understood that it was time to take his turn with the fearful task of carrying it.

"I have an idea," answered Tilke. "Can you take Server-master Wido with you? He can carry the kernel without being intimidated." Elenn hesitated. He was not sure it would be a good idea to have Server-master Wido with them.

"Master Elenn . . . It is hard to carry the kernel of the Soft One without thinking constantly about its importance," explained Tilke with earnest. "It is a burden. Server-master Wido, on the other hand, will carry it with ease, just as he has carried me."

So the team included Wido, along with the hooded guards, the outfield worker threesome and various other hooded masters and server-masters who expressed an eagerness to join them. Before they left, Tilke approached Wido.

"We are both going, right?" asked Wido, kneeling on one knee as he always did to allow Tilke to climb up. He already had Tilke's seat strapped to his shoulders.

"Server-master Wido, can you take my seat off your shoulders?"

Wido did not understand the reason for this request, but he obediently undid the straps and removed the seat from behind his head.

"Now, please bring your other knee down, . . . yes, like that . . . and now kneel back . . . " Tilke led Wido to sit back on his feet so that Tilke could reach his head from where he stood. "Server-master Wido, you know I've been carrying the Soft One's kernel. Now I am going to ask you to carry it." He opened the carrier on his chest and removed the kernel. It looked twice as big in Tilke's small hands. Elenn handed him a piece of cloth needed to wrap the kernel and tie it. Tilke lovingly wrapped the kernel and then reached up and pulled the hood off Wido's head. The neck of the hood pulled across Wido's face. The back of his head revealed a bowl-shaped cavity surrounded by scars where his skullwomb had been crushed in the accident. Tilke carefully fit the wrapped kernel into the cavity and tied it in place firmly with a long strip of cloth around Wido's head. "That is a perfect place for you to hold the Soft One's kernel for us."

"I'm sorry," said Wido, a bit confused.

"You're fine, Server-master Wido," said Tilke. "We are very glad that you can carry the kernel for us."

Wido nodded and smiled, and the attached kernel on his head held nice and firm, staying in place as he nodded.

"Let's put your hood back on," said Tilke. He stretched the hood over Wido's head, pulled it down and fixed the corners of the base section. "That looks very good!" he said.

Elenn saw how the protrusion of the kernel at the back of Wido's head looked exactly like a skullwomb. Wido turned to both of them, smiled happily, and brought hands to face. "Thank you!" he said, aware that he now had a bulge where uedin were supposed to have one.

The two-handed blades they used to cut their way through underbrush had, since leaving the capital, only been used for the hooded masters' ceremonial partaking of Substance. Now the team cut through brush and vines as they worked their way north northeast.

Elenn didn't mind the sweaty and tiresome slow movement as much as the nagging pessimism he couldn't seem to shake. Since adopting the rouedin into the expedition, he had wrestled with doubts from time to time about its success. It wasn't that the decision to take them along in any way doomed the expedition by disobeying the Instruction—he wasn't that superstitious. But that had been the first development which had made him think seriously about the Instruction's warning that nothing was guaranteed. Since then, the further they got from the capital, the more he felt disconnected from the basic hope for a future for uedin. When he tried to imagine a new capital coming under construction in the dense forest where the permanent camp was getting set up, all he could think of was futility and failure. The uedin population would die of starvation before they could produce crops. Furthermore, the tree-covered hill where they were headed with the kernel was woefully unlike the bluff where Lern Beyana's Substance had resided. Elenn hid his doubts about finding the needed environment for the kernel to develop into a new lern. And there were other bad signs. They all counted on the health of the new lake to produce healthy fertile wetuedin once the capital was moved . . . what about the frogs that hid there? He and Tilke had acknowledged the danger that they threatened. He had chosen not to talk about the possibility that they might eat wetuedin, but it remained in the back of his mind. The transition from old to new was fraught with too many things to go wrong. He was glad that he did not have the additional burden of carrying the kernel on his person, and he was glad that Wido had been employed to carry it.

The second day out, they came upon a great nest bearing a single, very large egg.

"What is *that?!*" exclaimed Pelto.

It was like nothing any of the group had ever seen before. It looked like the nest of any scavenger chick, but it was enormous. Elenn immediately looked around to see if the nest's owner was nearby. There was nothing unusual in the woods around them. Wido was curious, and neither Elenn nor any of the others were used to keeping an eye on him as Tilke had done. They didn't know what to say when he walked right up to the nest, bent over, and touched the egg.

"It's too big!" said Wido.

"Yes, it's very big," said Elenn, "Too big to resemble the eggs we've seen before. But you shouldn't touch it. Birds don't like it when uedin touch their eggs."

"Maybe there are many many birds inside," Wido commented.

"Probably just one big one," said Elenn.

"One big bird?" said Wido. "I want to see that bird."

No sooner had the words come out of Wido's lips than did a large white creature trot out from behind some trees. It stared at them from one eye. It was as tall as a newly-named. It appeared to be flightless, having no indication of spreadable wings.

"Some kind of . . . bird?" whispered Pelto.

"It's huge!" said Serka.

The bird turned its head and regarded them from the other eye, then quickly and loudly pecked at something on the ground. It seemed unconcerned about their presence.

"It's not even afraid of us," said Jeber, "how strange!"

The bird tilted its head in jerks as it looked at them, seemingly as curious about them as they were about it.

"It's beautiful!" said Pelto. Elenn did not disagree. The creature was pure white, with big round black eyes and a rounded greyish brown bill. It continued to cock its head to one side and then the other, pondering their presence. Then it suddenly did a strange little gallop in place, pecked hard at something on the ground, turned toward its nest, and took a few jerky steps toward them.

Wido's eyes were wide, and his mouth was open. He was absolutely amazed. He looked at Elenn and smiled. "It's too big!" he said with a laugh.

Elenn beckoned Wido to back away from the nest. "Let's be quiet and watch it. It is a quiet bird."

"And friendly," said Wido. "It is a friendly bird." He stood up tall and faced the bird, completely without concern.

"Come this way," said Elenn gently, trying to discourage Wido from going closer to the bird.

"Hello, friendly bird!" called Wido.

"Shhh!" whispered Elenn urgently, "It's a *quiet* bird!"

Wido looked at Elenn with understanding and raised a hand to face in apology.

"Let's get away from its nest," said Pelto. They all backed away and left the way open for the bird to return to its nest. They stood back and watched the bird for a long time. Finally, it approached the nest, checked its egg carefully, and then stepped into its nest and rested on the egg.

Elenn, satisfied that the bird was not disturbed, called out in a somewhat muted voice, "We don't want to disturb the bird. Let's go!" He regarded the clingstone, stepped around a tree, and pushed some shrub branches out of his way. He led them away, whispering, "Stay quiet until we get a little ways off!"

For the rest of day and every day thereafter, Elenn, along with the others, kept looking for more of the birds, but they didn't see another. The group made slow painstaking progress toward the hill that Daga had identified. As day after day passed crossing the forest, it began to feel as though time was dragging on with just as much tedium as the long time they'd spent crossing the hill country. Elenn was perplexed by the distance. The hills had been visible from the treetop back at the drystream. How could they have been visible from there if they were this far away? Perhaps, he thought, it only seemed far because of the manner in which they had to plod through the forest, cutting their path as they went. Whether it was distance or pace, it gave him a sense of dreadfully slow progress toward a goal that he didn't quite believe in. At times, the best he could do was continue along without questioning the point of it.

There was no more sign of the large flightless birds, but they did encounter small, tree-dwelling birds of unusual color and song whose presence cheered the group as they walked the dark forest floor under the canopy of trees. One afternoon when they were stopping for a short rest, Wido took a few steps off into the woods and crouched to have his toilet. Elenn carefully kept Wido's white hood in the corner of his eye while respecting his privacy. When Wido stood up and started walking further into the forest, Elenn quickly went after him.

"Server-master Wido," he called, "We're this way!"

Wido obediently stopped, turned around, and looked at Elenn. "Is the friendly bird here?" he asked.

Elenn looked around. There was no sign of any large bird. "I don't think so," he said. "Did you see one?"

"No," said Wido sadly. "I want to see the bird."

"Maybe we'll see one again," said Elenn. "But we have to stay together. Come back now."

Wido followed him back, and they concluded their break and continued on.

There were regular tree-climbing checks during which Pelto would climb as high as he could to see if they were still on track toward the highest hill and whether it was appearing closer. Though he could only report that it was hard to tell if the hill was appearing closer, they began to notice that they were going slightly uphill. It was apparently a hill of very gradual rise.

As the trek through the forest grew more laborsome for its uphill tendency, Elenn actually wished that they would experience a harder climb. This was the hill they had been aiming for. It was too easy to climb. It did not at all feel like a high place. He hoped that in the next day or two, they would experience some sort of steep rise.

They did not. In fact, it began to rise less.

Pelto came down from a treetop check with a worried face. "I think this is the top," he said. "We're already there."

Elenn sighed with dissatisfaction. "This can't be the top. It's not high enough."

"I looked all around," said Pelto. "There's nothing any higher in sight." He looked at Elenn gravely, and Elenn understood it to be the look of a former *new one* communicating a truth to his immediate *new one* successor. "This will have to be our high place," Pelto said, "What other choice do we have?"

"We were only to climb to half its height . . . " said Umat, standing among the other trekkers.

"What do you think, Elenn?" Pelto asked.

Elenn felt empty and hopeless. "There's nothing to do but bury the kernel right here and go back to the permanent camp," he said. He knew how this all must appear to the others. It was obvious that they had failed to locate a proper high place. None of this matched with the Instruction. They had imagined a scenario in vain. This hilltop was the best place they could find.

The team was demoralized. The Instruction had given them the idea of a high place, and this did not match anyone's expectations. As they took off their packs and looked around, Elenn heard sighs and grumbling. He thought of Tilke and what he would say. Tilke, he thought, would probably shrug and say, "My hope is great, and my comfort is great." There were no other words with which to respond. He decided that he had to call out the words to the group. "MY HOPE IS GREAT, AND MY COMFORT IS GREAT!" he yelled defiantly.

Umat nodded, with understanding. "My hope is great and my comfort is great!" he repeated just loudly enough for the others to hear that he was in agreement with Elenn's leadership.

With exhaustion and disappointment in their voices, they all repeated in unison, *"My hope is great and my comfort is great . . . "*

But strangely, Elenn soon started hearing the little excerpt being repeated from time to time as they settled in. By the time they started digging the next day, it was becoming like the reciting of the Names, or the recitation of the larger Instruction, only this was a single line being repeated over and over, the excerpt all by itself. *My hope is great, and my comfort is great.*

They used the shovels they had carried all the way from the capital, produced and presented with ceremony by the metalwork masters. At the beginning of their digging, they had no use for the pick axes. While they had anticipated the difficulty of breaking through rock, their more pressing concern at this point was how to cut through green tree roots. Elenn could feel the frustration of everyone involved as they commenced with the dig that would need to continue to a depth of one hundred forty handlengths. They were burying the kernel in a place that was simply wrong. The hill country they had crossed had contained many places that were much more suitable for a chosen high place. But the Instruction had required a high place close enough for the new lern to achieve communion, and the hill country they had crossed was too far away from Tilke's lake.

Over the following days, they cut through tree roots and dug through the layers of dirt, clay, and rock, finally using all their tools, shovel and pick ax alike. At a depth of eighteen hand-lengths, they started using rope ladders and sacks to remove the debris.

They didn't mind the hauling up of rock and clay. They were barren. They were large-body uedin. The physical work was not the hard part. The hard part was in believing that the kernel would survive and thrive there. The recitation of the single line, however, persisted. Elenn did at times grow weary of hearing it. He was sure that many of them, just like himself, found the phrase to be encouraging at times and aggravating at other times. The server-masters chanted it so constantly that at any hour of the night, he would hear one of them whispering it. Why did they keep repeating it? Was it because they believed it more than he did, or because they needed it more?

Then, after two days of digging, when they were at a depth of one hundred ten hand-lengths, they hit underground water. It so happened that a few of them were repeating, "My hope is great and my comfort is great" when the water was discovered. The chanting immediately stopped.

Everyone was at a loss for words. Water?! What would they do now? Should they keep digging and basically dig a *well*? If so, would they place the kernel in water? That would be so unlike the dry rock environment where the Substance of Lern Beyana had thrived.

Elenn sought Pelto's advice, but Pelto only shook his head and declined to speak. Pelto, more than anyone else there, knew the dry cave of the whitesponge, and he knew this was nothing like it. He expressed his disappointment with silence.

This will be as far as it goes, thought Elenn. He thought about the Instruction. *If we perish, we will at least perish with the comfort of our mutual love.*

"Wido, will you come here?" Elenn called out. Wido soon stepped to the front of the group. He did his own awkward hands to face and said, "Yes, Guard Master Elenn?"

"I'm going to ask you to do something for us now," said Elenn.

"Can I dig?" asked Wido eagerly.

"No, we're not going to dig any more," said Elenn.

"What can I do?" asked Wido.

"Come here, Server-master Wido. Turn around for me."

Wido stepped close to Elenn and turned around. He had done it once before when Tilke had put the wrapped kernel under his hood.

"I'm going to take off your hood now," said Elenn. He took the corner of the piece of hood that went around Wido's neck and over his shoulders. Wido reached for the other corner with his own hand, helping. Together they pulled the hood from Wido's head, and Elenn carefully took the wrapped kernel from the cavity in Wido's head and held it in his hand.

"We're going to push some big rocks into the hole. Then we're going to have you go down the rope ladder. Do you remember when you did the laddering exercise? You can climb up and down."

"Yes, I remember," said Wido, and Elenn could clearly see that the memory was not a happy one for Wido.

"You can climb down there, and put Lern Beyana's kernel on top of the rocks and come back up. Do you think you can do that?"

"I think I can do that," said Wido.

"We think you can, too," said Elenn. He felt tears in his eyes.

After a good number of large rocks were dropped into the hole, the rope ladder was put in place, and Wido was given the kernel.

"Should I take this off?" he touched the wrapping cloth.

"What do you think?" asked Elenn.

"I think I should leave it on," said Wido.

"Then please leave just like that, and put it just like that on top of the rocks," said Elenn.

Wido proudly held the wrapped kernel to his chest and started down the rope ladder. He had a little glimmer of confidence in his eyes that reminded Elenn of when he had first met Wido before his accident at the longhouse at Redrock outvillage.

For the long minutes that it took for Wido to carry the kernel down the ladder, place it on the rocks, and climb back up, there was absolute silence. No one repeated the line about hope and comfort. Elenn looked around and saw that some of them had tears in their eyes, others only gazed at the hole.

When Wido reappeared, they all cheered and clapped, but it was not in a celebration of success, since they had not even reached the prescribed depth of one hundred forty handlengths. It was only to make Wido smile and feel good. Wido did smile, and started clapping with them.

The piles of soil and clay that had accumulated around the excavation were shoveled back into the hole until it was full. As soon as that was done, they were eager to leave.

The return to the permanent camp went much faster because the trail they had made on their way was waiting for them. In just a few days, they reached the place where they had seen the nest with the large egg, and they found that it was still there. However, there was no sign of the large bird, even though they lingered there for a long while to indulge Wido who longed to see it again.

When they reached the camp, there was initial excitement at their return. Elenn did his best not to express his pessimism about how the kernel had been buried. Wido met Tilke with joy and reported that he had put the kernel at the bottom of the hole. Tilke listened happily. Elenn felt uninclined to provide great detail.

Even when Elenn and Tilke had a chance to speak alone, Tilke did not ask about the burial of the kernel. Instead, he said, "Oh, Master Elenn, you must find Master Pavis and speak with him. He's very upset."

"What now?" asked Elenn.

"While you were gone, the Quarterhouse masters killed a large bird and roasted it. Pavis was extremely unhappy about it. He said he had seen the bird before—with you. Do you know what he's talking about?"

Elenn was already feeling heavy-hearted about returning to the permanent camp with a disappointing tale. Now he felt the blood drain from his face.

"They killed it?" he asked.

"So you *did* see a bird like that, with Master Pavis?"

"No, but we saw one like that on our way to the hill. We've only encountered one. I fear it may be the same one the masters killed."

"I hope you will speak with Master Pavis. He was quite upset about it."

"Server Tilke, please don't mention it to Server-master Wido. He was so fascinated by the bird we saw."

"He will hear about it one way or the other," said Tilke. "Pavis expressed anger at the masters, and it caused much controversy. Everyone is still talking about it."

"Server-master Wido called it 'friendly bird.' He will be sad."

"Well, perhaps there will be more of them. Where there is one, there are usually many," said Tilke.

"Usually," said Elenn, "Perhaps there are others."

But when Elenn found Pavis and spoke to him, Pavis was unwilling to be comforted by the notion that there could be others out there.

"I told them they must never kill such a creature," said Pavis, "but they had already killed it, and it was too late. So they roasted it on a fire and ate its muscles. They tried to give me some . . . Can you imagine?"

"I will speak to all of them," said Elenn. "I should have done it before."

"But they are hungry for muscles!" cried Pavis. "Do you think they will listen to anyone?"

"Uedin are not normally eaters of animal muscles," said Elenn. "They will listen."

Pavis embraced Elenn, and spoke quietly in his ear, "The Soft One would have shrunk from such killing." Elenn was moved by this. He rarely saw Pavis as a uedin who had been raised to be a server.

That evening, when the hooded masters gathered for their partaking of Substance, Elenn and Tilke got their attention before they started.

"Masters, something needs to be announced," called out Elenn, getting all their attention, "I've asked Server-master Wido to make the announcement."

Wido stood up courageously, looked around with his peculiar unbalanced eyes, and addressed them. "You should not kill the big birds," said Wido.

None of the masters spoke.

"Don't kill him. He is a friendly bird," said Wido.

A hooded master who was not from Quarterhouse spoke out in defense of the Quarterhouse masters who had killed the bird. He looked at Elenn as he spoke, rather ignoring Wido. "The Quarterhouse masters know they made a mistake in killing the creature," he said, "They've already apologized to Master Pavis."

Elenn did not respond. He let Wido speak.

"I am sad because they killed that bird," said Wido back to the master. "He is a friendly bird. Don't kill him."

No more was said.

In short order, discussions began about the organizing of a return to the old capital to bring back the first group of settlers. They thought it would be possible to bring two hundred across the hill country in one trip along with stockpiles of food and Substance. Elenn had already worked out most of the plan with help from Pelto and the hooded guards. He was giving Tilke a rundown of the departure details.

A Quarterhouse master appeared with a bag. Elenn knew it was cooked muscles. He had to concentrate on appearing casual about it.

"It's roasted," said the master. "It's easy to chew." He handed Elenn a few pieces of the cooked muscle.

Elenn was tongue-tied for a moment as he looked at the slightly charred pieces. Then he saw Tilke watching him, seeing how he hesitated.

"Give me a piece," said Tilke, "Why should I be spared when you are required to worry?"

"No, Server Tilke. You should not eat this. We have enough food for you."

"I can eat this just as you can," said Tilke. "I am a uedin."

"We are the barren," said Elenn. "We have always known shame. We have always known worry. This is part of our duty. We'll eat the wild dog muscles. You should have yam gruel. If uedin survive, generations to come will eat yam gruel."

"But it is only for a short time of survival," argued Tilke. It was true. But Elenn just felt deep down that it would be wrong to let Tilke take on the burden of eating animal muscles. The same went for the rouedin.

"You don't give this to any of the rouedin, do you?" he asked the master who had brought the bag.

"No, Guard-master Elenn. We all know the rouedin should not be given wild dog muscles to eat."

Even if it was only for a short time of survival, the problem, to Elenn, was not so much about future uedin. The burden of eating wild dog had an aspect that Elenn was ashamed to talk about. It was intoxicating, but not like smelling sourembers or drinking yeastdrink. It was intoxicating like sharing necks—not to the same degree, but somehow in the same realm of pleasure. At a certain point came wisdom that taking pleasure in something so offensive to uedin identity was dangerous and wrong. The taste of the wild dog muscles lured them into something uncontrollable. Already there were many of the server-masters who were eagerly learning how to search out and kill wild dogs. They ate wild dog muscles with smiles and laughter.

"What does it smell like to you? Does it smell like something you want to eat?" Elenn finally asked Tilke.

"I want to eat it to reassure you," said Tilke. "It is not acceptable that the barren know a shame that other uedin do not know. The Soft One shrank from such an discrepancy."

"Then there is just one caution that I must give you," said Elenn.

"And what is that?" asked Tilke.

"Once you eat it, you may find, to your own displeasure, that you like it."

Tilke, hearing this, stared at Elenn for a long time, saying nothing.

"Think about whether you really want this," said Elenn, and he lifted a piece of roasted dog muscle to his mouth while maintaining eye contact with Tilke. He put it in his mouth and began to chew, watching Tilke for any reaction.

Tilke neither smiled nor expressed disgust. He looked back with rather sad and forgiving eyes. "Ancient uedin did this also," he finally said. "The Soft One is not with us now."

"Server Tilke, you say things that cross one another. You say Lern Beyana—the Soft One—doesn't like discrepancy if we barren carry a special burden, but when it comes to eating animal muscles, which we've always known Lern Beyana shrank from, you say that the Soft One is not with us now. How can both things be true?

"It's because I was the Soft One's Most High," said Tilke. "I was able to read the thoughts of the Soft One until the Soft One possessed me, and I remember Soft One's style of thinking. It is not just that I say things that cross one another. Ancient uedin ate animal muscles. We know that. The Soft One must have known also. But if the thought of it made her shrink, it did not make her love uedin any less."

Elenn held up a hunk of wild dog muscle. "You want to eat some of this?" Elenn asked Tilke, making an unpleasant face to convince him to decline.

"Yes," said Tilke. "I do want to." He took the piece from Elenn's hand, and thoughtfully put it in his mouth and chewed. He swallowed and spoke, "Don't worry, Master Elenn. We have become wild dog eaters, and we will be wild dog eaters as long as we must to survive. But we will never become wild dogs. We are still uedin, as long as we fully understand what we are doing."

Return to the Capital

The return party were at the beginning of their trek back to the old capital, and they were stopping at the place where the two smaller streams came together to form one large one. They would camp one night before following the main drystream up to what was now being called Tilke's Lake. The travelers included most of those who had gone to bury the kernel, with the exception of Wido. In addition, a number of the Childless were returning to the capital as well, for they planned to do a full inventory of the remaining Substance in storage at the capital warehouses. Elenn, Pavis, and Yulig were digging marshflowers at the edge of the drystream. It had a starchy tuber that had been offered, when found, only to Tilke and the rouedin.

"Some of the rouedin say they like it," said Elenn.

"They're just being polite," said Pavis.

"Well, we used to eat it once in a while at Flatpools."

"What does Server Tilke say about it?" asked Yulig.

"He eats it," said Elenn. "He seems to like it all right. But it's a lost cause. He still insisted on eating a bit of the wild dog muscles."

"Server Tilke ate wild dog muscle? Out of curiosity?" asked Pavis.

"He felt it was something he needed to do," said Elenn, not wanting to explain that Tilke did so in order that Elenn might feel less ashamed about eating it himself.

"Server Tilke cares deeply about you. He missed you every day when you were taking the kernel to the high place," commented Yulig.

"I'm glad you have befriended him," said Elenn. "Other than Server-master Wido and myself, there are few in the expedition who talk with him."

"I'm glad Server-master Wido stayed behind to keep him company," said Yulig. Then he added, "Did you know Server Tilke gave me a letter to take to the temple?"

"Is it for the high servers?"

"No, just for the primary advisor."

"Oh yes, Server Tilke and the Primary Advisor are very close. I'm sure they are both eager to meet again."

"How does one gain entrance to the compound?"

"I'll introduce you to Guard Master Amit at Central Station. He has regular contact with the temple emissary. He can make the arrangements."

Pavis spoke up. "Master Elenn, how long do you think it will take to reach the capital?"

"Well," said Elenn with a sigh, "we're moving much faster since we don't have the whole caravan, and these packs are small . . . "

"A full mooncycle?"

"Maybe that long. Probably not."

"I wonder if Server Tilke will read any Lern thought by the time we get back," said Pavis, innocently.

"Lern thought? Oh, I think it could be a long time before that happens." Privately, Elenn imagined that Tilke would probably never have any contact with a new lern, because he felt it was likely that no lern would ever hatch in the miserable hill where they had buried the kernel. With time, the failure of contact would tell Tilke that the kernel had failed to develop. It was going to be a terrible predicament for Tilke whose main purpose for being there was to receive contact. Elenn tried not to think about it.

"Master Pavis, do you have your woodflute with you?" asked Yulig.

"I always have it with me," said Pavis.

"Can you play us a short little song? Get us in the mood to start walking again?"

"I can do that," said Pavis. He reached into his pocket and took out the woodflute. Leol and Serka, sitting nearby, turned and listened with smiles as Pavis played a single verse of a cheery little tune without repeat.

"Very good!" said Elenn. "Let's keep on now! We'll be at Tilke's Lake before nightfall!" It felt so strange to refer to the new lake as "Tilke's Lake," but the server-masters had absolutely named it thus. Elenn hated to admit that he worried Tilke would probably have to be transported to the lake when the day came for his pilgrimage. The Instruction described a new home with its own lake and its own high place, and the home must be where Lern Beyana's offspring could achieve communion from the high place. *When he whom you have called Most High receives guidance from my offspring for his journey to the lake, you may know that my offspring has awoken and your new Lern will be with you.* But Elenn could only think of the many ways the Instruction had gone unfulfilled. The new capital was going to need new traditions. Passing-of-life, for future generations, might require that rouedin be transported to the lake. With that in mind, as Elenn led the trek up the drystream to arrive at the lake that evening, he imagined how a permanent road might have to be built all the way there.

They reached the lake, hiked around it, and retraced their path through the forest for the next few days, heading back toward the hills. When they had left the permanent camp, many were excited and eager to return to the capital. They talked about friends and acquaintances waiting there. But in the course of their return to the capital, everyone began to share the strange feeling of knowing that the permanent camp was going to be their new home and become their new capital. They were going back to a place that had been their home, but it would no longer be. Pavis mentioned it one day when they were gaining elevation and knew they were on their way to the series of three cold water lakes in the high hills.

"The new capital will eventually have a library," he said, "Maybe we can bring some of the collection back each time we go to the old capital."

"At least the codes," said Elenn. "But I will let the masters council decide everything from this point."

"Master Jutef and Master Yenca have increased their influence in recent years," said Pavis.

It was true. Jutef and Yenca had both acquired rank on the masters council. Elenn hadn't thought about either of them for a long time. "You know Master Yenca of Quarterhouse?"

"I met him though Master Jutef. They had a great debate about giving the hooded masters permission to carry out a self-extermination."

"Really?" said Elenn, curious. "What were their positions on that?"

"Yenca was against it. He said the numbers of syndrome-afflicted unnamed was too high to allow for any of that. He was afraid it would become an expectation that would shift onto their generation."

"And Master Jutef disagreed?" asked Elenn.

"Master Jutef didn't want to deny the hooded masters their free choice to self-exterminate. He said that the caretakers just needed to be very clear in their message to the unnamed. The unnamed needed to be taught that such a thing was a freedom, but would never be an expectation."

"Master Jutef always has an interesting way of looking at things, doesn't he?" commented Elenn.

"He is not proud of being associated with the hood statute," said Pavis.

"He never was. But he shouldn't be ashamed of it," said Elenn. "The hooded masters would not be who they are without the hoods."

"I hated the idea of taking hood," said Pavis. "Remember when you convinced me to accept one?"

"Apparently you don't mind it anymore. You would not have to wear it now if you didn't want to."

"What about you, Master Elenn? When you came back from the bluff, you were without hood. When did you start wearing it again?"

"When I went to see the Flatpools District guards, they made a terrible fuss over me. They gave me this new suit of guard's garb." Elenn touched the sleeve of his green robe. "Then, when I met the other squadron guards and found them all in hood, I decided that I would wear the hood again."

"I'm sure the Flatpools District guards are very proud that you came from their station."

"Maybe, but I'm sure they also remember all the grief I caused them."

"I know a few of the Flathouse District guards," said Pavis, "Do you know Master Ippal?"

"Of course I do. Master Ippal substituted for Master Nula when he was ill."

"I've drunk yeastdrink with Master Ippal before—he's very funny!"

"I would love to have a cup of yeastdrink with Master Ippal," said Elenn. "Maybe we'll have a chance to do that together." Elenn made a mental note to propose a party at Flatpools District station house after they got back to the capital. Master Wanba could be easily persuaded to go along with something like that. It would be good to raise a cup with all the old Flatpools guards. He thought of Master Deben who had helped him in his apprenticeship at Flatpools, and Nemis with whom he had camped at Murro. Master Henik had been so kind to him. Ribol,

Simol, all of them! It was going to be wonderful to see them again. Of course he would pay a special visit to Master Benar's hut, as he always did. And certainly he would have a chance to talk more with Master Jutef.

He noticed that Pavis had fallen silent and probably had his mind on the capital, just as Elenn did. All the uedin who had remained in the old capital during the expedition were there now, waiting for their return. It was strange to straddle two worlds—the old capital, which claimed all of uedin memory, and the permanent camp, buried in forest and largely unorganized. It was the presence of familiar faces which would make it their new home.

As they gained elevation for the next few days, they continued following the path they had created coming down. They had to duck under branches here and there as they climbed, and they noticed that the needle-leaf trees gradually appeared, predominating the landscape only to eventually give way to the empty rugged terrain of the highest hills. There, to their relief, they experienced none of the water dust that had rained on the caravan when they had come across the first time.

By the time they got to the three lakes, the server-masters among them insisted that they camp for a few days so that they could search out wild dogs and replenish their supply of muscles. This they did, and Elenn tried to hide his discomfort by eating it without showing reluctance.

Before they knew it, they were packing up to follow the cold water stream that spilled from the lowest of the lakes. It had been a long climb up. It felt very different going down. They finally reached the spot where Cebik and the Quarterhouse masters had discovered the cold water stream in the first place, close to where they had been attacked by wild dogs. Now the uedin were the killers of wild dogs. They scouted the area seeking to take more, but there were none around, and the next day they left the cold water stream behind and started across the stretch of hill country west of the Lake of Ceulan. They reached the mudstream a little north of the place where it split into two. They could see their old tracks in the mud. They followed the path down, and this time, followed the drystream that the rouedin had traveled. It would take them back to the capital in a more direct route.

When they came to a place where a very huge pile of rocks had been obviously stacked by uedin for generations, they figured out that that was how pilgrims to passing-of-life marked the edge of the drystream for future pilgrims to follow. From that location they could head south to the lichen fields and then on to the capital.

By the time the return party reached the lichen fields, they were all tired of wild dog muscles and the foul-tasting water from the mudstream. They were thirsty for good water and eager to eat good food in the capital. Elenn thought about the fact that the caretaker hut was so close to the capital gate. He wanted to stop to greet Jutef, but there would not be enough water there for the return party. There was no one in sight when they crossed the Northgate Bridge.

Elenn told Posha, "Master Pavis and I will stop briefly to see Jutef at the caretaker hut. The rest of you can go ahead to North-gate Station; we'll join you there shortly."

They reached the gate. Elenn and Pavis headed down the path to the caretaker hut as the others went on ahead.

"I will only stay long enough to greet Master Jutef," he told Pavis. "You can stay and talk with him longer if you like, then join us at Northgate Station. Perhaps Master Jutef will come with you." Pavis agreed.

But when they reached Jutef's hut, they found it empty. There was no water or food there. The inside of the caretaker hut was dusty and had the appearance of not having been occupied for days. An unfinished basket was on the floor beside Jutef's chair. The pile of reeds he had been using to weave it were completely dried out.

"If he moved out, why did he just leave everything like this?" asked Pavis.

"I have no idea," answered Elenn, equally befuddled.

When they heard the approach of running feet outside, they weren't sure who might be coming. A hand smacked the door tarp, and a server-master from the return party pulled it aside and addressed them.

"Something wrong!" he yelled, out of breath from running there, "We aren't finding anyone! Northgate District is empty!"

Elenn and Pavis hurried after him back to the gate. They entered the capital and saw the empty streets. The weirdness of not seeing any uedin sunk in as they neared Northgate Station. The return party was there waiting for them, stunned expressions on all of their faces.

Onnek met them first. "Master Posha and I are going to Southgate to see if we can find out what's going on."

"Nobody here at all?" exclaimed Elenn in disbelief.

"Master Umat said he's searched the whole station grounds. Not a guard or anyone in sight."

Elenn entered the station house.

"Aren't there any notes here?"

"I told Master Kobi so many times that we should be keeping a log," said Umat. "He didn't think it was important."

"There must be something happening in another part of the capital. I'm going to Flatpools," said Elenn. "There's always at least one guard on duty at the station house."

"I'll go with you," offered Pelto.

"Ordinarily there would always be someone here, too," said Umat. "It has to be some kind of emergency."

"I'm going to see if Master Yenca is at Quarterhouse," said Pavis.

Elenn tried to stay focused. It seemed to him that since they were back in the capital now, maybe the return party could disperse to their own residences. "Let's all go ahead and return to our own districts," he said, "If anyone needs me, look for me at Flatpools."

So they all headed out from Northgate toward their own residences and assumed that they would meet uedin there who would explain why Northgate was empty. But as Elenn made his way through the streets, with Pelto following, the absence of uedin was deeply troubling. Where was everyone?

Elenn ducked under the doortarp at Flatpools Station, calling, "Hello? Who's on duty?"

The front office was empty, and there was no response from anywhere. They searched the bunkhouses and found unmade bedding but no uedin. He went back to look for log books in Henik's desk. There was a stack of them sitting right on top of the desk. Elenn got a strange feeling that Henik had left them out for him to see. He opened the top volume.

The only thing written was a list.

> *Master Lobu, 6th gen, Bells cook, lost passing-of-life*
> *Master Ranow, 5th gen, Quarterhouse tutor, lost*
>   *passing-of-life*
> *Master Soren, 5th gen, Capital custodian, lost*
>   *passing-of-life*

It went on and on, page after page. Elenn put it down and picked up the volume beneath it. Its more distant entries went into slightly more detail but still consisted of a basic list of uedin who had lost their passing-of-life.

Master Nappo, 5th gen caretaker, was picked up at Bramble where the masters reported he had suddenly succumbed to the tem-

ple fever and lost his passing-of-life. His body was transported to the depository at Claybridge.

Then Elenn saw a familiar name.

Guard-master Deben, 6th gen, one of our own, was struck with temple fever yesterday and died during the night. Henik and Simol carried his body to Claybridge.

Master Deben?! Elenn much loved Master Deben! He was gone? . . . with all these others? And . . . The gravity of the situation struck him. The capital had been annihilated. But surely there were survivors. Maybe the survivors had concentrated in one part of the capital. Elenn closed the log and picked up the whole stack to take with him. "We have to find somebody," he said. "Where would be the best place to go?"

"I think we should try the infirmary," said Pelto. "If there are survivors, they might be there."

"It's still light out," said Elenn. "Let's go back to Northgate and get Masters Cebik and Umat. They can go with us to the infirmary." Elenn was imagining a grim scene of many ill uedin.

On the way to Northgate, they passed the Bramble domicile.

"I want to see if anyone's in there," said Elenn.

It was getting dark, but they walked through the courtyard at Bramble, and Elenn started entering rooms to look for anyone. Again, they encountered only dark, silent rooms. Then, Elenn found himself in a room that he recognized. It was the room where novades before he had met with Nula's counselor, the caretaker Master Yinob. On a ledge beside the window, Elenn found Yinob's diary.

He took it out to the courtyard where there was still enough light to read it. He opened it in the middle and saw an entry about how annoyed Yinob was with one of the custodians about some neglected chore. He jumped ahead to the last written section. His eagerness to learn what had happened did not allow him to actually read it. Instead, he impatiently flipped the pages, looking for key words. He saw the word illness and stopped to look at what was written.

I saw Master Yenca today, and he told me that the masters council has been notified that a strange illness has spread through the temple compound. The servers took so long to report it to anyone outside the compound that some servers have actually died. Yenca looks worried and exhausted. I don't envy his position on the masters council. We just got through those horrible experiences with the mice and then with the fleas. Everyone here at Bramble was miserable with flea-bites. What can the masters council do about any of this? Nothing. Yenca needs a rest.

Elenn flipped ahead. There was a mention of "Redrock."

The masters council finally released the capital guard report about Redrock outvillage. It has no survivors. They don't know how the illness even reached the outvillage.

Elenn thought of Master Nehu. He was gone too. Elenn quickly flipped ahead to the last entry. It was written with uneven, scribbled handwriting.

I am too sick to go for water anymore. The Instruction ends with comfort and hope, but I am going to lose my passing of life, and I have little comfort or hope. I am glad I went to learn about desert-watching exercises. I can look out and see the wind in the trees. I can watch that. I am not required to think about comfort and hope that I don't have. I'll watch the wind. That was the last thing he wrote.

When Elenn and Pelto reached Northgate Station and went inside, they expected to find only Cebik and Umat, who were Northgate guards. Elenn had figured it would only take a short explanation to get them to come along to the infirmary. But many from the return party were there. Among, them, Onnek and Posha—with traumatized looks on their faces. Pavis was there too, back, obviously, from Quarterhouse. Pavis approached them with red and swollen eyes. He closed his eyes and whispered, "The bodies of the dead have been piled up in the gully under the Clay Bridge. There are thousands of them. Southgate Station was also filled with dead uedin. The whole population of the capital seems to have died from some illness."

Posha saw Pavis whispering to them and cried out, "The stench outside the South Gate is so strong, it's impossible to breathe!"

"Has anyone been to the infirmary?" asked Elenn.

"We went in the main entrance and hollered to see if anyone was there . . . " said a hooded master in Crafting robe, "There was no answer. It was dark and quiet. I don't think there's anyone in there."

"Pelto and I are going to the infirmary to investigate," said Elenn, "We'll need lamps."

"We'll go with you," said Cebik. He looked at Umat, and Umat nodded.

They quickly prepared lamps and left for Central District.

As they were walking, Umat asked Elenn, "Where do you think the disease came from?"

"We know it started in the temple compound. It was referred to as 'temple fever' in the Flatpools log."

Cebik suddenly suggested, "Do you think the servers fell ill for sorrow over the loss of Lern Beyana and their Most High?"

"Oh my, that's a sad thought . . . but it might be true," commented Umat.

"Who can say where a disease comes from. This is too horrible to have ever imagined. The capital that we loved is gone."

"It's true. It hardly matters where a disease comes from. It only matters that it comes," said Pelto.

"We can try to determine where the disease came from later on. Right now I just want to know if there are any survivors. We haven't even found one survivor!" Elenn was embarrassed by the panic in his own voice. In a voice more suited to a guard, he said, "It's getting dark. We better go."

They arrived at the front entrance and entered with lamps held out in front of them.

"ANYONE HERE?" shouted Elenn.

After a moment, Umat shouted, "HELLO!!"

"HELLO!" shouted Cebik.

"HELLO!" echoed Pelto.

There was no sound. They started down the main corridor.

Before they could reach any of the rooms, the smell of decay assaulted them. They looked at one another in sober understanding.

"We should probably check every room," said Umat.

"Do we need to split up?" asked Cebik.

"We can stay in a group. It might take a little longer, but it will be easier for us all," said Elenn, and the two nodded agreement.

They went together from room to room. Not all of the rooms contained the bodies of dead uedin, but most of them did. They had to force themselves to breathe the air. The guards held up their lamps in each case and shouted, "ANYONE ALIVE?"

"ANYONE ALIVE?"

"ANYONE ALIVE?" they repeated into one room after another. They somehow knew it would not be wise to get too close to the dead bodies.

By the time they finished checking every room, they were all feeling nauseous.

As they came out the front into the street, Cebik nervously confessed, "I hate to say it, but I'm feeling sick. I'm afraid I might have breathed in the disease."

"I feel it too," said Umat, "but it's just nausea from the smells."

"I hope you're right!" said Cebik.

"I feel sick too. I think it's from the smell," said Elenn.

"Let's hurry back!" said Umat. They jogged through the capital streets. Elenn's mind was overwhelmed, and he had no doubt that the others were equally overwhelmed. But he didn't have the energy to try to engage in any discussion, so he was glad to jog, and breathe hard instead of talking. He was glad that he could breathe the good air, far away from those dead bodies.

He recognized a common shortcut to Quarterhouse, and had a thought which made him call the others to stop. "Masters, I would like to check one hut at Quarterhouse. The rest of you should go on back without me."

"No, we'll go with you," said Cebik.

They went down the side road at a walking pace. Umat and Cebik weren't as familiar with the short-cut as Elenn was. They turned a couple corners and came to the clearing that had served as a playing field for the unnamed, back when there *were* unnamed. From there they passed under some greenbark trees and walked up an earth ramp to the Quarterhouse and its adjacent facilities. They relit their lamps, and Elenn led them to a group of huts near the kitchen. He approached one of them.

"This is the hut of Master Benar, one of the first caretakers to the barren. He preferred being called a 'caretaker to the afflicted.'" Elenn stopped in front of the door.

He could not bring himself to call out, "Master Benar?" as he had done so many times.

Cebik, Umat, and Pelto were all looking at him through the lamplight. He looked up bravely, but he knew they saw his fear and sorrow.

"Oh Master Elenn, was this your counselor's hut?"

"Master Benar!" Elenn shouted through pain and tears. "Master Benar!"

"Do you want to go in?" Cebik asked him in a kind voice.

"Yes," said Elenn, now beginning to let his tears flow, "I do want to."

They pushed the door tarp aside and held it high so they could enter with their lamps.

There was no stench. The hut was neatly kept. There was a made bed with no one in it. On the table was a note. It was addressed to Guard-master Elenn of Flatpools Station. Cebik and Umat both held lamps up so that Elenn could open it and read it.

He read aloud. *"My dearest Master Elenn, if you are reading this, you have come back to the capital. How I would love to hear you tell about your time away."* Elenn paused to think about Benar saying this. It would have been hard to tell Master Benar about all that they had been through, but certainly Benar would be very eager to hear about it. He continued, *"We don't know what brought the illness to us, but I hope it will be spent by the time you arrive. I know you will be sad to see what has happened to us. It has been terribly sad to watch it unfold. Sometimes I have to sit and look at the roof of Quarterhouse because I can't stand to think about all the passing-of-life that is lost. I can see just a corner of the roof of Quarterhouse from the little yard in front of my hut. I sit and look at the roof, and it makes me feel better."* Elenn stopped here to swallow and fight back emotion. He went on, *"I wish I could advise you about how to best look after survivors. I'm afraid you will have to depend on your fellow guards for help with that."* Elenn stopped momentarily and looked up at Cebik and Umat. They were listening with sympathetic faces. Elenn went on reading, *"Master Elenn, please know how proud you made me. You were my counselee, and I dare to think that I had some influence on you, but even if I didn't, it was very wonderful to have you visit me. Sincerely, Benar of Quarterhouse Caretakers."* He took a deep breath and folded the letter. "We can go," he said. He put the letter in his pocket and held up his lamp. "Let's hurry back," he said.

In the following days, the Childless Yulig, Daga, and Leci completed an inventory of Substance, demonstrating an amazing coolheadedness. Their calm in the midst of the tremendous grief of the situation was a reassurance to Elenn. He was glad to follow them on a tour of the warehouses where waxed urns of Substance were stacked to the ceilings. They reported that all together, between the stockpiles of six different warehouses, there were more than fifteen hundred of the urns, all full of undisturbed Substance. They would have to make many return trips to the capital to get it all.

"We've only seen three warehouses," said Elenn, "I'd like to see them all."

"Do you have time, Master Elenn?" asked Yulig.

"I'd like to see the entirety of Substance. I'll have a better idea if I see it," said Elenn. He did not need to tell them that he was glad to spend this time away from the search for survivors. Everyone else in the return party was combing the capital, just as they had been for three days. They were finding no survivors, and Elenn was greatly relieved to be looking at the urns of Substance instead of helping them search.

At some point in the tour of warehouses, Elenn remembered that Yulig had a letter from Tilke for the Primary Advisor at the temple. The temple had already been thoroughly searched and found to have only corpses, no sign of a living uedin. "Yulig, do you still have the letter from Server Tilke?" Elenn asked.

"Yes," said Yulig, "But there is no one to give it to."

"Have you read it?"

"No. I was planning to give it back to Server Tilke when we get back."

"Perhaps we should read it," said Elenn. "If there was anything that Server Tilke wanted from the temple, we might be able to take it back for him."

Yulig reached into his pocket and retrieved the letter. He handed it to Elenn, and Elenn opened it and read aloud: *"To my dear Primary Advisor, The kernel has been buried. We shall see if an offspring of the Soft One comes into being. It could be a long time. I would be glad if you would come with the first migration. The Childless of the Bluff practice a mental discipline of watching that is much like our mindstilling exercise. They are willing to assist with the transition of the temple. I am asking one of them to deliver this letter. Please speak with him. Ask him anything you want to know about the expedition. I hope you will keep company with him during your travel coming here. Thank you for helping me when I was serving as Most High. I look forward to seeing you again. Server Tilke.*" Elenn looked at Yulig to see his reaction to being recommended as a traveling companion for the Primary Advisor.

Yulig's face betrayed a measured sadness. "It doesn't sound as if Server Tilke was requesting anything be brought back from the temple—other than his Primary Advisor." Then he added, "I was indeed looking forward to helping the servers establish a new temple. I do believe the servers and the childless would have had much to learn from one another." What Yulig only alluded to, Elenn felt as a deep and disturbing realization. There had been no barren servers in the expedition because they had all self-exterminated. Pavis had become a master, and Tilke had had such a unique role as Most High that he had little knowledge of regular server life. The entire culture of server life was gone.

Onnek had reported that the workhouse in the western outfields was found with many dead inside. Every neighborhood was checked and checked again. Some of the hooded masters who had grown up in Southgate even took it upon themselves to check through the piles of dead bodies under the Clay Bridge. They found no living uedin there.

Gradually the return party's attention shifted to salvaging any food they could find which was in jars or carefully stored. The Childless determined what number of the Substance urns could be carried back to the permanent camp. Elenn was finally returning to the Flatpools logs which he had taken from Henik's desk. He started reading them from the beginning, looking for clues about how things had transpired. The first indication of trouble was a message from the masters council that the servers were being given broad privilege to bury their dead outside the east and west walls of the capital after many of them had taken ill and lost their passing-of-life. Then there were some unrelated entries. The footwear masters apologized for being late with a promised production of footwear. And then there was something which caught Elenn's eye as being very important. An entry read: *Master Jutef, caretaker and masters council member, missing. G.M. Ippal says that Master Jutef often went on walks to see how far he could go into the hills and find his way back. G.M. Ippal and G.M. Nemis looked all day for him in the hills, but were not able to find him.*

The very next entry was about the illness. *Fever that started in the temple - now in the capital. Formal request for help received from infirmary. G.M. Simol and G.M. Ribol dispatched to assist.*

From there, regular notes about the progress of the illness were entered into the log. There was only one further mention of Jutef. The entry read: *Search for Master Jutef is suspended. Given rapid spread of temple fever, it is likely Master Jutef was not lost in the hills but took ill somewhere else in the capital.*

Elenn thought it strange that Jutef would have acquired the illness and disappeared so early. The illness was only being recognized at the time he was reported missing. In any case, the first uedin whom Elenn felt must be shown the log was Pavis. Pavis would want to know any details about Jutef, however incomplete.

Pavis was also perplexed by Jutef's disappearance. "Might he have gone to the temple compound? I can imagine him having some meeting or something there. He was very active on the council and often made proposals. He could have gotten illness right there when it was starting."

Elenn sighed. "But there was communication between the temple and masters council. They certainly would have reported the illness and death of a masters council member."

412

"Master Jutef probably did get lost in the hills," said Pavis thoughtfully.

"I'm inclined to think so," responded Elenn. "They gave up looking for him because they were overwhelmed with the illness."

"I have gone along many times with Master Jutef for his practice at finding his way. He always wanted me to follow him until he went as far as he could go. When he felt lost and disoriented, he would call out for me, and I would lead him back a bit so he could then find his way home."

"Did he actually get into the hill country?"

"He got to a section of it with me," said Pavis. After a moment of recollection, he suddenly asked, "How long ago was that log entry written?"

The logs had their own numeric; they were not associated with the temple calendar or any such thing. But by counting the number of entries that followed, especially those pages and pages of names, Elenn could estimate the time that had passed since the entry about Jutef's disappearance had been written. "I think the entry about Master Jutef's disappearance was probably written about two moon-cycles ago," he said. "I don't think Master Jutef could have survived for two moon-cycles lost in the hills."

"Shouldn't we at least look?" asked Pavis.

Elenn, too, felt the obligation to make a good faith search, just in case Jutef might be out there. "I'll check with the hooded guards when they get back."

"I would like to help look for him," said Pavis. "I know the area he reached before, and I know how he moves."

"Of course you will help. I'd like to search with you, if you don't mind. But it wouldn't hurt to have the other hooded guards help us cover territory."

They met the next morning at the caretaker hut.

"It feels good to get out of the capital," said Posha. They all agreed. The fruitless search for survivors among the dead was becoming unbearable. They were going to have to start preparing for a departure.

"I'm afraid that if we do find Master Jutef, it will be his body that we find. I don't think it's likely that he would still be alive. But I feel we must spend one day looking, seeing as he was never found."

They walked down toward the drystream, and Pavis pointed out a large rock. "That's one of his markers," Pavis said. "A few of the Flatpools guards placed them in different spots for him. There are markers all around here. He had quite of few of them placed . . . they lead half-way into the hill country."

"Do you know which way he usually went?"

"Yes," said Pavis. "He always went by the spot where he thinks Master Nula was put into the ground at the bottom of the drystream. I can show you where he climbed down to that spot, and I can show you where he always went up the other side."

Elenn felt his chest ache when Pavis mentioned Nula. He sometimes wished he had been strong enough to visit the pile of stones that had marked Nula's buried body. He could never bear to do so. Jutef, he knew, had visited it almost daily up until the Great Rains came and washed it all away.

They followed Pavis down to the bottom of the drystream and across. Pavis paused at one spot and suggestively waved his hand in a certain area, letting them know that this was about where Nula's stone pile had once been. Elenn let his eye linger on the spot for a moment. It was like any other spot at the drystream bottom, growing with weeds. The stones had long been washed away by not one but two Great Rains. So much had come to pass in two novades, but Elenn could still remember Nula's voice and face.

Would Master Jutef be gone too? So many were gone. They were all such remarkable uedin and good friends. It didn't seem real that they could be gone, just like that. Master Nemis, with whom he had camped under the stars at Murro and joked about Alka, back before he got famous for proposing the observation deck. Gone. Master Ippal, who went from being Nula's substitute to Elenn's permanent hood squad partner. Elenn would never forget how he kept that little mouse in a brush box. Gone. Master Henik, who led Elenn out into the eastern desert on that night of Moon's Crossing. Master Deben had been there too . . . Master Deben who, long ago, had met him in the library that time when he had that terrible dream about being barren. Master Deben had shown him the first compassion he had ever known. He was gone too. And Master Benar. He had taught Elenn so much about how to behave in the world of masters, with humor and good-natured flexibility. What was left of the world of masters? Only the hooded masters, and the rouedin. The thought of the rouedin made Elenn want to speak seriously with Pavis. He decided it was time for the search party to break up and try to comb the area.

"Let's break up into pairs," Elenn suddenly shouted. "We'll give it the full day and meet at the caretaker hut at dusk! Is that all right with everyone?"

"I agree!" said Umat. "We have plenty of water."

"Masters Posha and Onnek, do you have plenty of water?" Cebik asked.

"Three gourds," said Posha.

"All right . . . If you find Master Jutef's body, just leave it. We don't need to take it back to the capital."

They all nodded their agreement.

Elenn let a bit of time go by walking with Pavis before he started speaking. "Master Pavis, how does it feel to be the one who saved nineteen rouedin from dying of temple fever?" Pavis was silent for a long time. "Your action was very brave," Elenn finally added.

"I don't think I would have been so brave without Master Jutef's encouragement. He was completely against it at first, but we talked, and I told him that it was my server instinct that I felt compelled to follow, more than the Instruction. Then he told me he was weaving seats just like the one he had made for Server Til-ke, and he was going to try to make twenty seats for my rouedin."

"Is that what he called them? Your rouedin?"

"Yes. And I thought it was a bit of sarcasm, but he made all those seats. I knew when he was making all those seats that he really supported me."

"They are your rouedin, Master Pavis. You have shown them great respect. We will have to give them our very best care, especially now."

"It boggles my mind to think about it, but it's true," said Pavis, "Server Tilke and the rouedin are the only fertile uedin alive."

"Passing-of-life is not going to be easy for them."

Pavis was a bit confused by this. "Tilke's Lake will be easier to reach than the Lake of Ceulan was for uedin here in the capital," he argued.

"Well, I guess it depends on how much you pay attention to the Instruction," said Elenn. "There's something in the Instruction that could be a problem."

"What's that?" asked Pavis.

"The Instruction talks about when the *'Most High receives guidance from my offspring for his journey to the lake,'* and I think that means lern guidance has always aided pilgrims to passing-of-life."

"Well, won't we have Lern Beyana's offspring, just as the Instruction says?"

"That's what I'm afraid of, Master Pavis. I'm afraid that we won't."

Pavis was silent in response to this. Elenn hoped it wasn't a mistake to reveal his worry. In this case, there was a reason. "Master Pavis, Server Tilke and the rouedin will not have an easy passing-of-life. Without the guidance of a lern, we have no idea what ecstasy will be like for them. They may need to be given great care and attention. They may need to be transported to Tilke's Lake and led to its bank. We will probably have to follow them every moment through to their passing-of-life, since we can't count on the guidance. Will you remain dedicated to the rouedin? It will be a great burden to you."

"I'll do what I can," said Pavis. Elenn felt bad for Pavis. It was more bad news for him to absorb—the idea that they were going to have to live without a lern.

Indeed, there was turning out to be little reason to build up the new capital. What was the future if only twenty uedin completed passing-of-life and bore twenty wetuedin? There was no future for the capital. There would be no point in building a road from the permanent camp up to Tilke's Lake. And yet Elenn knew they couldn't abandon the Instruction completely.

The wind was cool and made waves of the grass that grew in patchy stretches through the hills.

"Are any of Master Jutef's marker stones set this far out?" asked Elenn.

"Oh yes, we got further than this, in lots of different directions. Master Jutef could get around these hills quite well."

Elenn and Jutef followed and backtracked different possible paths all day. They searched beyond the farthest marker stones in all directions. They crossed paths once with Posha and On-nek, who likewise had seen nothing. Elenn was sadly reconsidering the possibility that Jutef might have indeed died somewhere in the capital, just like it said in the Quarterhouse log. When the sun began to sink in the sky, they headed back to the caretaker hut. It was starting to get dark when they arrived, and they could see from light in the window that there was already a lamp burning.

The scene they walked into was one that Elenn had not dared to let himself imagine. Onnek, Posha, Umat, and Cebik were all seated around a figure who lay on Jutef's bedding. As Elenn and Pavis pushed aside the door tarp and entered, they all turned and looked at them. They said nothing but took a step away so the two could have a good look.

Jutef was breathing. His face was chapped, and his eyes, which usually already had a sunken look, now looked like deep holes in his head. There were purplish stains all around his mouth.

"Who found him?"

"Master Umat and I found him," said Cebik, "It was much farther off than we thought he would ever go."

"Did you find him just like this?" asked Pavis. "Has he made any noise at all?"

"Not a sound. We found him unconscious, just like this, in a large patch of vineberries. That must be how he survived."

"I have some Substance," said Pavis. "Let's try to give him some."

"We've already given him some," said Cebik. He held up a bowl. "We made it very watery. He can swallow. We've been giving him sips."

"Master Jutef is alive!" said Pavis, and he threw his arms around Elenn. Elenn hugged him back and patted his shoulder. He looked around at the smiling faces of his fellow guards. It was a moment of joy after a long period of misery in the death-drenched capital.

"I hope we can nurse him back to health quickly," said Elenn. "As soon as he can walk, we're going to pack up as much Substance as we can carry and leave. Nobody wants to stay in the capital any longer than necessary."

Smaller Fields and Adjusted Hopes

Serka pulled and released the fatwire saw being used to down one of the trees in an area designated for clearing. The whole camp was in deep disappointment and grief. It was a good thing, at least, that they had started clearing right beside the permanent camp and not in the far corner of the area they had initially mapped for clearing. The large area they had surveyed was equal to that of the western outfields back when they anticipated a need to feed a new capital with waves of immigrants coming by the hundreds. Now they would only need a small portion of that land.

The trees were bigger than the ones that grew in the woods near the western outfields, but he and Leol put their considerable weight into the sawing and seemed to be bringing them down with efficiency. Jeber was gone. He had joined the second return party which departed without delay to go after some of the stockpile of Substance left in the capital. He promised to bring back more tools from the outfields. Serka was there with Leol, and he was worried about him. Leol had hardly spoken since the camp had learned of the capital's demise.

Serka felt that he and Leol were much more upset about the capital than Jeber was. Jeber had kept a cool head about it right away. It almost seemed like the news didn't even affect him, so quickly had he made arrangements to join the second return party, gotten organized, and gone off. How could he be so quick to adjust to something so . . . unthinkable. Serka felt much more empathy with Leol, who seemed to be wholly devastated.

They got through the mid-sized tree trunk and stepped aside for it to fall. They had sawed specifically to direct its fall toward the already cleared area so that it wouldn't get hung up on other tree branches. It fell with a swoop and slammed on the ground. Serka stretched and sat for a short rest, and Leol sat beside him.

For a long time, they were silent. Serka thought about what he might say to brighten the mood.

Finally he spoke, "Amazing that Master Jutef of the caretaker hut was found alive, don't you think?" He looked at Leol for a reaction.

Leol nodded and smiled sadly. "Yes, amazing," he said, making an obvious effort to not be so glum. They sat there for another long moment, and Serka couldn't think of anything else to say that might make it better.

He was very encouraged when Leol volunteered, "Did you see the yam patch today? They're big enough to start eating some of the greens."

"Yes, I saw them," said Serka, "They're looking great!" The enthusiasm in his voice was a little too strong.

Leol forgave him for that. He continued, "It won't be long before we can feed ourselves without eating animal muscles."

This was a topic about which Serka didn't need to hide his true feelings. "The Quarterhouse masters are already talking about calling a halt to the killing," he said. "I have a feeling some of them don't want to stop."

"They'll stop," said Leol, "We're still uedin."

Serka wasn't as optimistic as Leol. He worried that some of the Quarterhouse masters actually enjoyed the killing. He didn't like the idea of it, but that's the way it seemed to him. If that was the case, there was nothing he could do about it. Nothing, but try to get some successful cultivation started.

"Yams do better than fieldpears here," he said, "and they do make beautiful greens."

"I think we might be able to cultivate marshroot," said Leol. "It doesn't grow as big in dry soil, but it does grow."

Serka said nothing. He thought about the peach orchards in the western outfields, and it made him remember some of his outfield worker companions there . . . all gone now. There was nothing that didn't lead him back to his sorrow about the capital.

They sat silently for a while, gazing at the sunshine on the felled trees. The wood would serve good purpose, and the crops planted in new fields would help them get away from eating the muscles of woodrats and wild dogs. Serka himself had gotten used to the taste of it, but when he ate it, he always thought about how much he would love to have some of Master Ghera's cooking. The thought struck him: he would never see Ghera again. "Let's cut one more," he yelled, choosing to put sad thoughts out of his mind and get back to work.

After they had cut down their last tree for the day, the two made the short walk through the small patch of cleared forest with its stumps and vines. The camp was looking more and more like a village every day. With such a small community there, it would never be the "new capital" that everyone there had had in mind before they knew that the migrations wouldn't be coming. But it had a character of its own. By now, there were well-worn footpaths which winded through the camp. The lean-tos had all been converted to fully supported huts, some with make-shift roofs of large fronds laid over branches, others with proper thatching that looked like the huts of the old capital.

Serka was fascinated by the section of the camp occupied by the Childless. He had been watching them, particularly during the time when the first return party was away. With many of the leaders of the expedition gone back to the capital, the camp had gotten very quiet. It was then that the Childless seemed to come to live, thriving on the silence and inactivity. They were so calm. Serka figured it must be the result of novades eating a diet of Substance, even though their rations were now small like everyone else's. When the return party came back reporting that all uedin in the capital, save for one, had died of a fever, Serka had looked to see how the Childless would take this news. The Childless, like everyone else, were all shaken. But they recovered their balance quickly. It was impossible not to respect them.

Since everyone now knew that the apportionment of land was not going to involve incoming migrations, there was discussion about how permanent residences should be arranged. Serka felt, along with many of the hooded masters, that the Childless should have their choice of land, not as a group, but as individuals. Each of the Childless could decide whether to stay where he had haphazardly landed, there with other bluff dwellers, or, at his fancy, go somewhere else in the camp to set up residence. They were welcome anywhere. A few of the Childless accepted this invitation, and went off to other areas of the camp to find a suitable spot, but most chose to stay right where they were. Serka thought this was politeness on the part of the Childless. Even if they wanted to stay together, they should have more than the small patch they currently occupied. But they insisted that they wanted no other location and no more space.

As Serka neared his own spot in the camp, he thought about whether he would end up moving or not. Before the return party came back, he had made plans with Jeber and Leol to set up their own camp about midway into the area planned for outfields. It was a good thing that they had been too busy to get anywhere with those plans. They would have found themselves living out in the middle of woods that would never need clearing.

"Master Serka, look at this tree!" said Leol, looking up. They were very near their own hut.

"What about it?" said Serka, "Do you think it should come down?"

"Oh no, not this one. This is a mola tree—isn't it?"

Serka looked up. He certainly didn't see any mola beans hanging from any branches up there, but the foliage and branching pattern did look somewhat familiar. "I'm not sure I would recognize mola unless it had beans in it," he admitted. "Do you think this is mola?"

"I'm pretty sure," said Leol. "Maybe we can make mola stew someday!"

"That would be nice," said Serka, still peering up into the dark canopy. He wondered if they could reproduce a stew like the stew Master Ghera used to make.

First Rouedin is Guided to Tilke's Lake

Pelto put his hand on the shoulder of the rouedin, half comforting and half directing him. The poor rouedin had abstained from Substance in order to come into his ecstasy so that he could go back to Tilke's Lake. These days, all the surviving rouedin were known to talk about nothing but Tilke's Lake. Pelto knew that it must have been extremely difficult to go from a generous allowance of Substance to none at all. And this poor rouedin—name of Master Linib he was told—went into raving with a sense of panic. Master Linib didn't feel the instinct to go. He said he wanted to go, but he didn't feel drawn *anywhere*. Ros in ecstasy were supposed to feel drawn to their pilgrimage. Pelto had never seen a pilgrimage departure in the capital, so he wasn't exactly sure what they were like, but he felt sorry for Master Linib. Raving, for him, was clearly an experience of great distress, so much so that they had to escort him to Tilke's Lake.

Pelto was glad that the ro had gradually grown incoherent and docile. He could be easily guided along, although Pelto didn't think he would go on by himself if they tried to get him to complete the pilgrimage without them accompanying him.

The rouedin was becoming exhausted and needed to sleep. They stopped for the rest of the day and following night. A few times, since leaving camp, he had woken in the night and started to wander, and when that happened, they treated it as his natural pilgrimage movement and intervened only to keep him going in the right direction.

Pelto felt that Linib's troubled pilgrimage was a bad sign. The thought of bad implications had been particularly sobering when they had left the capital. Poor Master Linib had pressed back against their guiding hands, afraid to go.

For the moment, he was sleeping peacefully. Pelto set up his spot with his bedding and gourds. He ate silently with the other escorts. They would offer the rouedin food when he woke up, though he no longer showed signs of any appetite. After the brief meal, Pelto excused himself and went to sit on his bedding and watch the forest. Knowing that the rouedin was asleep made it easier to concentrate on looking at the forest. It was beautiful, just like the bluff was beautiful. Back at the camp, the Childless had come to understand that the forest could be watched with the same clean wonder with which they had always watched the desert.

But Pelto found it hard to put worry out of his mind. He wished he could stop thinking about the kernel. The thought of it carried with it a great deal of unpleasant emotion. Pelto was the one who had told Elenn that they should just get the kernel in the ground and accept that no suitable high place had been found. At the time it was a simple matter of accepting the facts of the situation. But now it seemed entirely unacceptable. Master Linib had no lern to give him a sense of where to go, and neither would any of the other rouedin who waited for their passings-of-life. Furthermore, they had to wean off Substance in order to go into raving for their pilgrimage, so they could not enjoy its calming benefit.

Pelto let his eyes hover at the place where sky was visible in a cleared section. He looked at the evening sky. It certainly was a different sky from the faraway sky at the bluff. This sky looked touchable.

The sky was touchable but the place was lonely. It was lonely because this forest had been envisioned as a home for many, but it was now going to be home to a very few. Assuming these rouedin produce healthy wetuedin, there would be only twenty of them. And when those uedin grew up and needed assistance in their pilgrimage, who would be left? They would have to assist one another to Tilke's Lake.

Out of the corner of his eye, Pelto thought he saw something white, and he immediately thought of the large white bird that he had seen on the way to bury the kernel. No, it wasn't one of those. It was just a little section of white flowers hanging on a vine and blowing in a breeze. For a long time, Pelto tried to look at the flowers. They were beautiful, and one could try to absorb their beauty. But as much as Pelto might find a mental shelter in watching the forest, he had an unignorable ache. The kernel. He had lifted it from its bed of whitesponge. He had pulled it out from deep mud. Then he had understood that it would have to be abandoned. Uedin would be lonely and alone evermore.

Comfort in Small Numbers

Tilke sat in the shade under the extended awning of his hut. He felt uneasy. How hot the sun was here, once trees were cleared. It seemed hotter than any sun that Tilke had experienced in the temple courtyards back during his server career. Patches of trees were left standing here and there, but mostly the scene was of small huts like his own, outdoor kitchens, uedin walking, doing various chores.

Some server-masters were delivering water. The hoods they now wore were trimmed down to small skullwomb covers with a thin strip for tying under the neck. They carried urns that had once held Substance and were now used as water jars. Their robes were removed from their shoulders and tied to hang down from their waists. Their large upper bodies were so strong and muscular that they hardly looked like uedin. One of them approached.

"Server Tilke, do you need water?"

Tilke looked at the smiling figure holding the sweating urn of cold water. An urn full of water was too heavy for him to lift, but this server-master carried it easily. "I still have half full," Tilke said.

"Let's replace it anyhow. Fresh water is always nice to have," said the server-master. Tilke raised hands to face, and the server-master stepped past him to put down the full urn, pick up the half-empty one, and slide the fresh water urn to the exact spot where the other urn had set.

"Thank you," said Tilke. The server-master raised hands to face and held them there a little longer than he needed to. Tilke was mildly annoyed by the deference that was constantly demonstrated to him. It felt a little bit like pity. His primary advisor had often looked at him with the same kind of concern. But that was when he had had communion with the Soft One. He had nothing like that now, and now that there was open admission that the kernel had been buried incorrectly, even the Instruction failed to provide any sense of purpose. The chanting of it had fallen into disfavor. Tilke himself only grew depressed when he thought of it.

The server-master walked off, stopping to empty the urn of its day-old water by tossing it to the side of the path. Tilke noticed that he was wearing the footwear that was being produced here now. It was sewn from cured greenbark. In addition to the full stockpile of Substance, every sort of tool had been brought from the old capital. The most recent caravan had brought back equipment for brewing yeastdrink along with most of the library collection.

Tilke leaned back on his chair, another import from the capital. He closed his eyes. Perhaps he would be able to nap. Sometimes his mood improved after a nap.

Before he could let himself drift off, he heard uedin approaching and opened his eyes. It was Elenn and Yulig coming. Yulig carried a small wrapped bundle and Elenn had a crate. Tilke stood up to greet them.

"Hot sun today," said Yulig.

"A good day to enjoy shade," answered Tilke. "I just got fresh water. Can I give you some?"

"Yes, thank you," said Yulig. Elenn nodded.

Tilke filled a cup and handed it to Yulig. "How is Master Banfa?" he asked. Banfa was the last of the rouedin. His decline had dragged on long after all the others had been taken to the lake.

"He left last night," said Elenn. "Master Pavis and Daga went with him."

"Good!" said Tilke. "He waited a very long time." Even though no one talked about it, Tilke knew that the rouedin had all suffered greatly during their declines, experiencing nothing like the ecstasy that the uedin of the old capital enjoyed.

"I have some of those sour fruits for you," said Yulig, opening his small bundle, "and some dried muscle if you want it." The sour fruits were in a sack. The dried muscle was in long dark strips.

"I thought there wasn't going to be any more of that," said Tilke.

"The Quarterhouse hooded have some of this dried stuff left. Only if you want it."

"No . . . " said Tilke. "But I'm grateful for the sour fruits." He raised one hand to face and accepted the sack of fruit.

"And what's that? From the library?" Tilke looked at the crate full of small bound books and tied scrolls.

"We're dividing it up until we have a proper place to build a new library," said Elenn. "This is all server writings. Maybe you'll want to look at some of it."

Tilke lifted a booklet on the top and peered at the gathered pile of server writings. He really had absolutely no interest in reading any of it. "I can keep it here if you like," he said. "I may not read it."

"That's fine," said Elenn, quick to reassure him. Everyone was quick to reassure him these days.

"Do you have enough Substance?" asked Yulig.

"I have plenty," said Tilke. They were always encouraging him to consume more Substance. Quotas had been doubled since it was all brought back. They had talked him out of refusing it like the rouedin. He was only fifth generation, and though the Instruction said to wait for his ecstasy, there was no indication of it happening early. So he glumly consumed a daily portion and tried to be thankful for the relaxation it provided.

"Will you join Leci and me this evening?" asked Yulig. They had been meeting regularly to walk to the edge of the new capital and watch the forest.

"Yes, gladly," said Tilke.

"We'll come for you after evening meal," said Yulig.

Tilke knew that watching the forest was a way of accepting life without a lern. There was nothing anyone could say to console him about the kernel. It was hard not to be upset about it, not to think of it as having been abandoned in an unsuitable place. He was learning to train his mind away from such unpleasant thoughts, thanks to the customs carried on by the Childless. How fortunate that they had befriended him.

Tilke waited that afternoon for Wido to come in from the outfields. He was helping there with the first harvest of new yams. Wido came every day and met Tilke to walk together to have evening meal at the nearest kitchen. While he waited, he poked through some of the little bound books in the crate that Elenn had left with him. He lifted a thin booklet bearing the title, "In Defense of Games." He opened it and started reading.

The Soft One shrinks at the playing of games, but this does not mean we should not play them. It is her nature to sleep, and when she sleeps, it is our nature to play games. Reading this, Tilke felt a great revulsion that made no sense to him. The lines of the booklet were true. There was no reason to refrain from games. They had always been an important part of the balance of life for servers. Why did Tilke feel such a disgust when he read that? He closed the booklet and put it back in the crate, then turned to the sack of sour fruits. He spread a small towel on the ground and dumped the sour fruits from the sack. They spilled out, some rolling off the towel. As he picked up the ones that had rolled off, Wido appeared.

"What is that?" asked Wido, pointing to the crate.

"Things to read," said Tilke.

"Can I see one?" said Wido.

"Go ahead," answered Tilke, giving the crate a little push in Wido's direction.

Wido picked out a scroll and untied it. He paid no attention to the calligraphy on it. He was fascinated by its ability to curl up into a roll and be pulled open.

"Master Elenn brought that stuff," said Tilke.

"Master Elenn let me put the kernel at the bottom of a big dark hole," said Wido. "I climbed a ladder down there."

"Do you remember Yulig the Childless? Yulig was here too. He brought me these sour fruits."

"Yulig helps in the outfields sometimes," said Wido.

"No, you're thinking of Pelto. Yulig is another of the Childless. Probably has nine generations."

"How many sour fruits?" said Wido.

"Oh, let's see," said Tilke. He looked down at the sour fruits gathered on the cloth. He reached out his hand and divided them. "Four, and four more, and four more, and three more." As he divided them with one hand into small clusters, he felt a strange release.

"Four and four and four and three!" said Wido, seeing how the bunch had been divided. Tilke looked at Wido's happy smile. Something about dividing a large number into smaller ones was amusing to Wido. Tilke noticed, with some fascination, that he shared Wido's enjoyment on an unusual level. Ordinarily he might enjoy seeing Wido taking playful delight in something, but in this case, the division into small numbers gave him a weird satisfaction that felt alien. What was it about spreading out that sourfruit in small clusters that gave him that peculiar satisfaction? There was a comfort in the small numbers. This was a thought that felt like one *not his own*. It immediately reminded him of the time when he had heard the first words form in his head based on a communication from the Soft One. "Let us be at peace," had been those words. Tilke had read the thoughts of the Soft One many times before that, but the formation of actual words had been a shocking and unexpected communion. That is what he was feeling right now—an unexpected communion! He picked up one of the sour fruits and stared at it.

"Now it's four, and three, and four, and three!" said Wido playfully, "You have one!"

Tilke suddenly felt a tremendous rush of humility. He was experiencing lern contact. He was overwhelmed with awe. He looked at Wido, who was still smiling, innocently unaware of what was happening.

"Wido!" said Tilke, his voice cracking with emotion.

Wido quickly stopped smiling and looked back with confusion.

"Wido, you put the kernel at the bottom of the hole, didn't you!"

"Yes!" answered Wido with a smile. "I went down the ladder!"

When Tilke heard these words, he felt a rush of surprise in his own veins. He couldn't tell if the surprise was coming from himself or from the new lern!

For the rest of the evening, Tilke experienced multiple occurrences of surprise feelings that seemed not to have any association with anything he was personally perceiving. He was quite sure this was communion, but he didn't want to announce it to everyone. The attention would certainly frighten the new lern. He did his best to act normal as he proceeded to go with Wido to evening meal as usual and be greeted by nearly everyone he met. It made him nervous to conceal what was happening, but doing so, he felt, was necessary.

After the meal, Wido walked with him back to his hut. Tilke found himself silently counting his steps as he walked, one-two-three-four, one-two-three-four. He wondered if he was doing it to give comfort to the lern. Wido said good night and left him at his hut. He stood for a moment before telling himself that it would be suitable to sit and wait for Yulig and Leci whom he had promised to join for a forest-watching.

While he waited, he noticed a fringe of loose threads at the end of his sleeve. They were twisted and bunched together. He carefully straightened the threads and drew them out over his wrist. Then he pinched groups of three threads and divided them into little bands. He was doing with the fringe of his sleeve what he had done with the sour fruits, and it was having the same effect. Comfort and relaxation came to him from outside himself.

When Yulig and Leci arrived, Tilke remained silent about having received contact. He wanted to maintain as much calm as possible. He followed Yulig and Leci toward the new outfields where they could sit in an open space and view the forest from a distance.

They sat in an empty place and gazed at the forest darkening under the evening sky. Tilke was able to clear his mind. He did not forget that the new lern was in communion with him, but he managed to rest with the thought of it. After a long period of silent watching, Leci stood and stretched. It was getting dark, and this was a signal for them to return to their huts.

Tilke decided to tell them. "I have something important to say," he said as they started back.

"What is it, Server Tilke?" asked Yulig.

"I have received contact from the new lern," answered Tilke.

Both Yulig and Leci were quiet for a long time. They stopped walking. "Are you sure?" asked Yulig.

"I'm pretty sure," said Tilke.

"Because it would not be impossible for you to imagine such a thing," said Leci. "And we know that the kernel did not reach any place like it was supposed to."

"It's just like it was with the Soft One," said Tilke, "I'm sure of it. But I don't want everyone to know. I must hide the communion as much as I can, to protect it."

"But you'll at least tell Master Elenn, won't you?" asked Leci.

"I intend to go to him in the morning," said Tilke.

"I hope you will also consider telling Pelto," said Yulig. "Pelto is vexed about burying the kernel in a poor location."

"I will tell Pelto also," said Tilke. He was grateful that Yulig and Leci neither overreacted nor asked many questions.

The next morning, Elenn received Tilke's news with caution.

"I think you should continue to eat Substance," said Elenn.

"I will see," said Tilke. "I will see how it effects communion."

"And I think it is very wise that you refrain from telling many others," said Elenn.

"I've only told Yulig and Leci," said Tilke, "and now two others—you and Pelto. I won't tell anyone else."

"You feel confident about this?" asked Elenn, wanting to be convinced. Tilke noticed the odd look on Elenn's face. Elenn was having trouble believing it.

"Master Elenn, wherever you put the kernel, it must have been good enough," he said.

Tilke Leaves for His Pilgrimage

Since quitting Substance, Tilke felt a muddle of confusion about most things. It didn't matter who had leaked the news of his communion with the new lern. Maybe it was he who had told others himself. The only thing that mattered was that now it was known to everyone, the situation was impossible, and now that he saw a path forward to Passing-of-Life, he couldn't wait to go.

Master Elenn hovered over him insufferably. Elenn's attention, along with the attention of everyone Tilke encountered, caused the new lern to shrink. Pelto also refused to stay away. Pelto seemed to feel some special connection to the new lern, since it was he who had first retrieved the kernel, and it was he who had protected it and seen it all the way to its burial location. But Pelto had been pressing Tilke much too much about the application of a name to the new lern. Tilke felt the lern shrink when this idea was pondered at any level. So Tilke simply refused to discuss it, and refused to discuss anything about his new communion. He understood that uedin were hungry for any mention or description of the new lern, but their eagerness made the lern shrink away, and Tilke was not willing to let that happen. Since there was no temple into which he could retreat, the only answer was to go to his passing-of-life as quickly as possible. He was on track to make *that* happen, having refused Substance for many days. Elenn and the others had fair warning.

Tilke was unsure, when he experienced the muddled states of mind, whether they were signals of raving which would indicate that he might soon be ready for his pilgrimage. Or, were they simply the natural sensations of a uedin who was overwhelmed? He leaned on the hope that it was soon time to leave for his pilgrimage. It was all he could think about. And this longing did not seem to cause any shrinking on the part of the new lern. Her communion was quite congruent with his longing for passing-of-life.

One evening, he decided he would initiate the event by telling Wido of his plans. Wido had walked with him, as he always did, to evening meal and back to his hut. Instead of bidding him goodbye, Tilke invited Wido to sit with him for a short while.

"Why do you want me to sit?" asked Wido.

"It's because I want to talk to you about something important," said Tilke.

"Is it about the new lern? I know you talk to the new lern, even though the new lern is far away in the hill," said Wido. "Master Pavis told me about that."

"It's not about that," said Tilke.

"It's another important thing?" asked Wido.

"Yes. I want to tell you that I'm going to my passing-of-life."

Wido immediately looked very worried and upset. "I was there when Master Banfa was leaving. Master Banfa was crying!"

"It's different for me, Server-master Wido. I won't cry."

"But it's very sad to go to passing-of-life! Please don't go!"

"It's not sad. I want to go."

"You want to?" asked Wido. "But I'm not going."

"I know," said Tilke. "You won't go to passing-of-life. But that's all right. You will stay here. There will be wetuedin here someday soon, and you will be a friend to the unnamed. That's your job, Server-master Wido."

"I can do that job," said Wido.

"Please be a friend to the unnamed like you have been a friend to me," said Tilke.

"I will," said Wido.

"That's all," said Tilke. "That's all I wanted to talk about. You can go now."

Wido casually raised his hands to face and left.

As Wido walked away from his hut, Tilke had a strange sensation. He felt as if he were seeing two versions of Wido, one coming and one going. It was another moment of that confusion that he was unable to interpret. He would call it his raving. He would consider such sensations as signs that he was ready to go.

The next day Elenn and Pelto came to his hut. They brought him food.

"I know you don't like going to the kitchens anymore," said Elenn.

"It's true, I don't like walking about," said Tilke.

"No one means to cause you any upset," said Pelto, "we only want to know our new lern."

"Server Tilke," said Elenn, "I know you don't like to discuss a name for the new lern, but . . . "

"I have no idea what to do about that," said Tilke. "I have no idea how a lern is given a name. The new lern doesn't like when I think about it."

"That's why we think it's up to us to name her," said Pelto. "We just need your help."

"The new lern has no need of a name, nor any desire to have one," explained Tilke, feeling frustrated again.

"But uedin need a name for their lern," said Pelto.

"Server Tilke, do you think it would be acceptable to use one of the old names? We could choose one of the names we are familiar with."

"It doesn't matter," said Tilke, "That would be fine. Anything is fine."

"We want to try something," said Elenn. "We're going to recite the old names of the Lern Beyana. All you have to do is tell us when to stop."

"You want *me* to choose?"

"Just tell us when the new lern shrinks."

Tilke nodded in agreement, just because he had no will to argue. The truth was, the new lern was nowhere near present to him at this moment. She was already withdrawn. It was too late to see when she would shrink. But Tilke decided he must play along, for there was no other option.

Elenn and Pelto then began a very methodical recitation of the Names, spoken in unison and not in the usual repeating chant style.

"Lehera Beyana yana ya," they said, watching Tilke for his reaction. Tilke stared hopelessly at the ground.

"Lerna Beyana ulrana uedina," they continued. Tilke knew he was going to have to tell them to stop at some point, and it would be with no particular shrinking from the new lern who was already absent.

"Lern Beyan kiman kiman uedin olor," they slowly enunciated.

How long should he let them go on?

"Hunna Bah muh Lor," they said, watching him.

"Why can't you name the new lern?" he wanted to ask. But that would be too insulting to Elenn and Pelto. It was unthinkable that any uedin would interrupt a recitation of the Names. He was the Most High Server of the temple, and he could not interrupt.

"Mei nar Lalem Lalem Pa--," they said.

"Stop now," said Tilke.

Pelto jerked forward. "Is that it? Is it Lalem?"

"Yes, that will be the name of the new lern," said Tilke, feeling very much like a liar. "She will be Lern Lalem." He watched them lower their eyes in humility. For them, this was a great revelation. Their new lern was Lern Lalem. He felt guilty because he knew it did not in any way reflect any name that the new lern would embrace, but he was leaving them to their own inclination to accept it.

"Thank you, Server Tilke," said Pelto. "Everyone will be very relieved to know this name." Perhaps Pelto suspected that Tilke had only arbitrarily stopped the recitation. It didn't matter. That was taken care of. Now Tilke wanted to let them know of his intentions.

"My friends," said Tilke, "I want to leave the capital. I'm going for my pilgrimage."

Elenn didn't hide his objection. "Server Tilke, you're not ready, not even close. You've only recently stopped consuming Substance."

"I'm ready," said Tilke. "I don't need to be in full ecstasy."

"What if you're wrong? You would linger at the lake for many days, starving."

"I know that I'm being guided properly. I'm feeling very ready."

Pelto and Elenn looked at each other to see what the other thought.

"We must at least be given the chance to give you departure ceremony," said Pelto.

"But I want to leave tomorrow," said Tilke.

"Tomorrow?!" exclaimed Elenn.

"I would like to leave with as little commotion as possible. I've already spoken with Server-master Wido."

"Don't you want to say goodbye to Yulig and Leci, at least?" said Pelto, "They have been with you through much of this."

"We will accompany you, of course," said Elenn.

"Accompany me? To the lake?"

"We have accompanied all the rouedin," said Elenn. "If you were in full ecstasy and you had a strong instinct, perhaps it would be all right for you to go on your own, but you are not in full ecstasy."

"Yes, Master Elenn and I will accompany you," said Pelto. "But I'm going to tell Yulig and Leci that we are leaving. They, at least, deserve the chance to bid you farewell."

Tilke imagined a scene of the next morning. He knew Yulig would embrace him. Leci would raise hands to face. He would feel distressed about insulting others by leaving them out—Daga, and Master Pavis. Maybe he should be giving some parting words to Master Jutef. Jutef would be the only uedin left with passing-of-life ahead of him. But he just wanted to go, as quickly as possible. "Very well," he said. "If you would be so kind to meet me here at the first light of dawn. I will be honored to have Yulig and Leci come to give me farewell."

He noticed Elenn looking at him with a puzzling worried look that he didn't understand. It reminded him of the Elenn he first knew before he had entered the temple. The look on his face suggested that he was thinking, *Aren't you forgetting something?* But Tilke didn't think he was forgetting anything. Elenn had the Childless to guide him now, and soon the new capital would become acquainted with their lern. What name did they want? . . . *Lern Lalem.* Only those who learned not to call her that would have any chance of reading her thoughts. He thought about telling Elenn that directly, but that would not be appropriate. The uedin needed a named lern, and he had just given them one. Better to let the generations find out for themselves.

"Well then, this will be your last night with us," said Elenn. "I hope you have a restful sleep. We will be back in the morning to leave with you."

Pelto spoke. "Server Tilke, thank you for sharing your communion. After we left the kernel in that place, I never thought there would be a lern. For letting us know that there is, I will be grateful to you for the rest of my life."

Tilke accepted Pelto's gratitude with a slow nod and hands to face. Perhaps it was a very good thing that they had their Lern Lalem.

They left him alone with his lamp. It was now dark, and the lamplight fell on the objects in his hut. He decided he would fill his gourds now so that they would be ready to carry in the morning. He had two of them. One was a plain one that the expedition had provided. The other was an etched gourd that had been picked up on the way to the Lake of Ceulan. That poor server who dropped it had borne his offspring in the dead lake, and they had watched it die in the foul water there. Tilke filled both gourds from the urn. He gazed for a moment at the crate of server writings. Was there anything there he needed to look at? No, there was not. It was all just a defense of games. He prepared his bedding and blew out the lamp.

During the still hours in the middle of the night, Tilke drifted in and out of sleep. He felt himself sleeping *with* the new lern, and he recalled times when he had felt the same thing with the Soft One back in the temple. It was such a comfort to share a common sleep. But Tilke dreaded the morning. The lern would withdraw as soon as he got up and started the anxious task of seeing Yulig and Leci and being chaperoned by Elenn and Pelto to the lake. *Tilke's Lake* . . . how strange that it was now named after him. But names didn't matter. They didn't matter if they weren't recognized and they didn't matter if they were. The only thing that Tilke regretted was that the lern would shrink from him during his pilgrimage. The thought of it bothered him until he could stand it no more. He decided suddenly and resolutely. He would elope.

He quietly got up from his bedding, rolled it neatly and pushed it to the inner corner of his hut. Then he put on his server wrappings, attached the filled water gourds to his sash, and left.

By the time the first light of dawn appeared, Tilke was far up the drystream and away from the new capital. The same path had served caravans for many trips back to the old capital, and it was easy to follow. He trusted that Elenn and Pelto would understand, and they would not come after him. His communion with the new lern was undisturbed. She seemed to know exactly where he was going. Tilke felt the lern's joy. It gave Tilke such vigor and thrill for his pilgrimage.

First Descent

Elenn walked through the newly constructed domicile looking up at the row of windows that lined the tops of the walls on both sides. Though of wood construction, it was reminiscent of the Redrock longhouses in shape. The sky outside was dark and cloudy, so little light filled the space. After the Great Rains, light would pour in. This would serve as a home for both the server-masters and whatever upcoming generation might arrive.

He stepped outside and stood on the extended along the full length of the building. The heat and humidity were the same inside and out. Below was a scene of gullies and canals carved into the land between the capital and the drystream. The cabins and huts of the capital stretched out behind him on both sides. All wood construction, the buildings of the capital looked particularly dark under the overcast sky.

He often thought about how naturally and easily they had all taken to calling their new home "the capital." The old capital had been a place much defined by its surrounding landscape, open and dry. The new was a place of intimacy with the forest, something quite different. Normally noisy with the sounds of birds and chirping insects, it had grown quiet in the days leading up to the Great Rains. The rains were about to arrive. Uedin settlement at this location had occurred in time to allow two years to pass, the last two years of the novade, and it had been a period of intense labor. All their work was about to be tested.

Elenn had frequent nightmares of giant frogs in Tilke's Lake, chasing and swallowing tiny wetuedin. None of the escort groups who had taken rouedin to the lake ever mentioned seeing them, but Elenn knew they were there. Elenn had stopped himself from mentioning his anxiety to Tilke ever again, and when Tilke went off to his pilgrimage, it seemed that he had quite forgotten about the frogs. Tilke had been blessed with a very good ecstasy, and Elenn had no problem forgiving him for disremembering the frogs or for leaving alone without the departure ceremony that they had agreed on.

But there was no way to know whether Tilke's Lake would produce wetuedin, or whether they had already been eaten up by frogs, and there was nothing to do but prepare for their arrival. If there were any wetuedin coming, the canal system was in place for them. The project had been immense. Most of the buildings of the actual capital were small and temporary, built far back from the drystream so as not to be washed away. The real effort had gone into the delivery system for wetuedin. The wetuedin would be guided through a series of canal branches and directed with nets to a manageable stream and finally into a hatching pool.

Elenn knew that few if any wetuedin would arrive, but he and the others would do all they could to safely receive them, and then continue building a small capital to give them a home. In the distance, there was still a team of server-masters adding yet another reinforcement to the dam. It was built to divert water to two canals, one fitted with massive nets to guide wetuedin into the other, smaller one. Upstream at the place where the drystream split into two branches, a wall of heavy nets had already been put in place to ensure that no wetuedin would go the wrong way. Elenn was hopeful that it was going to work. He could think of no project in the old capital which had received such careful and intense effort. He was sure that no construction, neither the Grainhouses of Murro nor the Clay Bridge, had ever been undertaken with such urgent and grand attention. The canals were a marvel. One look at them revealed that they were a labor of the large-bodied barren. The rocks dug from deep underground and transported to placement in the dam were more than ordinary uedin could ever have managed. The masters council of the old capital would not have dared such an ambitious movement of earth and stone.

Someone was coming around the corner of the porch. Probably someone else with a question. Elenn leaned to see who it was. It was Master Pavis. Pavis looked up at him.

"Oh, Master Elenn, there you are. I wanted to speak with you one time before the rains arrive."

Elenn raised hands to face. "Hello, Master Pavis. Yes, the sky looks very ready." Ever since it was understood to Elenn that Pavis's plot to bring rouedin to the new capital had turned out to provide the only fertile population to survive, he regarded him with deep respect.

"I haven't been here for a while . . . I can't believe how big this delivery system is!"

"Yes, we think we're ready."

"It's stupendous!"

Elenn thought it would be inappropriate to say "thank you," since the achievement was not his to claim. He couldn't help, at any rate, feeling a bit proud. "Was there something you wanted to speak with me about, Master Pavis?"

"Yes . . . " said Pavis, "It's about Master Jutef."

"Is Master Jutef getting along all right? I'm sure the Childless are making him feel very welcome." Jutef lived with Pavis in a hut in the cramped Childless neighborhood. The Childless had chosen to remain on the small section of land which they had occupied when the capital was first forming as a permanent camp. It was made even more crowded by their early decision to set aside a plot of land within their small neighborhood for a preserved patch of forest on which they focused their forest-watching exercises. Everyone who lived in that part of the capital had become very focused on the lern. Elenn had his doubts about whether any uedin other than Tilke had ever achieved any reading of the thoughts of the new lern, but the Childless were convinced that she favored the stillness of forest-watching.

"We are very glad we were able to join the Childless. They make both of us feel welcome."

"I may move to the Childless neighborhood someday," said Elenn, "I think we should let the Server-masters build the capital over the next few novades."

"It would be very good to have you living closer," said Pavis, "I'm sure Master Jutef would be delighted to hear you say that."

"What can I do for Master Jutef?" asked Elenn.

"Would it be all right to bring him here when the wetuedin descend? He won't be able to help much, bu—"

"Of course Master Jutef can be here. He is most welcome."

"Oh, thank you, Master Elenn! He was afraid to presume."

"It may be any hour, you know. Will you bring him?"

"I could, but I would not be useful either. I've been at forest-watching with the Childless most days. I'm afraid I haven't contributed much here."

"You're all focused on the lern, and that is as it must be. I'm afraid I haven't contributed to *that*."

"You will fit in nicely if you join us someday."

"Well anyhow, I think you should accompany Master Jutef. You will describe it to him, and he will be glad to have you along."

"I am only worried about what he might feel if . . . Well, you know, we can't be sure."

"If no wetuedin arrive," said Elenn. "Yes, we all think about that."

"Master Jutef would be in such an awful place if he, and he alone, were the only uedin left to bear an offspring—and what awful life would that offspring face alone? But Master Jutef has never said a word about that. I think he is hopeful. He wants to come."

"We are hopeful that wetuedin will arrive . . . some, at least."

"Twenty uedin have gone to passing-of-life in Tilke's Lake," said Pavis.

Elenn thought about Pavis's relationship with the rouedin. He knew them all individually. Elenn had only been slightly acquainted with Master Obu. "But think about it, Master Pavis. They would not have been able to come here had it not been for your risk-taking."

"I had no idea we would lose the capital," said Pavis gravely.

"The wetuedin who do arrive here will face a difficult future," said Elenn. It was hard to imagine living with a very small group of uedin with no population around them. But that was the fate that awaited those who might come, and their future offspring.

"They will have a very young lern to accompany them," said Pavis.

"Master Pavis, when you were a server, in your youth, did you not feel drawn to the Soft One?"

"It was nothing like what I feel now," answered Pavis. "I feel entirely drawn to Lern Lalem. Even though she is shy, she is happy that we are here."

"That's very encouraging, Master Pavis. It's good to know that whatever wetuedin do arrive, they will have Lern Lalem."

"Thank you, Master Elenn. I will tell Master Jutef that he is welcome here during the descent of wetuedin."

"If the drystream here is anything like the one that went to the old capital, it will flood within hours of the of Great Rains' arrival," said Elenn.

Thunder often occurred in the later days of a Great Rains, but rarely at the beginning. Elenn was startled when a crash of thunder woke him during the night. He looked around at the other hooded guards. They were likewise roused and responding.

"Here it comes," said Cebik.

Within seconds, a blasting rain hammered the thatched leaf roof of the guards' hut. It sounded like a great thudding rumble above them. Water began to trickle through the thatching and fall in tiny streams on and around them in the dark. The guards rose quickly from their bedding and put on wax-cloth capes which they had brought from the old capital.

They set out into the rain and toward the new domicile. The drystream was diverted at a sufficient distance to allow the series of canals to be branched and netted to bring in the wetuedin. How had wetuedin always found their own way to the hatching pools at the old capital? Elenn had no idea. Catching them from a Great Rains river was an entirely different affair.

The rain fell in torrents. They could hear it hammering down upon the forest canopy all around the camp, while in the cleared range of their huts and all the way to the canals, rain fell in an unimpeded downpour to the ground. The dirt was quickly turning to mud under their feet. The capital would need a drainage system for the future.

Uedin were now coming from all directions. Elenn saw some server-masters carrying bundles of back-up replacement netting, and they had Wido with them. The server-masters had totally embraced and employed Wido after Tilke's departure. Elenn was happy to see him working alongside his fellow server-masters. As for the back-up replacement netting, he hoped it wouldn't be needed.

As they walked past the new domicile, the view of the canals would ordinarily have been visible, but in the dark and rain, they could see nothing of them. Elenn felt a need to hurry. He knew that water would not start running into the canals for at least a few hours, but he had to see how they looked in the rain. Was the rock fit going to be tight enough for the canal walls to stay in place?

When they got close enough to see the rockwork through the dark, the canal wall looked very good with the washing of the rain. Hopefully it would be as strong as it was beautiful. The other guards met with recruits and moved on to the other critical positions. Onnek and Posha were heading to the top of the first canal where the drystream was completely netted, and, if planning had served well, half of the Great Rains river would be diverted. Cebik and Umat had offered to monitor the three interior branches where nets and canals reduced to the last branch. There, most of the water would be diverted away while a last net directed any wetuedin to the final stream leading to the hatching pool at the domicile.

"Go ahead!" shouted Elenn to Cebik and Umat. *"Master Serka is right over there! I'll send him if I need you!"*

Serka must have heard his name, for he looked up and waved at them. Wido and his server-master companions were also standing close by with the back-up nets. Other uedin were taking their positions at intervals up and down the canal. The hooded guards raised hands to face and started off for their respective watchpoints.

The waiting began. The waxcloth cape kept the top part of Elenn's body dry while his feet got soaked. By the first light of sunrise, small puddles were forming at the bottom of the canal. He watched them and let his mind wander. His thoughts bounced to Nula, and to Tilke. He thought about the supply of Substance. He thought of rain falling on the empty structures of the old capital and how the dwellings of the bluff would be dry but empty. He thought of Cebik and Umat having to rotate up and down the branches at the mid-section to keep checking on the nets, and he thought about his old friends from Flatpools Station, . . . if only they could be here with him now. He thought also of frogs, and the possibility that their preparation for wetuedin was all in vain.

When Pavis and Jutef arrived mid-morning, there was still no flow in the bottom of the canal, only deep puddles.

"All I hear is rain," shouted Jutef, *"No stream yet?"*

"Not yet! I'll tell you when we see a stream!"

They waited together until Elenn could clearly see a small stream that trickled from one puddle to the next.

"There's a stream forming now!" he said. *"It's flowing right into the netted section!"*

"Bless the Lern!" shouted Jutef, clapping his hands.

"It might be two days before we get the floodwaters from Tilke's Lake!"

The stream grew steadily through the day, but Elenn suspected that it was all rainwater and not yet any floodwater from the lake. In the late afternoon, Pavis and Jutef returned to their hut, promising to come back the next morning. Elenn was also exhausted, but there was no question of leaving the net. He stood in the continuing rain, and looked out at the other uedin stationed at a distance who likewise held their vigils through the long hours.

It was the middle of the night again when the stream seemed to suddenly swell, and Elenn sensed that they were getting the floodwaters of Tilke's Lake. The importance of the moment sunk in. He thought of sending for Jutef and Pavis, but he decided that they need not be called back until the wetuedin were received. Until he saw a wetuedin, he would have that annoying thought that none might come.

At the spots where the Great Rains river was diverted, and at the other branch canals between here and there, there was every possibility that a wetuedin would rush past without being spotted, but here at the final net where wetuedin were to be delivered directly to the hatching pool, there would be no missing them. By morning, Elenn was exhausted by the urgent watching. To give himself some relief, he called Serka over.

"Yes, Master Elenn?" hollered Serka through the rain, a little out of breath from running.

Elenn had to shout so Serka would hear him through the rain. *"Go up and see how the other guards are doing, then come back and tell me!"*

Serka raised hands to face, quickly turned, and ran upstream. Elenn watched him until he was out of sight. He grew nervous as he waited. If Serka came right back, it would be because nothing had been spotted, and there was nothing to report. If there were any news, it would delay his return.

Suddenly, Elenn saw a wetuedin come through! Seeing it felt dreamlike! It was not really swimming, but rather simply rolling with the turbulent flow. Elenn's eyes widened and he was transfixed. The wetuedin clumsily flopped against the net for a moment and rolled right into the stream going to the hatching pool. A wetuedin! A wetuedin had actually arrived! The dam must have held! The delivery system was working!

Elenn heard the treading of feet in mud and turned to see Serka, back with news. Before Serka could say a word, Elenn shouted, *"We have a wetuedin!"*

"Four!" shouted Serka. *". . . so far!"*

"FOUR?!"

"So far! . . . One came just when I got there! There are probably more alread-- Look! Now!"

The second wetuedin was luckily carried by the water and disappeared quickly down the stream that led to the hatching pools.

Elenn felt no trace of the exhaustion that he had been feeling when he sent Serka for news. Now he was full of excitement. *"Master Serka, can I ask you another favor?"*

"What can I do, Master Elenn?"

"Go get Masters Pavis and Jutef. Do you know where they live? In the Childless neighborhood?"

"I'll find them!" said Serka. He raised hands to face and ran off.

By the time Jutef and Pavis arrived with Serka, Elenn had counted nine wetuedin. Now that he had gotten a fairly good look at them, he noticed that they looked small to him. But perhaps that was because he had never seen wetuedin until they were at least a few days in Quarterhouse hatching pool. Maybe they grew more quickly than he had imagined.

"*Master Serka says we've received four wetuedin!*" shouted Jutef, trotting up with his hand on Pavis's arm for guidance.

"*We have nine!*" announced Elenn.

"*Are they beautiful?*" asked Jutef. Elenn felt a momentary awkwardness, sadly aware that Jutef would not be able to see them.

"*Very beautiful!*" asserted Elenn.

"*Of course they are!*" answered Jutef with a happy laugh.

They stood together, waiting for the next. After a while, it came. The tenth wetuedin was like the others, smallish, unable to properly swim in quick-flowing water, and inexplicably beautiful.

The eighteenth wetuedin came through a day later, a very late arrival. It seemed inappropriate to think about the fact that nineteen uedin had gone to passing-of-life, and only eighteen had come back. To grieve the absence of one would be to lack gladness for the arrival of the eighteen. Pavis and Jutef had remained through the long night, celebrating each arrival. Gradually the rain subsided, but the canals continued to swell and filled to full capacity. For a few hours, they feared that the water would overflow the canals, but then it started to slowly diminish.

A few hours later, when Elenn saw the other guards coming all together, he was a little aggravated that they had decided to call it quits without communicating. Maybe it was time to do so, but it should have been agreed upon.

"I know the flow is going down, but this water could still be floodwater from the lake! There might be another in there, for all we know!"

"What do you mean, Master Elenn? Didn't you see the last one come through?" asked Onek with concern.

"No! You saw the nineteenth wetuedin?"

"Yes . . . but we took our time walking down here. It should have gone through by now. Do you think you might have missed it?"

"No. The net directs them right in there. They're easy to see!"

"Could one be caught up in the net?" asked Umat.

Elenn looked at the net that directed the wetuedin to the delivery stream. It was taut. It had held very firmly for the whole time. But the base of the net was in deep water, and it was muddy water that couldn't be seen through.

Without consulting, Elenn stepped into the rushing water. The flow was strong, but the rocks that lined the canal gave him leverage to first stand and then maneuver through the stream. He made his way to the net and started across, keeping his feet close to the edge. The water was cold, the flow was strong, and the rocky surface he stepped across was uneven. At the very middle of the net, he felt the body of a wetuedin rolling around in place where the flow was strongest. It had been trapped by the flow. He couldn't tell if it was alive or dead.

"There's one here!" shouted Elenn, *"Right at my feet!"*

"Go ahead, Master Posha," said Umat. Posha stepped down into the canal to help Elenn guide the wetuedin to the delivery stream. Together they placed their hands on the wetuedin and pulled it away from the net. At first Elenn had a terrible thought that it might be dead. But it soon wiggled from their hands, and they had to reapply their grip to guide it. They led it up to meet the water that flowed into the delivery stream and then let it go. It sputtered its tail as it was whooshed away to the hatching pool. Again, Elenn pondered the appearance of the wetuedin which seemed somehow different. Was it just their smallness? Or was there something else?

The new capital was full of uedin eager to see the wetuedin, but they understood that a day would come to observe them after the wetuedin had adjusted to the hatching pool. For now, only caretakers and guards could be there. The muddy water that had flowed through the canals was finally settling in the hatching pool, and the shapes of wetuedin could be seen making little movements under water.

Jutef approached Elenn and said, "Master Elenn, one of those third—well, I guess now fourth generation caretakers—wants to inspect the wetuedin for any cuts or scratches they might have from the canals. I don't think it's right to do so until they've adjusted to the pool. It's too much stress."

"What does he intend to do for the scratches?"

"He said wetuedin who came to the hatching pool at Bramble were said to suffer a lot of cuts and scratches, and they always put oilwax on if there were any nasty cut, to help it heal faster."

"It might be better to just do it right away," said Elenn. "Otherwise, they're just calming down to be disturbed again."

Jutef turned and spoke to the caretaker, "Go ahead. We trust you know what to do."

The caretaker signaled to three others, and they all stepped down into the hatching pool. Two of them took hold of a long wooden pole placed there, and they each held an end down into the water. They then commenced to move it up and down to guide and control the wetuedin. They stepped toward the other two caretakers. One held a small jar of wax oil. The other waited while one of the wetuedin was singled out for inspection.

Elenn watched as the caretaker from Bramble gently placed his hands on the body of the wetuedin and turned it to take a look. He suddenly looked up, "Master Elenn! Come and see this!"

"What?" Elenn carefully stepped down into the water and approached slowly.

"Look!" said the caretaker. He turned the wetuedin so Elenn could see the back of its head. Where a single little bump would normally appear, there was a skullcap divided into three separate protrusions. Three! The wetuedin had multiple skullwombs!

"What? What is it?" cried Jutef.

Elenn was stunned with the discovery, but he turned and looked at Jutef.

"Master Jutef, can you crouch down and find the edge? Can you sit on the edge of the pool?"

Jutef dropped his cane and Pavis stepped over to guide him down. He crouched at the side of the hatching pool, and then somewhat awkwardly sat down and lowered his feet into the water.

"Let's take it over to show him," said Elenn. He and the Bramble caretaker gently led the wetuedin to the edge. "Can you hold it firmly for a moment?" Elenn asked.

"Like this?" The Bramble caretaker knew how to hold the wetuedin in such a way that made it relax and sink into his grip.

"Yes! Over here, now," said Elenn. When the wetuedin was right in front of Jutef, Elenn reached up and took Jutef's arms in his hands. He slid his hands up Jutef's arms to draw his sleeves up. He felt the crookedness of the bones he had once broken with a similar grip. He lowered Jutef's hands to touch the back of the wetuedin's head.

Jutef ran his fingers over the humped skullcap. For a moment his look was one of confusion. Then he turned his head abruptly. "Three humps! Three humps on this wetuedin's skullwomb!"

"Yes!" said Elenn.

"There will be more than nineteen . . . Someday there will be more!"

"Yes, Master Jutef! There will be more!"

The caretakers with the wooden pole were already moving to check another wetuedin. After a moment, one of them cried, "*This one has two!*"

From there they moved on, announcing, "*This one has three, like the first!*" and then "*This one also has three!*"

Elenn looked up at Jutef. Jutef's eyes were, as usual, looking nowhere, but there were tears coming out of those dim eyes and dripping down his cheeks. Elenn felt a choking lump form in his own throat as the tremendous significance of the event set off his emotions. All nineteen wetuedin had descended, despite the misplanting of the kernel, despite the unpleasant ecstacies of the rouedin, despite the danger of frogs and the guesses of the delivery system. They had all descended! And they seemed, amazingly, to have multiple skullwombs. Elenn and Jutef both knew what that meant, and they could not respond with anything but tears. It meant that the new capital was going to be a true capital! It was going to have a future!

The day that the new capital learned of the full descent of nineteen wetuedin with multiple skullwombs was a day of drunken celebration. The uedin could not contain their joy without the help of yeastdrink. Fortunately the camp had long since set up a brewery with equipment and key ingredients carried back from the old capital.

When Elenn got back to his shared hut, it was late, and he was mildly drunk. The other guards were still at the domicile, singing and drinking with the server-masters. Elenn was there alone. He didn't bother to light a lamp. He stumbled out of his guard's garb, grabbed his bedding, and flung it open. As the patter of light rain on the thatched roof increased to a harder rain, he flopped down, drew a blanket over him, and pulled the wheel pillow under his face. A sudden few drops of rain made their way through the thatching and formed a stream of drips that came directly down to the back of his head. He laughed into the darkness. Of all places for the little stream of drops to fall, it had to be right onto his empty skullwomb! And yet he wasn't bothered. He didn't mind the leaky roof.

◆ ◆ ◆

THE END